There are boats on the river, barges sailing past, the sun glinting on the water. Down below, people are strolling along the Embankment, past the gardens of Cheyne Walk – young men in sports shirts and flannels; girls in summer dresses; a girl in a forget-me-not-blue dress, with royal blue collar and cuffs, a girl who looks a little bit like –

Oh, God, it couldn't be – could it?

She's walking along quickly, she'll be gone in a moment. Don't waste any time – go after her now!

...You run blindly along the pavement; you stop at the corner of Oakley Street. Strangers push past you, but she's nowhere to be seen. You must have imagined it. It was only imagination, or a trick of the light, because Jo is dead. She died years ago.

You are alone. You have always known that.

Peter Ling wrote his first published novel when he was eighteen. After a career in journalism, he became a television scriptwriter, creating numerous children's programmes as well as writing for adult audiences. With Hazel Adair he created the much-loved series *Crossroads* which ran for over twenty-three years. He has scripted episodes of *Dr Who* and *Dixon of Dock Green* and has written plays and serials for radio. Married with four children, Peter Ling now lives in East Sussex.

By the same author

Crown House

Crown Papers

Crown Wars

High Water

Flood Water

Storm Water

Halfway to Heaven

Happy Tomorrow

PETER LING

ORION

An Orion Paperback
First published in Great Britain by
Orion in 1995
This paperback edition published in 1997 by
Orion Books Ltd,
Orion House, 5 Upper St Martin's Lane,
London WC2H 9EA

A CIP catalogue record for this book
is available from the British Library.

ISBN: 0 75280 330 1

Printed and bound in Great Britain by
Clays Ltd, St Ives plc

This book is dedicated, with all my love,
to Vicky, Katy, Ted and Ellie,
who went to Battersea Park a long time ago.

My sincere thanks are due to Lita Brooker, Tony Bateman and Richard White for their expert advice, to John Bignell for his photographic memory of the past, to Yvette Goulden for her invaluable help in setting me on the right lines, and above all to Tony Shaw at the Local History Section of the Battersea Reference Library, who guided me to so much background information on the place and the period – though I must stress that the story and all the characters are entirely imaginary, as are the houses they lived in.

Prologue

'CAN YOU HEAR ME?' Through the choking darkness, Jo heard her mother's voice: 'Where are you? Are you all right?'

It was Saturday, 10 May, 1941, and the bomb had just landed. That was when Josephine Wells lost her home, and her world fell apart.

Jo lived in Battersea, just off Albert Bridge Road, in a warren of narrow streets and workmen's cottages behind the riverside wharves and warehouses. Number 18 Mill Street was home for the Wells family – eleven-year-old Jo, her sister Vera (known as Vee) who was two years younger, and their little brother Charlie, aged three, together with their mum.

Gracie Wells used to say she was glad she had three children, because good things always came in threes; but Jo soon found out that bad things could happen in threes too.

The first bad thing had happened a year ago in 1940, when Dad, Corporal Tom Wells, was killed on the beaches of Dunkirk. Somehow Gracie pulled herself together and managed to struggle on, bringing up the children on her own. She received a widow's pension, and earned a little extra by 'charring' for some well-to-do people on the Chelsea side of the river, in the big houses along Cheyne Row and Oakley Street.

The Wells's house was very small: just one room and a kitchen and scullery downstairs, and two bedrooms upstairs. Gracie slept in the front bedroom, in an old-fashioned double bed which she shared with little Charlie, while the girls had two narrow iron bedsteads in the back room.

1

The second bad thing had happened tonight – Saturday night – when the moon was full, and wave upon wave of German planes flew in through a cloudless sky.

Gracie hadn't taken her children to the public shelter; she preferred to stay at home, with the kids wrapped in blankets around her, in the cupboard under the stairs – she put her trust in God, and the solid Victorian staircase above their heads.

When one of the bombs landed uncomfortably close, Vee had clutched Jo's hand and squeaked: 'Bloody 'ell!'

Instantly, Gracie reprimanded her: 'Don't you ever let me hear you talking like that! We may not be rich, but in this house we speak proper English, like they do on the wireless.'

As a result, the girls had grown up to be bilingual, 'talking proper' at home, and reverting to cockney at school, as protective colouring in the playground.

But when the bomb fell on Mill Street, demolishing number 19 opposite and taking the roof off number 18, for the first few moments none of them said anything at all. Plunged into total darkness, they were too shocked to speak; then Gracie flung her arms round her children, gripping them fiercely and saying: 'Can you hear me? Jo – Vee – Charlie – are you all right?'

Their ears were still ringing, but as the echoes died away, all three children mumbled: 'Yes, Mum – we're OK . . .'

None of them cried – not even little Charlie – though they began to cough and splutter. As the pall of brickdust dispersed, they looked up and saw the stars overhead, and searchlights flailing the sky. Only the skeleton of the staircase was left – a staircase ending in mid-air, leading nowhere. The rest of the house had fallen into rubble.

'Thank God for that,' gasped Gracie. 'We're not hurt; that's all that matters.'

Marooned in their little refuge, they were unable to clamber out until the Heavy Rescue party lifted them to safety.

They had nothing left but their ragged blankets and the nightclothes they wore – now tattered and filthy – and a few treasures like Mum's handbag, Charlie's teddy-bear and Vee's beautiful doll; Bella had been a present last Christmas and had gone to bed with her every night since then. Everything else had gone for good.

One of the rescue team put them into a car and drove them to the nearest Emergency Aid Post, across the river, at St Luke's Hospital in Sydney Street. Along with other survivors they were given cups of hot sweet tea and biscuits, and made themselves as comfortable as possible on camp-beds.

Gracie sat in a deckchair, but the children were too excited to settle down, and Vee wandered off, getting into conversation with a little girl about her own age – another Blitz refugee.

As she began to relax in her deckchair Gracie said: 'Don't let the others get lost, Jo. We've had enough trouble for one day, without that.'

Outside, the anti-aircraft barrage continued, accompanied by the drone of planes overhead and the occasional crump of an exploding bomb. Jo glanced at the clock on the wall, which said ten minutes past twelve, pointing out: 'It isn't today any more, Mum – it's tomorrow . . . Sunday morning.'

She was pleased to be given something to do, and set off obediently. Vee was still chattering to the little girl, but Charlie seemed to have disappeared. Vee's doll was lying on the floor, together with Charlie's teddy-bear – it had chocolate-brown fur, and he called it 'Chockie' – so she picked them up and went to the other end of the dormitory. Charlie was standing at an open doorway – a small figure in pyjamas, looking up at the night sky.

'Charlie!' she called to him. 'Mum wants you!'

Grinning cheekily, he turned and waved. That was when she heard the whistle as the bomb fell. The sound grew louder and louder, and she began to run towards him, calling: 'Charlie! Come here!'

But he just laughed. That was her last memory of him.

The bomb that landed on St Luke's Hospital in the early hours of Sunday morning, 11 May, demolished the Emergency Aid Post completely – and that was the third bad thing that happened to Jo Wells.

A few hours earlier, she had lost her home; now she had lost everything.

Everything except her life.

Chapter One

IT WAS THE SAME DREAM; the one Jo dreamed so often. She was back in their little house at Mill Street, with Mum and Vee and Charlie, happy and laughing; she was eleven years old again and they were all together.

The dream never went beyond that, because the alarm clock always woke her – just as it did now – and her warm feeling of happiness burst like a bubble. She switched off the alarm and swung her bare feet on to the cold lino, because if she stayed in bed she might slip back into sleep – and that would mean trouble.

Half-past six was getting-up time. Crossing to the window, Jo pulled back the curtains; a grey, damp morning, though the chimneys of Battersea Power Station were touched with sunlight.

In the other bed, her cousin Chrissie rolled over, burying her face in the pillow. Seven-year-old Chrissie always had an extra half-hour in bed. Yawning, Jo shrugged into her flannelette dressing-gown and trailed downstairs to put the kettle on, trying to remember if she had done all her homework last night before she went to bed—

Then she remembered what day it was, and smiled.

It was Tuesday, 8 May, 1945, and last night they'd announced on the wireless that today would be V E Day – for 'Victory in Europe' – a public holiday. The war was over at last. It was like an unexpected present – a gift from God.

Or it would be – if there really was a God. For the past four years, Jo had not been too sure about that.

Four years ago, the bomb that demolished the Emergency Aid Post

5

had killed Gracie Wells instantly. When Jo came to, she found herself being lifted into an ambulance. She could still remember seeing the other stretcher next to her: her mother's face, chalk-white under dirt and brick-dust, and the wide-open eyes staring up at the roof. Jo did not need to be told that her mother was dead.

At the hospital, she asked about her brother and sister, but no one could tell her anything. Someone had seen a little boy who must have been about three years old, running away down Sydney Street – terrified and naked, his clothes stripped off by the bomb-blast – but in the confusion nobody knew what had become of him. They assured her he would be found very soon; but the hours turned into days, and days into weeks, and there was no news of him.

And no news of Vee. She had not been dug from the wreckage; she had simply disappeared.

A nurse gave Jo some pills to swallow, and a cup of cocoa, and told her she was a very lucky girl. By some miracle, she had emerged without a scratch; when the shock wore off, she would be as right as rain, able to go home again.

Except she didn't have a home to go to.

In this emergency, it was Mum's sister, Mrs Topsy Bone, who offered her a home.

As she finished laying the table for breakfast, then filled the kettle and put it on the stove, Jo gazed around Auntie Topsy's kitchen and thought how strange it was; for nearly four years, she had lived here at Agar Road, in the three-storey terraced house under the shadow of Battersea Power Station, yet she had never thought of it as home.

Of course it was very good of Auntie Topsy to take her in: if it hadn't been for her generosity, she would have been packed off to an orphanage – Auntie Topsy never let her forget that.

It was hard to remember that Mum and Topsy had been sisters; they were so different. Topsy was married to Chief Petty Officer Norman Bone, RN, and as the wife of a serving naval officer, she had always looked down on poor Gracie, whose husband had never risen above the rank of corporal, and had also been inconsiderate enough to get himself killed in battle, leaving her with a family to support. Topsy considered three children to be excessive – almost indecent. She and Norman just had the one, pretty little Chrissie, born the same year as her cousin Charlie.

Jo sighed. It was funny to think that Charlie would have been seven now, if he were—

Then she broke off, scolding herself. Of course Charlie was alive – he had been seen running down the street, hadn't he? One of these days he would turn up again. And so would Vee: after all, they never found her body, so there wasn't any proof that she had been killed. Four years after their disappearance, Jo refused to give up hope.

When she had filled the teapot, she arranged four cups and saucers on a tray. As soon as the tea had drawn, she poured it out and set off upstairs.

On the first floor, she tapped on her aunt's bedroom door and went in.

'Morning, Auntie,' she said. 'Here's your tea.'

Auntie Topsy lifted her head from her pillow on the double bed; even though Uncle Norman was half the world away, she kept to her own side of the bed, taking care not to roll over and trespass on her husband's territory.

'Mmmm,' she mumbled, and groped for her dentures in the glass on the bedside cabinet; she would not speak to Jo until she had put in her teeth. Then she asked: 'What's the weather like?'

'A bit cloudy, but it's not raining. They've got a nice day for it.'

'Nice day for what?' snapped Topsy, frowning.

'The holiday – VE Day.'

'Oh, that . . . The Government should have had more sense; what's the good of making a holiday out of it? Just an excuse for people to hang about doing nothing, except drinking and carrying on . . .'

Auntie Topsy disapproved of drinking and carrying on; most of all, she disapproved of people doing nothing. Sipping her tea, she continued: 'Seeing you don't have school, I thought we'd make a start on the spring-cleaning. It'll be a chance to give the kitchen a proper going-over.'

'It might be nice to go out for a while,' said Jo, bravely. 'They started hanging the flags out yesterday. I'd like to go and have a look.'

'You've got better things to do, my girl! You can stay here and make yourself useful.'

From the day she moved in, it had been impressed on Jo that her role in the household was to 'make herself useful'. So she said nothing, but picked up her tray and left the room, crossing the landing. Putting

7

down the second cup of tea, she shook Chrissie's shoulder.

The little girl pulled the covers over her head. 'I've got an awful headache – tell Ma I'm not well enough to go to school today.'

'No need.' Jo smiled. 'It's a holiday – remember?'

'Oh!' Chrissie surfaced, and grabbed her cup. 'I think I'm feeling a bit better after all.'

'That's right, you can save your headache for another day,' said Jo.

Chrissie stuck her tongue out, and began to unwind the 'crackers' from her hair – knotted ribbons that Topsy put in each night to keep her daughter's corkscrew ringlets in place.

When she first welcomed Jo into the house, Topsy told her that she and Chrissie would be great pals – but it hadn't worked out like that. The eight-year difference in age was too wide a gap, and there had never been much love lost between them.

Taking the tray, she continued on her way up to the top floor.

'Morning, Mr Penberthy!' she called, knocking at another door. 'Here's your cup of tea!'

'Leave it there, I'll have it presently,' came the muffled reply.

Mr Penberthy was one of Mrs Bone's two lodgers: a fifty-year-old clerk, who worked in some Government office in Whitehall. Topsy Bone would never have lowered herself to go out 'charring' like her sister, but she was happy to supplement her marriage allowance from the Royal Navy by taking in 'paying guests'.

Mr Penberthy kept himself to himself; no one ever saw him until he was fully dressed, with a few sparse strands of hair carefully combed across his bald patch. He left the house at eight sharp every morning, and returned at six-thirty. After supper he retired to his room, where he listened to the wireless until bedtime. He was dyspeptic and very fussy. Jo did not care for him.

With relief, she knocked and entered the last bedroom.

Old Mr Mulligan was already sitting up in bed.

'It's a grand day for the race,' he began cheerfully.

Jo chimed in: 'The human race!'

The old Irishman winked as she handed him his tea. He took it in his left hand, for his right pyjama-sleeve hung empty at his side.

As a young soldier in the First World War, Mr Mulligan had lost an arm, and was discharged with a meagre pension, making a little money by doing odd jobs: as a caretaker, a nightwatchman, and even painting and decorating – though how he managed to put up wallpaper Jo could not imagine. But he never kept any job long; apart from his missing arm, a gas-attack in the trenches had left him with damaged lungs and bouts of bronchitis.

In spite of his disabilities, he remained incorrigibly cheerful. Cocking his head on one side, he asked: 'You'll be off gallivanting later, I daresay?'

Jo shook her head. 'Auntie says we're going to begin spring-cleaning.'

His eyebrows shot up. 'I thought yer man on the wireless said we'd two days' holiday?'

'Auntie doesn't believe in holidays. She wants to make a start on the kitchen.'

'On a day like today? I'm sure you'd sooner be out celebrating, wouldn't you now?'

'Well, yes, but—'

'But me no buts, Miss Wells! It's your patriotic duty to go and celebrate, so it is. Tell me – how old would you be now?'

'I'm fifteen – I'll be leaving school at the end of this term.'

'Fifteen, is it? Mother of God, you'll soon be a fine young woman. It's time you stood up for yourself. Tell your aunt the spring-cleaning can wait.'

Jo laughed. 'I couldn't do that – she's always been so good to me—'

'Oh, yes – as she never stops reminding us. But you've been very good to her as well, fetching and carrying and slaving from morn to night, with never a word of thanks. One of these fine days, you'll spread your wings and fly away – and today's as good a day as any to make a start.'

She stared at him. 'You are joking, aren't you?'

'I was never more serious, my darlin'. Go on now – get out and make a new life for yourself.'

She went back to her bedroom in a thoughtful frame of mind, and began to put on her Sunday best. Auntie had bought the dress at a jumble sale, thinking it might do for her daughter – it was far too big, and would need cutting down – but Chrissie had refused to wear it, so it was passed to Jo.

It was forget-me-not blue, with royal blue collar and cuffs, and a wide, sash-type belt of the same colour, and it fitted perfectly.

9

When she went downstairs to start the breakfast, she put on an overall to keep it spotless. Breakfast was a simple meal: slices of bread and marge with a scrape of homemade carrot marmalade – they couldn't get the oranges for love or money – and dollops of porridge with a little milk and no sugar. They had got used to making do with the meagre rations by now, and although the war was over, there was no hope of the food restrictions being lifted yet.

Afterwards, Jo did the washing-up, while the others made their plans for the day. Chrissie was going round to one of her schoolfriends, and Mr Penberthy had arranged to have lunch with an office colleague who lived in Ealing.

Mr Mulligan turned in his chair, calling over his shoulder to Jo: 'And what do you propose to do today, Miss Wells?'

She emptied the washing-up water down the drain as she replied: 'Oh, I was thinking of taking a stroll to Buckingham Palace . . . If I see the King and Queen, shall I give them your regards, Mr Mulligan?'

'Certainly, certainly – wish 'em all the best from me,' he chuckled.

'Don't talk nonsense,' frowned her aunt. 'Have you forgotten you're going to give me a hand, cleaning the kitchen?'

'No, Auntie – but I thought I'd leave that till tomorrow,' answered Jo politely. 'There's no hurry, is there?'

Topsy stared at her niece, unable to believe her ears. 'What did you say?' she demanded.

'I said I'm going out. Well, it is a holiday. I'd like to make the most of it.'

Mr Mulligan chipped in: 'I told her, it's her patriotic duty to go out and celebrate—'

'I'll thank you not to encourage her, Mr Mulligan,' snapped Topsy Bone, and turned to Jo again. 'You ought to be on your bended knees today, mourning your nearest and dearest, not larking about – you that lost both parents in the war, and your brother and sister dead and gone as well – what have you got to celebrate?'

'They're not dead.' Jo began to take off her overall. 'I'll find them one of these days . . . Today, perhaps?'

Chrissie exclaimed shrilly: 'Ooh, Ma – she's got her best dress on!'

Topsy rose to her feet. 'I'm sure I don't know what's wrong with you, Josie. What's got into you, my girl?'

'I told you, I feel like some fresh air. I don't know what time I'll be

10

coming back – and I am not "your girl"!'

With that, Jo marched out of the house and the front door slammed behind her.

A breeze came off the river, and a flock of seagulls overhead wheeled and screamed in exultation, flashing white wings in the sunlight.

Jo took a deep breath. A new day had begun – the first day of peace. Throwing back her head, she stepped out to meet it.

By midday she was beginning to feel less confident. For one thing, she was hungry.

It had all happened so suddenly, she hadn't thought about taking any money with her. As Jo walked over Albert Bridge, then along the King's Road to Sloane Square, admiring the Union Jacks and red, white and blue bunting that had appeared overnight, she felt a pang of emptiness. She would have liked to stop at a café for a cup of tea and a bun, but that was impossible.

Heading for Buckingham Palace, she noticed so many couples. Some of them were middle-aged or even elderly: ARP wardens, whose jobs had come to an end overnight, together with off-duty nursing sisters or silver-haired ladies in WVS uniforms – husbands and wives, perhaps, sharing an unexpected day off. But most of all there were the servicemen in khaki, navy or air-force blue, with their arms round their partners – pretty girls in bright summer dresses . . .

She began to wish she hadn't come out. Perhaps Aunt Topsy was right; perhaps it was wrong to try and celebrate, when the people she loved best in the world had gone for ever.

No, not for ever, she told herself fiercely, she would never believe that. Now the war was over, everything was going to come right again. Surely Charlie and Vee would turn up soon – round the next corner, even?

But the next corner was the end of Buckingham Palace Road, and Jo found a huge crowd assembled there; thousands of them, packed tightly together, staring through the railings at the palace, where the long balcony was draped in crimson with a gold fringe. The french windows were open; at some time the King and Queen would step out on to the balcony and greet the patient crowds, who were happy enough to stand and wait.

Jo had never seen so many people. Even if Vee or Charlie were here, she could search all day and all night without finding them.

Depressed, she turned away and walked round the fringes of the crowd, into St James's Park.

There were plenty of people here too, making the most of the spring weather. Many of them had brought picnics, sprawling on the grass beside the lake. Jo decided to sit down, hoping she wouldn't get grass stains on her dress – Aunt Topsy would never let her forget that. As she relaxed, she couldn't help overhearing the conversation of a young couple near by.

'Is there anything left, Malcolm?' asked the girl.

A pale youth in spectacles burrowed in a paper bag. 'Just one sandwich.'

His companion pulled a face. She was a dumpy girl in her teens with a sallow complexion, not helped by the olive-green twin-set she wore, though she had done her best to brighten it by pinning a red, white and blue rosette to her bosom.

'I don't want it.' She tossed her head. 'I've had too many already – I'm sick of them. Let's throw it to the ducks.'

'Oh, Nora! Throw away a perfectly good sandwich?' Malcolm was shocked. 'They'll have us up for wasting food!'

'For goodness' sake!' Nora grabbed the paper bag and rummaged inside it, then realised she was being watched.

By this time Jo was very hungry, and her face must have betrayed her feelings because Nora addressed her with a ladylike smile: 'Would you care for a sandwich? It's only Spam, but it seems a pity to waste it.'

'Well, if you're sure you don't want it . . .' Jo accepted the offer gratefully. 'I was feeling a bit peckish, as a matter of fact. Thank you.'

'Don't mench! We had some digestive biscuits as well, but I'm afraid they're all gone . . .'

She chattered on, talking about VE Day, and how lucky they were with the weather – didn't it rain during the night? Had Jo come a long way?

When Jo explained that she lived in Battersea, Nora gave a little squeal of amazement. 'There now – it's a small world, and no mistake. We've come over from Clapham ourselves, haven't we, Malcolm? We work at Bryden Brothers – you know, the department store near the Junction.'

'I'm not sure,' said Jo doubtfully. 'I know Arding and Hobbs.'

'We're the other department store – a bit further up the hill, on the opposite side. You must have seen it.'

Jo remembered it vaguely – an old-fashioned establishment which had probably not changed much since it was founded by the Bryden family in the 1890s – but she had only been inside the shop once, when she accompanied her aunt on an expedition to buy blackout material.

'So you're Battersea and we're Clapham – that makes us practically next-door neighbours!' Nora introduced herself briskly: 'I'm Nora Topping, and this is my friend Malcolm Jones. I'm in Haberdashery, and Malcolm's in Hardware and Kitchen Utensils – he's waiting for his call-up papers, then he'll be going in the Army.'

'But I thought – now the war's over—' began Jo.

'Only the war in Europe,' Malcolm corrected her, looking over the top of his spectacles. 'We've still got to settle matters with Japan, remember.'

'So poor Malcolm's going to do his bit in the Far East,' Nora continued. 'It does seem unfair because it's not as if he was medically A1 – he's been graded B2 on account of his eyesight . . . And where do you live, Jo?'

Between mouthfuls of Spam sandwich, Jo outlined her situation as briefly as possible, while Nora made sympathetic noises and finally exclaimed: 'So you're only a year younger than me! You don't have to stay on at school now you're fifteen, you know. You could leave and get yourself a job, like I did. Tell you what – I know Bryden's have got a vacancy, why don't you come and see Mrs Spenlow? She's the manager in charge of juniors. I'm sure if I put in a word for you, she'd take you on. Don't you think so, Malcolm?'

Jo struggled to get a word in. 'It's very kind of you, but I don't think my auntie would like that. I mean, as long as I'm living in her house—'

'But that's what I mean – you wouldn't have to live there any more!'

Nora explained: Bryden Brothers kept up the old traditions and provided accommodation on the premises for the juniors; at the top of the building, among the attic store-rooms, were two dormitories, one for male and one for female staff.

'So you'd get board and lodging as well as wages. When could you come for an interview?'

Then she broke off, interrupted by a strange noise, a great rumbling that seemed to roll around the sky, and they realised it was the sound of people cheering, outside the palace. The King and Queen must have come out on to the balcony at last.

'Quick – let's go and see!' Nora jumped up. 'Oh, buck up, Malcolm, for goodness' sake – we don't want to miss them, do we?'

Dragging him to his feet, she set off towards the palace, and Jo followed.

The figures on the balcony looked very small, but as they smiled and waved Jo felt an unexpected rush of affection; in a funny way, they seemed almost like old friends. After all, they had stayed in London throughout the war – bombs had fallen on Buckingham Palace too, and after particularly heavy raids, they had gone out to the worst-hit areas, visiting the survivors and giving them words of encouragement.

So Jo stood and cheered like all the others. Then the Queen turned to the open windows and beckoned, and the great roar of enthusiasm redoubled as the two princesses, Elizabeth and Margaret Rose, came out shyly to join their parents. Tears pricked Jo's eyes. Of course, that was what it was all about – they were a family, too.

When the royal party disappeared, the crowd began to break up; Jo walked along to the Horseguards Parade with her new friends, and Nora returned to the topic of Bryden Brothers.

'It couldn't do any harm to have an interview, could it? I'm sure you'd be happy there. Don't you think so, Malcolm?'

Malcolm, who had not taken much part in the conversation, became positively enthusiastic: 'Oh, yes, it's quite a jolly crowd – in fact I'd describe us as one big, happy family.'

Family – that word again. Impulsively, Jo said: 'It does sound nice. Perhaps I could come and meet your Mrs Spenlow on Saturday? I generally have Saturday afternoons to myself.'

Walking between the two girls, Malcolm linked arms with both of them as they strolled along. Jo felt a glow of happiness she had not known for a long, long time.

Oddly enough, it was Nora who withdrew into a thoughtful silence now.

When they reached Whitehall the crowds were thicker than ever, and the road was completely jammed. They discovered the reason for this when, upon another balcony, another famous figure appeared.

The Prime Minister, Winston Churchill, together with several members of his wartime Cabinet, stood beaming down at the upturned faces below him, waving his Homburg in one hand and clutching a cigar in the other. He spoke into a microphone, and the familiar voice – a little thick, a little overripe – boomed from a dozen loudspeakers: '. . . This is your victory,' he told them. 'It is the victory of the cause of freedom in every land. In all our long history, we have never seen a greater day than this . . . God bless you all.' Then he threw back a command over his shoulder: 'Give me the note, somebody!'

One of his Ministers obliged. Churchill cleared his throat and led the audience in a tuneless version of 'Land of Hope and Glory', followed by Ernest Bevin, who clapped him on the shoulder and struck up 'For He's a Jolly Good Fellow'.

It was a touching moment, and again Jo felt near to tears. She started to say something to Nora and Malcolm, and found that they had vanished. That wasn't surprising; it was easy to get separated in this mass of people. Pressing on, she pushed through the crowd, looking for her new friends, and eventually reached Trafalgar Square.

Some jazz musicians were playing at the foot of Nelson's Column – 'When the Saints Go Marching In' set everyone's feet tapping. Boys in shirtsleeves, guardsmen in paper hats, GIs in trimly tailored uniforms began to jitterbug, swinging their partners around; the girls gave themselves up to this outburst of joy, their skirts flying wide, their hair streaming behind them.

Jo watched, and marvelled – and envied them.

Then someone grabbed her. She found herself looking into the eyes of a curly-haired serviceman in khaki with two stripes on his sleeve, who drew her into the dance.

He had soft brown eyes with black lashes, and a smile so warm, it melted her heart. She could not utter a word as the music swept her away; he led her on, faster and faster, until she was breathless.

Jo did not really know how to dance, but it didn't seem to matter; she could have followed him to the end of the world . . . Then, with a last defiant crash on the drums, the music stopped.

'Ta very much,' said the soldier. 'I reckon we could both do with a drink after that.'

Jo didn't come down to earth until they were about to enter the pub, somewhere off the Haymarket. Hanging back in the doorway, she said: 'I can't – I'm sorry.'

He stared at her. 'What's wrong?'

'I– I'm under age.'

'Ay-oop! How old are you, then?'

'I'll be sixteen next month.'

'Blimey.' He grinned. 'Flippin' 'eck, let's take a chance. They'll be too busy to trouble about a little thing like that today.'

And he steered her into the crowded saloon bar.

'What'll it be?' he asked. 'Fizzy lemon? Or do you want to go mad and have a shandy?'

'Fizzy lemon,' she said, feeling very small – then added: 'Please.'

He grinned again, and pointed to the far corner. 'There's two seats there if you can get through. I'll fetch the drinks.'

She was afraid someone would accuse her of breaking the licensing laws, but she remembered what Mr Churchill had said – something about 'the cause of freedom'. Well, this was her day of freedom, and she was going to make the most of it.

The soldier reappeared with two glasses, saying: 'How about that, eh? I've not spilled a drop.'

He talked in a funny way; it wasn't the kind of voice she was used to. It reminded her of one of those men on the wireless who used to read the news – the one who sounded different from all the others – Wilfred Pickles.

Sitting close beside her, he raised his glass and launched into song: 'Happy V-Day to you, happy V-Day to you, happy V-day, dear—' He broke off. 'Dammit, I don't know your name – what is it?'

'Josephine Wells. My aunt calls me Josie, everybody else calls me Jo.'

'Pleased to meet you, Jo. I'm Pete. Corporal Peter Hobden, born and bred in Sheffield.'

'Oh, yes.' Of course, Wilfred Pickles was a Yorkshireman. Shaking hands, she said: 'Jo Wells – born and bred in Battersea.' To keep the conversation going, she volunteered: 'It's funny, my dad was a corporal too.'

'Was?'

So she told him about Dad being killed at Dunkirk, and that led on to Mum and the air raid, and Vee and Charlie, and Aunt Topsy. By the time she had finished, he wasn't smiling.

'So, what are you going to do with yourself, Jo?' he asked.

'I'm going to get a job.'

'What sort of job?'

'Working in a shop, I hope – one of the department stores at Clapham Junction. I'm going for an interview on Saturday.'

'Well, I wish you luck. I hope you get what you want.'

Without stopping to think, she blurted out: 'Will I see you again?' Then she added quickly: 'I mean, if you want to know how I get on at the interview, I could tell you afterwards.'

He put his hand over hers; a large, muscular hand, yet his touch was very gentle.

'No – I can't do that,' he said.

She felt herself blushing, and went on hastily: 'I'm sorry, it was a stupid thing to say. I shouldn't have asked—'

He interrupted her. 'I'm glad you did. I'd like to see you on Saturday, but I won't be here. I've got to get back to barracks tomorrow – Catterick.'

'Is that a long way?'

'North Yorkshire. Further still.' He squeezed her hand. 'I'll get another leave one of these days – we'll keep in touch, eh? And we've still got the rest of the evening . . . Bags of time, really.'

She sat watching him, listening to the soft, unfamiliar music of his voice, and when he smiled at her she thought she had never seen anything so beautiful in her whole life.

By the time they left the pub it was dusk, and the street lamps were coming on one by one; the blackout was a thing of the past.

Jostled by the noisy crowd, Jo had to put her lips to Pete's ear before he could hear what she was asking him: 'Can I write to you sometimes?'

''Course you can. And I'll write back an' all. When we get out of this mob, I'll give you my address, OK?'

Their faces were very close, and when he kissed her, it was the easiest, most natural thing in the world. They stood still, holding one another, while the boisterous tide surged around them – a tiny island of peace and happiness.

When they reached Piccadilly Circus, Eros had been boarded up for safety, though some intrepid climbers were scrambling over it, trying

17

to cling on; others were shinning up lamp-posts, or swarming over the top of a marooned taxi. A conga-line emerged from nowhere – a sinuous caterpillar of boys and girls – stamping out the rhythm, weaving in and out of the crush.

'C'mon – let's join in!' Pete shouted, and as the last girl danced past he caught her round the waist, calling to Jo: 'Follow me!'

She hesitated for a second, afraid of making a fool of herself, and in that second another girl grabbed Pete, and another man tagged on after her.

Jo called out: 'Pete!' but he couldn't hear her above the din – and at the same instant the taxi crawled forward. Jo had to step back, waiting as it inched past her. As it moved away, she pressed forward, but by then the conga-line had been swallowed up in the crowd. She searched for a long time, but Pete had disappeared.

At last she was forced to give up. She would have to make her way home and face Aunt Topsy, who would certainly be waiting up.

Slowly, she began to retrace her steps. Slowly, she faced the truth – she did not have Pete Hobden's address, and he didn't have hers. Slowly, she tried to accept the fact that she would never see him again.

Chapter Two

Aunt Topsy had waited up.

As soon as Jo walked into the kitchen at Agar Road, her aunt began: 'What time do you call this? Where have you been?'

Though she was very tired, Jo tried to answer politely, telling her aunt that she had seen the Royal Family, and Winston Churchill, a jazz-band in Trafalgar Square, and people dancing in Piccadilly Circus—

Topsy Bone cut in: 'You went to Piccadilly Circus – all by yourself? You silly girl, anything could have happened to you!'

Jo bit her lip. It was true – anything could have happened. But she wasn't going to tell her aunt or anyone else about Pete Hobden. Quickly, she explained how she had got in conversation with a nice young couple in the park, who shared their sandwiches with her.

Topsy interrupted again: 'How many times do I have to tell you – you must never talk to strangers! Those sandwiches could have been drugged!'

'It wasn't like that. They were very nice – they work for Bryden Brothers, at Clapham Junction.'

'Oh?' Topsy raised her eyebrows. 'Well, I must say that's a reliable shop. They have a good reputation.'

'Yes . . .' The chance was too good to miss: 'That's why I thought I might try and get a job there myself. They said they might be able to get me an interview with one of the managers.'

'Did they indeed!' Topsy pursed her lips. 'You mean, when you leave school?'

'I could leave school now, I'm old enough. And if they do offer me a job, I could start right away, couldn't I?'

Topsy considered the possibility; it sounded respectable enough.

'I suppose it was bound to happen one day,' she said at last. 'And I can't go on giving you free board and lodging till kingdom come. If you're earning, there's no reason why you shouldn't pay me a fair rent. It would be better than having you round the house, under my feet all day long.'

'That's what I thought,' Jo agreed. 'In fact, you wouldn't have to put up with me at all – because I'd be living-in at Bryden's.'

Topsy's face hardened. She had assumed that Jo would come home every evening, and help with the washing and ironing and other household chores.

'You mean you're prepared to turn your back on me and walk out at a moment's notice – after all I've done for you?'

'Well, like you said, it had to happen some time, so I think the sooner I go the better, don't you? It's time I started to earn my living.'

'Oh, yes, you've got it all worked out, haven't you? This is how I'm to be treated – me, that's worked my fingers to the bone all these years, giving you a home and bringing you up . . .' Topsy pulled out a handkerchief and blew her nose loudly. 'This is all the thanks I get!'

'Cheer up, it's not as if I were going far away.' Not somewhere far away, like Sheffield or Catterick, she thought, and managed to force a smile. 'I'll come round on Sunday afternoons for tea – how's that?'

When she arrived at Bryden Brothers on Saturday, Jo found Nora trying to serve two customers at once – measuring petersham ribbon for one lady and trying to match a particular shade of darning-wool for another.

'Two and a half yards exactly . . . Excuse me, madam – yes, I think that's the same shade of beige, but if you'd like to take it out on to the pavement to compare it in daylight . . .' Seeing Jo, she said unenthusiastically: 'Oh, hello, I thought you'd probably be dropping in. You've picked a very busy time.'

When Nora had finished dealing with her customers, she came back to Jo and said: 'Mrs Spenlow's expecting you. You'll find her in her office – first floor, through Toddlers and Baby Linen, next to Accounts. Her name's on the door.'

Jo followed instructions, and soon found the Manager's sanctum. Mrs Spenlow, a large lady, studied her suspiciously.

'What did you say your name was? Wells? Are you sure?' She flipped through her appointment book. 'Oh – Wells! Here it is. I thought you said Miss Topping from Haberdashery introduced you? Is she a friend of yours?'

'Well, not exactly – I mean, I do know her—'

'Your name was given to me by Mr Malcolm Jones in Hardware. According to my notes, he arranged this interview.'

'Oh, did he? Well, yes, I know Mr Jones too – slightly—'

'Oh, yes? Very well, you may sit down. I must ask you to answer a few questions, Miss Wells.'

The questions were fired like bullets from a machine gun – questions about her home, her family, her school, her academic achievements, her previous experience (if any) – and at the end of the inquisition Mrs Spenlow leaned forward and asked: 'Have you ever been in trouble with the police? At Bryden Brothers, we insist on absolute honesty at all times. We also require two personal references – one from your head teacher, together with a copy of your latest school report. After that, we may take you on for a trial period of three months. Very well, you may go.'

When she went to school on Monday morning, Jo had to explain to the headmistress about the job at Bryden Brothers. The head – who knew something of Jo's family background – said kindly: 'We don't approve of girls leaving before the end of term, Josephine, but in your case I think we might make an exception to the rule. I shall be sorry to see you go, but I realise these are difficult times for everyone. I shall of course give you a first-class reference.'

Mr Penberthy provided the second reference. As the letter was typed on Government stationery with a Whitehall address, the final result was impressive.

When Mrs Spenlow had studied these documents, she summoned Jo again and informed her that she could begin work next Monday. As a junior assistant (female) she was entitled to £3.15/- a week, but as she was living in, two guineas would be deducted for board and lodging, leaving £1.13/- in her weekly pay-packet.

'I shall ask your friend who recommended you to show you where you will be sleeping – let me see, who was it?'

'Malcolm Jones—'

'Male staff are not permitted to enter the female living-quarters. Didn't you say you had another acquaintance – someone from Haberdashery, wasn't it?'

She sent for Nora, who appeared within a very short time, looking flustered and wondering what she had done wrong. Mrs Spenlow handed Jo over and told Nora to show her round the building.

They climbed an echoing stone stairwell in silence. Once again, Jo was struck by the change in Nora's manner – she'd been so friendly, that day in the park – but decided she must be tired.

The girls' dormitory was dark and chilly, with small windows set under sloping ceilings, and smelled of fish. Nora explained: 'I hope you're fond of boiled cod, the canteen does it two or three times a week.'

Jo's bed was narrow, with a lumpy mattress, but she had a metal locker with its own key, her own bedside table, and a cane-bottomed chair.

'Seen all you want?' Nora asked. 'It's not too late to change your mind, you know. You don't have to come here.'

'I'm sure I'll like it. You said you were all one big, happy family.'

'I didn't say that,' Nora corrected her. 'Malcolm did.'

'What's all this, then?' Malcolm was lounging in the doorway. 'Someone taking my name in vain?'

'What are you doing here?' Nora asked sharply. 'You'll get into hot water if anyone catches you.'

He smiled. 'A little bird told me you were showing Jo around. I thought I'd come and say hello, and pass on a few useful tips. Has Nora warned you about the canteen?'

'She did say something about boiled cod—'

'When we're desperate, we go over to the Greasy Spoon.'

'The Greasy Spoon?'

'It's what we call the caff across the road. Sausage and chips are sixpence, and baked beans tuppence extra. Anyhow, it'll be nice to have a new face around the old place. I hope you'll be very happy here.'

It was arranged that Jo should move in the following Sunday evening, ready to start work on Monday morning.

On Sunday afternoon, Aunt Topsy lent her an ancient suitcase and sat on the edge of Chrissie's bed, watching her pack – just in case, as she pointed out, any of Chrissie's things got mixed up with Jo's by mistake.

Not that Jo had much to pack anyway; when she began to fold up her flannelette dressing-gown, Aunt Topsy reached out and took it from her.

'That's not yours,' she said firmly. 'I lent it you when you first came here – this is mine.'

'I'm sorry, I thought you'd given it to me,' said Jo. 'But I'm going to need a dressing-gown at Brydens, for when I go to the girls' washroom.'

'Oh, so you have to share a washroom, do you?' Topsy sniffed. 'I don't know why you're so keen on the idea of going there. I suppose you've got it into your head that you're going to do better for yourself, eh? I blame it on your mother – Gracie always did give herself airs.'

Controlling herself with an effort, Jo managed to say: 'Let's not argue about it, Auntie. I think I'm doing the right thing. But you've been very good to me all these years, and I'll always be grateful for everything you've done.'

'I was only doing my duty,' mumbled Topsy. 'Oh, very well then, if you're going to need a dressing-gown, I suppose you might as well hang on to this one. You can have it as a going-away present. I just hope you're not making a big mistake, that's all. And I certainly hope you're not going to turn up on the doorstep in a few weeks' time, saying you've changed your mind, and asking me to take you back!'

'No.' Jo folded the dressing-gown and went on with her packing. 'I shan't do that.'

When everything else was inside the case, she fetched the most important things she owned, which she had left till last: her best blue dress, together with the doll called Bella and the teddy-bear called Chockie.

Still watching every move Jo made, Topsy remarked: 'What do you want those for? You're too old for toys, a girl your age. Chrissie might like to have them – why don't you leave them here?'

'I couldn't do that. They're all I've got to remind me of Vee and Charlie. When they come back, they'll be glad I've looked after them.'

After tea, she said goodbye to Chrissie, and to Mr Penberthy, who

23

gave her his good wishes for her success in her new employment, and told her to be respectful to her superiors. Lastly, she said goodbye to Mr Mulligan, who slipped a half-crown into her palm when no one was looking.

'Don't forget us now,' he told her. 'I'm going to miss you, my darlin', and that's no lie.'

Aunt Topsy and Chrissie came to the front door to see her off, and she kissed them both, then picked up her suitcase and set off down the street. When she reached the corner of Thessaly Road, she turned back to wave, but they had already gone in and shut the door.

It was a long walk to Clapham Junction, but she wasn't going to waste money on buses or trams. The old suitcase, which had seemed quite light when she set out, soon became heavy, and she had to keep changing it from hand to hand.

At last she reached the alley behind Bryden Brothers, and rang the bell at the staff entrance; the nightwatchman let her in. It was a long climb up to the top floor, and when she got there she couldn't remember where the girls' dormitory was. Taking a chance, she turned left, but she had only gone a few steps along the corridor when a voice called: 'If you're looking for Malcolm, you're wasting your time – he's out.'

Startled, Jo turned. Nora was watching her from the other end of the corridor.

'I was looking for our dormitory. I forgot where it was.'

'Oh, yes? You'd better be careful you don't make that mistake again, or you'll be asking for trouble.'

In the dormitory, Nora stood and watched while Jo unpacked her case. When she went to put her nightie under the pillow, she found a small box of chocolates, and turned to thank Nora. 'Oh, you are kind, but you really shouldn't—'

'I didn't.' Abruptly, Nora turned away. 'I suppose that was Malcolm's idea – he's been saving up his sweet-coupons this month. Anyhow, I can't stick around here all night, I'm off out. If you want a cup of tea, the canteen's open for another half-hour. I'll show you where it is.'

The canteen was almost empty, and a tired-looking woman in a green overall was wiping down the tables. Malcolm – who had been sitting at the far end of the room with two other young men – got up and came to meet them with his hand outstretched, saying: 'Hello again! Good to see you. Is everything OK?'

Nora was tight-lipped. 'I thought you'd gone to the pictures. You always do, on Sunday nights.'

'I waited in to say hello to Jo first. Did you find the chocs I left for you?'

'Oh, yes, thank you very much, but you shouldn't—'

'My pleasure. I was going to ask – if you haven't got anything else to do, would you like to come to the pictures?'

Jo looked uncertainly at Nora. 'Well, I don't know . . .'

Nora said quickly: 'They have dreadful old films on Sundays, they're not worth paying good money for.'

'This will be my treat,' Malcolm insisted. 'And it's a good 'un this week – *The Wicked Lady*, with Margaret Lockwood and James Mason. How about it, Nora? What d'you say we all go together?'

Nora shrugged. 'If you like. But I'll have to powder my nose first. You two go on, I'll catch you up.'

The film was a little scratchy in places, but to Jo – who had hardly ever been allowed to go to the cinema – it seemed wonderful. Malcolm sat between her and Nora, and once she thought he was pressing his knee against hers, but it didn't happen again, and anyway he and Nora were holding hands, so it was probably her imagination.

At the end everyone stood to attention for the National Anthem, while a picture of the King appeared on the screen, then the lights went up and the show was over. Nora seemed to have recovered her good humour, and kept up a flow of chatter all the way back to Bryden Brothers.

At the top of the stone staircase, they said goodnight to Malcolm and Jo thanked him for an enjoyable evening, then they went to their respective dormitories.

The long room was full of young women; they seemed to be a cheerful, good-natured crowd, and her spirits rose. At last happiness seemed to be a possibility, if not right away, then very soon – tomorrow, perhaps.

Taking her nightclothes with her, Jo went into the washroom to undress and clean her teeth. Before she got into bed, she went to her little bedside cabinet; it would be nice to offer Nora a chocolate. The box was empty, except for the paper cups and shavings.

When she showed Nora the empty box, Nora beckoned her, and said in a low voice: 'I should have warned you – you mustn't leave your locker-key lying around. You can't trust anyone these days, can you?'

Another Sunday, in late September, summer was sinking into autumn. A month ago, Japan had surrendered to the Allies and the world had become a peaceful place once more, but there was a wintry chill in the air.

Now the Thames was deserted except for a string of blackened coal-barges. Somewhere in the mist, a ship's hooter sounded mournfully. The light was going; soon it would be dark.

The front door of a house in Cheyne Row opened, and someone stepped out, moving so quietly, even a footfall on the glistening pavements made no sound.

Someone was setting out for a solitary walk, shrouded by the rising mist and the shadows that closed in gradually upon Chelsea Embankment . . . Someone who was almost invisible.

There was very little traffic about. The stranger did not look right or left but walked across the Albert Bridge and over the river towards Battersea. Tall trees in the park stood like watchful sentinels; cranes along the wharf were poised, waiting for something to happen.

The stranger moved on, along Albert Bridge Road into Anholt Road where blank windows on either side watched and kept their secrets, then into a warren of narrow streets and workmen's cottages behind the wharves and warehouses – past a cracked name-plate, bearing the words: 'Mill Street'. One or two houses had lamps burning in their windows; most were dark and derelict – in some, a little daylight showed through a crack in the wall, or a gaping hole in the roof – and a barrier had been erected across the road, with the sign: 'Danger – Keep Out'.

Beyond that there were no houses, nothing but a pile of dirt and rubble, like a burial-mound.

The stranger stared at this wasteland for several minutes, while the last traces of daylight seeped from the sky.

There was nothing left here now but loss and desolation.

Darkness fell, slower than a bomb but with its own destruction, wiping everything out, and the stranger was swallowed up in the night, like a ghost.

Someone who had never died – someone who had never been born – someone who had no existence at all . . . What else could such a stranger be, except a ghost?

Throughout the long winter, London was trapped in the grip of frost and fog, clenched like an iron fist.

The staff quarters at Bryden Brothers had no heating. Fuel was still rationed, and though there was a little warmth in the shop, it was switched off every afternoon, as soon as the last customer had gone.

The staff grumbled about their cheerless living conditions, but Jo didn't mind. Life with Aunt Topsy had never been particularly comfortable, and she never felt any regrets about Agar Road. Here she had the company of other young people, and she revelled in her newfound freedom.

Not that she made friends easily – perhaps she had been on her own too long, and had lost the knack – but the other girls in the dormitory were pleasant enough. Only Nora was unpredictable: sometimes she would be perfectly sociable and then for no apparent reason she would become cold and withdrawn.

These changes of mood seemed to have something to do with Malcolm Jones, and Jo soon realised that if she wanted to remain on good terms with Nora, it was best to keep out of his way.

In any case, she was concentrating most of her energies upon her work. As a rule she enjoyed dealing with customers, and if she had to serve someone who was being difficult, she tried to rise to the challenge and handled them tactfully.

For the first few months she was put to work in Haberdashery, and that had not been easy. Nora treated her as an underling, making her fetch and carry, only letting her serve customers when they were busy.

Perhaps Mrs Spenlow had noticed this, because Jo was transferred to Ladies' Lingerie, where she had to cope with the continuing nightmare of rationing. Coupons were still required for all clothes, including underwear, and Jo had to cut out the little squares of paper carefully: three for a vest or a pair of knickers, two for stockings. She also mastered the till system, learned how to make up bills, count out the correct change, and make certain that the till-roll tallied exactly with the cash and cheques she paid in to the Accounts Department at the end of each day. She prided herself on her accuracy, and made no serious mistakes.

That was why she was all the more annoyed when – during the spring sales – she lost the key to her dormitory locker. She felt sure that she had put it down on her bedside cupboard while she changed out of her shop uniform, into her skirt and jumper. When she went to shut the locker the key had vanished, and though she searched high and low, it was nowhere to be found. So she had to confess that she had mislaid it. Mrs Spenlow gave her a lecture on carelessness, and provided her with a duplicate.

When the canteen meals were particularly unappetising, she sometimes went over to the Greasy Spoon for supper: sausage and chips, or Spam fritters and chips, or even a fried egg and chips, if there were any eggs to be had. 'Big Wally' Grice, the café proprietor, would never explain where he got his occasional supplies of eggs. He used to tap the side of his nose, saying: 'Ask no questions, and you'll be told no lies!'

Everyone suspected he had some black-market connections, but they weren't going to complain about that, as long as the food continued to appear on the tables in generous portions.

One evening when the café was half empty, Jo queued up, looking hopefully at the menu chalked on the blackboard. Eggs were never listed, but he might have one or two under the counter.

When it was her turn, she asked: 'Any chance of egg and chips?'

'Sorry, love, the hens ain't laying today.' Wally wiped his moustache with the back of his hand and leaned over the counter. 'Tell you what – d'you fancy a nice bit of rabbit stew? With potatoes and carrots, an' if you're lucky, you might even find a bit of onion floating round as well – how does that tickle yer fancy?'

'It sounds lovely. Wherever did you get rabbit?' she asked.

He tapped his nose. 'Me lips are sealed, love. But it's been simmerin' on the stove all day – real tasty, it is.'

'How much?'

'Anyone else, one-and-a-kick – but only a bob to you, gorgeous.'

She checked the contents of her purse; it was a Thursday evening and she wouldn't get her pay-packet till tomorrow.

'I'm sorry, I don't have that much on me. It'll have to be sausage and chips.'

Behind her, Malcolm said: 'She'll have rabbit stew, and so will I. Rabbit stew twice, Wally.'

'Oh, no, I couldn't possibly—' she began.

''Course you could. No arguments – let's bag that table in the corner.'

As they faced one another across the table, he said: 'Bit of luck, running into you like this. It's rather a special occasion.'

'What do you mean?'

'I got my call-up papers this morning – report at Brentwood Barracks for basic training in ten days' time.' His glasses had steamed up. He began to polish them on the end of his tie, saying: 'This is what you might call a farewell party.'

'Oh, Malcolm – but you'd been expecting it, hadn't you?'

'That doesn't make it any better. I'm glad you're here, I didn't feel like being on my own this evening.'

'Why, where's Nora?'

'Ask me another – I haven't seen her. She'll only get all worked up about it, and make a big song and dance. You know how she is.'

'But I thought you and Nora were – well, you know – together . . . ?'

'Oh, lor', no. She's all right in her way, but she talks too much.'

He broke off as Big Wally shouted: 'Grub up! Come and get it!'

The rabbit stew was very good, though they had to be careful to pick out all the sharp little bones. It wasn't until some time later, over cups of watery coffee, that Malcolm referred to his call-up again.

He began by saying there was a dance on Saturday at the Town Hall, and asked if Jo would like to go with him. Remembering Trafalgar Square and the jazz-band and Pete Hobden, she looked away, saying: 'It's very nice of you, but I'd rather not. I've never learned how to dance – not properly.'

When they left, Malcolm suggested a quick drink at the Falcon, but she refused that too.

They left the café and crossed the road. When they got to Brydens, he put his arm round her waist as they climbed the stairs. When they reached the top floor she thanked him for supper, and said goodnight.

She was about to turn away when he grabbed her hand, saying: 'Don't go, I've got something to tell you.'

'What is it?'

'Not here, people might come along. I know somewhere.'

He took her along the corridor, and opened a door into one of the store-rooms which was piled high with furniture; there was no light, except the glow of street-lamps through the windows. Malcolm pushed the door to, and began: 'I've been wanting to tell you for a long time – I expect you can guess. You must know the way I feel about you, Jo.'

Suddenly he grabbed her and tried to kiss her. His glasses bumped against her forehead, and he took them off, stuffing them into his breast pocket.

Jo did not want to hurt his feelings, but she felt very awkward and uncomfortable. Trying to disengage herself, she said: 'No, Malcolm, I don't think we should—'

'I'm mad about you, Jo. It's you I want, not Nora, and now I'm going away – I've got to tell you, before it's too late . . .'

He pulled her down on to one of the sofas, and she began to struggle, saying: 'Please, let me go—'

'Don't you understand? This is our last chance! Soon I'll be in the Army. I might never see you again – you've got to be nice to me. I've always been nice to you, haven't I?'

He was fumbling with her clothes now, trying to unbutton her coat – she could feel his breath, hot and moist on her cheek – for a moment they wrestled together, and then the door creaked open behind them.

At once Malcolm let go of her. They stayed quite still, listening, then heard a faint rustling sound, followed by footsteps moving away.

He heaved a sigh of relief. 'They've gone, it's all right. Jo, where are you going?'

Running for the door, she made her escape, down the corridor and into the dormitory. She was glad Nora wasn't there, but the other girls stared at her in surprise.

'What's up?' someone asked. 'You're out of breath – have you been running?'

'It's the stairs,' she gasped, then turned away and started to undress.

It had been a difficult evening; and the following day was worse.

★

A small delivery of nylon stockings had come in, and as soon as word got round, the Ladies' Lingerie department was besieged with customers. The whole lot were snapped up before midday, but women continued to pour in from all over south-west London, and some turned quite nasty: 'What are you doing – taking them home and flogging them on the quiet?'

Jo tried to remain calm, but it wasn't easy, and since many of the would-be customers decided that rather than go home empty-handed they might as well buy something else, she was kept busy all day.

Nora had been sent in to help because things were quiet in Haberdashery. Jo wondered how much she knew about the previous evening, but she was all smiles – more friendly than usual, if anything.

During a few moments' lull, Nora remarked: 'I suppose you've heard Malcolm's news? We shall miss him.'

'Yes,' said Jo, and changed the subject.

At the end of the afternoon she cashed up, taking the till-roll and the money to Accounts. She returned to her counter to tidy up, and then one of the cash-clerks came through and told her she was wanted in the office.

Jo was surprised to find Mrs Spenlow in conversation with the Chief Cashier. They both looked at her gravely, and Mrs Spenlow said: 'Shut the door, please, Miss Wells. I'm sorry to have to tell you that a discrepancy has come to light in your receipts. When the money was checked against the till-roll, there were twenty pounds missing.'

'There must be some mistake.' Jo stared at her; it was impossible for so much money to have gone astray.

'I'm afraid not. It has been checked and double-checked. That is why I must ask you if you can throw any light on the missing cash?'

'Surely you don't think I—'

Mrs Spenlow interrupted: 'Did you have a purse or handbag with you at the counter?'

'No!' Of course she didn't – it was strictly against the rules. 'I always leave my purse upstairs in my locker.'

'Then I must ask you to accompany me to the dormitory and open your locker.'

The dormitory was crowded. The girls were all talking at once, but they fell silent when Mrs Spenlow marched in and asked them to leave the room. They eyed Jo curiously as they went out; she saw Nora among them – smiling.

'Your key, please,' said Mrs Spenlow.

Jo took it from her pocket and handed it over. Mrs Spenlow opened the locker, found Jo's purse, and emptied the contents on to the bed.

Jo stared speechlessly at the money on the counterpane: two five-pound notes, eight pound notes, and a handful of silver and coppers.

Mrs Spenlow counted the money and collected it up again, saying: 'You realise you are the only person with a key to this locker?'

Jo said quickly: 'No, there was another key – don't you remember? I lost mine, and you gave me a spare one. Somebody must have taken my key and kept it.'

Mrs Spenlow sighed. 'Are you suggesting that someone took the money from the till, then put it into your purse – inside your locker? I hardly think that's very likely. I shall instruct the cashiers to make up an extra week's wages in lieu of notice. Please pack your belongings and remove them from this dormitory, then go to the Accounts Office to collect your pay-packet, and leave immediately. Under the circumstances, I cannot provide you with a reference.'

Chapter Three

'HERE Y'ARE LOVE – another coffee.'

Jo looked up in surprise as Big Wally put a brimming cup in front of her; some of it slopped into the saucer.

'I didn't ask for another one—' she began.

'I reckon you could do with it. On the house.'

The Greasy Spoon was almost empty. When she left Bryden Brothers, Jo had not been able to think of anywhere else to go. She had ordered a coffee, but nothing to eat; she wasn't going to waste her money – there was no knowing how long her pay-packet would have to last.

Wally Grice pulled out a chair and sat down opposite her.

'You've been given the push, aincher?' he asked.

'Who told you?'

'Nobody, but you've got your suitcase under the table, and from the look on your face, I reckon you're not going off on yer holidays! You've had the order of the boot – right?'

'Well – yes.'

'Thought as much. And now I suppose you've got nowhere to go?'

'I can go back to my aunt at Agar Road if I have to. I don't suppose she'd turn me away, only—'

'Only you don't want to – is that it?' When she nodded, he went on: 'Maybe I can help. I used to have a girl to clear the tables and help in the kitchen, doing the washing-up and that, but she left me in the lurch. Walked out without so much as a by-your-leave, and that's the last I saw of her. So if it's a job you're after, you're welcome to it.'

At that moment it seemed too good to be true, but she had to confess: 'I haven't got any references.'

He grinned. 'Why? What've you bin up to?'

So she had to tell him, and wound up by saying: 'But I didn't do it, honestly I didn't.'

'I'll believe you, thousands wouldn't. All the same . . .' Wally looked thoughtful. 'I get a lot of 'em coming in from Brydens. It might be a bit awkward for you, like.'

'I've done nothing wrong – I've got nothing to be ashamed of,' said Jo.

'Good for you, girl! OK, then, you can start first thing tomorrow. All right?'

As he pushed back his chair and stood up, Jo added: 'There's just one thing . . . I was living-in at Brydens – you don't know anywhere round here where I could get a room, do you? Somewhere not too expensive?'

Wally scratched his moustache. 'Not round the Junction, I don't. There's old Sarah's place, down by the river – that might be worth trying. Number 1, the Rope Walk, near St Mary's Church. Ask for Sarah Venus and tell her I sent you. 'Course, she might be full up, I wouldn't know.'

The Rope Walk was about a mile from Clapham Junction, and Jo's suitcase seemed heavier than ever. The drizzling rain soaked through her coat and her headscarf, and by the time she arrived she felt half-drowned. Sarah Venus sounded very grand – Jo hoped she would not turn her away.

It was quite dark by now, and she had some difficulty in finding the Rope Walk. This was the oldest part of Battersea and the streets were narrow, with houses crammed in, higgledy-piggledy, but at last she found a gaslamp with a name-plate below it, saying: 'The Rope Walk', and a fingerpost that said: 'To The River'.

The river itself was invisible in the darkness, but the Rope Walk was only a hundred yards long, and Jo knew that at the far end, across Battersea Church Road, a black tide lapped against brown girders and sucked at sea-green stones. She recognised the smell of muddy water and tar and engine-oil and drains, and sniffed the air, remembering her childhood.

The house with the gaslamp had the word 'One' painted on the half-moon fanlight over the door. It was tall and thin, and once upon a time it must have been very elegant. Through the murk, she could see that the stucco was peeling and some of the window-panes were cracked, but there were lighted rooms behind the curtains. Jo tugged at the old bell-pull and heard an answering jangle in the depths of the house, followed by footsteps on a creaking floor.

The front door swung open, and a husky cockney voice asked: 'Who is it?'

'Can I speak to Mrs Venus, please?'

'Who wants her?'

'My name's Wells – Josephine Wells. Walter Grice sent me. Mrs Venus doesn't know me.'

'No, I don't think she does, 'cos you're speaking to her. You'd better come in out of the wet.'

A little old woman in a long velvet dressing-gown trimmed with moth-eaten fur thrust her face up at Jo. Her short-sighted eyes were large and luminous. Scrutinising Jo carefully, she said: 'You must be drenched. Come into the kitchen and get warm.' Leading the way along a passage to the back of the house, she threw back over her shoulder: 'Mind how you go, this carpet's seen better days – well, who hasn't?'

Avoiding the holes and worn patches, Jo followed the old woman into the kitchen, where a fire burned in an old-fashioned range. For a small room, it held a lot of furniture: apart from the sink and the dresser and the kitchen table stacked with pots and pans, there was also an armchair, a rocking-chair and a wardrobe. To her surprise, Jo noticed there was a mattress on the floor beneath the table, with rumpled bedclothes, pillows and an eiderdown.

Sarah explained cheerfully: 'I got into the habit of sleeping down here during the bombing, and afterwards there didn't seem much point moving upstairs.'

Next to the larder there was a dressing-table, with jars and powder-bowls and scent-sprays and an old telephone. Sarah squinted at herself in the mirror, picked up a large powder-puff and dabbed her nose and cheekbones. The air was heavy with an aromatic perfume, and Jo sniffed again.

'Patchouli – it's my favourite,' said Sarah. 'Now then, take off those wet things and sit down. You can have the rocker, push Tibbles on to

35

the floor. He'll probably jump up again as soon as you sit down.'

So Jo sat down, and the grey tabby jumped up immediately, circled round a couple of times, then settled comfortably on her lap.

'Tell me your name again, dear. My memory's falling to bits nowadays, just like everything else.'

'Josephine Wells. I'm usually called Jo.'

The old woman plumped herself down in the other armchair and leaned forward, screwing up her eyes. 'You're a pretty girl, and no mistake. You might not think so now, but I was quite pretty myself, a long while ago.'

In spite of her peroxide hair and the thick powder and paint which failed to hide her wrinkles, the ghost of Sarah Venus was still there; no longer pretty, yet still – somehow – a beauty.

'Let's see, what were we talking about?' Sarah continued. 'Who was it sent you?'

Once again, Jo had to tell her story. When she had finished, Sarah nodded several times, then said: 'If you're going to work for Walter Grice, you'll have to keep your eyes peeled – likes to get up to a few tricks, he does.'

'I don't really know him very well, but he's been very helpful.'

'Oh, he's helpful all right – and he likes to help himself at the same time, so you'd better watch out. But I do have a room going vacant, as it happens. One of my regulars moved out last week. Would you like to take a look at it? I hope you've no objection to stairs, 'cos it's on the top floor. We'll take it nice and slow, 'cos I'm not as young as I used to be, and I run out of puff.'

As they left the kitchen, she added: 'I've got a phone, but I don't let the girls use it unless it's an emergency, otherwise I'd have them chattering away till all hours. If you want to ring someone, there's a phonebox round the corner.'

It was a long, slow climb to the top floor, and Sarah was wheezing by the time they got there. Pushing open a door, she struck a match, and a gas-mantle blossomed into a brilliant yellow light.

It was an attic room, sparsely furnished with a bed, a wash-stand, a cupboard, a chest of drawers and a chair. There was a gas-fire in the hearth, and a small gas-ring with a kettle on it.

'I don't allow cooking in the rooms, but you can hot up water for washing, or make yourself a pot of tea. You'll need sixpences for the meter,' Sarah told her. 'The convenience is on the half-landing, and there's a bath on the first floor. It's got a hot-water geyser, and you'll have to watch out you don't let the flame blow back, or we'll all finish up on the other side of the pearly gates, dear.'

The rent was thirty shillings a week, but Jo agreed at once. To her, this was luxury: for the first time in her life, she would have a room of her own.

'I'll take it,' she said.

'And I'll be glad to have you here,' said Sarah. 'When would you like to move in?'

'Well, I was hoping – would tonight be all right?'

'No time like the present.' Sarah folded her arms, looking very solemn. 'I hope you've got the money, 'cos the rent must be paid one week in advance. I have to be strict about it. Cash on the nail, every Friday, or out you go!'

For the next month or two, Jo was happy – or as happy as she could be, up to her elbows in washing-up water. When she wasn't at the sink, she was opening tins of baked beans, or cutting doorsteps of bread and spreading them with marge, or brewing gallons of tea in a fearsome urn that threatened to explode at any moment.. The only time she was allowed out of the kitchen was when Big Wally sent her into the café to scrub the floor, or give the tables a wipe-over with a smelly old dishcloth.

It was on one of these occasions that Nora Topping walked in with one of her colleagues from Haberdashery.

As their eyes met, Nora's face grew bright red, and she turned on her heel, saying: 'Come on, let's go somewhere else.'

And she dragged the other girl into the street, never to return.

Other members of Brydens' staff still patronised the Greasy Spoon. They generally passed the time of day and asked how Jo was getting along. One of the girls said: 'Nobody thinks you took that money, whatever Mrs Spenlow says.'

That was some consolation, though as a rule Jo never met the customers. Work in the kitchen was hard and monotonous, but she soon found she could get on with her duties – slicing carrots, or peeling and cutting up potatoes for chips – while her mind was on something quite different, like the film she'd seen last Sunday, or the library-books she read every night at bedtime, or the memory of a crowded pub in the Haymarket and the touch of a man's hand, that night. Was it really a year ago? It seemed like yesterday.

The only man she spoke to nowadays was Big Wally. As long as she got on with the tasks he gave her, he was quite satisfied, though she sometimes caught him watching her out of the corner of his eye.

It wasn't a bad life. Just a bit on the lonely side.

She hadn't made any new friends at the Rope Walk either. Sarah Venus was always very pleasant if they happened to pass in the hall, or when Jo paid her weekly rent – on the dot every Friday, without fail! – but she hardly ever saw the other lodgers.

They were all girls, she knew that much, but they seemed to keep very odd hours. Jo thought they might be nurses on night duty at the Battersea Hospital, because as far as she could tell they stayed in bed in the mornings, and were getting ready to go out when she came home in the evenings.

During the night they seemed to come in and out at all hours. She was often woken up by footsteps on the stairs, or smothered laughter, and bedroom doors opening and shutting.

One evening, not long after she had come home from work, there was a knock at her door. A girl with her hair in curlers and a kimono draped round her shoulders said brightly: ''Scuse me for barging in, but you couldn't spare me a spoonful of tea, could you? I got to the end of a packet last night. But I'll pay you back out of next week's ration, cross me heart and hope to die.'

Jo said there was no need for that, she was just going to make a pot anyway, and the girl seemed very grateful.

While they waited for the kettle to boil, she sat down and introduced herself: 'I'm Peggy Hooper. What's your name? You've got a day job, haven't you? I sometimes hear you getting up and going out in the mornings.'

Jo explained that she worked at the Greasy Spoon, and Peggy said: 'Wally Grice's place?'

'Yes – do you know him?'

'We have met,' said Peggy darkly. 'If you don't mind me asking, has he given you any trouble?'

'No. Why? What sort of trouble?'

'Oh, nothing . . . It's just that he thinks he's God's gift, so don't say

38

I didn't warn you. Funny, I'd never have pictured you working in a place like that.'

'Really?' Jo changed the subject. 'You work at the hospital, do you?'

'Whatever gave you that idea? I've never been that struck on nursing myself. Blood and bandages and bedpans – I wouldn't fancy it myself.'

'So what do you do? For a living, I mean?'

'Oh, part-time work, mostly – nothing regular. Bit of this and a bit of that . . .' Peggy crossed her legs. 'Goodness, that kettle's taking its time.'

Jo laughed. 'Well, you know what people say—'

'No, and I don't want to!' Peggy looked affronted. 'I never listen to what people say about me. What right have they got, passing remarks behind my back?'

'No, I didn't mean—' Jo tried to explain. 'I meant – you know the old saying – watched pots never boil.'

'Oh, that . . .' Peggy subsided. 'Yes, of course. Silly me.'

They were both grateful when the kettle boiled, and Jo filled the teapot. Peggy took her cup of tea and disappeared, with repeated expressions of gratitude. Afterwards, Jo wished she'd questioned her a little further about Wally Grice. Sarah had made some cryptic comments about him as well, and she couldn't help wondering what they meant.

A week later, she found out.

It was a lovely summer day, too good a day to sit indoors. Wally grumbled that most of his regular customers must have taken sandwiches into Battersea Park, or up on Clapham Common. The café was hot and stuffy, and the kitchen was hotter still.

Wally, frying bubble-and-squeak and warming up baked beans at the stove, had taken his shirt off, and his vest clung to his sweaty torso.

'Blimey, it's like flaming Timbuctoo in here!' he said, wiping his face on a teacloth. 'You must be boiled alive, girl, wearing all them clothes – you wanna strip off, like me.'

'I've only got a summer dress on,' Jo protested.

'Yeah, but what have you got underneath, eh?' He stretched out a bearlike paw. 'That's what I'd like to know!'

'Stop that!' She moved further away, out of reach. 'I can't get on

39

with the washing-up if you keep messing about.'

She retired to the sink at the other end of the room, keeping the kitchen table between them, but he went on teasing her.

'What kind of knickers have you got on, sunshine? Pretty little frillies, eh? Come on, give us a quick shufti!'

'Mind your own business!' she retorted.

For a while they worked in silence, until he exclaimed: 'I need some more fat, the potato's starting to catch. Fetch us down another packet of lard, there's a good girl.'

'Where is it?'

'You know where it is – up here!' He pointed to the shelf above his head: 'Buck up about it, before the spuds stick to the pan.'

She came over to the stove, standing on a chair to reach the top shelf.

At once, he put his hot, sticky hand right up her skirt, with a great guffaw. 'Gotcha!'

Without stopping to think, Jo picked up the first thing that came to hand and brought it down on his head. It happened to be the hot saucepan of baked beans. With a squeal of pain and rage he staggered back, clawing the beans and tomato sauce from his eyes and mouth.

'You little bitch!' he spluttered. 'You're fired, do you hear? Fired! Get out of here, before I bloody kill you!'

Jo had already torn off her apron, and was halfway to the door. Thank goodness, she thought, as she walked out of the smelly café into the fresh air. I won't ever have to go there again.

At last she understood the warnings about Wally Grice. She guessed why his previous assistant had 'left him in the lurch' so suddenly.

She was out of a job again; without a reference, she had very little chance of getting another. And Wally Grice still owed her a week's wages. Obviously, he would never pay her now. And to crown everything, today was Thursday . . .

'Cash on the nail, every Friday, or out you go!'

On her way back to the Rope Walk, she tried to think of a solution, but without success. As luck would have it, she met Sarah Venus on the doorstep.

'Hello dear, you're home bright and early today,' said the old woman, blinking at her like an owl.

'Yes, aren't I?' Jo tried to smile.

Sarah frowned. 'Are you all right, dear? You're not ill or anything?'

'No, I'm fine – really. Excuse me.'

And she darted in, running upstairs before Sarah could ask any more questions.

She sat in her room for some time, until a knock at the door made her jump – perhaps Sarah Venus had come up to find out what was wrong – and she said guiltily: 'Come in.'

But it was only Peggy Hooper from next door, saying: 'I know I'm being a real nuisance, but I wonder if you'd be very sweet and let me have another cup of tea, 'cos I seem to have run out again. Would you mind?'

'Of course not, sit down.' Jo put the kettle on, then added abruptly: 'Can I ask you something?'

'Depends what it is,' said Peggy.

'When Mrs Venus says "Cash on the nail on Friday, or out you go", is she really serious? Would she let me stay if I promised faithfully to pay two weeks next Friday?'

'Oh, lor' – are you skint? What happened to your job at the caff?'

When Jo had told her story, Peggy wagged her head sadly and said: 'That's the sort of rotten sod he is. He's barred from this house – Sarah won't have him no more.'

'Mr Grice, he's been here? Is that how you met him?'

'Oh, yes, he used to be one of the regulars at one time, until he started playing silly buggers. I mean, business is business, but that man tries to take advantage.' Then, seeing the look on Jo's face, she added: 'You must have caught on by now. Don't you know most of us are on the game?'

Jo understood at last. Girls in the school playground had often talked about women being 'on the game': neighbours, aunties, older sisters – mothers even, sometimes. Like all her classmates she had acquired a sketchy knowledge of the facts of life very early.

'Does Mrs Venus know what's going on?' she asked.

'She may be short-sighted, but she'd have to be blind and deaf and dumb not to!' retorted Peggy. 'She don't object, so long as we don't get in trouble with the law – and provided we pay the rent.'

The kettled boiled, and Jo began to fill the teapot. As she waited for it to brew, she asked: 'About the rent . . . What would happen if you couldn't pay?'

'She'd have us out, and no messing! Well, you can't blame her. It's the rule of the house, and once she made an exception, she'd have everybody living here rent-free before you could say Jack Robinson. No, you'll have to pay up tomorrow, duck, or it'll be "O-U-T spells out!" Haven't you got anywhere else you can go? No family, or nothing?'

'Of course I've got a family . . . Only I don't know where they are. We got sort of separated, during the war.'

She found it hard to get the words out, and Peggy eyed her speculatively over the rim of her teacup.

'You're in a real pickle, aren't you?' she said. 'Never mind, I might be able to help.'

'Could you?' Jo brightened up. 'D'you mean you could lend me some— ?'

'Oh, no, nothing like that. But I could teach you how to make some.'

'How do you mean?'

'It's not that difficult. I could show you where to go, what to say, how much to ask for.'

'You mean "on the game"?' Jo was horrified. 'Oh, I couldn't—'

''Course you could. That's how we all started – we had no choice. And from what you tell me, it looks like you've got no choice, neither.'

'I know you're trying to help, and I'm very grateful, but – I couldn't.'

Peggy stared at her and asked: 'You mean to say you're still a virgin? Haven't you ever been with a man?'

'Yes, of course I have.' Jo felt herself blushing. 'Well, sort of . . .'

'What d'you mean – just kissing and cuddling? Or all the way?'

'Well, no, I wouldn't do that – not unless it was somebody I loved. Not with a stranger.'

'In the long run it don't make that much difference, believe you me. There's not many women can say they've never gone to bed with a chap they didn't love. You might as well make up your mind to it. We all have to, sooner or later.'

Jo sat as if she were hypnotised, gazing at the steam rising from the spout of the kettle.

Putting down her cup and saucer, Peggy stood up. 'Hang on a tick.

I'm just going to fetch something.'

She returned a few moments later with a bottle and a couple of glasses, saying: 'Here, I owe you for two cups of tea, don't I? How about a nice drop of port instead?'

In the last rays of the setting sun, the wine glowed like a stained-glass window. Jo sipped. The taste was unfamiliar – Aunt Topsy would never have strong drink in the house – but it was rather nice. Soon she felt a pleasant glow, listening dreamily as Peggy continued: 'There's only one way you can make some money between now and tomorrow. I'll tell you exactly what you've got to do, then you'll have nothing to worry about.'

She went on to describe the whole procedure. It was shockingly frank, but it was straightforward and practical, and when she refilled Jo's glass, and that warm glow spread through her body, right down to her toes, Jo began to think it didn't sound so very terrible.

According to Peggy, everyone had to learn how to do it sooner or later, so why not now, when it would make all the difference between having a roof over her head, and being thrown out?

'I expect you're right,' she said at last. She felt as if she were floating above the rooftops, looking down on the scene, watching herself drinking port and listening to Peggy. 'Yes, that's what I ought to do.'

After all, there was no harm in trying, was there? If she didn't like it, she could always say she'd changed her mind, couldn't she?

'Where do I have to go?' she asked. 'To find somebody to do it with?'

'I'll take you out presently, when it's dark. Vicarage Gardens, down by the river, that's a good place for picking-up. I'll show you where to stand and wait, under the trees, and I'll teach you what to say. And I'll find you some other clothes. You need a bit of sparkle – the come-hither look. I've got plenty of things you can borrow.'

Peggy gook her into the other room, and pulled half a dozen garments out of her cupboard, holding them up against Jo. She finally settled on a lace blouse cut very low, and a bright red skirt, saying: 'That's the idea – now they'll be able to see you in the dark. And I'll give you a hand with your make-up.'

Jo let Peggy get on with it. She felt as if she were a doll being dressed, and remembered Vee's beautiful Bella, safely tucked away on the top shelf of her own cupboard, next to Charlie's teddy-bear . . .

'Oh, come on, give us a smile!' Peggy told her. 'Take a look in the mirror – you're going to be the belle of the ball tonight!'

A stranger stared back from the glass, with mascara'd eyes and rouged cheeks, and a cupid's-bow mouth like a spoonful of raspberry jam. Jo began to giggle – it seemed so silly.

'That's more like it!' said Peggy, proud of her handiwork. 'Men always go for girls who laugh. It makes 'em think they're going to have a good time.'

When they left the house, Jo felt as if she were going to a party.

Arm in arm, they went along the Rope Walk and crossed Battersea Church Road. Jo could just see the outline of St Mary's spire silhouetted against the night sky. They skirted the slipway that ran down to the Thames; lights shining from the wharves on the opposite bank were reflected in the river.

As they passed an old public house, they heard the buzz of voices from the saloon, and Peggy said: 'When they've had a skinful, they often come out for a breath of air. That's a good time to get them talking.'

Further on, Jo felt grass beneath her feet, and saw leafy branches overhead.

'This is Vicarage Gardens, where I generally hang out. Stay here and wait to see who comes along. If you want, you can stroll over to the river-wall and back again, but don't go too far or the other girls will get narked, being as you're new round here.'

Jo felt reassured: at least she would not be completely alone.

'Where will you be?' she asked.

'I'm going to take a chance down Vicarage Crescent – I don't want to queer your pitch. Remember what I told you: don't let 'em start anything till you've seen the colour of their money.'

Then she was gone. Suddenly Jo felt very lonely, and shrank back into the shadows. Far away she could hear a dog barking, followed by the thunder of a train crossing the railway bridge over the Thames. Then it was silent, except for the slow pad of footsteps along the path. Somewhere a man cleared his throat and there was a whispered exchange, too faint for her to hear.

The glow of the port was wearing off, and she began to wish she had not come out – but she must earn some money tonight; that was the important thing.

Now there were heavier footsteps approaching – unsteady, uneven – and the sound of a man belching. She could see the shape of him against the lights across the water. He seemed to be enormously fat, and from his lurching gait she guessed that he was drunk. To her relief, he passed on. There was one flickering gas-lamp at the end of the path, and she saw him stumble through the circle of lamplight for a moment before he disappeared.

Perhaps if she stayed here nobody would see her – but that was stupid.

Another man passed under the gas-lamp, coming towards her. She only caught a brief glimpse of him, but just for a second, he looked a little bit like Pete Hobden, except that he wasn't in uniform. In the past year, she had seen so many passing strangers who had resembled Pete for a moment – in busy streets, on buses or trams, a profile seen in a shop window, the back of a head in a crowd – but of course it had never been Pete.

Whoever he was, he was coming this way. He couldn't possibly see her in her dark hiding-place, and Jo knew she must make the first move. Summoning every scrap of courage, she took a step forward and said softly, in the words Peggy had taught her: 'Evening, dear. All on your own tonight?'

He moved closer, trying to see her through the blackness.

'Eh?' he grunted.

'Feeling a bit lonely, are you?' she went on, repeating her lesson. 'Looking for a nice time?'

He fumbled in his pocket for a packet of cigarettes, and struck a match. The flame illuminated their faces.

'Pete!' she gasped, overwhelmed with joy, and he stared at her as if he couldn't believe his eyes.

'Flippin' 'ell!' he said, then the flame burned his fingers, and he dropped the match, leaving them in the dark.

'I can't believe it,' she said. 'It's like a miracle.'

'That's not what I'd call it,' he said, and his voice was hard and sharp as Sheffield steel. 'I've been looking for you ever since last year. Every bit of leave I had, I came down to London. You told me you'd got a job in some big store at Clapham Junction, and I went to Arding and Hobbs, but they said they'd never heard of you.'

'It wasn't Arding and Hobbs, it was the other one – Bryden

45

Brothers.'

'I didn't even see that one. Daft, really, I kept coming to Battersea, wandering round on the off-chance I might run into you . . . And now I have.'

'I don't understand. How did you know where to find me?'

'I didn't know! How could I? Only tonight I was in this pub, see, and after I'd had a couple I got talking to some chap, and he said if I was on me own, I might pick up a bit of company around here. I take it you're not working in a shop these days?'

She heard the sarcasm in his voice but was too excited to understand.

'No, I got the sack from Brydens.' Her words tumbled over one another. 'They said I'd stolen some money. Of course I hadn't, but—'

'Don't tell me!' he cut in harshly. 'I don't want to know. So this is how you finished up.' He mimicked her: '"Are you looking for a nice time?"'

When the full realisation hit her, she thought she was going to faint. 'No – I haven't—' she stammered. 'It's not like that—'

'Don't come that with me.' He gripped her wrists tightly. 'D'you live around here?'

'Yes, I've got a room quite close by. But—'

'That's handy. C'mon then, let's go.'

He threw his arm round her shoulders, sweeping her off her feet. As he dragged her roughly along the path, she stumbled and nearly fell.

'You don't understand,' she panted. 'I couldn't, not like this, not with you.'

'What's wrong with me? My money's as good as any other man's, isn't it? Come on, Jo Wells, give me a nice time!'

Chapter Four

'SO . . .' PETE LOOKED ABOUT HIM. 'This is where you live?'

'That's right.' She put a match to the gas-fire and it lit with a pop. 'Sorry the room's a bit chilly. It'll warm up presently.'

'I daresay it will,' he grunted. Unbuttoning his coat, he hung it over the back of the chair, then sat down.

Jo sat by the fire, trying to stop shivering. Making conversation, she said: 'You're not in uniform. Aren't you in the Army any more?'

'Not for long, this is my demob leave. Once I get out, I'll be off to Sheffield, and I won't be coming south no more. I've had enough of London.'

On the way back from Vicarage Gardens, Jo had tried to explain – to argue with him – but he refused to listen to her, and they finished the journey without another word. He said nothing as she produced her key and unlocked the front door. Climbing the stairs, they passed two of the other girls on their way out. One of them fluttered her eyelashes at Pete, while the other gave Jo a knowing smile, saying: 'If you can't be good, be careful!' Then they clattered away downstairs, giggling.

On the second floor, a half-open door revealed a middle-aged man, peeling off his braces; he kicked the door shut as they passed.

Now, as the gas-fire deepened from yellow to orange, Pete stared at Jo. 'I certainly got you figured out wrong,' he said.

'No, you didn't.' She began again: 'It's not like you think.'

He looked away. 'Any fool can see what sort of place this is. I didn't come down in the last shower of rain. Have you got any booze? I could do with a drink.'

'No, I'm sorry. I can make some tea, if you like.'

He smiled sarcastically. 'Is that all you offer your visitors – a cup of tea?'

'I don't have visitors. You're the first.'

'Oh, yes?' The smile turned to a sharp laugh that made her flinch. 'I'm your first customer, is that it?'

'The first – and the last.'

'Get away, you must think I'm a right barmpot.'

'It's the truth! I needed the money, 'cos I got sacked today and—'

'Sacked – again?'

'Yes. I hadn't got enough to pay my rent, but I wasn't really—'

She broke off, unable to finish the sentence, so he finished it for her: 'You weren't really looking for pick-ups? Oh, come on. I was there, wasn't I? I *saw* you!'

A sudden anger flared up in her. 'Yes, and I saw you too. You were looking for company, you told me so. I did it for the money – you were doing it for fun!'

They glared at one another, and he muttered: 'I'd had a few drinks, that's all.'

'So had I. I wouldn't have done it otherwise.'

'D'you expect me to believe that?'

'I don't care what you believe!' She stood up. 'I've had enough of this. I think you'd better go.'

As she made a move to the door, he caught her arm. 'Oh, no, you don't. You picked me up, didn't you? You say you need money – all right, I've got money. How much?'

He began to unfasten his tie and unbutton his waistcoat, and she tried to stop him. 'Don't do that. Please!'

'What's up now? You were ready to go with the first chap that came along. What's wrong with me, all of a sudden?'

'There's nothing wrong with you, only—'

'Only what? Would it be easier with a stranger – is that it?' Without giving her a chance to reply, he went on: 'Because if that's the case, you've nothing to worry about. My God, you and me are strangers all right! We only met the once, and I was soft enough to think I was in love with you. Well, I'm not that stupid any more, but I still fancy you. Take your clothes off, and get on with it.'

Slowly, as if she were in a trance, she began to pull off her blouse,

48

and unhooked her skirt. Then she stood in front of him in her underclothes, while he sat on the bed, unlacing his shoes. When he looked up, something in her expression made him ask: 'What is it?'

She wanted to say: 'I still love you,' but she could only shake her head, backing away.

'Do I disgust you, or something? Is that it?'

Jo took a deep breath, and heard herself say: 'I'm sorry, I think I'm going to be sick . . .'

Then she grabbed her dressing-gown and fled from the room. Running down the stairs, she collided with Sarah Venus on the half-landing and burst into tears.

'Whatever's the matter?' exclaimed the old woman.

'I can't pay you, I haven't got enough money,' she sobbed. 'Please don't turn me out, not tonight.'

Sarah patted her shoulder, saying: 'There, now, don't take on so, dear. It'll be all right, you'll see. Here, take my hanky. Dry your eyes, and we'll go downstairs.'

In the kitchen, Sarah helped Jo into the rocking-chair, and began to make her a cup of cocoa, while Tibbles jumped up, kneading Jo with his paws, and turning her lap into a cosy nest. Purring loudly, he gazed up at her so adoringly, she nearly started to cry again – it was comforting to be loved, if only by an old tabby cat.

Sarah took the other armchair, and Jo began to drink the cocoa. In between sips, she tried to tell her landlady the whole story.

'. . . so when I walked out of the café, I hadn't been paid. That's why I – I was trying to get some money, to pay my rent.'

'I suppose Peggy put you up to it? Yes, she's got a good heart, but no more brains than a sparrow. When you came back with that young feller, I was quite worried. What happened? Did he step out of line?'

'No, not exactly. He—' Jo lifted her head, listening; someone was coming downstairs two at a time. 'Do you think that's him?'

Sarah got up to have a look; the front door banged, shaking the house. Sighing, she closed the kitchen door.

'That was him all right, in a nasty temper by the sound of it. That's the worst of going with strangers, you never know how they'll turn out.'

'He wasn't a stranger,' said Jo. 'I'd met him before, about a year ago. Somehow I thought that would make it all right – but it wasn't.'

Sarah's big eyes dimmed. 'And you're fond of him – is that it?'

'No!' Jo spoke so violently, Tibbles looked up in astonishment. 'I don't like him at all. I hate him.'

Sarah nodded. 'So it didn't turn out the way you wanted, and you didn't make any money?'

'I meant to pay you tomorrow. I would have done, if—'

'You did your best, nobody can do more than that. I daresay I could stretch a point and let it run on till next week, but you'll have to get yourself a job by then, 'cos I won't be so soft another time – understand?'

'Yes, thank you. Only I don't know how I'm going to get a job between now and then. I've got no references.'

'Maybe not, but good looks are worth any amount of references.'

'You mean I ought to try again, like I did tonight?'

Sarah frowned. 'I don't mean anything of the kind! You're not cut out for that sort of caper, and if Peg had a penn'orth of sense, she'd have seen that for herself. But you've got a good figure, pretty eyes, and good bones. Bones are important. Face and figure won't last, but if the bones are right, you'll go a long way. Can you sit still?'

Jo blinked. 'Sorry, was I fidgeting?'

'No, no. I'm asking you a question: can you sit still for more than five minutes? Could you keep still for half an hour, even an hour, if you had to?'

'I don't know. Why?'

'Because you'll need to, if you're going to be a model. I used to do a bit of modelling meself, once upon a time. It don't pay much, but it's not a bad way to earn a living, and it'll suit you better than the other thing! How about it, eh?'

'I wouldn't know how to begin.'

'I could probably start you off. Augustus John, now, I sat for him several times when I was a girl. He's got a studio over the river, in Tite Street. I could look out the address, and send you over with a little note. He doesn't paint much these days, but he might be interested.'

Her violet-shadowed eyes grew misty as she rummaged through memories of a long-distant past, then she shook her head. 'Perhaps not. He's a fine painter, but he does have his little ways. Perhaps we ought to start a bit nearer home. There's always Galleon House.'

'Galleon House? Where's that?'

'Just a few steps away, at the other end of the Rope Walk. A great big house, hundreds of years old, mostly studios now. There's three or four painters working there – and Russell Wade. Have you heard of him?'

'I'm not sure. Is he a famous painter?'

'He's done a few drawings and paintings, but that's not his line. He's a sculptor, and a damn good one. Anyhow, I'll introduce you to the whole lot tomorrow.'

Sarah was as good as her word. The following morning she spent a long time at her dressing-table, brushing her fine, white hair and smudging powder and paint on her face. Jo waited patiently, wearing her best dress – the one Aunt Topsy had meant for Chrissie – while Sarah pulled on a floppy velvet turban and wound a silk scarf round her neck.

'That'll have to do,' she said at last, and turned to face Jo. 'How do I look? Not too much like an old baggage?'

'You look very smart,' Jo assured her.

'You're a terrible liar!' Sarah patted her hand. 'Sorry I kept you waiting, but it's no use calling at the studios too early – most of them don't turn up till ten o'clock.'

'Oh, don't they live there?' asked Jo, as they set out.

'Bless you, no! They rent the studios, and come in by the day. Except for Mr Wade. He's got a flat on the top floor; the house belongs to him. He lets out the rest as studios and keeps one for himself. He's very clever – brilliant, they used to call him. You've seen his *Diana the Huntress*, haven't you? In Kensington Gardens, near the Serpentine. A goddess, she is, holding a bow and arrow and a blooming great dog on a lead . . . I was Diana,' she added modestly.

Jo was very impressed. 'I shall go and look for it.'

'You won't recognise me, I was slimmer in those days. I got dreadful cramp, the pose was a real devil: one leg stuck out behind me, leaning forward, hanging on to the lead – oh, dear . . .'

As they approached the end of the street, she said: 'Here we are. That's Galleon House, on the corner.'

It was a double-fronted Georgian house in mellow red brick, with a front door under a centre portico, and a small L-shaped wing on either side. The ground-floor windows were very tall, looking on to the river.

'Artists like to have a north light,' Sarah volunteered, 'though I don't know why – it's very chilly in winter.'

'It looks rather like a ship in full sail,' said Jo. 'Do you suppose that's how it got its name?'

'Ask me another,' said Sarah, opening the front gate, and they crossed the tiny patch of garden. There was a row of bell-pushes beside the door. Four of them were numbered, but the top one had a visiting-card printed with the name 'Russell Wade', and the words 'No Callers' scribbled across it in ink.

'He doesn't seem very keen on visitors,' said Jo, doubtfully.

'Not too sociable, p'raps, but if it's anything to do with his work he's quite different. We won't trouble him if he's upstairs; I'll try the studio. He's got number four, 'cos it's the biggest.'

Sarah pressed bell number four, but nothing happened.

'Seems like we're out of luck. Ah, well, let's try Reggie Bentley; he's bound to be in. He does illustrations for books, and magazines, and all that sort of thing. He's always looking for models.'

She pressed number three, and a few moments later the door was opened by a slight, nervous-looking man who peeped out anxiously, then said: 'Sarah, thank God it's you. I thought it might be somebody from the publishers, because I was supposed to deliver on Monday, and they're turning ugly. Who's this? I don't think we've met.'

Sarah introduced Jo, and Reggie escorted them into his studio. It was a glorious clutter, piled high with furniture. An easel, a drawing-board, tables covered with books and prints, open portfolios over-flowing prints, pictures of all kinds everywhere.

When Sarah explained the reason for their call, he pulled a long face and turned to Jo.

'I'd like to be able to help, but I've got nothing to offer, alas! I'm doing the illustrations for a boys' adventure serial about pirates, and you don't look much like an old sea-dog to me. And the next job's equally hopeless: a book about the war in the Middle East – Monty and Rommel, hundreds of Desert Rats, and the only females in sight are a pair of camels. If you'd like to try again in three or four weeks, I might have something.'

Sarah asked. 'What about Russell? D'you know what he's working on now? I rang the studio, but there was no reply.'

'He hasn't been there a great deal lately – I think he's sort of in between commissions. I should try the flat if I were you.'

'No, I don't like to bother him if he's upstairs. Is that Welsh feller still in number one?'

'Yes, though I don't know if he's there now. And I think he's given up figure studies; flower-pieces sell better. You could try the new man in number two. I think he goes in more for abstracts, but you never know.'

As they crossed the hall, Jo heard footsteps. A tall, broad-shouldered man was coming down the stairs. As their eyes met, she felt a tingle along her spine. His eyes were sea-green, steady and penetrating.

'Who are you?' he asked in a deep voice. 'What do you want?'

He must have been in his middle forties; there were streaks of silver in his shaggy black hair, but he had strong, vigorous features: wide cheekbones, a flattened nose like a boxer, and a firm, square jaw.

'We want you, Russell,' said Sarah.

'Dear God – Sarah Venus!' he exclaimed, and his face relaxed. 'How are you, my dear? Still living in the same old house? It's been a long time . . .' He took her hand for a moment. 'Why do you never call and see me these days?'

She shrugged. 'Time goes by so quick nowadays. I seem to be on the go all day; I daresay it's the same with you.'

'Oh, yes, I'm always busy.' He released her hand, and looked again at Jo. 'And who is this young lady?'

Sarah performed the introductions, and as their hands touched Jo felt the same electric tingle pass through her. She could not take her eyes from his face; at close range, the intensity of his gaze was extraordinary.

'So you want to find work as a model,' he said at last. 'Well, that might be possible. Can you spare me a few minutes now? I'd like to make some preliminary notes.'

'Yes, all right,' she answered, and turned to Sarah. 'We're not in any hurry, are we?'

'That's all right, I won't detain Sarah,' said the sculptor. 'You can get on with your busy life, my dear. I'll send your friend back shortly, safe and sound.'

'I'm sure you will.' Sarah flashed a smile at Jo. 'See you later.'

Mr Wade saw her out. Through the half-open front door, Jo could see them exchanging a few last words in the garden. When he returned, his lips were puckered in a quizzical expression, as if he were sucking an invisible lemon, and she wondered if he were already regretting his offer, but his voice sounded cheerful enough as he said: 'Shall we go into the studio?'

Studio Four was very different from Reggie Bentley's overcrowded studio. At one end there was a dais with an old oak chair upon it, rather like a throne, and the walls were lined with shelves, which held rows of books and small pieces of sculpture – a girl's head, a dancing figure, the bust of a bearded man – while beneath the shelves stood a line of large metal bins with lids, spattered with clay. At the other end stood an old sofa, covered in faded chintz, behind a table laid out with various cutting and shaping tools – coils of wire, and odd pieces of wood and metal twisted into fantastic shapes. In the corner, upon another dais, a monolithic piece of timber was surrounded by wood-chippings – a piece of work barely begun, Jo guessed, for nothing was visible but a curve that might have been a shoulder, and the line of an arm.

The windows were veiled in cheesecloth curtains. When Russell Wade pulled them aside a cloud of dust flew up – caught in rays of sunlight, the motes hung in the air.

Now Jo could see dust everywhere, even on the unfinished piece of wood. Nothing in this studio had been touched for some time.

Mr Wade grabbed a clay-stained rag and flicked it over the model's throne, raising still more dust, and said: 'Forgive the mess. I've been working on several ideas, but they're still at the thinking stage. I have to get them clear in my head before I can knock them into shape. Would you care to sit here, so I can take a look at you?'

When she sat down, he remained several feet away, fixing his eyes upon her. His scrutiny was so powerful, she could almost feel it on her skin, like the heat from a furnace.

Without turning his head, he put out a hand and groped for a sketchbook and a pencil, then made a few swift marks on the page. Slowly, he began to move around, studying her from every angle. At one point he cupped her chin in his hand, lifting her head slightly. Again, his touch was electric – she wondered if he felt it too. But he said nothing, and continued to prowl, making the occasional jotting in his sketchbook.

She sat very still, hardly daring to breathe. The silence was suffocating.

Once he cleared his throat and took a deep breath. She looked at him expectantly, and he said: 'Please – don't move.'

'I'm sorry. I thought you were going to say something.'

'I hardly ever talk when I'm working. It breaks my concentration.'

Time stretched out endlessly; she felt she had been sitting still for ever. At last he tossed the sketchbook on the table, saying: 'That's it. I've seen enough.'

Eaten up with curiosity, she dared to ask: 'Can I see?'

He made a purring sound, like a vocal smile. 'It's not a drawing, if that's what you think. I doubt if it will make much sense to you.'

But he held the book towards her. The page was covered with tiny drawings – one ear, the corner of her mouth, the tilt of her nose – others were simply curves and angles, like pieces of a jigsaw.

'Notes to remind me of my first impressions,' he told her. 'When can you come again?'

'Whenever you like,' she said.

'Fine. I pay a guinea a day, and a day usually means six or seven hours. I'd like you to be here at ten tomorrow, and ten every day after that, until the job's finished.'

'Tomorrow?' She thought for a moment. 'Tomorrow's Saturday.'

'I'm aware of that,' he said, with a touch of impatience. 'Why? Do you have a prior engagement?'

'No, nothing, only I wasn't sure you'd want to work at weekends. What about Sunday?'

'As far as I'm concerned, one day is the same as another. We work every day until further notice. Any questions?'

'No.' She stood up. 'Oh, just one thing – what do you want me to wear?'

He frowned slightly. 'I don't want you to wear anything.'

She stared at him. 'Oh, you want me to take my clothes off?'

She remembered last night, when she and Pete had begun to undress. To her dismay, she felt her cheeks flaming. She despised herself – and hated Pete more than ever.

'Don't worry about that.' Russell twisted his lips into the same quizzical expression as he explained: 'I'm proposing to model your head and shoulders; your clothes will be irrelevant.'

She gave a small sigh of relief. 'I didn't understand.'

He asked with a hint of amusement: 'Would it have bothered you?'

'I don't know . . . I haven't really thought about it.'

'If you propose to take up modelling as a career, you might have to think about it in future – but not for the moment.' He took the sketchbook over to the window, examining it in the sunlight. 'That will be all for now. Tomorrow at ten, don't be late.'

Since he appeared to have no more to say, she began to walk to the door. As she reached it, he asked abruptly: 'What did Sarah say your name was?'

'Jo. Josephine Wells.'

'Jo Wells.' For the first time, he smiled; a genuine smile, full of warmth. 'I won't forget again.'

Then the smile vanished. But the memory of it stayed with her as she left Galleon House – and she knew it would stay with her for ever.

Sarah met her in the hall, asking: 'Well? How did you get on?'

'He wants me to start tomorrow.'

Sarah hugged her, then said: 'You were so long, I'd begun to wonder what had happened to you.'

'He did a lot of sketches. He's going to pay me a guinea a day – he said that usually means six or seven hours.'

'Mind you keep an eye on the clock! Once Russell gets down to work, he forgets about time, but he's a good sort.'

When Jo went upstairs to change out of her best dress, she met Peggy on the landing, wearing her old kimono and looking half-asleep.

'Good morning!' said Jo. 'Have you been having a lie-in?'

'No. Why? What time is it?'

'Almost midday.'

'That's when I generally get up.' Yawning, Peggy began to pass by, then her face changed. 'Oh, lor', I nearly forgot. How did you get on last night? Margie and Roz said they saw you coming in with a feller. I thought you must have struck lucky. Wasn't he any good?'

'No, he wasn't,' said Jo. 'No good at all . . . But it didn't matter, because I've got myself another job now.'

When Jo explained, Peggy drew down the corners of her mouth, and said: 'I shouldn't fancy that. I know what them arty blokes are like – a lot of big chat, and no money at the end of it.' She shook her head sceptically as she trailed off to the bathroom. 'Don't say I didn't warn you!'

Next morning, when Jo entered Studio Four, she found Russell had set up his easel.

'I sometimes make a few charcoal sketches before I start work with the clay,' he told her. 'Forms and shapes, not a photographic likeness.'

When she took up her pose, he asked her to change position several times – to lift her head; to move to one side; to turn and look over her shoulder – but when he started work, there was no more talking. The morning passed in silence, though he sometimes gave a smothered exclamation when a stick of charcoal snapped, or if he accidentally smudged a line.

Again, time stood still. Jo began to feel hungry, and was afraid her stomach might rumble. Eventually Russell broke the silence, saying: 'That's enough for one day. Same time tomorrow, please.'

The following day, Russell started to make another charcoal sketch, but this time she gathered that the work was not going well. After a while he suddenly ripped the drawing up, and flung the pieces on to the floor.

'Hopeless,' he muttered, under his breath. 'Completely hopeless . . .'

Jo did not know if she were to blame in some way; perhaps she had moved without realising it, and lost the pose. Making a great effort not to relax, she tightened her muscles, and he barked immediately: 'Sit still, for God's sake!'

She began to say: 'I'm sorry—' but he interrupted.

'And don't talk. When you open your mouth, your whole face changes.'

Why was he in such a bad mood today, she wondered? Yesterday she had felt very close to him, but now a gulf seemed to have opened between them. He still gazed at her with the same intensity, yet she had the impression that he wasn't seeing her as a human being, but as an inanimate object – not as a person at all.

She longed for the session to come to an end, and again she began to suffer hunger-pangs. Sarah's lodgers were not allowed cooking facilities – the girls stocked up with things like cornflakes, tins of sardines or jars of meat-paste – and now Jo wished she'd had more than a cup of tea and an apple for breakfast. There was no knowing how long she would have to wait for her next meal.

Suddenly an awful realisation struck her – it was Sunday today, wasn't it? The shops would be shut. She tried to remember what she had left in her cupboard – would there be the heel of a loaf? Did she finish up the cheese last night?

Then she remembered something else . . . Aunt Topsy would be expecting her for tea.

Ever since she started work at Bryden Brothers, Jo had gone back to Agar Road for tea every Sunday. After she was dismissed from Ladies' Lingerie, she had continued to go back each week, but decided it would not be wise to tell her aunt that she had changed her job – Topsy Bone would not have considered working at the Greasy Spoon a respectable occupation for her niece.

Mr Wade had already abandoned one drawing, and started another. He might go on working for hours, and if she didn't turn up at four o'clock as usual, there would be trouble.

Jo stole a look at him from the corner of her eye. He seemed to be in a towering rage – this was not the moment to break in and say: 'Excuse me, but I've got to go at half-past three . . .'

She felt scared, and empty. Worst of all, she was beginning to feel dizzy.

She tried to take deep breaths, but it didn't do any good. Her heart was thumping, and she could feel the blood draining down from her head. The room seemed to be growing darker . . . She must get out into the fresh air—

Trying to stand up, she found that one leg had gone to sleep; then she slipped sideways from the throne, off the edge of the dais, and was swallowed up in a great darkness . . .

When she came to, she found herself staring at the ceiling. There was a funny, burning taste in her mouth, and someone was holding a glass to her lips. Russell Wade's face loomed over her, troubled and sympathetic.

'Have another sip,' he said. 'It'll do you good.'

Jo tried to swallow, but it was like liquid fire going down her throat.

She choked and spluttered, trying to sit up, but he stopped her.

'Stay where you are for a few minutes,' he said gently. 'You need to rest.'

She was lying on the faded chintz sofa, at the other end of the studio. 'What happened?' she asked.

'You passed out – keeled over before I could catch you,' he said. 'You were out cold for several minutes. Luckily I had some brandy; your colour's beginning to come back. How are you feeling?'

She looked into his eyes; no longer the cold, professional observer, he was all concern and tenderness.

'All right,' she said. 'I'm sorry to be so stupid.'

'I was the stupid one, keeping you here so long. When did you last have anything to eat or drink?'

'At breakfast . . . I'll be fine now.'

'I'm going to fetch you a hot drink. Stay there till I get back.'

She heard him running upstairs, and imagined him picking her up in his arms and carrying her across to the sofa. Feeling strangely happy, she closed her eyes.

'So there you are, Josie,' said Aunt Topsy. 'We'd nearly given you up!'

Chrissie bounced up and down impatiently, nudging her mother and saying: 'When are you going to ask her, Mum? Go on – ask her now!'

'Give over, Chrissie,' snapped her mother. 'Leave this to me, please.'

Sunday tea was a formal affair in the Bone household. The table in the front room had the best lace cloth on it, and the best china was set out. There were places for Chrissie and Jo at one side, with Mr Mulligan and Mr Penberthy seated at the other, and their hostess at the head of the table.

Jo slid into her place. 'Sorry I'm late – I got held up.'

'I daresay you did,' said Topsy darkly, as she began to pour out. 'Another ten minutes, and I'd have gone to the police!'

Jo blinked. 'I'm not that late, surely?'

'How was I to know what might have happened?'

Chrissie rattled her cup and saucer. 'Go on, Mum – ask her now!'

Mr Mulligan tried to intervene. 'Never mind. The girl's arrived in one piece, so you've nothing to worry about.'

'That's hardly the point, Mr Mulligan. Josie's my niece, and that gives me the right to make enquiries – wouldn't you agree, Mr Penberthy?'

Mr Penberthy poked a loose strand of hair back across his scalp and intoned heavily: 'You have every right, dear lady, and it's your bounden duty. In such cases, you must leave no stone unturned, until light is shed upon the darkness, and the truth is revealed.'

Aunt Topsy leaned forward, speaking slowly and clearly, aiming each word like a poisoned dart. 'Then perhaps you'll be good enough to tell us, my girl – what have you been keeping from me, eh?'

Jo's heart sank, but she tried to brazen it out. 'I don't know what you mean.'

'I think you do. You've been deliberately misleading us, all this time. I might never have found out, if it weren't for the summer sales.'

'I don't understand.'

'The sales – at Bryden Brothers. I'd been thinking of buying some new sheets. I wanted to try Arding and Hobbs, but they were so crowded, I went to Brydens instead – and while I was there, I thought I'd drop in to Ladies' Lingerie and pass the time of day. But you weren't there, were you?'

'Well, no, not exactly—'

'Not at all!' Topsy Bone interrupted her. 'Because when I enquired they told me as how you'd been dismissed, months ago! And ever since then you've been coming here to tea of a Sunday under false pretences. All these weeks, you never said a word about it. I'd call that deception – wouldn't you, Mr Penberthy?'

'It certainly appears to require some explanation,' he agreed.

Jo said: 'Yes, I was sacked – unfairly – for something I didn't do. They said I'd stolen some money, and I hadn't. They wouldn't even listen to me. I didn't tell you, because I knew you'd be upset.'

'There now, she was trying to spare your feelings, the darlin' girl,' Mr Mulligan began, but Topsy waved him aside.

'What I want to know is – what have you been doing since then? Where have you been living, might I ask?'

Jo told them, as briefly as possible, that she had taken a job in a café, and Topsy exclaimed: 'That's not what I'd call a suitable situation for a young girl!'

'No, I thought you wouldn't. That's why I didn't tell you. So I took

60

a room in a boarding-house, and I've been living there ever since.'

'What did I tell you?' interjected Mr Mulligan. 'Didn't I say there'd be no harm in it?'

'How do we know there isn't? What sort of people are there at this boarding-house of yours?' Topsy wanted to know. 'A crowd of loose-living young men, I'll be bound!'

'There aren't any men living in the house,' said Jo. 'The landlady only takes young women; she's very particular about that.'

'Oh. Well, that does make a difference, I suppose . . .' Topsy simmered down slightly. 'So that's how things stand, is it? You're living in a girls' hostel, and working as a waitress?'

'Well – no, as a matter of fact, I gave that job up as well. I didn't like the man who owned the café; he wasn't very well behaved.'

Aunt Topsy sipped her tea. 'What are you up to now? What kind of job have you got?'

Jo held her head high. 'I'm modelling for an artist – Mr Russell Wade.'

'Modelling?' The teacup slipped from Topsy's hand, spilling tea over the lace tablecloth. 'Now look what you've made me go and do. Chrissie, fetch a dishcloth – and shut the door behind you!'

As soon as Chrissie left the room, Topsy whispered: 'You mean to tell me you pose – undressed – for some low-down painter?'

Jo said indignantly: 'Certainly not! He isn't a painter, he's a sculptor. He's a very famous man, with letters after his name. There are statues by him in Hyde Park. And I don't pose in the nude – it's just head and shoulders.'

'I'm sure your auntie didn't mean to hurt your feelings,' said Mr Mulligan. 'It's all been a misunderstanding, and now it's cleared up, why don't we all get on with our tea and say no more about it, eh?'

Chrissie burst in with the dishcloth, asking: 'Have I missed any good bits? What did Jo say?'

'Nothing,' said her mother, flatly. 'Give me that cloth, and eat your bun. You've missed nothing.'

When Jo arrived at Galleon House on Monday, Russell met her at the front door and asked: 'Are you sure you're well enough to work today?'

'Oh, yes, I'm fine. Don't worry.'

The furniture in the studio had been moved. The chintz-covered sofa had replaced the throne on the dais, and Russell explained: 'When you were lying on the sofa, you looked so young and vulnerable, somehow. I'd like to draw you like that – curled up, with your head resting on your arm, like a sleeping wood-nymph.'

She sat on the couch. 'With my feet up, like this?'

'Yes, you'll probably find it more comfortable. And I promise I'll keep an eye on the time. At one o'clock, we'll have coffee and sandwiches – all right?'

'That sounds very nice.' Jo tried to get into the correct position. 'Did you say, my head on my arm?'

He hesitated, then continued: 'There's one other thing. The other day, I said it wouldn't be necessary, but, well, for this particular subject, being neo-classical . . . How would you feel about modelling – nude?'

Of course she had to say no, but she couldn't help smiling. It was such a coincidence, after the tea-party argument. Then she looked into his eyes – and in that moment everything changed.

'All right,' she said. 'If you want me to.'

Chapter Five

He did not seem particularly gratified by her decision, but nodded in a businesslike way.

'Then I shall leave you to get ready,' he said. 'Take your time, there's no hurry.'

With that, he turned and walked out.

Then Jo noticed another change of furniture in the studio. A three-panel folding screen had been set up at the far end, and when she went to investigate she found a silk dressing-gown laid over the back of a chair.

Slowly, she began to get undressed. She had worn her best dress again today; now she thought, as she fumbled with hooks and eyes, she need not have bothered.

Taking the dress off was easy enough; the next stage was more difficult. It seemed hard to slip off her petticoat in a strange room, in a strange house, and stepping out of her knickers was even more difficult. When she stood naked, it felt like a dream; one of those dreams where she was in a busy street with no clothes on, and everyone was staring at her.

Hurriedly, she pulled on the dressing-gown, and as she did so she knew that Russell had worn it himself. It smelled of him – a mixture of tobacco, and Pear's soap, and the lotion the barber put on his hair. She closed her eyes, wishing that her heart would stop thumping, wishing that he would come back and start work, wishing that he would never come back . . .

But he was paying her to do a job of work; that's all it was – a job, just like any other.

Breathing deeply, she walked the length of the studio. The bare boards were cold beneath her feet, and she hoped there wouldn't be any splinters. Mounting the dais, she sat upon the sofa and waited.

After some time, the door opened and Russell appeared.

'All right?' he asked, without looking at her.

'Yes, thank you,' she said, and her voice sounded shrill and thin.

'Let's start work, then,' he said. 'Take up the pose, as I told you.'

He moved away, busying himself with sheets of paper and sticks of charcoal. While his back was turned, Jo stood up, letting the dressing-gown slip from her shoulders, telling herself that it would only be like stepping into the water at the swimming baths – once you were in, it wasn't as bad as you'd expected.

But she still felt embarrassed, as she lay down on the sofa – her knees drawn up, her head resting on one arm. He hadn't looked at her once; he was fixing the paper to a drawing-board, moving it from one place to another, glancing up at the soft sunlight through the curtained windows, switching on an overhead light – a workman, going through the motions of his trade.

Jo forced herself to speak. 'Is this right?' she asked, in the same high unfamiliar voice.

He looked at her; a swift, professional summing-up.

'Left knee raised a little more . . . Right arm forward – not too much . . . Keep it like that.'

Taking up a stick of charcoal, he began to draw.

Gradually she relaxed. Because there was nothing else to look at, she looked at him, looking at her. She saw the way his hair curled back from his forehead, and the beauty of his high, wide cheekbones – and his eyes, deep green, and glittering . . . She could not stop looking at his eyes.

She stared at him openly, because he scarcely glanced at her face; those piercing eyes were intent on her body – examining her shoulders, moving slowly over her breasts, down to her thighs, and the shadowed valley between her thighs – and she felt the same tingle of electricity that had startled her at their first meeting. It was as if his intense gaze was a physical contact upon her skin like the touch of his hand. A strange joy grew within her, a joy she had never known before.

It was as if he were slowly caressing every part of her – tenderly, lovingly – and her body responded like a flower unfolding its petals to the sun. As she basked under that radiance, her skin was glowing, her muscles relaxing, her inmost secrets open to him, warm and melting . . .

When Russell announced that it was one o'clock, she said: 'Already? The time seemed to go so fast today.'

'For me, too; the work's coming on well. You didn't seem to be as tense as last time.'

'I was afraid I might feel a bit, you know, awkward. But once we started, it was easy.'

Not only easy – exciting, thrilling, wonderful . . . But she couldn't tell him that.

'Put on the dressing-gown, while I go and rustle up some food.'

When he came back with a flask of coffee and a plate of sandwiches, they sat on the edge of the dais, chatting about this and that – trivial, ordinary topics.

'I hear they've started rationing bread now, on top of everything else,' he said. 'Anyone would think we'd fought the war and lost!'

It was hard to imagine Russell fighting, and Jo asked: 'Were you in the Army?'

'Not exactly, though it's kind of you to suggest it. I was a touch too old for active service, but I managed to get into uniform, after a fashion. I volunteered as an official war artist; they sent me over with the landing-forces in Normandy. I had quite a jolly time of it, until a stray bullet cracked my chest open and made a mess of my left lung.'

'Oh, how terrible.'

'Not really. I had a spell in hospital, and now I'm right as rain. Anyhow, that's enough about me. What were you up to during the war?'

'Oh, I didn't do anything.' She didn't want to go into all that. 'I didn't leave school till the war was over.'

'Of course, I keep forgetting how damn young you are . . . More coffee?'

After lunch, he carried on working for a couple more hours, and at last announced that he had done enough for one day. 'I've got all the sketching I need. Tomorrow I'll start on the clay.'

'May I look?'

'If you want to.'

The sketch was very good, she could see that. It was a real girl, resting her head, sleeping peacefully – warm, and vivid, and alive.

'It's just a preliminary outline,' he told her. 'I rather wish I'd worked it up with some colour. Your skin has an unusual quality – soft and glowing, like a peach. Never mind; the real work starts tomorrow.'

'How long will it take?'

'It depends how long I take to get it right! Weeks, probably – months, even. You'll be bored stiff by the time it's finished.'

'Oh, no,' she smiled. 'I won't be bored.'

When she left Galleon House, she was still smiling.

It was too good a day to go straight back to Sarah. She decided to go for a walk – over Battersea Bridge, and back across the Albert Bridge. A tug whooped cheerily on the river, where the water shone and sparkled; the spire of St Mary's soared up to a clear blue sky; a flock of seagulls spiralled around it, their white wings outspread – and Jo's heart lifted with them.

Last week she had been in the depths of despair; her world had collapsed in ruins, and it was all Pete's fault. But today everything had changed, and Pete Hobden would never be able to humiliate her again. And she was in love – really in love this time – with the most wonderful man in the world.

Pick up the pen, sit with it in your hand, poised above the paper. It's one of the smart new ones – what's it called? Oh, yes – a 'Biro'.

You'd like to write someone a letter, but you can't. Because there's nobody you can share your thoughts with.

You could write a private diary, but if someone else were to find it, and read your secrets, that would be the end of everything.

Don't write anything down. Never confide in anyone. You are alone, and you will always be alone, for the rest of your life.

If you can call it a life.

Outside the window, it's a beautiful sunny day. Stand up, walk to the window and look out. Up here on the third floor, you have a wonderful view across the river, to the trees in the park. But you don't go to the park any more, because just over the bridge there's the turning off to Mill Street, and Mill Street has gone now. There's nothing left; the houses that were still standing after the bomb fell have

66

been wiped away altogether. You've seen the bulldozers, and the excavators, and the lorries unloading bricks and scaffolding.

Mill Street had been swept away, along with everything else; you can never go back.

There are boats on the river, barges sailing past, the sun glinting on the water. Down below, people are strolling along the Embankment, past the gardens of Cheyne Walk – young men in sports shirts and flannels; girls in summer dresses; a girl in a forget-me-not-blue dress, with royal blue collar and cuffs, a girl who looks a little bit like—

Oh, God, it couldn't be – could it?

She's walking along quickly, she'll be gone in a moment. Don't waste any time – go after her, go now!

Out of the bedroom, down the stairs, round the second-floor landing; down again, past the dining-room and the drawing-room, headlong down the last flight, clutching at the banisters—

Clattering over the tiled floor in the hall, fumbling for the handle of the front door, the safety catch, the double lock—

Out into Cheyne Walk, where the sunlight hits you like a lightning flash, dazzling and confusing you—

Screw up your eyes. Where did she go, the girl in the blue dress?

You run blindly along the pavement; you stop at the corner of Oakley Street. Strangers push past you, but she's nowhere to be seen. You must have imagined it. It was only imagination, or a trick of the light, because Jo is dead. She died years ago.

You are alone. You have always known that.

Breathless, you walk home again. The front door is still wide open. You walk up the steps, into the cool, shady hall. From the first-floor landing, a familiar Scottish voice calls down: 'Is that you, dear? I thought I heard you go out.'

You call back: 'Yes, I thought I saw someone go by – somebody I used to know. But I made a mistake.'

On Tuesday Jo arrived at Galleon House ten minutes early, but Russell opened the front door very promptly. He was wearing an artist's smock with a big pocket at the front; it was stained and grubby, in striped blue-and-white canvas like a butcher's apron.

'Forgive my working-clothes,' he said. 'You're early, but I've done most of the setting-up already. I've been at it since the crack of dawn.'

When she entered the studio, she saw he had been busy. A modelling-stand was set up in front of the dais – a four-legged wooden stool, waist-high, with a flat board on top, and on the board lay a weird construction of metal rods and twisted wire.

Intrigued, she asked: 'What's that?'

'That's you,' he told her. 'At least, it will be. That's your skeleton – the armature, if you prefer the technical term.'

Looking more closely, she recognised a faint resemblance to her pose – the curved backbone, two cross-pieces for shoulders and hips, and bent wires representing her arms and legs.

'I put this together from the sketch I made yesterday,' he went on. 'But I'll need your help to put some flesh on this bony creature. I warn you – this is a long job, so don't expect miracles.'

She went behind the screen to undress. Today, she felt no embarrassment at all. She put on the silk dressing-gown to cross the studio floor, but as soon as she reached the dais she slipped it off without any hesitation, and took up the pose.

He threw in a few trivial corrections: 'Your chin's tucked in, I can't see your face. Open that hand, don't clench the fingers. It's not a fist.'

He dragged over a metal bin with a damp cloth lying across it. Rolling up his shirtsleeves, he plunged in his hands wrist-deep, then flicked handfuls of clay on to the metal framework. As the morning ticked away, a figure began to emerge on the modelling-stand – faceless and formless, more like a scarecrow than a human being.

His technique was so different from the deft artistry of the previous day, Jo felt a twinge of disappointment. Today she had become an object once again, a shape – lumps of sticky clay flung together, nothing more.

Yet he was so energetic and cheerful, like a boy absorbed in his hobby, she loved him more than ever.

By the end of the day, he had achieved something very like the human form. Surely at this rate the work would not take long. But the next day the pace slowed down. In the days that followed it became slower still, and she realised that this was where the real skill came in.

Now he was not throwing on lumps of clay; he was cutting, paring, shaving it with a wooden spatula, a wire loop, a blade like a scalpel, and using the tips of his fingers to make the smallest, most delicate touches. He was as intent as ever, but it was a slow, serious process.

He was not whistling now.

One morning she arrived to find the front door already open. She rang the bell of Studio Four, but nothing happened, so she walked in and found that the door of Russell's studio was ajar.

On the modelling-table, a damp cloth covered the clay figure, with a message propped up against it: 'Had to go out – make yourself at home. R.W.'

She had never seen his handwriting before. It was full of character – a thick black script with broad down-strokes and narrow up-strokes. Beneath his initials, a few words had been added in scrawled capitals: 'COME UP TO TOP FLOOR.'

It was obviously an afterthought. He must have come back already, and was waiting for her upstairs. Jo felt a surge of excitement; he had never invited her to his flat before.

She had tried to imagine him up there, and wondered how he managed to fend for himself. Remembering the days when her mother had gone out to 'do' for wealthy families in Chelsea, she decided he must have someone to keep the place clean and cook his meals. Perhaps he employed a housekeeper.

Inquisitively, she made her way up the broad Georgian staircase. At the top of the stairs was a closed door. Painted green, it had a small round window of frosted glass set into it, shaped like a daisy. She rapped on the glass, and a woman called out: 'Push the door, it's not locked.'

The door opened halfway along a passage like the corridor of a train, running the full width of the house, with doors on one side.

Immediately facing her, she could see into what seemed to be a drawing-room, and the woman called again: 'I'm in here.'

The drawing-room was a long, low room, furnished with smart modern sofas and deep armchairs, upholstered in faded chintz. The floor was covered with a thick white carpet. There was a white baby-grand piano, and a huge radiogram. The fireplace at the end of the room had a large glass jar of madonna lilies in it. Jo saw several photographs in silver frames: glossy portrait studies of a glamorous, dark-haired woman, smiling, laughing, or looking soulfully into the camera – and the same woman was seated in one of the armchairs, still glamorous, though several years older. She held out her hand, saying in a deep, husky voice: 'You must be Jo. I've been longing to meet you. I'm Laura Stanway . . . Russell's wife.'

She never knew how she got through the rest of the day. Somehow she kept smiling, talking easily and politely, determined not to give way.

That evening, when she got back to her room in the Rope Walk and shut the door behind her, she threw herself down on her narrow bed and waited for her grief to overflow. But the tears stuck in her throat.

Russell's wife had been very nice to her. She insisted on making coffee, and pressed her to have a chocolate biscuit. 'We manage to get them off the ration, under the counter. I happen to know this darling little man at Fortnum's . . .'

She had explained why her name was Stanway and not Wade: 'I'm an actress. I don't suppose you ever heard of me, because I haven't made any movies in donkey's years, and I don't expect you often go to plays in the West End, do you? Anyhow, Laura Stanway is my stage name, and after I married Russell, I hung on to it because otherwise it would have muddled everyone so dreadfully . . .'

She asked Jo a stream of questions.

'Where do you come from, my dear? . . . Oh, heavens, dear old Sarah Venus. Is she still alive? . . . But where did you live before that? . . . Near the Power Station? How magnificent. I always think those huge chimneys look just like some ancient Greek temple, don't you? So what made you decide to take up modelling? . . . Russell never tells me a thing about his work, but I guessed he'd discovered a new model, because all of sudden he became frightfully energetic. When I asked him, he said he'd found this lovely child called Jo Wells. I've been simply dying to meet you.'

She went on to explain that Russell had had a phonecall last night from an old friend who ran a gallery in Chelsea, and this morning he'd gone rushing off to talk about dates for an exhibition of his recent work.

'Not that there's been very much recent work, actually, but he has high hopes of this new thing he's started. He told me he was going to leave a note for you in the studio, so I thought I'd tiptoe downstairs and take a little peep at the work in progress. No wonder he's been so enthusiastic; it's going to be simply divine when it's finished, I can tell . . . You have such a perfect figure, my dear – but at your age that's hardly surprising.'

Laura stood up, stretching her legs and gazing thoughtfully at her reflection in a long mirror. 'People say I've managed to keep my figure pretty well, but I'll never look the way you do. I expect it's what they call the bloom of youth.'

Jo broke the silence by asking: 'I suppose you must have modelled for Mr Wade heaps of times?'

'Modelled? Goodness, no, he pays people to do that.' Laura added quickly: 'Oh, dear, I didn't mean to be rude. But I've always been too busy working, you see – plays and films and so on.'

'Oh, yes. Are you in a play at the moment?'

'Not at this very moment, but I get sent masses of scripts, all the time. It's a question of picking the right part; one has to be so careful.'

Then the door had opened, and Russell came in, frowning.

'Ah, there you are, my sweet.' Laura held out both arms to him, and he went over and kissed her, before greeting Jo.

'Sorry I wasn't here when you arrived. I had to go and see someone, unexpectedly.' He turned back to Laura: 'I found your postscript on the note in the studio.'

'So dreary for poor Jo, sitting there all by herself. I thought I'd ask her up for coffee. You don't mind, do you?'

'Why should I mind? Is there any left in the pot?'

As he poured himself a cup, Laura continued brightly: 'Jo and I have been getting on like a house on fire – haven't we, my dear? You should have introduced us ages ago. I'm sure we're all going to be such good friends.'

Staring into the shadows, Jo saw Laura's face before her – the raven-black hair, those heavy-lidded eyes and full, sensual lips – and heard again that husky voice: '. . . *He said he'd found this lovely child called Jo Wells . . .*'

A 'lovely child', that was how Russell thought of her – when he thought of her at all.

A soft tapping at the door roused her from these bitter thoughts, and she tried to pull herself together, asking: 'Who is it?'

'Only me,' said Sarah. She turned the handle and walked in, saying: 'Sorry to bother you, dear, but I saw you just now, when you came in, and you looked as if – I don't know – as if something terrible had happened.'

'Did I? No, nothing's happened. Nothing at all.'

Sarah came closer, peering. 'Are you sure? You still seem—' She began again. 'Is it something to do with Russell?'

Suddenly, Jo blurted out: 'Why didn't you tell me he was married?' And then the tears came.

Sarah hugged her, patting her shoulder and murmuring: 'That's right, have a good cry . . . I suppose I should have guessed. What's he been saying to upset you?'

'It wasn't anything he said,' Jo sobbed. 'It was her – Laura.'

'That Laura Stanway, she's got a wicked tongue when she's in one of her moods. But she's no right to go taking it out on you!'

'She didn't. She invited me up for coffee – she was very nice. That's what made it so awful!'

And then she could not speak at all, because her tears were choking her.

That night she lay awake for a long time, dreading the day ahead, having to face Russell as if nothing had happened.

Except – nothing had happened. That was her only comfort: Russell had no idea she had fallen in love with him. Thank goodness, he would never know.

But she still found the thought of working at the studio hard to bear; modelling for Russell, being close to him day after day. She thought wildly of sending a message to say she had been taken ill, but that meant leaving him with the statue half-finished, which wouldn't be fair. No, she had to stay on, as long as he needed her.

Besides, although it would be painful to go on seeing him, not seeing him would be worse still.

Next day she hoped he would not notice how tired she was, or remark on the dark circles under her eyes.

All he said was: 'You're looking pale and interesting today. There's something different about you – is it a new dress?'

It was one she had worn several times before, but when she told him so he only shrugged and said: 'I hadn't noticed. Anyway, it suits you. By the by, Laura asked me to tell you how much she enjoyed meeting you. She said any time you feel like dropping in for a cup of coffee, you only have to ring the top bell.'

'Oh, I wouldn't want to bother her.'

'No bother. She doesn't see many people; she gets rather tired of her own company.'

'I'd have thought she met lots of people, being on the stage – all those actors and actresses.'

Russell sighed. 'It's quite a while since she appeared on stage. Between ourselves, she's not been terribly well for the past few years. Not well enough to tackle a long run in a play.'

'I'm sorry. What's wrong with her?'

'It's a combination of things, really . . .' Russell took the moist cloth off the clay model and examined it thoughtfully as he went on: 'She has good days and bad days. You know how it is.'

Jo sensed that he didn't want to go into details. The subject was dropped, and he started work.

The months that followed were difficult for Jo. She kept telling herself the torment would soon be over. But this would create more problems: when Russell no longer needed her, she would be out of work.

One day, as she arrived at Galleon House, she met Reggie Bentley on his way out shopping and he greeted her cheerfully: 'Hello! I was thinking about you last night. Russell's still keeping you busy, I suppose?'

'Well, yes, but I think the job will be coming to an end soon.'

'Good. I've got a commission to illustrate a woman's magazine serial, and I need someone to model for the heroine. Would you be interested?'

'I certainly would. How soon do you want me?'

'I'm hoping to start on it next Monday. Would that suit you?'

'I think so. Of course I'll have to ask Mr Wade first – can I let you know?'

Feeling more cheerful, she went into Russell's studio. He was spraying a fine haze of water on to the clay figurine, and said without any preamble: 'We have to keep her damp. If she dries out, she'll crack. But she's looking pretty good, don't you think?'

'Yes. She looks to me as if you'd almost finished.'

'So I have. A couple more days, and then she'll be ready for firing.'

'Firing?'

'Baking in a clay oven.' He threw her a quirky smile. 'Don't worry, you're not going to be fired!'

As she went behind the screen to undress, she called out: 'But you won't be needing me after this week, will you?'

She was just going to tell him about Reggie Bentley's offer, when he went on: 'I've been meaning to talk to you about that. You'll be looking around for other work, and I was thinking . . .' He paused again, as if he were faintly uncomfortable, then plunged ahead: 'When we knock off at midday, perhaps you'd come up to the flat? I have one or two ideas I'd like to discuss, some new possibilities.'

This was the moment to tell him about Reggie. It was what she'd been hoping for, a chance to work with someone else and put an end to the strain of seeing Russell every day – and yet . . . When she opened her mouth, she heard herself saying: 'Yes, thank you. I'd like that.'

Her head told her she should put an end to her misery over Russell, but her heart was pulling her in a different direction.

As she lay on the sofa with her head on her arm, her mind was racing, wondering what the 'new possibilities' might be.

At midday, when Russell took her up to the flat, Laura was waiting for them. She had made a plate of sandwiches, and the coffee-pot was steaming.

'Jo, I'm so pleased Russell persuaded you to come up for a chat. Has he told you about our wonderful idea?'

Our wonderful idea? Jo turned to Russell, who was helping himself to sandwiches.

'Not yet,' he said. 'I never talk when I'm working.'

Laura clapped her hands gleefully. 'Then I'll tell you myself. I had this brilliant idea . . .'

While Jo sipped coffee and began to eat a sandwich, she rattled on: 'To begin with, I have to confess I'm the world's worst housewife – isn't that right, darling? I'm not bad at cooking, and I like arranging the flowers, but apart from that, I'm simply hopeless! After I've made the beds they look as if they've been trampled on by water-buffalos, and the vacuum-cleaner blows up the minute I lay a finger on it. Russell never complains, but he has such a lot to put up with, poor darling.'

'Things aren't that bad,' he growled.

'Oh, yes, they are. We used to have a little woman in every day, but she turned out to be worse than useless. For one thing, she was tippling on the sly. I couldn't leave her alone with the decanter, and when I screwed my courage up to mention it in the kindest possible

74

way, she flew into a towering rage and rushed out.'

'We advertised for another daily, but without success,' added Russell.

'My dear, you should have seen them!' exclaimed Laura. 'The only people who turned up were monsters and halfwits, so I tried to cope on my own. But what shall we do when I get my next play? I can't be expected to do eight performances a week and run a house as well, can I? Then I suddenly had this absolute brainwave. Why don't we ask darling Jo to be a ministering angel and become our lovely housekeeper?'

The sandwich turned to sawdust in Jo's mouth. She managed to swallow it, then asked Russell: 'Is this what you meant, about new possibilities?'

'Yes. Of course if the idea doesn't appeal to you—'

'It's not that so much, but . . .' Jo tried to think fast. 'You see, now I've started modelling, I'm really enjoying it, and Mr Bentley's asked if I'd sit for him, when you finish the statue. I was going to tell you.'

Russell puckered his lips. 'Well, that's entirely up to you, of course.'

He appeared to be rather cross, and Laura broke in: 'Well, why not? Couldn't Jo do both? Mornings up here, and afternoons with Reggie – how about that? I used to pay the last woman two shillings an hour. It worked out at £4. 10/- a week. Of course if you're only doing mornings, it would be half that. Do say yes – from the moment I saw you, I felt certain we'd all get on well together. I can feel it in my bones!'

She squeezed Jo's hands in hers as she urged her: 'I know people don't like the idea of domestic service nowadays, but it won't be like that. We shan't think of you as a servant, you'll be one of the family! You will say yes, won't you?'

And Jo had to agree.

At the end of the afternoon, she told Reggie: 'Mr Wade says he'll be finished by Friday, so I can start with you on Monday. But it'll have to be afternoons only, do you mind?'

'Not at all, I've never been one of nature's early risers. Have you got another job in the mornings?'

When she explained that she was going to become the Wades' part-time housekeeper, his eyes widened. 'Working for the lovely Laura? Well, the best of luck. You're not going to live up there, are you?'

'No, I'll still have my room at the Rope Walk. Why?'

'It's just – she can be a bit difficult sometimes, by all accounts. But as long as it's only the mornings, I'm sure it'll be perfectly fine.'

To begin with, it was.

Laura treated Jo like a favourite niece, offering to share some of the chores, discussing menus and making out shopping lists together, though Jo did all the shopping since Laura hardly ever left the house ('You've no idea what purgatory it is when people recognise you in the street, my dear. I was once stopped in Westminster Abbey and asked for my autograph'), and apologised profusely whenever Jo had to tackle some rather messy job ('Do you think you could bear to clean the oven some time? I simply hate asking you, but it is getting to be the teeniest bit uggy – would you be an absolute poppet?'), never failing to thank her for everything.

Sometimes, Laura would tell Jo to leave the hoovering, and invite her to sit down for a gossip instead. She enjoyed reminiscing about the roles she had played, and talked about Hollywood before the war, when she had been an international movie star. There was one film, *The Angel Has Wings*, which cropped up again and again, and she asked Jo several times: 'You never saw it? What a shame. I suppose it was before your time.'

Jo hardly saw Russell: while she worked upstairs, he was busy down in the studio. One day, as she cleared away the plates, she asked if the little statue was finished, and was amazed to learn that the clay model he had been working on was only the first stage of a long process.

'That's what they call the "maquette" – a small-scale version of the real thing. Now I'm using an enlarging machine that makes a lifesize copy,' he explained. 'Next I'll take a plaster cast and make a mould, then it will be sent away to the foundry for the last stage of all, when they pour in the molten metal and cast it in bronze.'

Jo couldn't really understand the various procedures, but she said she would like to see it when it was finished.

'So you shall,' Russell told her. 'I'm having an exhibition at the Chenil Galleries in the spring. You must come to the private view, as the guest of honour!'

Every afternoon, when Jo had done the washing-up and left the kitchen tidy, she went down to Reggie Bentley and spent a happy couple of hours in some absurd tableau – a daring cliff-top rescue, clinging to a stepladder which played the part of a sheer rock-face – talking about everything under the sun. Unlike Russell, Reggie chatted while he worked.

When he asked how she was getting on with Laura, Jo told him how friendly she was: 'Today she got out some of her old scrapbooks, and showed me photos of herself in some of her plays and films. She must have been so beautiful when she was young.'

'Oh, she was. No doubt she told you all about *The Angel Has Wings*? That was her big triumph.'

'Yes, I wish I'd seen it.'

'You haven't missed much – it's only a B-movie. But she was playing opposite Harold Stanway. That's how they met.'

Jo stared. 'Harold Stanway?'

'He was her first husband – didn't you know? He made a few cowboy pictures, and they had a passionate romance. After they were married, I gather it cooled off pretty quickly. The divorce was about a year after the wedding. I don't think Laura's the marrying kind.'

'But, she's married to Russell—'

'Yes, but they don't spend a lot of time together, do they? I mean, they're not exactly Darby and Joan.'

She should have guessed, really. When she started to work for the Wades, she discovered that they occupied separate rooms. Laura explained that she was a very poor sleeper, and often sat up reading half the night: 'I couldn't keep poor Russell awake, it would be too unkind.'

Even so, Jo sometimes wondered why the two bedrooms were at opposite ends of the flat.

The year slipped away, and Russell told Jo that the finished statue was now being cast in bronze. Every day he travelled to a foundry in Rotherhithe, to keep an eye on the process.

By now Jo had her own keys for Galleon House: one for the front door, one for the studio, and another for the top flat, so she could let herself in without disturbing Russell when he was working, or, if he had already left the house, Laura.

When she unlocked the green door at the top of the stairs one morning, she found him in the corridor, putting on his overcoat.

'Hello, there,' he said, and glanced back along the passage – the door of Laura's bedroom was firmly closed. 'I'm just off. I woke up rather late this morning.'

As a rule Jo's first task was to wash up the breakfast things. Going into the kitchen, she saw there were no dirty plates or cups on the table, and called out to Russell: 'Haven't you had any breakfast? Shall I make you something?'

He followed her into the kitchen, lowering his voice: 'Don't bother. I'll stop off somewhere and grab a coffee on the way.'

'Well, if you're sure. I'll take a tray in to your wife, shall I?'

'No, she had rather a broken night, I'm afraid. She has these bad patches sometimes – better not disturb her. You've got other things you can get on with, haven't you?'

'Yes, but what about lunch? Do you know what she wants?'

'She may not want anything. I should just leave her, if I were you. And be as quiet as you can; don't do any hoovering.'

She looked at him uncertainly. 'When she wakes up later, shall I ask her if there's anything she—?'

'Don't worry about it. She'll be fine when she's caught up on her sleep. I mustn't stop, I'm late already.'

And with that, he was gone.

Jo went to his room and began to make his bed. When Laura was around, she got through this particular task as quickly as possible, but today she lingered over it. Before she folded his pyjamas she pressed them to her face, imagining that the thin silk still retained a little of his warmth.

Then she tidied up the drawing-room, emptying ashtrays and plumping up cushions. There were a couple of dirty glasses on the drinks cabinet. She picked them up – then noticed that the whisky bottle was missing. That was odd; it had been nearly full when she left yesterday.

There was still no sound from Laura's room, so she decided to take this opportunity to give the kitchen a thorough turn-out. Taking down the pots and pans from the cupboard, she began to scrub the shelves. When they were spotless, she started to put back the saucepans; unluckily, one slipped through her fingers, crashing to the floor.

As she picked it up, a door was flung open, and an angry voice shouted: 'What the hell's going on? Why can I never get one single minute's peace in this damn house?'

Jo hurried to Laura's room, and found her scrambling back into bed. As she walked in, a gust of warm, fetid air came out to meet her, heavy with Laura's perfume – the electric fire must have been burning all night.

'I'm sorry. Did I wake you?' she began.

'Of course you bloody well woke me! Crashing and banging about. I thought the Blitz had started again.' Laura's voice grated harshly. 'What in God's name were you playing at?'

Jo had never seen her like this – her hair unkempt, her face without any make-up, she seemed to have aged ten years overnight. Her eyes looked small and malevolent, in folds of sagging yellow skin.

'I'm very sorry,' she said again. 'Mr Wade told me not to disturb you, but now you're awake, can I get you anything?'

'I just want to be left in peace. God knows that's not much to ask, surely? Where is Russell? Why isn't he here?'

'He had to go to the foundry. He said you weren't feeling very well.'

'I feel like death.' Laura picked up a hand-mirror from the bedside table and winced away from her reflection. 'Jesus Christ. Give me a comb, and my make-up. And fetch my tablets. They're in the bottle on the dressing-table. No, you fool, not that bottle, the other one! What's the matter, are you blind?'

Jo was gazing at the litter of cosmetics, medicine-bottles and pillboxes that covered the dressing-table. In the middle of the clutter stood the missing whisky bottle – completely empty.

Laura must have been drinking heavily half the night, alone in her room; now she had woken up with a crushing hangover – and she was still drunk.

'Here are your tablets,' Jo said quietly. 'I'll get you a glass of water, then I expect you'd like some coffee.'

'Don't tell me what I'd like!' Laura screamed hoarsely, her face darkening with anger. 'Get the hell out of my room, do you hear? Get out!'

When she left the house, Jo went for a long walk.

At first she had been tempted to follow her predecessor's example and give up the job, but in a strange way, she felt sorry for Laura. After all, it was a kind of illness, and when she was sober, she had been very friendly. But, most of all, Jo felt sorry for Russell. It must be terrible for him. If she left Galleon House, she would be deserting him; if she carried on, she might make his life a little easier.

Turning these thoughts over in her mind, she found that without realising it she had walked to Battersea Park.

When she was a child, this had been her favourite place. Whenever life seemed hard to bear, she had come here with Vee and Charlie, playing hide and seek among the trees, or wandering through the flower-beds. It had never failed to cheer her up. Instinctively, she had come back, looking for the same magic escape.

Only this time she was alone.

Winter had set in, and the trees were shedding their leaves. A clammy mist drifted off the river, and an old man in a shabby uniform was walking along the path, sweeping the fallen leaves into a heap. Idly, Jo noticed that one of his sleeves was hanging empty. He was wielding his broom with one arm. Suddenly she raced towards him, calling joyfully: 'Mr Mulligan! Hello!'

The old Irishman dropped the broom, his face shining with happiness. 'Me darlin' girl, is it yourself?' he cried. 'How ever are you, Jo?'

She told him she was very well, and he said she was a sight for sore eyes, then scolded her because she never came to visit Agar Road any more.

'I've been busy,' she said lamely. 'I often have to work on Sundays. Besides, Aunt Topsy didn't approve of me being an artists' model. Tell her I'm a housekeeper now. That should please her – it sounds respectable.'

'Why not tell her yourself?' Mr Mulligan suggested. 'I'm certain she's wanting to see you.'

'Perhaps, one of these days. I suppose Uncle Norman's home for good? He must have been demobbed by now, surely?'

'No, your uncle signed on as a regular in the Navy. The last we heard, he was off in the China Seas. I think your auntie gets lonesome. Will I tell her you'll call in next Sunday?'

'I don't know, I might be working . . .' Jo changed the subject. 'How long have you been a park-keeper, Mr Mulligan?'

'It's only temp'ry. They take on help this time of year, sweeping.

Still, the extra cash comes in handy for beer and baccy.' He looked her up and down. 'And I'm not the only one that's been making changes – you've grown into a fine young woman, so you have.' He winked at her. 'That's maybe why we don't see so much of you now, I daresay?'

'What do you mean?'

'Ah, get along with you, you've gone and got yourself some young fella – isn't that the truth of it? Why not bring him home with you next Sunday?'

Jo turned up her coat collar and said flatly: 'There isn't any young fella, there's nobody at all, and I won't be coming home on Sunday. It isn't my home – it never was.' She backed away. 'I'm sorry, I've got to go, it'll soon be dark. Goodbye!'

As she ran towards the gates, she said to herself: 'It doesn't matter, none of it matters. I'm not going to be unhappy. Things will be different tomorrow. Tomorrow I'll be happy – it's not long to wait.'

Chapter Six

'HERE WE ARE – 181 King's Road. This is where we get out.'

The Chenil Galleries were next door to Chelsea Town Hall. Russell helped Jo to alight, then paid the fare. It was the first time Jo had ever ridden in a taxi. That alone made it a memorable occasion, but to be escorted by Russell to the private view of his new exhibition – that was like a dream come true.

He slipped her arm through his, and they crossed the pavement. Other people were going in: smart, beautiful ladies and gentlemen, all talking at once. Entering the gallery, the buzz of chatter swept over them like a breaking wave, punctuated by ripples of laughter and sudden, startling pops as champagne corks exploded.

'What a pity your wife decided not to come,' said Jo. 'I'd have thought she would enjoy parties.'

'She enjoys theatre parties, where she knows people. She never feels comfortable with the arts crowd,' said Russell. 'They don't speak the same language.' He hailed a passing waitress with a tray of champagne, and commandeered two glasses. 'Your very good health,' he said.

'And good luck to your exhibition,' she added, as they clinked glasses.

'Well, it's not all mine. I'm sharing it with an old friend, Sir Hugh Fern-Pryce. He goes in mostly for high society portrait busts – that's why he's always rolling in money. I pick my subjects for their beauty, not their bank accounts.'

Jo didn't really understand, but she smiled anyway. It was the first time she had tasted champagne, and she hoped it wouldn't give her hiccups.

When the gallery manager came up to speak to Russell, Jo was introduced briefly, and the manager asked: 'Would you forgive me if I monopolise Mr Wade for a minute or two? We've got a reporter from the *Chelsea News* here, and he wants to ask a few questions.'

'Don't go away,' Russell told her.

They disappeared into the crowd, and when they had gone Jo stood quite still, wearing a fixed smile, while a stream of people flowed around her.

Suddenly a familiar voice said: 'All on your own?'

She found Reggie Bentley grinning at her over the rim of his champagne glass. 'I thought I should give my landlord a bit of immoral support. You look as if you could do with a drink.'

'No,' she raised her glass, 'I've already got one, thanks.'

'That's empty. We both need a refill.' He took it from her and returned with two brimming glasses. 'First rule of private views: make sure you know where the refreshments are. What do you think of it so far?'

'I haven't seen any of it. Russell had to go and talk to a man from a newspaper.'

Putting one hand under her elbow, Reggie steered her through the crowd, then said: 'There you are, Number 11 in the catalogue: *Sleeping Dryad*, by Russell Wade . . . Why are you looking so startled? You must have seen it dozens of times.'

'Not like this.'

The statue had taken her breath away. She had never imagined how it would look with the sheen and lustre of bronze. And it was so much bigger than the little maquette; a naked girl, fast asleep, before a crowd of staring strangers.

'It's wonderful, but – it makes me feel shy. Do you think they'll recognise me?'

'Nobody's looking at you; they're admiring her.'

She saw that this was true, and she realised that the sculpture had nothing to do with her any more. It had acquired a life of its own.

Beginning to feel more confident, she was able to admire it objectively. 'It's very good, isn't it?'

'Best thing in the show. It knocks old Fanny Fern-Pryce's stuff into a cocked hat – oops!' Reggie put a finger to his lips. 'Talk of the devil – he's heading this way. I'm off!'

Jo grabbed him. 'Don't leave me on my own—'

'Sorry, my love, I can't stand the old phoney. You'll be all right, he's got Russell with him.'

As Reggie melted into the crowd, Russell appeared with a silver-haired gentleman sporting a monocle and a goatee beard.

'Hughie, let me introduce you to my friend Jo Wells – my model, and my inspiration. Jo – Sir Hugh Fern-Pryce.'

The old man bowed over Jo's hand, and screwed his monocle more firmly into his eye.

'Delightful . . .' he purred. 'A great pleasure.'

'Wasn't that Reggie B. I saw sloping off just now?' Russell continued.

'I expect he saw me coming and made himself scarce,' said Sir Hugh. 'Poor Reggie. As a commercial artist he must feel out of place on an occasion like this.' Still hanging on to Jo's hand, he added roguishly: 'Have you had an opportunity to look at any of my humble efforts, my dear?'

'Not yet. We've only just arrived.'

'Then perhaps you'll allow me to take you on a tour of the gallery?'

To Jo's relief, he was interrupted by a young man with a flash-camera, who asked: 'Could I have a photo for the *News*, gents? The two of you together?'

'Why not?' said Sir Hugh, abandoning Jo and putting an arm round Russell's shoulders. 'Something like this, perhaps?'

'If you wouldn't mind dropping your eye-glass, sir. We don't want it to flare on the plate, do we?' said the cameraman. 'Nice big smiles, please . . . Here we go, hold it—'

The bulb flashed like a bolt of lightning, and Jo blinked.

'One more to be on the safe side . . .' Another flash, and the photographer lowered his camera. 'Thanks a lot, gents.'

'How about one more, with the young lady?' suggested Sir Hugh. 'After all, she's a great deal prettier than we are.' He stood back, indicating the sleeping nymph. 'And of course she was the model for this excellent piece of work.'

'Is that a fact?' The photographer looked at the statue, then at Jo. 'Good idea – the three of you together, and the sculpture, of course.

Our readers are partial to a nice drop of art.'

Jo looked at Russell. 'You don't want me in the picture, do you?'

'I've no objection,' he said. 'They say that any publicity is good publicity – unless of course you'd rather not?'

'Nonsense!' exclaimed Sir Hugh, putting his arm round Jo's waist. 'Every picture needs a pretty girl in it. Come along, all together now, say "Cheese"!'

Not wanting to make a fuss, Jo did as she was told. While the photographer adjusted the camera, she felt Sir Hugh's hand slip from her waist to her hip. As the flashbulb exploded, he pinched her bottom.

'Thank you, my dear fellow,' said Sir Hugh graciously, then turned to Jo: 'And thank you, my dear, thank you very much.'

'Don't mention it,' she said coldly.

Unabashed, he slapped Russell on the back, saying: 'I must congratulate you, my dear chap. A charming creature, and a first-class bronze. But why did you call it a dryad?'

'Why not? A wood-nymph in a forest glade . . .'

'Didn't you say you found her in Battersea? A water-nymph, surely, resting after a dip in the river? Rather like that little mermaid in Copenhagen – only without the tail, of course.'

Ignoring Sir Hugh, Jo addressed Russell: 'Is it all right if I walk round on my own? I'd like to see the rest of the exhibition.'

She hoped she might find Reggie again. The sooner she got away from that old goat, the better.

On the way back to Galleon House, Russell said: 'You're very quiet. Didn't you enjoy the afternoon?'

'Most of it. Parts of it were rather embarrassing.'

He chuckled: 'Getting your picture in the papers? Don't worry, you'll get used to it.' As the cab rattled over Battersea Bridge, he went on: 'I was just thinking about Sir Hugh.'

'So was I.'

'I know, he talks a lot of rot sometimes. Still, he said one thing that appealed to me.'

'Oh? What was that?'

'When he talked about you being a naiad – a water-nymph. I've been casting around for a new idea – a sort of companion-piece – and I think that might be the answer. Did you hear what he said about the

Little Mermaid? She's a character in Hans Andersen—'

'I know. We used to read Hans Andersen when I was at school.'

'Well, in Copenhagen, they've got the Little Mermaid on a rock in the harbour, and it struck me – I might be able to persuade Battersea Council to find a place for mine beside the river. The spirit of the Thames! What do you think?'

When she turned to look at him, she felt she would drown in those deep green eyes as she said: 'I think – it sounds – very exciting . . .'

The following week, Laura ordered a copy of the *Chelsea News*.

When Jo arrived for work and went round collecting up the breakfast-things, she found her sitting up in bed, saying: 'I only bought it to read Russell's notice – which isn't at all bad, I'm happy to say. But imagine my surprise when I saw the photo they've put next to it. Have you seen yourself?'

She passed the folded newspaper to Jo, who glanced at it and groaned: 'Oh, dear, I look awful.'

'Nonsense, you look simply divine, and you're in the picture twice – dressed and undressed!'

'I didn't want them to take a photo of me, but they seemed to think it was a good idea.'

'Quite right. It's time they put the model in the picture for once.'

'I wish you'd been there. They'd have had you in the photo instead.'

'Me? Why would they want a picture of me? I had nothing to do with it. No, it's really very good of you, darling. It's rather a shame they sprang it on you without any warning, that's all.'

'We knew the man was taking it – he told us to smile.'

'I don't mean that. If you'd had a couple of days' notice, you could have had your hair done and put on your best dress, couldn't you?'

'That is my best dress,' Jo admitted.

'Oh, I didn't realise, I've seen it so often. It's very nice, of course, but it is looking a teensy bit old-fashioned now, don't you think? I mean, look at these . . .' Laura picked up the *Daily Mail*. 'The latest style, all the rage at the latest Paris collections – it's called the "New Look".'

Jo saw a series of photographs: exquisite girls, wearing saucy feathered toques, stand-up collars, tight bodices and narrow waists – but their skirts were very full, billowing out over layers of frothy petticoat.

'They must take yards of material. What about the coupons?'

'Don't be silly, darling, you can always get round that if you know how. I happen to have some very good friends in the rag trade.' She sat up, brimming with enthusiasm: 'You're not modelling today, are you, my sweet? Good. Let's not bother about lunch. I'll have a bath and put my face on, then you can telephone for a cab. We'll both go up to the West End and see what we can find!'

It was a long, tiring day, as they dashed from one salon to another in a succession of taxis. To begin with, Laura made a point of introducing Jo to everyone ('My darling friend and helper – I don't know what I'd do without her'), but gradually Jo's role became fetcher and carrier, as she had to struggle with a growing number of cardboard boxes and carrier bags.

On the return journey to Battersea, Laura sank back against the upholstery, flushed and a little dishevelled. 'So many gorgeous things – and all for me! Russell's going to kill me when the bills come in, but who cares?' As an apologetic afterthought she exclaimed: 'Oh – and I didn't buy you a single thing, did I, angel? Never mind, when I turn out my wardrobe, you can have first pick of anything that takes your fancy. The rest can go to the Red Cross.'

Jo tried to look suitably grateful, while Laura continued: 'Of course, you don't earn nearly enough – artists' models are paid an absolute pittance. You should give it up and start modelling for a photographer instead. As soon as I saw that picture, I knew you were photogenic. You've got a good skin, and I'm sure you could make a fortune, modelling for *Harpers* or *Vogue*. Why don't you try it?'

'I wouldn't know where to begin,' Jo told her. 'Besides, I'm perfectly happy, modelling for Mr Wade – and Mr Bentley.'

Laura narrowed her eyes. 'No, you must widen your horizons – I insist. Leave it to me. I'll ring round some of my chums and get them to take a look at you.'

'It's very kind of you, but—' Jo shook her head. 'Mr Wade might not like it.'

'Serve him right; he's becoming too dependent on you. He can easily find himself another model – it's your career we've got to think about.'

Jo might have worried about this, but she knew from past experience that like so many of Laura's enthusiasms, it would all be totally forgotten the next day.

Still, Laura remembered one of her promises: she presented Jo with a loose summer dress in cream moss-crêpe – a little too big for her, but it had a tie belt so that didn't really matter. It was the simplest thing in Laura's wardrobe, and it suited Jo very well.

No more was said about modelling for fashion photography, and the following week Russell started to make some sketches of her for his next project, the water-nymph.

Summer in London – and nothing to do.

You wish you'd stayed up in Scotland. At least in the Highlands, you could go for long walks with the dogs and tire yourself out. You always slept soundly there, with the scent of the heather and the mountain air in your lungs . . . But not in London.

You don't like walking all by yourself; there are too many other people about. London is the loneliest place of all. Ah, well, there might be a good film somewhere that would help to take your mind off things.

So you reach for the local paper and turn the pages, searching for the cinema advertisements. Yes, there they are, tucked in between the variety bill at the Chelsea Palace, and an art exhibition at—

And then you stop, frozen.

It's only a blurred photograph – two sculptors at the Chenil Galleries, beside a nude statue – but it's the girl who catches your eye . . . The girl you saw once before, going along Cheyne Walk.

'. . . Sleeping Dryad, *by Russell Wade, together with his young model, Miss Josephine Wells . . .*'

So you did see her last year. She's still alive.

How dare she be alive, happy and smiling, as if she hadn't a care in the world? And she's not alone, she's got friends, she has a life of her own . . . You really hate her for being alive.

After staring at the photograph for a long time you get up and go to the bureau. You find the little pair of scissors, and then, slowly and carefully, you cut the picture out of the newspaper, and fold it up. You will study it later – many times.

You long to see her, and speak to her, and tell her everything. Only you know you can never do that.

Because Jo is alive – and you are dead.

★

When Russell had explained the pose he wanted, he saw that Jo was looking doubtful.

'What's the matter?' he asked. 'Is something wrong?'

Standing on the modelling-dais, about to take off the silk dressing-gown, she hesitated.

'No, not really, only . . . It's different, isn't it?'

'What's different about it? You didn't mind being nude last time.'

'I was curled up then. Now you want me to stand up straight, with my arms out.'

'The water-nymph is about to dive into the river. What's wrong with that?'

'Because of the way I was lying then, with my knees bent, you couldn't see . . . all of me.'

'For heaven's sake! You're not ashamed of your body, are you?' He moved a little closer, speaking gently. 'Everything about you is pure and beautiful, every part of your body is beautiful.'

Bravely, she made up her mind.

'All right . . .' She let the dressing-gown fall, then held her arms out straight, palms together, a diver about to take the plunge. 'Like this?'

'Like that . . . That's perfect.'

But although she had managed to throw off her self-consciousness, she found it was a difficult pose to maintain. As a sleeping dryad, she had been able to relax; now she could not relax for a moment – her outstretched arms became heavier and heavier until they felt like lead weights.

Russell had to keep reminding her. 'You're letting those hands drop again. Lift them up – no, a little more, level with your shoulders.'

He tried to give her regular rest periods. Each time he released her from the pose, she massaged her arms, helping the blood to circulate. During one of these modelling breaks, when she was lying on the sofa with the dressing-gown thrown over her, they heard the sound of raised voices outside the door.

'What the devil's that?' Russell asked, making some minor altera-tions to the sketch on the easel.

'It sounds like Reggie, arguing with somebody.'

Through the closed door, everything was muffled, but she recog-nised Reggie's voice, and she could hear a woman shouting angrily:

'don't you try to stop me, young man – I want to see her!'

Jo gasped, then the door burst open, and Reggie appeared on the threshold, apologising: 'Sorry about this. I was just on my way out, and this lady marched in before I could stop her—'

Mrs Topsy Bone pushed past him, grasping ten-year-old Chrissie's hand, and demanding: 'Are you Mr Wade? I've got a bone to pick with you!'

As Jo scrambled to her feet, the dressing-gown slipped open. Hastily, she tied the belt, but the damage was done.

'You wicked girl. I saw you, flaunting your nakedness . . . Chrissie, don't look!'

Saucer-eyed, Chrissie took no notice, but Reggie did his best to intervene, asking Russell: 'Do you want me to call the police?'

Topsy turned on him furiously. 'It's me what ought to do that. You deserve to be locked up, the pair of you – leading young girls astray! That's our Josephine, that is, and I've come to do my duty by her!'

Russell turned to Jo. 'Do you know this lady?'

Miserably, Jo said: 'She's my Aunt Topsy. And Chrissie's my cousin.'

Hearing herself identified, Chrissie began to jig up and down, squeaking excitedly: 'Ma, Josie's got nothing on underneath – I saw her! And that's rude, isn't it?'

'Hold your tongue, Chrissie!' Topsy advanced upon Russell, hissing with indignation: 'If you don't let my niece go, I'll have the law on you!'

Wearily, Russell said: 'All right, Reggie, I'll deal with this. Shut the door behind you. We don't want to disturb the whole house.' Then he faced Topsy and asked: 'Now then, madam, what exactly are you saying?'

'I'm saying she's my niece and she's coming with me! You could be sent to prison, you could – interfering with young girls.'

Russell appealed to Jo: 'Have I interfered with you?'

Crimson, ashamed of her aunt, ashamed of feeling ashamed, Jo mumbled: 'Of course not. I work as a model, Auntie, I told you that.'

Topsy glared at her. 'Oh yes, and you told me you never took your clothes off, and all. That was a pack of lies, wasn't it?'

'It was true – when I said it. It was just my head and shoulders then.'

'It's no use pretending, my girl, I seen your picture in the paper!

One of my neighbours made it her business to show it me.' She shook her fist at Jo. 'You bad girl – bringing sin and shame on our family, and your uncle a Chief Petty Officer, too. You told Mr Mulligan you was working as a housekeeper – you said they kept you so busy, you'd no time to come and visit us. A likely story!'

'I am a housekeeper, upstairs, in Mr Wade's flat—'

'Up in his flat?' Topsy snorted. 'So you admit it?'

Russell broke in. 'I'm getting rather tired of this. I employ your niece to look after my flat, and to help my wife, who is not in the best of health. If that doesn't satisfy you, I'll take you up and introduce you, though I would prefer not to disturb her, since she isn't very well.'

This came as a surprise to Topsy. She drew back and tossed her head. 'I'm sorry to hear that, I'm sure, but all the same . . . What does your wife have to say about all this undressing and suchlike?'

'My wife has seen the photograph you mentioned, and was kind enough to congratulate Jo about it. She understands that I have to employ models when I'm working on nude studies; I make no secret of that. Now, unless you have anything further to say, I'd be grateful if you would leave me to get on with my work.'

Topsy addressed Jo: 'I still say it's not decent – you'd be better off at home with me and Chrissie. If it's housework you want, I'm prepared to take you back, and we'll say no more about it.'

'No, thank you, Auntie,' said Jo politely. 'It's very good of you. I'm sorry you've had a wasted journey.'

'I see.' Topsy drew herself up. 'So that's all the thanks I get – me that's worked for years to bring you up. Very well, my girl. I won't forget this in a hurry, believe you me. Come on, Chrissie, we're leaving.'

Dragging a protesting Chrissie after her, she marched out, and they heard the front door slam.

'What a dragon!' Russell apologised: 'I'm sorry, I know she's your aunt, but honestly . . .'

'I'm the one to be sorry, embarrassing you like that.'

'It wasn't your fault. It took me by surprise, because I never knew you had an aunt. You never talk about your family – why is that?'

'I don't know, it's rather difficult.'

He heard the pain in her voice, and put his arm round her. 'She said she brought you up. What happened to your parents?'

So then she had to tell him about Dad getting killed at Dunkirk, and the bomb falling on Mill Street, and the bomb on the Emergency Aid Post . . . And Mum lying beside her, stiff and cold in the ambulance; and Vee and Charlie missing, under the bricks and rubble. Her voice broke as she continued: 'All these years, I've been telling myself they'd turn up one day. I tried to pretend they were still alive, but I can't keep pretending for ever. I know it's not true really. I know they're dead and gone, both of them . . .'

She could not go on. Russell held her tightly in his arms, cradling her.

'Oh, my dear, my love . . . You mustn't cry.'

He kissed her forehead, soothing and caressing her; his lips moved lightly over her face, kissing her cheeks, finding her mouth.

Returning his kisses, she clung to him, telling him over and over again: 'I love you – I love you . . .'

After that, their hands seemed to be everywhere – his upon her, hers upon him – and when the silk dressing-gown slid to the floor for the second time that afternoon, neither of them bothered to pick it up.

Chapter Seven

IT WAS TERRIBLE, and it was wonderful. It was a kind of heaven – a heaven she had always dreamed about, but never quite believed in – and at the same time it was a kind of hell.

To begin with, Russell had been gentle with her; as soon as he realised it was her first time, he said: 'Don't be afraid, I won't hurt you. Just relax and leave everything to me.'

He was kind and patient, stroking her and kissing her, introducing her to the rites of love; waves of excitement began to flood through her, but as he grew more excited, his movements quickened, becoming thrusting and urgent, and he got carried away. The sharp, stabbing pain made her gasp, but he went on. Jo bit her lip, determined not to cry out – and then pain and joy and relief were mingled, and at last they lay breathless in each other's arms.

It was terrible, it was wonderful, and it was love at last – real, passionate love.

Afterwards, when they were getting dressed, he said very little; it was obvious that the afternoon's work had been abandoned. When she was ready to leave, he kissed her again and said: 'You'll never forget this day . . . And neither shall I.'

'Never . . .' Resting her cheek against his, she asked: 'What's going to happen?'

She felt him tense slightly. 'Happen?'

'Well, us, just now – you and me . . . Will it happen again?'

'Of course it will.' His voice rumbled in her ear. She shut her eyes with an ecstatic shiver. 'If you want it to.'

'You know I do . . . I really do love you.' She pulled back a little, searching his face; she knew she shouldn't ask, but she had to know: 'Do you – love me?'

He sighed, and let her go; turning away, he smoothed down his hair. 'I love you very much. But it won't be easy, for either of us.'

'You mean – because you're married?'

'That too.' He began to roam round the studio, picking things up and putting them away, setting everything neat and tidy, ready to start work again tomorrow. 'It's never easy, is it?'

'I don't know,' she said in a small voice. 'It never happened to me before. Your wife would be dreadfully hurt if she knew, wouldn't she?'

'Whatever happens, Laura must never find out. She can be very jealous.'

'I think perhaps she's guessed something like this might happen.'

Russell looked at her sharply. 'What makes you say that?'

'She told me I ought to work for a fashion photographer instead. She said you were getting too – dependent on me. I wasn't sure what she meant.'

'That's what she meant.' He was looking past her now, into space. 'She's always had this terrible jealousy.'

Again she couldn't stop herself asking: 'I suppose there were other girls – girls who modelled for you, like me?'

'Not like you. It was never serious.' He came up to her, about to take her in his arms again. 'The others didn't matter. You matter – very much.'

She pulled away from him. 'No, we mustn't – we mustn't hurt her.'

He pulled her round to face him. 'What are you trying to say? That we must never make love again? Would that stop you loving me?'

'No . . . But I'm thinking of her. We ought to stop, before it's too late.'

'It is too late,' he said. 'It was too late from the first minute I walked down the stairs and saw you in the hall. You knew then that this was going to happen, didn't you?'

'No! . . . Yes, perhaps . . .'

He drew her towards him, and she felt as if her whole body were melting.

'But what are we going to do?' she asked, when she could speak.

'I don't know. All I know is that we shall go on. We can't turn back now.'

She could not understand how she could be so happy and so unhappy at the same time.

The following morning, she kept out of Laura's way as much as possible. She counted the hours until lunch would be over and she could go down to the studio – to be with Russell.

When she got there, she undressed behind the screen as usual, then went to take up her pose on the dais. Russell started work, looking at her in the same, detached way she knew so well, his mind fully involved, his hand making swift, sure movements over the drawing-paper.

But something had changed. He spent more time looking at her – and he looked in a different way. After a while he put down the stick of charcoal, then took off the painting smock he was wearing, and unbuttoned his shirt.

'What are you doing?' she asked.

'We can work later. Sit down. I can't concentrate when I see you like that – you're driving me crazy.'

Pulling his shirt over his head, he walked over to the door and turned the key in the lock. Stripped to the waist, he returned to the dais and drew her down on to the sofa, and she could not resist him.

He kissed her lips, her neck, her breasts, murmuring: 'My darling girl, you're so perfect, so unbelievable . . . Am I really the first?'

'You know you are. Yesterday was the first time for me.'

'But haven't you ever been in love before?'

She remembered Pete Hobden, but thrust him from her mind immediately; that had been a mistake – it was never like this.

'No,' she told him. 'There was no one – before you.'

'First love . . .' The words were like honey on his tongue. 'That's what makes it so precious.'

And then there was a knock on the door.

They both tensed, and he whispered: 'Don't make a sound.'

Somebody tried the handle, and Reggie's voice called: 'Russell? I can't open the door, it seems to have jammed.'

Russell swore under his breath, then shouted back: 'It's locked! I'm working. I didn't want to be disturbed.'

'Oh, sorry!' Reggie sounded very surprised. 'Shall I come back later?'

'No, hang on.' Russell whispered: 'Put on the dressing-gown,' and scrambled into his shirt at the same time, fumbling with the buttons. A moment later he went to the door and turned the key. Puzzled, Reggie walked in, looking first at Russell, then at Jo.

'Sorry to interrupt,' he said awkwardly, then addressed Jo: 'I've got another serial to do, and I wondered whether I could book you again. I mean, have you any idea when you'll be finished?'

Russell cut in: 'I shall be starting on the clay tomorrow; after that I'm going to need her for several weeks at least.'

'I see . . . Then I suppose I'll have to try someone else. Sorry to barge in when you're busy.'

He sketched a wave in Jo's direction, and went out. Russell pushed the door shut.

'Bloody man . . .' he growled. 'Why the hell couldn't he have waited till this evening?' He looked at the sketch on the easel and touched it with the tip of his little finger, softening a line. 'Oh, well . . . That's that, then.'

'Do you want to carry on working?'

'I suppose we might as well. You were right; this wasn't a good idea. I'll have to try and organise something – somewhere else.'

As the days went by, and the clay-modelling began, Jo became accustomed to these unpredictable changes of mood. One moment he would be cheerful and optimistic, as if he hadn't a care in the world; suddenly he would plunge into anger and despair, snapping at her if she dared to ask a question.

It was a strain for both of them – wanting one another, and trying to control their feelings – but that didn't make it any easier.

And Laura had noticed the change in Russell.

'You must be an absolute saint,' she told Jo one morning, as she sat up in bed, turning the pages of the latest *Theatre World*. 'I don't know how you put up with it.'

'Put up with what?'

'My husband of course. He's been impossible lately – up one minute, down the next – and when dear Russell is down, everyone else has to suffer with him! How do you cope with the man?'

Jo tried to laugh it off. 'We all get bad moods sometimes.'

'Not like that! Have you any idea what's upsetting him?' Laura tossed the magazine aside and lowered her voice: 'Do you think he might be in love?'

Jo mumbled: 'I don't know what you mean.'

'Love, my pet. Whenever Russell gets bitten by the love-bug, it affects him in the weirdest way.' She smiled. 'Oh, don't look so shocked, darling. Russell and I have been married for a long time. Even the most devoted husbands stray now and then. The puzzling thing is that he never goes anywhere – heaven knows where he met his new heart-throb. I wondered whether he might have dropped any names lately, in passing?'

'No – he – he hasn't said anything,' Jo lied, and felt herself starting to blush. Averting her face, she began to polish the ashtrays vigorously.

'No clues at all? Oh, how disappointing,' sighed Laura. 'Never mind. I'll find out, sooner or later.'

The telephone startled Jo, but she welcomed the interruption.

'Shall I?' She picked up the receiver. 'Hello?'

'Don't say hello – say the number,' Laura told her.

'Oh, yes, sorry.' Jo recited the phone-number, but there was no response. 'Hello? Are you there?'

'What's happening?' Laura asked. 'Have they rung off?'

'No, there's somebody there, I can hear them breathing. Hello?' There was a click, and the dialling-tone began. 'Now they've hung up.'

'It must have been a wrong number.'

'I suppose so. I must go and start the lunch.'

Laura's questions had been bad enough; the mysterious phonecall was almost more disturbing. Jo could not explain why it had upset her so much, but she felt certain that it had not been a wrong number.

A few days later, when she was shopping in Battersea High Street, she had the same uneasy feeling.

She had just bought some potatoes and a cabbage at the greengrocer's, and was about to cross the road on her way to buy some fish – the meat ration had been cut again, so there was no point in going to the butcher's – when she felt a prickling at the back of her neck, and knew someone was watching her.

She turned her head, but could see nobody she recognised. It was a fine day and there were several people about, but they were all strangers to her, and no one was looking in her direction. Telling herself that it must have been imagination, she went on with her shopping.

At the fish shop, half a dozen women were queueing up to buy some herrings. While she was waiting, she felt the same uncanny sensation, and she saw from the shadow on the tiled floor that somebody was standing in the doorway, behind her.

When she turned round, there was nobody there. She ran out on to the pavement, but there was no one to be seen. This time, she felt sure she had not imagined it; there had been someone there. Once, she might have been mistaken; twice meant that someone was deliberately following her. It was not a pleasant thought.

When she went back into the fish shop, she had lost her place in the queue.

Sometimes there were good days, when the work went well and Russell whistled as he shaped the clay. And there were days when she didn't have to hold her arms up all the time, when he was concentrating on legs and feet.

And there was one particularly good day when he broke a long silence by saying suddenly: 'There, that's it. You can get dressed.'

'You mean you've finished for the afternoon?'

'I mean the job's finished. I won't do any more to the maquette. She's ready to be enlarged to full-scale.'

Slipping into the dressing-gown, Jo stepped down from the dais for a closer look. 'Yes. She's beautiful. Not much like me, though.'

'Stop fishing for compliments. You're alive – she's just a mass of cold wet clay.' He pulled her into his arms. 'On balance, I prefer you.'

When he kissed her, she could sense his mounting excitement, taut as a coiled spring.

'We ought to celebrate,' he went on. 'I know – let's run away together!'

'Why not?' She made an effort to play along with his joke. 'Where shall we go? Paris? Timbuctoo? How about a desert island?'

'No, I mean it. Let's play truant – give ourselves a holiday and go out for a day in the country.'

Hugging him, she asked: 'Could we really?'

'Of course we could. A whole day off, just the two of us, on our own.'

'That would be marvellous.' But already Jo could foresee problems. 'Only, what about—'

'Laura? I'll say I've got to go out of town, on business.'

'I'd have to be here all the morning, shopping and cleaning.'

'Not if we go on a Sunday.' Once a week, Jo had a day off, when Laura stayed in bed till lunchtime, reading the Sunday papers. Russell's mind raced ahead: 'I can leave her some sandwiches before I go. She'll have a glorious time, ringing all her cronies and complaining about me.'

'But you wouldn't be going out on business on a Sunday, would you?'

'I might. I could be going to see Hughie to discuss another exhibition. I promise you, it's going to be fine.'

And it was fine.

Russell's plans went smoothly. He asked Jo to meet him at Clapham Junction station at ten o'clock. She was determined not to be late, and set off soon after breakfast, wearing the cream summer dress that Laura had given her. The weather was radiant; a faint heat-haze promised a perfect day.

When she reached the station, Russell was already waiting for her by the booking office, carrying a bulging string bag – she could see the neck of a bottle sticking out of it. She ran to meet him.

When he kissed her, she glanced round. 'Suppose anyone saw us?'

'Nobody knows who we are. Anyway, I don't care. We're on holiday, we can do whatever we like,' he told her. 'I've got the tickets. The train will be here in ten minutes.'

The string bag clinked as they walked down the echoing metal staircase to the platform, and she asked: 'What have you got in there?'

'A picnic: some wine – I actually remembered a corkscrew! – apples, sandwiches . . . I was making some for Laura, so I made some for us as well. I left hers under a plate on the kitchen table; she was still asleep.'

There was hardly anyone else on the platform, and he kissed her again, saying: 'You look like a vanilla ice-cream. After the sandwiches, I might eat you as well . . .' Then he added in a different tone: 'I haven't seen you in that dress before, have I?'

'No, it's the first time I've worn it. I was saving it for a special occasion.'

'I thought so. Laura gave it to you, didn't she?'

Her face fell. 'I'm sorry, I should have thought.'

'It doesn't matter. It suits you.'

But his face was still shadowed, and she asked quietly: 'Are you worried about leaving her?'

'No. Let's drop the subject, shall we? We'll make a pact: for the rest of the day, my wife doesn't exist. Promise?'

They were both relieved when they heard the faint thunder along the rails, heralding the approach of the train.

Their destination was Guildford, and when they alighted, Russell went straight to the cab-rank. As they climbed in, he told the driver: 'Tall Trees, near Clandon Park.'

The taxi set off, and Jo said: 'That sounds nice. Is it a good place for a picnic?'

'Very good.' Russell grinned. 'You wait and see.'

It was some way out of Guildford, and when they turned into a narrow lane, she was astonished to read a rustic sign beside a gate, with the words: 'Tall Trees'.

She exclaimed: 'We can't go in there – it's somebody's house!'

'That's all right,' said Russell. 'We're expected.'

It was a large house, surrounded by plushy green lawns and herbaceous borders. Russell paid the driver, while Jo looked about, bewildered.

As the cab disappeared, she said: 'I thought it was going to be just us. Who lives here?'

'Hughie Fern-Pryce.'

'Oh, Russell . . .' She lowered her voice. 'Do we have to?'

'I said I was coming to see the dear old boy on business. What's wrong with that?'

She whispered urgently: 'I don't want to see him, I don't even like him. Can't I wait in the garden?'

Russell laughed. 'My darling, I'm not quite such a fool as all that. Hughie's in Scotland for a fortnight, and he's sent his domestic staff on holiday.' Producing a key from his pocket, he unlocked the front door. 'We've got the whole place to ourselves.'

'He lent you a key? Did you tell him about us?'

'Not in so many words. But I think he's got a pretty shrewd idea. Shall I lead the way?'

It was the most beautiful house Jo had ever seen. Walking through it, Russell unbolted the french windows. The gardens were like the setting for a fairy-tale. When they stretched out on the grass, they were surrounded by roses in full bloom, and the petals dropped lazily around them; the sun continued to shine, and time stood still.

There was a line of poplars at the far end of the garden, and when they had finished their sandwiches, Jo said: 'I suppose that's why he called it Tall Trees?'

'I've never enquired, but beyond those trees, there's another part of the garden you haven't seen. Let me show you.'

On the other side of the poplars was a small blue swimming-pool, shining in the sunlight.

Jo said: 'Can I ask you something? Why is Hugh Fern-Pryce richer than you, when you're a much better artist than he is?'

'Perhaps Hughie's patrons don't have your impeccable taste. Also he's a bachelor, and I'm – but we won't go into that.'

'Doesn't it make you feel envious?'

'I've got everything I want, though I must admit I wouldn't mind owning a swimming-pool. Well, if I can't have that, I'll settle for a swim. How about you?'

He was already tearing off his clothes. Jo began to follow his example, then stopped. 'I haven't brought a costume.'

'Neither have I. Today, you and I are the only people in the world.'

Today he was not an artist; he was her lover, and she lifted her face to the sun, stretching her arms wide, exulting in her nakedness.

They tumbled into the water together, and the icy shock was another kind of excitement. They rolled around like seals, under and over the surface, sunlight and water-drops glistening on their skin; embracing each other, splashing and caressing, legs around waists, hands parting thighs, mouths sliding over shining bodies . . .

At last they lay on the grass, letting the warm air dry them, and began to fondle one another – stroking, arousing, thrilling; opening, welcoming, entering; giving and receiving love.

This time, there was no pain – nothing but joy. This time it was perfect.

But time could not stand still. At last they began to feel chilly; the evening shadows had crept up on them. The sun was going down behind the poplars, and their holiday was coming to an end.

The train was packed with people going home after a day in the country; Jo and Russell were squeezed together, side by side, and she whispered: 'It was all perfect, every minute of it. Nothing can spoil that.'

But even as she said it, she couldn't help thinking, if it had been such a perfect day, why did she feel guilty?

As the months went by, the sense of guilt never left her.

Again, she tried to avoid Laura, finding things to keep her busy in another part of the flat: washing paintwork, polishing windows, taking down Russell's collection of art books that lined the long corridor, scrubbing the shelves, and dusting each book before putting it back.

All the time, she was aware of an indefinable menace that dogged her footsteps; a mysterious vengeance, waiting to strike.

More than once when she was out shopping she felt she was being followed; each time she whirled round, but there was never anyone to be seen.

During these weeks she hardly saw Russell. Now she had no reason to visit his studio, and he was fully occupied with the enlargement of the water-nymph maquette; soon he would make the plaster cast, and after that he would spend long days at the foundry, keeping a watchful eye as they cast it in bronze.

He encouraged Jo to look for other modelling work: 'Can't Reggie give you a job?'

'He's found himself another girl.'

'Well, have you tried Llewellyn, in Studio One?'

'He's still working on flower paintings. It's all right, I'm quite happy not to do any modelling for a while.'

'You don't look very happy.' Russell examined her more carefully. 'You're looking rather washed out.'

'I haven't been sleeping very well lately.' She couldn't describe the vague feeling of doom that oppressed her, but blurted out: 'I keep thinking I'm being followed, whenever I go out.'

Even as she struggled to put it into words, she realised how feeble it sounded. 'Yesterday, when I was going home, I thought I heard footsteps behind me, along the Rope Walk. By the time I got to the door of Number One, I was practically running, but when I turned round, there was nobody there.'

Russell tried to reassure her: 'Why would anyone do a thing like that? Who would want to follow you about?'

'You don't suppose it could be – your wife?'

He stifled a snort of laughter. 'I don't honestly think so. I mean, can you remember the last time she left the house?'

'Well, she took me up to the West End, that day when—'

'Yes, in a taxi. Can you really picture her trailing round the streets after you?' He shook his head. 'It's got to be your imagination, you know.'

But she was not convinced; and she continued to steer clear of Laura.

This was made easier, because Laura stayed in her bedroom most of the time. She felt sure she had an attack of 'flu coming on; she did not feel strong enough to get up and dress, but remained in bed all day, having snacks and hot drinks brought to her from time to time.

One afternoon, when Jo carried a tray of tea and biscuits to her room, Laura said: 'Don't run away, my pet, I don't seem to have seen anything of you recently. Sit down for a minute. We haven't had one of our little chats for simply ages.'

She pushed a heap of magazines off the bed on to the floor, and patted a space on the eiderdown.

'I ought to be getting on with the hoovering—'

'The hoover can wait! Anyone would think you were trying to avoid me – and we've always been such friends. It's time we had a proper talk.'

Uncomfortably, Jo perched on the side of the bed and Laura cooed: 'You can come closer than that, darling, I shan't bite.'

Moving a little nearer, Jo recognised the smell of whisky, not quite disguised beneath the powder and perfume; Laura's face was flushed and her eyes unfocused. It was the middle of the afternoon, and she was already half drunk.

'What did you want to talk about?' Jo asked.

'Oh, various things. I pick up all kinds of funny little items when I'm reading the magazines. For instance – I was glancing through the *Tatler* this morning – do you ever read the *Tatler*, my angel?'

'No, not as a rule—'

'Of course you don't. All those dreary society people – why would you? But this time they've printed a picture of somebody you've actually met.' With a smug look like a small child saying: 'I know something you don't know!' Laura began to hunt through the pages.

'Let's see, where was it? Ah, here we are . . . Look, darling – Russell's friend, Hugh Fern-Pryce. You did meet him, didn't you, at the private view? I felt sure you'd like to see it. Doesn't he look ghastly, with his mouth wide open? Those flashlight photos are always a mistake.'

Jo smiled politely, and glanced at the caption underneath, something about a charity ball at Holyrood House, last month.

'Yes, thank you,' she said, handing it back.

'You didn't notice the most interesting part about it – the date. According to this, that little gala took place on a Saturday night – the night before Hugh invited Russell down to spend a day at his lovely country place near Guildford.'

Jo stammered: 'I – I don't understand.'

'Neither do I, darling. I simply can't imagine how dear Hughie can have been painting the town red in Edinburgh, yet he managed to be in the heart of Surrey on Sunday morning. Quite a puzzle, isn't it?'

'They must have made a mistake.'

'Oh, no, it was definitely the same weekend. No, my mistake was to believe for one moment that Russell was telling me the truth.'

Jo made a move: 'Excuse me, I must go and—'

Laura gripped her wrist: 'Don't rush off, darling, I haven't finished yet. He didn't go to see his old friend Hughie that day; he nipped away to have a bit of fun with some little tart he's picked up. He probably went to amuse himself with one of the Sarah Venus girls; we all know she runs a brothel in that house—'

'No!' Jo interrupted her: 'Russell did go to the country that day.'

'Did he now?' Laura fixed her with a glittering eye. 'And how would you know that? Unless of course you went to the country with him? You know, I wondered about you, right from the beginning – after all, you're one of Sarah's girls yourself, aren't you? There you were, taking your clothes off for him, day after day – it was bound to happen, wasn't it?'

To Jo's surprise Laura smiled suddenly and pulled her closer, adopting a very different tone: 'Oh, it's not your fault. You couldn't help yourself, could you? I know what it's like – I let that man twist me round his little finger, and now he never gives me a thought. I'm still beautiful, aren't I? You don't need a man like that. I can give you a good time, truly I can . . .'

She pulled her closer still. The blend of sweat and whisky and scent made Jo feel sick as Laura gabbled desperately on, pleading, cajoling.

'Forget about Russell, he's a heartless bastard. You don't want him – I'll give you a wonderful time, I swear it.'

Jo struggled to get free, gasping: 'No, please – let me go!'

At last she managed to break away. As she fumbled with the door-handle, Laura screamed after her: 'Go on, then – bitch, slut, filthy whore! Get the hell out of my house! You're sacked, do you hear? Get out, and don't ever come back!'

Grabbing her coat and her bag, Jo fled. Halfway down the staircase she met Russell and he put out a hand to stop her.

'What is it? What's happened?'

Jo managed to say: 'She's given me the sack. I can't come here any more.'

'Of course you can. I know what she's like when she gets into these moods, but she doesn't mean half of it. Leave it to me, I'll talk to her.'

He tried to comfort her, but she wouldn't let him. 'It's worse than that. She knows – about you and me. I'm sorry, I can't stay here.'

Pushing past him, Jo made her escape, half running, half falling down the last flight of stairs. He called after her, but she did not stop. Flinging open the front door, she stumbled out of the house, and went on running, with Laura's harsh voice still ringing in her ears – a bitter mixture of hatred and loneliness.

Jo understood loneliness very well; now it had come back to claim her.

The past two years had been full of surprises, love and happiness – and now the happy times were over. She had lost the man she loved, and, once again, she had lost her job. She could not even model for Reggie, because that would mean going back to Galleon House.

More than anything, Jo longed to make a fresh start. She wished she could shut the door on her past and begin again; more than anything, she wished she could free herself from this overwhelming sense of shame.

In time, you might be able to accept guilt; you could own up to having done wrong, and hope to be forgiven – but shame never let you go. Shame was not being able to forgive yourself.

For no reason, Jo found herself thinking about her mother. She was glad that Mum would never know of her disgrace . . . What had made her think of Mum, all of a sudden?

Looking around, she recognised her surroundings. Lost in her unhappy thoughts, she had crossed over Battersea Bridge Road. The next corner would be Anholt Road; she must have walked along here with her mother a thousand times, helping to push Charlie in the pram, with Vee hanging on to her . . .

Automatically, she turned the corner into Anholt Road, heading towards Mill Street.

For a long while after the bombing, Jo had not been able to go back there; she didn't want to see the ruins of her childhood. But now the demolition squads had done their work; the broken buildings had been torn down. The old streets had disappeared, and now a new estate was springing up. A giant hoarding advertised the development of Mill Wharf – 'two- or three-bedroomed apartments, lifts to all floors, open walkways, with riverside panorama . . .'

Wryly, Jo realised that one of her wishes at least had come true: this doorway to the past had been bolted and padlocked. There was no going back.

The sun had set beyond the chimneys of Lots Road, in a mass of threatening purple and orange clouds. Soon it would be dark. Jo turned away, and prepared to go home.

But what was her home? A bed-sitting room in a rackety house? No, she didn't want to go back there, not until she had walked long enough to tire herself out, making certain that she would sleep soundly tonight.

Across Albert Bridge Road the treetops in Battersea Park seemed to sway and bow, beckoning her. Presently the park gates would be closing, but there was time to wander among the trees, and feel the grass under her feet.

Gradually the noise of the traffic began to fade behind her; she heard sparrows twittering sleepily, and the crunch of her own footsteps, crushing the fallen leaves. She remembered Charlie when he learned to walk, kicking up a flurry of leaves, laughing and calling: 'Look at me, look at me!'

Shivering slightly, she began to wish she hadn't come to the park. On a gloomy autumn day, it wasn't a very cheerful place. She would go home to the Rope Walk and have a cup of tea with Sarah.

Then, as she turned back, the bad feeling crept over her again. She knew that somebody was watching her.

She stopped, listening, and thought she could hear slow, regular footsteps crackling the dry leaves, but she knew that if she looked round, there would be no one there. And then she thought she heard a voice from the past, calling to her across the years: '*Look at me, look at me . . .*'

The hairs rose at the back of her neck; her heart was pounding like a drumbeat – but she dared not look round.

Far away, a handbell was starting to clang; somewhere a park-keeper bellowed hoarsely: 'Everybody out! Gates closing in five minutes – everybody out!'

And, much closer, another voice said softly: 'Time to go home, Jo . . .'

She had never been so terrified. For the first time since her mother died, she found herself praying: 'Help me, Mum . . . God, if you're there, help me now. Our Father, which art in heaven, help me . . .'

Because, this time, she would have to look round.

She was shocked to see how dark the path had become, so full of shadows, she could hardly see anything at all. But then one shadow moved, and Jo saw a young woman coming towards her. She was dressed in a winter coat with the collar turned up and a broad-brimmed hat pulled down over her face – but Jo knew her, even before she spoke.

In the same soft voice, she said: 'This was bound to happen, sooner or later. I knew I'd find you here.'

Slowly, Jo walked to meet her sister. 'Vee? Is it really you?'

'No, not really.' Then, with the ghost of a smile: 'Vee Wells is dead . . . I'm Vanessa Coburn now.'

Interlude

ACCORDING TO THE BIG CLOCK on the wall, it was dead on midnight.

This was something special; Vee had never stayed up so late before. When you were only nine years old, you were sent to bed at half-past seven. Being still up and about at midnight was very exciting.

There had never been a night quite as thrilling as this. First of all there was the bad part, with the bomb on the house opposite, and then when the dust had settled, there were the Heavy Rescue men in their big boots and tin hats, carefully lifting them out. Such strong men, but they'd carried you so gently to the waiting car.

That was exciting too – you didn't often get a car-ride when you lived in Mill Street – and when you looked out of the window as you drove away, it looked like a different place, with holes in the ground and broken bricks and dirt everywhere, and jagged shapes where some of the houses should have been.

Vee remembered clutching Jo's hand, and soon, too soon, they stopped at St Luke's and were taken into what Mum called an 'Emergency Aid Post'.

Then they came into this long, narrow room that seemed to go on for miles, with a row of beds along one wall. Mum got Charlie into one of the beds, but as soon as she turned her attention to Vee, the naughty boy slipped out again, dropping his teddy-bear, and pattered off towards the doorway in case he was missing something.

'Charlie, you come back this minute!' Mum called after him, but he pretended not to hear.

So she gave up and said wearily: 'All right, you can all have ten more minutes. After that it'll be straight to sleep – I mean that!'

She flopped into a deckchair and closed her eyes. It seemed funny that she was the only one who felt tired, when she was a grown-up.

Vee didn't want to go down to the entrance. She wasn't interested in seeing the cars and vans and ambulances coming and going. At the other end of the dormitory, there was another little girl, all by herself.

They were about the same height and they both had fair hair. When Vee moved closer, they both ventured a smile.

'Hello,' said Vee.

'Hello,' said the little girl. 'How old are you?'

'I'm nine,' said Vee, in her best voice, because the other girl sounded quite posh.

'That's funny,' she said. 'So am I.'

Vee was still dressed in her old cotton nightie, grimy with brick-dust, and a tattered blanket round her shoulders, but the other girl had a beautiful pink nightdress with broderie anglaise and pink ribbon laced in and out. She wore brown slippers like bunny-rabbits, while Vee's feet were bare.

'Did you get bombed out too?' Vee asked.

'Sort of. The roof caught fire, and the firemen came to put it out. I wanted to stay and watch, but Mummy said it was too dangerous, so we came here instead.'

'Our roof was blown right off,' said Vee proudly. 'Everything fell down except the stairs, but we were all right. That's Mum, in the deckchair, and that's my sister Jo talking to her and my brother Charlie – no, he's gone off to see what's happening outside. Have you got brothers and sisters too?'

'I've got a brother. He's called Alexander – only I call him Alec.'

Vee looked round. 'Has he gone outside, like Charlie?'

'Oh, no, he's ten years older than me. He's a pilot in the RAF . . . Well, he was. His plane was shot down over Germany last year.'

'I'm sorry. My dad was killed in the war, too.'

'No – we thought Alec was dead, but then we got a letter from the Red Cross to say he's in Germany.'

Vee frowned. 'How can he be in Germany? We're at war with Germany.'

'He's in a prisoner-of-war camp.'

'Oh, I see.' After a moment Vee asked: 'Where's your mum, then?'

'She went with Daddy to find a telephone. They've got to ring people up to let them know where we are, because tomorrow we're leaving England.' Sitting on the foot of the bed, the little girl explained: 'Since the air-raids started, we've been living in Falmouth.'

This meant nothing to Vee. 'Is that near here?'

'No, silly, it's in Cornwall.'

Vee didn't know where Cornwall was either, but she gathered it was a long way off, outside the range of German bombs. Much later, she learned that when the Blitz on London began, Mr and Mrs Coburn had shut up their house in Cheyne Walk and moved to Falmouth – until they heard rumours that the Germans were planning an invasion, when they decided it would be wiser to leave England altogether. Through influential friends, they managed to book passages on a ship to the USA.

The little girl chattered on: 'We only came up to town yesterday. They just opened a couple of bedrooms in the house while we were in town. Of course we aren't taking any staff with us, so we didn't bother about meals or anything, and tomorrow we're going to Southampton. That's where we catch the boat.'

Vee didn't quite follow this, but it sounded very exciting.

'You are lucky,' she said. 'Going to America.'

'At first I didn't really want to – I thought I'd have to leave all my toys – but they're packing everything into big trunks, and sending them on after us. Everything except Munk – he's my favourite.'

'Munk?'

'This is Munk.' The little girl reached down the side of the bed and produced a red woolly monkey; with patches of fur worn thin, he had obviously been much loved. 'I had to have Munk on the journey; he goes to bed with me. Have you got a favourite, like Munk?'

'I've got a doll called Bella – she's down there, with Mum and Jo.'

In her deckchair, Mum seemed to be half asleep, and Jo was looking up at the clock on the wall, saying: 'It isn't today any more, Mum, it's tomorrow . . . Sunday morning.'

Then Mum said something, so quietly Vee couldn't hear, but she guessed it was about Charlie, because Jo set off towards the open doorway.

Vee turned back. 'Did you hear that? It's after midnight – it's Sunday now.'

'Yes, I know. So she's Jo – what's your name?'

'Vera.'

She began to giggle. 'That's funny, my name begins with V as well. I'm Vanessa – Vanessa Coburn.'

'That's nice. I don't like "Vera" much. Everybody calls me Vee.'

'Mummy called me Van.' Then she remembered something else. 'Look!' Putting her hand to her throat, she tugged at the slender gold chain round her neck. 'Look . . . V for Vanessa.'

The small pendant had been hidden under her nightdress, but she lifted the chain carefully over her head – a letter V, in gold filigree.

'Ooh, it's lovely. Where did you get it?'

'Somebody gave it to me when I was born. Would you like to try it on? Then you can show me your doll.'

But Vanessa never saw Bella, because as Vee slipped the chain over her head, she heard the sound of the bomb whistling towards them, and Jo's voice echoing down the long dormitory as she called: 'Charlie! Come here!'

From a long way off, she heard Charlie laughing. Then there was nothing at all. No sound, no light, just darkness all around . . .

The next thing she knew was a pain in her chest. When she took a breath it hurt. And then she was dimly aware of an unfamiliar voice saying: 'She's coming round . . .'

She saw the pattern of sunlight on a ceiling and a face looming over her; but it wasn't a face she knew, so she shut her eyes, and the darkness swallowed her once more.

Presently a cool hand stroked her forehead. An elderly lady was sitting beside her bed, saying in a soft voice she had never heard before: 'At last . . . It's been such a long time.'

Vee didn't understand. She lifted her head, and saw that she was in a big room with three others beds in it. There were big windows, and dazzling sunlight, and everything was white: the bedspreads, the sheets and pillows, the walls and ceiling. She saw a man in a white coat, and nurses in white caps and aprons, and she knew she was in hospital.

'It's all right, my dear, don't worry.' When the strange lady kissed her, Vee smelled a lovely flowery scent. 'You're going to be all right.'

Vee tried to speak, but her mouth was too dry, and the lady continued: 'You don't remember me, do you? We haven't seen one another for an awfully long time. I'm your Great-aunt Elspeth – your daddy's auntie. And I wouldn't have known you either, if it hadn't been for this.' She held up the little gold pendant. 'I gave it to you years ago, as a christening present.'

Vee's head was aching, but she remembered the golden V; she had to try and explain about that.

'No – Van . . .' She managed to force out the words: 'Vanessa, and Munk . . .'

The lady was puzzled. 'What's that, dear? Something about a monk?'

'Munk. Woolly – red monkey . . .'

'Of course! I'd forgotten your toy monkey.' Her face cleared. 'So you do remember – that's a good sign.'

'Van – America – a big boat . . .' she blurted out. 'Tomorrow . . .'

Aunt Elspeth's smile faltered. 'No, the boat's gone. You won't be sailing to America now. You've been here for nearly a week, since – since it happened.'

Vee stared at her. 'What – happened?'

Gently and carefully, Miss Coburn told her about the people who had been bombed out of their homes and taken to safety, and how they had become the target for another bomb on the Emergency Aid Post. Vee tried to make sense of the news, but it was too much to take in. Miss Coburn said that she had had a miraculous escape, because she was the only one brought out alive . . . So they were all gone. Not just Vanessa, but Mum too – and Jo, and Charlie – and she was alone in the world.

In her lilting, unfamiliar accent, Miss Coburn went on: 'As soon as I heard the news, I came straight down from Inverness. When you're well and strong, I'm going to take you back with me, my dear. I'll look after you.'

'Thank you . . .' whispered Vee. 'I should like that.'

Then she closed her eyes and went back to sleep.

Chapter Eight

THEY STARED AT EACH OTHER for a long moment. In a kind of wonder, they put their hands out to touch one another, then they held each other close, laughing and crying.

Happiness rushed through Jo, like sunshine breaking through clouds. For the first time since Mum died, she was a whole person again. Except . . .

'What about Charlie?' she asked. 'Where is he?'

Vee shook her head. 'Charlie's dead – he must be.'

'Why? We're still here!'

'Yes, but – that's different.' Vee tugged at her coat collar, pulling it a little higher. 'Someone told me I was the only one found alive, after the bomb.'

'But that's not true. I'm alive, too.'

'I suppose she meant I was the only one left in her family.'

The bell rang for the last time, and the hoarse voice shouted: 'Gates closing now, everybody out!'

Holding hands, they broke into a run, arriving at the Albert Bridge Road gates just as the park-keeper put the key in the lock. He scowled at them – two silly girls, breathless and giggling – but all he said was: 'Cutting it fine, weren't you?'

When they were outside, Jo reminded Vee: 'That's what they used to say when we came here in the old days. It seems like another lifetime now.'

Vee said quietly: 'It was another lifetime. I told you, I'm not Vera Wells any more.'

'Why did you change your name?'

'Not just the name. I'll tell you presently. Where are we going?'

Without thinking, they had set out instinctively, as if the house in Mill Street were still there, waiting for them. They stopped and looked at one another.

'Where do you live now?' said Jo.

'Cheyne Row, just over the bridge. But we can't go there.'

'Why not?'

'It's too complicated. Can we go to your place?'

'It's further away. I live at the Rope Walk—'

'I know. And you work at Galleon House, for that sculptor—'

'Who told you?' Jo added suddenly. 'Have you been talking to Aunt Topsy?'

The idea made Vee laugh. 'Aunty Topsy! I haven't thought of her for years. Is she still alive? And little Chrissie?'

'They're still at Agar Street. I lived there for a while, after Mill Street. But how did you know where I—' Then Jo realised. 'It was you, wasn't it? You've been following me.'

'Ever since I saw your photo in the paper. I tried to telephone Russell Wade, to ask him where you lived. When you answered, it took me by surprise – I didn't know what to say. His address was in the phone-book, so I started watching the house – and you.'

'But why didn't you tell me? I was scared stiff!'

'I'm sorry. Like I said, it's all very complicated.'

As they walked along, they exchanged reminiscences of their childhood, asking each other again and again: 'Do you remember that time when . . . ?'

It wasn't until they turned into the Rope Walk that Jo broke off and said: 'We shouldn't have come here.' Jo looked at her sister under the light of the street-lamp; the smart coat, the expensive shoes. 'You'll hate it. I've only got a bed-sitter.'

'What difference does that make? I don't care what it's like.'

Jo led the way up to her room, where she lit the gas-fire and made a pot of tea.

Looking about her, Vee said: 'It's quite nice really. A bit on the small side, perhaps, but it's very cosy.'

While they drank their tea, Vee told the story of Vanessa Coburn, and when she had finished Jo asked incredulously. 'But how could you do it? Pretending to be somebody who was dead?'

'Somehow it seemed easier to go along with it than tell the truth. And I thought everyone else was dead. If I'd said: "I'm not Vanessa, I'm Vera Wells", I didn't know what would happen. I suppose I remembered those books we used to read, about orphans being brought up by cruel people, and Aunt Elspeth was so nice and kind.'

'I can't understand why she believed you. I mean, there must have been other people in the family who knew what Vanessa was like.'

'Her parents were killed when the bomb fell, and her brother Alec was a prisoner-of-war in Germany. The rest of the family lived in Scotland; they hadn't seen Vanessa for years, because of the war. I was quite like her: same size, same colour hair . . .' She added: 'Of course, there were the servants, but—'

'Servants?'

Vee smiled awkwardly. 'It's that sort of family. But the staff who looked after them in Falmouth never came to London, and by the time the war was over, and they reopened the house in Cheyne Walk, most of the London staff had got other jobs. Some were killed in air-raids, and the ones who did come back were so much older. They all said I'd changed, but they never guessed, not one of them.'

'But what about the brother? Did he come home from the prison-camp?'

'Oh, yes, he came home . . .' Vee said slowly. 'I was dreading it, but he'd been away for nearly six years. Van was only eight the last time he'd seen her, and now I was fifteen. He said I'd grown into a beautiful young lady – he'd never have known me. Then he kissed me, and – that was that.'

Jo felt a twinge of jealousy. 'So you've settled down nicely, haven't you? What are you going to do, now we've found each other again? What are you going to tell them?'

There was a long pause. The gas-fire roared, and from the next room, they heard the scratchy sound of a record playing on a portable gramophone: 'I'd like to get you on a slow boat to China, all to myself, alone.'

At last Vee said: 'I shan't tell them anything. I can't, can I?'

'Of course you can. You've got to—'

'They'd never forgive me. What good would it do if I told them? It would only make them unhappy. Don't you see? By now they are my family.'

'They're not, I'm your family!'

'It would break their hearts.'

Jo was growing angry. 'And it would break your heart to give up what you've got. As soon as I saw you, I could tell you'd done all right for yourself.'

'That's not fair! Just because I've got some decent clothes, and a comfortable home.'

Jo wasn't even listening. 'No wonder you took so long spying on me, before you let me know you were alive. You didn't want to run the risk of losing all that!'

They were arguing so fiercely, they never heard the knock on the door until Peggy walked in, saying: ''Scuse me, girls, sorry to bust in like this. I'm Peggy Hooper, from next door. You're new here, aren't you, dear?'

She was dressed in a bra and pants, with her wet hair tied up in a towel. She hadn't put her make-up on, and was not looking her best.

Jo began: 'She's not staying here, she's my—' Seeing the look in Vee's eyes, she broke off. 'She's a friend of mine. Vanessa Coburn.'

'I thought I hadn't seen you before. Vanessa – that's unusual, isn't it? Anyway, glad to know you, dear.' She addressed Jo: 'I just popped in to say me and Margie and Roz are going to throw a little party in my room tonight. I've asked a few fellers round and you're both very welcome to drop in and join us, if you feel like a bit of fun.'

'That's very kind of you.' Vee was at a loss. 'I'm afraid I—'

'She's not stopping,' said Jo firmly. 'And I'm busy this evening. Some other time, perhaps.'

'Oh, well, suit yourself. If you change your mind, you know where to find us. Nice to meet you, Vanessa!'

When she had gone, Vee said: 'I'd better be going anyway. Perhaps I shouldn't have come.'

'Oh, for goodness' sake, don't talk so daft. Shut up and sit down. Do you really think I'm going to let you go like that, after all these years?'

Vee made up her mind. 'I know what we'll do. Come on, get your coat, we'll go back to Cheyne Row.'

'But you said we couldn't—'

Vee glanced at her wristwatch. 'Aunt Elspeth goes to bed early, we'll have the place to ourselves by now.'

'Are you sure?' said Jo doubtfully. 'But what about—?'

'What about what?'

'I was going to say, "What about your brother?", only I can't call him that: he's not your brother.'

'Don't start all that again. Alec's away for a few days, staying with some schoolfriends. And we've got to talk.'

Half an hour later they reached the house in Cheyne Walk. Jo followed Vee up the steps, then hung back while Vee took a key from her purse and unlocked the front door, saying: 'Are you sure about this? Suppose anybody asks who I am?'

'They won't ask. It's none of their business. Come in.'

The door shut behind them, and Jo stepped into another world, one that was elegant and spacious. Their footsteps, clicking over a floor of black and white tiles, echoed up the curving staircase; a chandelier, glittering like a fountain of diamonds, shone down upon them, as Vee escorted Jo upstairs.

'This is the drawing-room,' she said.

It wasn't smart and modern like Tall Trees. The furniture was dark and heavy: a mahogany sideboard; a wall full of books that looked as if they hadn't been touched for years; an overstuffed sofa and two matching armchairs in worn leather; and occasional tables, side-tables, consoles and whatnots – all cluttered with framed photographs and family treasures. A log fire was burning itself out in the grate; there was a smell of wood-smoke, and old leather, and furniture polish, and dead rose-petals, and dust, and time.

'You actually live here?' Jo could hardly believe it.

'Most of the year, except when Aunt Elspeth takes me up to Scotland. Come and sit by the fire. Shall I go down to the kitchen and forage for some supper?'

'What about the servants?'

'Oh, they're used to me poking around and helping myself. They'll make us some coffee. How do you like it? Black? White? With or without sugar?'

'White, with one sugar. Won't they think it's funny if you ask for two cups? They'll want to know who the other one's for.'

Vee laughed. 'I'll just say I've brought a friend home – that's all they need to know. Shan't be long.'

Jo watched her leave the room. This was a very different Vee: poised and confident, on her own territory.

She began to realise that it wasn't as simple as she'd thought. It had been stupid of her to think that Vee could turn her back on all this . . . And yet it still seemed wrong for her to go on living a lie. But what could Jo offer her as an alternative? A shared bed-sitter at the Rope Walk? A job as a model, if she were lucky, or as a housekeeper?

Then she thought of Russell and Laura, and the humiliation of her last encounter at Galleon House hit her like a blow to the heart. She flinched away from the pain.

When Vee came back with a tray, she found her sitting on the hearthrug, gazing into the dying embers.

'What's wrong?'

'Nothing, just feeling a bit low . . . It's been quite a day.'

'For both of us. But a wonderful day, too.' Vee began to pour the coffee. 'Help yourself – there's bread and cheese, and Dundee cake. Will that be enough for you?'

They sat side by side on the floor, as if it were a picnic.

'Remember when we were little? Us having picnics in Battersea Park?'

'And that summer when Mum took us to Southend for the day, and you were sick in the charabanc on the way home?'

'Trust you to remember that. Well, I was only little then.'

'And Charlie wasn't even born.'

They were silent for a moment, remembering Charlie.

Jo asked: 'Do you really think he's dead? I always believed I'd find you both one day – and I was right about you, wasn't I? So he could be alive.'

'I'd like to believe it, but I can't,' said Vee. 'If he were alive, why hasn't he turned up?'

'He wouldn't know where to find us.'

'He'd have gone to Aunt Topsy, he'd make enquiries.'

'Why should he? You didn't,' Jo pointed out.

'I had a special reason, didn't I?' said Vee. 'He'd have got in touch with us somehow.'

'Give him time, after all, he's only—' Jo counted on her fingers. 'He'd be ten by now, if—'

'There you are: "if". You don't really believe it, either.'

'I do. I do believe. He'll turn up one of these days, you wait and see.'

They went on talking, and Vee asked Jo how she became a model, and Jo told her about all the jobs she'd done since she left the house in Agar Street.

The story about Big Wally and the baked beans horrified Vee. 'He put his hand up your skirt? I'd have died.'

'It was his idea of a bit of fun. That's the kind of man he was.'

'Tell me about that girl, the one who came into your room.'

'Peggy Hooper – she's all right. She tried to help me make some money after I left the caff – only I wasn't very good at it.'

'Good at what?'

Jo decided to be frank about it. 'Prostitution. Most of the girls in that house are on the game.'

'You don't mean – you actually . . . ?' Vee was speechless.

'I only tried once. I was absolutely hopeless.'

'I don't know how you could even try. I know I couldn't!'

Jo glanced around the drawing-room, and said lightly: 'It's surprising what you can do when you're desperate. Anyway, I got a job as a model instead. According to Aunt Topsy there's not much difference. Both jobs mean having to take your clothes off.'

'Yes, I saw the photo. That must have been embarrassing.'

'Only the first time. After that it seemed perfectly natural.' Jo yawned. 'Sorry, I'm getting sleepy.'

'Would you like some more coffee?'

'No, I ought to be going. It's getting late.'

Vee reached for her hand. 'Why not stay here?'

'What?'

'We've still got heaps to catch up on. Don't go yet – stay the night.'

'What would everybody think? The servants?'

'They won't know. You can sleep in my room.' Jo was beginning to weaken, and Vee realised it. 'It'll be like old times – do stay!'

Vee's bedroom was very pretty. There were little sprigs of flowers on the wallpaper and the curtains, and through another door there was a small, shining bathroom.

'Just for you?' Jo had never imagined anyone with a bathroom all to themselves. 'It's like living in a palace. You must be very rich.'

'I suppose the Coburns are what they call "comfortable". It's not the sort of thing they ever talk about.'

Vee put on a lacy white nightdress, and found an even prettier one for Jo, embroidered with daisies; then they both climbed into the big, soft bed, with sheets and pillows smelling faintly of lavender.

Jo sighed. 'It's all so beautifully clean. I can't get used to the idea of you, living like this.' Turning it over in her mind, she asked: 'I should have thought, in the beginning you'd have given yourself away over and over again. Why didn't anyone realise you weren't Vanessa?'

'There was the "V" round my neck, and the things I already knew, like them going off to America. And the woolly monkey.'

'But there must have been things you didn't know – who everybody was?'

'When I left the hospital, I was whisked off to Scotland. Van hadn't been there since she was little, so it was understandable that she wouldn't remember anyone. They weren't surprised when I didn't know my way round.'

'There must have been things about the family, things she would have known. Didn't you ever make mistakes?'

'Not really. I never pretended. When I didn't know something, I just said I couldn't remember; they thought the bombing had blotted out my memory. And if anyone asked difficult questions, I said I didn't want to talk about it – I said it made my head ache. That was true; I used to get lots of headaches at first. Then as time went on I got so used to being Vanessa, I stopped worrying. I suppose, in a way, I sort of became Vanessa.'

'And you stopped being Vee . . .' Jo lay back against the pillows, frowning at the bedside lamp with its rosebud-patterned shade. 'Didn't you ever think about us?'

'It sounds awful, but I was trying not to. Don't forget, I thought you were all dead. That was the worst part – the loneliness.'

'You must have made new friends, you must have gone to school—'

'Yes, with a lot of Scottish girls who made fun of me because I was English. In the end I got on quite well with them, but I had to pretend all the time. I could never tell them the truth about myself, so they were never proper friends.' She looked at Jo with a touch of envy. 'I expect you've got lots of friends.'

'Not many. Nobody close to me – except one.'

'Tell me about her.'

'It's not a "her", it's Russell Wade – the man in the picture. He's the best friend I ever had.' She took a long breath. 'The best thing that ever happened to me.'

'Better than family?'

'Not better, different . . . Closer, somehow.'

'How could anybody be closer than your family?' Suddenly Vee sat up and stared at Jo. 'You've in love with him – that's it, isn't it?'

'Yes.'

'And he's in love with you?'

'I don't know. Perhaps he is . . .' Jo rolled over, unable to face her sister. 'Stop looking at me like that – you're embarrassing me.'

Vee switched off the bedside light. The room was plunged into darkness, except for a faint glow from the window.

'Tell me about him,' she said.

At first Jo was reluctant to talk, but as she went on, she enjoyed describing each step of the relationship; it seemed to bring Russell nearer. She explained how they met, and how she started to model for him – she told how she had taken off her clothes for the first time – how he had looked at her with an artist's eye, not like a lover at all – and how, in time, that had changed.

She told Vee about Aunt Topsy marching into the studio, and how she had burst into tears afterwards and Russell had comforted her, and kissed her – and then—

'And then it happened,' she said simply.

'You actually let him . . . ?'

'I didn't *let* him – it just seemed the only possible thing. I suppose you never . . . ?'

'Of course not! How could I? I don't know any men – well, not like that. And even if I did, isn't it terribly dangerous? I mean, you might have had a baby!'

'When your body wants somebody so much, you don't stop to think about things like that. I'm sorry, Vee. You don't understand, do you?'

Vee did not reply. After a while she began again, in a small voice: 'What did it feel like? Didn't it hurt?'

'At first it did, then you stop minding about that, and soon it doesn't seem to hurt at all. It's no good, I can't put it into words.'

'Is it really that wonderful?'

'Well, I only know about Russell, but I think . . . if you love him, and he loves you, then it's wonderful. At least, it was – not any more, though.'

Then she sketched in the final stages of her story: the terrible scene with Laura; her last meeting with Russell; her flight from the house.

'And now it's all over. I keep telling myself that. That's why I was in the park, this afternoon, walking and walking, trying to make myself believe it. Getting used to the idea that I'll never see him again.'

'Oh, Jo, how awful.' Vee put her arms round her. 'I'm so sorry.'

When they were children, they had often shared a bed, and now it was oddly comforting; cradled in each other's arms, they drifted off to sleep.

The next thing Jo knew was Vee shaking her awake and saying: 'Time to get up. I just heard the church clock striking six. It will be better if you can slip out before anyone sees you.'

Jo yawned. 'Last night you didn't care what the servants thought.'

'If they found out you'd stayed the night, I'd have some explaining to do. I hate asking you to go, but—'

'That's all right – I understand.'

She rubbed the sleep from her eyes; in Vee's gleaming bathroom she splashed some water on her face and scrambled into her clothes, while Vee apologised.

'I feel dreadful, bundling you out like this without any breakfast.'

'I know – they mustn't see me.' As Jo combed her hair their eyes met in the mirror. 'Will I see you again?'

'Yes, soon . . . very soon.' Vee tore a page from her engagement book and scribbled on it. 'Here's my number. Ring up any time and ask for Van – Vanessa Coburn.'

'Suppose they ask who I am?'

'Just say you're Jo Wells. I'll explain that you're someone I met in the park. We'll make a date to meet again. We could spend a whole day together, perhaps – if you want to?'

'I'd like that.' Jo heard sounds of movement downstairs. 'I think somebody's up and about already.'

'They'll be doing the early-morning teas, and lighting the fires. I'll come down and see you out, just in case.'

Still in her dressing-gown, Vee went first, and they ran lightly down the carpeted stairs, their feet making no sound. She unbolted the front door to let Jo out. It was nearly dawn. There was a pale light in the eastern sky; an early thrush was starting to sing in the plane trees along the Embankment.

Jo said: 'Thanks – for everything.'

Vee hugged her. 'You said Russell Wade was the best thing that ever happened to you. This is the best thing that ever happened to me . . . knowing I'll never be lonely again.'

Jo got back to the Rope Walk just before sunrise; there was a strange half-light that made everything look grey and unreal, like shadows.

She fumbled in her bag for the key. To her dismay, she found a second key-ring – the keys to Galleon House. In her panic to get away yesterday afternoon, she had forgotten the keys. What was she going to do about them?

Wrestling with this problem, she entered the hall and shut the front door gently behind her, so as not to disturb the sleeping house, but she was not the only one awake at this hour.

'You're an early bird, and no mistake.' In her fur-trimmed velvet robe, Sarah stood at the end of the hall, beckoning her. 'How d'you fancy a nice cup of tea? I've just made a fresh pot.'

Jo hesitated. She wanted to go straight to her room, to try and decide what to do about the keys.

'Come and keep me company, there's a dear.'

Forcing a smile, she turned back and went to join Sarah in the kitchen, saying: 'You're up early yourself.'

'I'm not much of a sleeper these days. I was just mashing the tea when I hear the key in the door. "There now!" I said to myself. "There's someone else as can't sleep!"' Pouring two cups of tea, Sarah glanced sideways at Jo. 'Or p'raps you weren't at home last night?'

Jo tried to sidestep the question. 'You don't miss much, do you?'

'Well, that old kitchen door's never hung straight since the air-raids, it's always a little bit ajar, and sleeping so light, I generally hear people coming in and going out. I like to keep an eye on things.' She handed her the cup. 'Get that inside you. You look as if you could do with it.'

It was too hot to drink. Feeling she owed Sarah some explanation, Jo said: 'While I was out yesterday evening, I met somebody I used to know, a long while ago. We got talking, and – I stayed out all night!'

'Fancy . . .' Sarah's large dark eyes glowed like lanterns. 'Would that be the friend you brought back once before? I seem to remember, you met him when you were out walking that time, as well.'

'Oh, no, not him!' Jo was quick to reject this suggestion. 'It was nothing like that. This was a girl I knew when I was a kid. We went back to her place, talking about old times, and she asked me if I'd like to stay the night – so I did.'

'Ah . . . I wouldn't have asked, only you seemed a bit upset.'

Though she was short-sighted, Sarah Venus could still see a good deal. To give herself time to think, Jo sipped her tea and nearly scalded her mouth.

'No, I'm perfectly all right,' she said. Then she realised that sooner or later she would have to tell Sarah she was out of work again, and admitted: 'Well, the fact is, I've got to start job-hunting. I wondered whether you knew any other artists I could try?'

'Doesn't Russell want you to model for him any more?'

'He's busy – doing other things. And I think it's time I made a break. You can't stay in one place for ever, can you?'

Sarah peered at her. 'But what about the housekeeping and all that? Laura Stanway will still be needing you, surely?'

'No, not now. We had a bit of a disagreement, and she sacked me.'

'Oh, that's her all over, flying off the handle at the least little thing. She'll have forgotten all about it by this morning. Go back and start getting their breakfasts ready, and you'll find she won't say a dicky-bird – I'll take a bet on it!'

Jo tried to laugh. 'I'm afraid you'd lose your bet – this isn't something she's going to forget in a hurry.'

She gulped, aware that her laughter was close to tears.

'Ah . . . so that's it. Russell's been making up to you, has he? Well, he was bound to try his luck, sooner or later. And Laura twigged what was going on – right?'

'You don't know what it was like.' Jo began to get annoyed, and the threat of tears subsided, as Sarah had intended. 'He really does love me – he said so.'

'I'm sure he did, my duck, and I do know what it's like. You don't get to my age without breaking your heart a few times, I can tell you.'

'Then you must see I can't ever go back.' Another thought struck her. 'Only I've still got their keys. Could you drop them in for me?'

'I could, but it'd be much better if you took them back yourself.'

'Oh, no, I can't possibly—'

'There's a right way and a wrong way of doing things; I don't suppose you waited long enough for them to pay you what you're owed, did you?'

'Oh, the money doesn't matter – that's not important.'

'It's important to me – and it will be to you, if you don't pay your rent next Friday! You stand up for yourself, dear. Take what's your due!' Then she asked in a different tone: 'Did you get a chance to say goodbye to Russell, before you went dashing off?'

'Well, no – not properly.'

'That's what I thought. All right, tidy yourself up, put on your best bib and tucker, then go back and finish the job – nice and dignified.'

Half an hour later, Jo was at the front door of Galleon House, with the keys in her hand. She felt slightly sick, and wished she had not let Sarah talk her into this.

She had decided that she wouldn't set foot in the house; she would just drop the keys through the letter-box and come away again. That would be sufficiently dignified, surely?

She was on the point of pushing them under the flap, when she thought: Suppose somebody else finds them? After all, lots of people go in and out of Galleon House. There's no telling who might pick them up.

She had opened the door and was already in the hall when she asked herself: What am I doing here? I said I'd never come back . . . Only I couldn't leave the keys lying about; I've got to make sure Russell gets them safely. But whatever happens, I'm not going to see him – that's definite.

Breathing a little faster, she went upstairs to the green-painted door. This too had a letter-box in it. She only had to put them inside and—

Again, she hesitated. They'd make a terrible clatter when they landed on the floor. Suppose the noise woke Russell up? Or Laura? Suppose they came to the door, to see what was going on?

As she stood there with the keys in her hand, she saw a blurred movement through the round coloured-glass panel. Someone was there, looking at her.

Russell opened the door, barefoot, and in his pyjamas. They looked at each other in silence, and then Jo said: 'I took your keys – by mistake.'

'You'd better come in,' he said, and held the door wide.

'No, really – I—'

'Come in,' he repeated.

In a trance, she followed him into the kitchen. He shut the kitchen door, and turned to face her; then she was in his arms, and her unhappiness disappeared as if it had never existed.

'My dearest,' he said, as he kissed her: 'My dearest love . . .'

Even then, her joy was shot through with second thoughts: 'We shouldn't. I told you what happened.'

'After you'd gone Laura told me all over again. Of course it was the booze talking – God knows how long she'd been knocking it back.'

'But she knew: about you and me, about Tall Trees. She saw something in one of the magazines. Mr Fern-Pryce was in Edinburgh that weekend, so she guessed about us.'

'Yes, she told me that too. She threw an ashtray at my head – luckily it missed by a mile. In the end she screamed so much, she exhausted herself and I haven't heard a peep out of her since. Give me a kiss, for God's sake.'

'Russell, we can't go on like this. I can't come here any more.'

'Of course you can! I'm not going to let you go – and when she sobers up she'll realise she doesn't want to let you go, either. She needs you here, to look after the place.'

'But she could get someone else.'

'Yes, I expect she could, in time, but there's no guarantee she'd find anyone half as good. And while that's going on, who do you think is going to do the cleaning and the shopping and the cooking? Certainly not Laura!'

'I don't understand – what are you saying?'

'I'm simply telling you that when Laura wakes up with a splitting head, she's going to realise she went too far last night. For the sake of one big dramatic scene, where she could play the leading lady, she's thrown our lives into chaos – and she'll wish she hadn't done it.'

Studying her carefully, he went on with some concern: 'You're very pale. Have you been skipping breakfast again?'

'I had a cup of tea, but I haven't had anything to eat.'

'Neither have I. I'll tell you what – you make some tea and toast while I have a shave and jump in the bath. And while I'm doing that, you can lay up a tray and take it along to Laura, with a couple of aspirins on the side.'

'I can't – she'll be furious.'

'She'll be delighted. Just say good morning, and she'll say good morning and carry on as if nothing had happened. Believe me.'

'But Russell, we can't go on pretending – the three of us . . .'

He patted her shoulder. 'Don't worry about that. The main thing is that we must all try to be reasonable. We must talk things over quietly and calmly and work out a solution to the problem.'

Jo tried to believe that he was right, wanting to believe it, and asked: 'You really think that's possible?'

'I'm certain of it.'

He kissed her once more, then left the kitchen. As she made the toast and laid up Laura's tray, Jo tried to understand what Russell had meant. Of course it would be perfect if they could arrange everything so that nobody was hurt – if they could go on seeing one another, loving one another . . . But what could they do in a situation like this?

As she walked down the corridor, carrying the tray, she told herself that she mustn't be afraid. But when she knocked at the door she was feeling very frightened indeed.

There was no response, but that was hardly surprising – Laura rarely woke up until she put the tray down and pulled the curtains. Screwing up her courage, Jo opened the door.

The room was very stuffy, heavy with whisky-fumes and cigarette-smoke and stale perfume, but it wasn't warm, so that meant she had remembered to switch off the electric fire before she went to sleep – that was a good sign.

Putting down the tray, Jo said: 'Good morning,' then went across and pulled open the curtains, dreading what Laura would say.

But Laura said nothing at all. When Jo turned from the window, she saw her lying slumped at an awkward angle against the pillows, with an empty tumbler clutched in her hands, her mouth gaping, her face turned up towards the ceiling. With an icy shock of fear, Jo remembered Mum, lying beside her in the ambulance . . .

Even before she touched the stiff, cold body, Jo knew that Laura Stanway was dead.

Chapter Nine

THE ELDERLY CORONER cupped one hand behind his ear and leaned forward. 'What did you say your name was? Speak up, please.'

'Wells . . . Jo Wells.'

'Did you say "Jo"? Is that an abbreviation? You must give us your full name, Miss Wells.'

'I'm sorry. It's Josephine . . . Josephine Mary Wells.'

The inquest upon the death of Mrs Russell Wade, also known by her professional name of Laura Stanway, was held in the dead of winter, when the days were at their shortest. By three o'clock in the afternoon, the Coroner's Court in Sheepcote Lane, off Latchmere Road, was so dark they had to turn the lights on, and one of the hanging lamps was shining straight in Jo's eyes, dazzling her as she tried to concentrate on the Coroner's lined, anxious face.

'I understand that you were employed as a part-time housekeeper by Mr and Mrs Wade?'

'Yes, sir.'

'And how long have you been working for them?'

'Well, I've been working for Mr Wade for just over two years now, but only about eighteen months as their housekeeper.'

Confused, the Coroner shook his head irritably. 'I must ask you to speak clearly, Miss Wells. Would you repeat your answer, please?'

When she said it again, he still seemed mystified. 'In that case, what were you doing before you became a housekeeper?'

'I began by modelling for Mr Wade – he's a sculptor – and then Mrs Wade asked if I'd like to do some part-time housekeeping as well.'

'So you were originally an *artist's model*?' He stressed the final words as if they had some double meaning, and there was a ripple of amusement in the courtroom. 'Silence! I will not have these interruptions. If there are any more disturbances, I shall instruct the usher to clear all members of the press and public from this court.'

He cleared his throat and resumed his interrogation: 'At what hour did you normally commence work, Miss Wells?'

'About eight o'clock, sir.' As he started to cup his ear again, she repeated loudly: 'About eight o'clock!'

'There's no need to shout. I am not deaf.'

He asked her to cast her mind back to a particular morning, some four or five weeks earlier, and invited her to tell the members of the jury what time she had arrived at the Wades' flat that day.

'I'm not sure. I might have been a bit later than usual.'

'What makes you think that?'

'As a rule, I made the breakfasts straight away, then took trays in to Mr and Mrs Wade. They liked to have breakfast in bed.'

'On the morning in question, was there some departure from the usual routine?'

'Well, yes.' This was where Jo had to be careful. 'That morning, Mr Wade was already up and about when I arrived. He was walking along the passage, and he saw me through the glass panel in the door.'

'So he was already up and dressed?'

'He wasn't dressed, he was in his pyjamas.'

Another buzz of comment from the court was quelled by the Coroner angrily rapping his pencil on the top of his desk. 'Quite so. And what happened after that?'

'I went to the kitchen and began to make the breakfasts. I laid up a tray for Mrs Wade, then I took it along the passage to her bedroom.'

Jo went on to describe how she had set down the tray and opened the curtains, and how she had seen Laura lying in bed.

'She might have been asleep, but somehow I knew she wasn't. When I touched her, she felt terribly cold . . .' For a moment Jo could not continue.

'Try not to distress yourself, Miss Wells. Just tell us what was in your mind at that moment. What did you think had happened?'

If she were to tell the truth, she would have to say that there was something wrong about the way Laura was lying there . . . something out of place, something that should have been there, but was not. But she knew this would make no sense.

She answered lamely: 'I was almost sure – that she was dead. I tried to feel her pulse, but I couldn't, so then I ran along the passage to Mr Wade's room—'

The Coroner's hand shot up, arresting her. 'Mr and Mrs Wade occupied separate bedrooms, did they? But they were not adjoining rooms?'

'No, sir. They were at opposite ends of the flat.'

This time there was an excited outburst, and the Coroner exclaimed: 'Silence! I will not have this hullabaloo!'

When calm had been restored, he turned back to Jo. 'You were about to tell us how you broke the news to Mr Wade?'

'Yes, sir. He ran to Mrs Wade's room at once. He did the same as me – he felt her pulse, then he took a mirror from the dressing-table and put it to her lips, but she wasn't breathing. That's when he rang the doctor.'

'Thank you, Miss Wells. You may stand down.'

Jo returned to her seat, and Russell was called to the witness-box. He was dressed in black and his face was very pale; his green eyes added the only note of colour.

After he had given his name and agreed that he was a professional artist, sculptor and Royal Academician, he tried to relate the events of that terrible morning; how he had telephoned Dr Hawthorne, who had a fashionable practice in Chelsea, and had said he would drive over from Paulton Square immediately.

'But I knew there was no point in hoping. I knew Laura was already dead.'

'Let me ask you to turn your mind to the events of the preceding day, Mr Wade. When was the last time you spoke to your wife?'

'It was the early part of the evening – I think it was somewhere between six and seven.'

'Where did that conversation take place? In the drawing-room?'

'No, in her bedroom. She thought she had 'flu coming on, so she'd stayed in bed all day.'

'And how would you describe her state of mind?'

'She was feeling very low. In fact, I really think that damn 'flu was to blame for everything.'

The Coroner's eyebrows arched again. 'Are you trying to tell us that your wife's death was caused by influenza?'

'No, no – but the 'flu had a very depressing effect on her, and she'd been drinking – more than was good for her.'

'Drinking? You mean – alcohol?'

'She had a bottle of scotch by her bed. She'd started on it for medicinal reasons, you understand, but I'm afraid she'd had a couple too many. That's what started all the trouble.'

'What do you mean? What "trouble"?'

Russell passed his hand across his face before he replied: 'We had an argument. I suppose you might call it a domestic quarrel.'

'And what was the cause of the quarrel?'

Seated on a hard wooden chair, Jo held her breath.

'Do you know, I can't tell you.' Russell tried to smile. Beads of sweat stood out on his forehead. 'It was probably about her hitting the bottle. Anyway, it was so damn trivial, I can't remember it.'

Jo's finger-nails bit into her palms as he went on: 'Isn't that how tiffs generally start? A tiny disagreement, and before you know it the balloon goes up. We're both very emotional people – I mean, we were – both inclined to be temperamental. She must have said something that caught me on the raw, and I snapped back without stopping to think: something cruel, something wounding. I remember her telling me to go to hell, and I stamped out and slammed the door. I threw on my coat and walked out of the house. God forgive me, it was the last time I saw her – alive.'

The Coroner said: 'I'm sorry, Mr Wade. I shall try not to pursue this very much further, but I must ask you a few more questions. When you left the house, where did you go?'

'I can't tell you that either. All I know is, I walked for miles. I must have been gone a couple of hours, I suppose. Then I came home again.'

'Did you go to your wife's room?'

'I did – I had some idea of trying to make it up with her. But when I opened the door, I could tell that she was asleep, so I went to the kitchen and made myself a bite to eat. I think I had a couple of drinks myself. Then I went to my own room, undressed, and went to bed.'

'And you did not see or hear anything more of your wife?'

'No, sir. Next morning, I was on my way to her room to see how she was, when Jo – Miss Wells – arrived. You know the rest.'

'One final question, Mr Wade. Did your wife at any time mention the possibility of taking her own life?'

Russell lifted his head and looked the Coroner squarely in the face. 'No, sir. It wasn't in Laura's nature.'

'Thank you, Mr Wade. You may stand down.'

The last witness to be called was Dr Hawthorne. It was because of the doctor's reluctance to agree on a definite date that the inquest had been delayed; he had so many other important – and lucrative – commitments in his Chelsea practice.

He entered the witness-box with a smile on his lips and a perfect rose in his buttonhole, and graciously acknowledged that he was Dr Reginald Hawthorne of Paulton Square, and that he had acted as personal physician to Mrs Wade – or as he always thought of her, Miss Laura Stanway, for he was a keen playgoer and one of her devoted admirers.

The Coroner asked him to describe how he had been summoned to Galleon House on the morning of Mrs Wade's death, and Dr Hawthorne corrected him: 'Possibly the morning after her death: whether she passed away before or after midnight, we cannot be absolutely sure. All I can say with certainty is that death had taken place not less than eight hours earlier, or more than twelve.'

He gave the medical details arising from the autopsy, then went on to say that in his opinion, death had been caused by an overdose of sleeping-tablets, combined with an excessive amount of alcohol.

Jo shut her eyes. Russell set his jaw and gazed steadily at the coat-of-arms on the wall above the Coroner's head.

The Coroner continued: 'I take it you had prescribed these sleeping-pills for Mrs Wade, Doctor?'

'I had. I impressed upon her that she should only take them when she felt she was unable to sleep without medical assistance, and I warned her that she must never, under any circumstances, exceed the stated dose. I also said it would be unwise to imbibe alcohol in conjunction with the tablets.'

'Because the combination might prove fatal?'

'Not directly. They would create a high level of toxicity, certainly, though that would not necessarily have amounted to a fatal dose. But the alcohol might make the patient forget whether she had already taken the tablets and so repeat the dose. That, I fear, is what must have happened in this case.'

'Thank you, Doctor. Now let me put to you the same question I asked Mr Wade. Had the unfortunate lady ever mentioned the idea of suicide to you?'

Dr Hawthorne's smile disappeared altogether, as he replied coldly: 'No, sir. The lady was highly strung, certainly, with rather too much dependence upon alcohol. I was forced to remonstrate with her on more than one occasion – I implored her to control her drinking. But I can assure you that she never showed any suicidal tendencies. If such a suspicion had entered my mind, I would never have prescribed sleeping-tablets for her. It would have been an act of criminal negligence to do so.'

The Coroner reassured him: 'Believe me, Doctor, I never intended any such implication. We may therefore conclude that in your opinion, Mrs Wade became confused by alcohol, and swallowed too many pills, without realising what she had done?'

'In my expert opinion, yes, that is so.'

No more witnesses were called. In his summing-up, the Coroner ran over the principal facts and took the opportunity to deliver a short homily upon the tragedy of a life cut short by the excessive use of alcohol. The jury brought in a verdict of accidental death, and the proceedings were concluded.

When Jo left the courtroom, several flashbulbs exploded in her face, and a crowd of strangers fell upon her, all talking at once.

Half-blinded, and badgered by so many questions – about Laura, about Russell, about her life at Galleon House, and did she ever pose in the nude? – she stammered: 'I don't know. I don't know anything. Please let me go.'

A hand gripped her elbow, and Russell's voice said firmly: 'Get out of the way. We've had enough questions – we've nothing more to tell you!'

By his force of personality and sheer physical strength, he manhandled her through the mob and into a waiting taxi.

As she slumped back against the leather upholstery, the press surrounded the cab, banging on the windows, and in that crazy kaleidoscope of faces, Jo thought she saw one face she knew – but then the taxi moved away.

She must have been mistaken – it couldn't possibly be Pete Hobden. He'd gone back to Sheffield long ago.

Beside her, Russell asked: 'How are you feeling? Are you all right?'

'Yes. I was very scared when I had to stand up in the witness-box, but the worst part was those people outside, yelling at me.'

'I'm sorry you had to go through that ordeal.'

'It wasn't as bad as I expected. I hope I told the truth – I tried to.'

'I think you showed great courage and presence of mind. You gave your evidence very tactfully.'

'I think I was more frightened for you than I was for me. When he asked what the quarrel had been about—'

Russell put his finger on her lips, and nodded towards the driver; the glass panel was open, and he could overhear their conversation.

'I'm sorry,' she murmured.

He drew his finger slowly, lovingly, down from her mouth, stroking her chin, then said softly: 'Don't be sorry. We must simply be grateful that it's all over.'

She edged away a little – the driver might be able to see them in his rear mirror – and gazed out of the side window as they crossed Battersea Park Road.

When they reached Galleon House, Russell paid off the cabbie, and turned to Jo. 'Will you come in for a moment? Have a coffee or something? We've still got things to talk about.'

She had not been inside Galleon House since Laura's death, and she said uneasily: 'It's just – I feel awkward about going back to your flat.'

'I know what you mean. It's been difficult for me, too. We could go into the studio, if you like?'

'All right.'

It seemed extraordinary to walk through the front door and across the hall. She glanced up at the staircase, and averted her eyes quickly.

At first sight, the studio looked the same, as if nothing had happened since the last time she modelled for him. But then she saw the dust lying thick on everything; the room was bitingly cold.

'I'll switch on the fire, it'll soon warm up,' said Russell. 'I'm afraid it's in a terrible mess – the whole house needs cleaning.' He sat on the edge of the dais, hugging his knees. 'Actually, that's one of the things I wanted to talk to you about.'

Jo stared at him. 'About cleaning the house?'

'You can see what a state it's in. So I wondered – how would you feel about starting work again? I shall need a permanent housekeeper now.' Seeing the look on her face, he asked: 'What's the matter? I thought you'd be pleased.'

She frowned at her clasped hands, and said: 'I thought you wanted to talk about something else . . . About everything that's happened – about your wife.'

He stood up and took a few paces towards the windows. 'I don't think there's much to say. Laura's gone – in an odd way I find I'm missing her – but talking about her won't bring her back, will it?'

'I'm sorry, I've no right to ask about her, but I was worried about what you said – in court – about the quarrel you had.'

'What about it?'

'You said it was a domestic tiff – you couldn't even remember what started it – but that wasn't true, was it?'

'What did you expect me to say, for God's sake? We had a row because my wife found out I'd fallen in love with someone else?'

'You were supposed to tell the truth. You'd taken an oath.'

'I happen to think you're more important.' He swung round to face her. 'Don't you see? I was trying to protect you! And if that means I'm going to roast in hell, that's too bad. It's you I care about – nothing else.'

She saw that he was telling the truth, yet she was still haunted by the feeling that something was wrong.

'You don't really think she committed suicide, do you?'

'Good lord, no! You heard what the doctor said – she wasn't the type.'

'If I thought it was on account of me, if I'd driven her to it—'

'Laura was a fighter, you know that. She might have tried to kill one of us – both of us, even! – but never herself.' He held out both hands to her. 'You've got no reason to feel guilty. I need you now, more than ever. I need someone to look after me.'

She took his hands in hers. 'All right, then. I'll be your housekeeper, if that's what you want.'

'I'll always be grateful. I'll want you to go on modelling for me as well, of course – you can organise the housework around the modelling – and you must give up your room at Sarah's house. You can live here. You can have Laura's room now.'

She let go of him. 'I won't leave the Rope Walk. I don't want to move into this house – I couldn't.'

'You feel sensitive about it now, I appreciate that, but in time, when things have settled down—'

'No, Russell, I'm sorry.'

They looked at each other like strangers, and then the silence was broken by the front door bell.

'Who the hell is that?' he growled.

'I'll go and find out,' said Jo. 'If I'm going to be your housekeeper, I might as well get used to answering the door.'

She opened the front door, then stopped dead.

'Evening,' said Pete Hobden.

'So it was you – I thought I saw you. What do you want?'

'Well, this'll likely surprise you, it's Mr Wade I'm after.' He flashed a press pass at her. '*Evening News*,' he explained. 'Our photographer got his picture after the inquest, but we'd like a few words to go with it.'

'You're a newspaper-man?'

'That's right. This old world's full of surprises, int it? Could you ask him if I can have a quick word?'

'Well, I don't know if—' She heard Russell calling: 'Who is it, Jo?' and added: 'Wait here. I'll go and ask.'

Leaving Pete on the doorstep she went back to explain to Russell; but as soon as he learned that the caller was from a newspaper, he exclaimed savagely: 'Bloody ghouls, the lot of them. Tell him I'm not seeing anyone.'

She shut the door behind her when she left the studio, then led Pete out into the darkened garden, saying: 'He won't see you – he's not seeing anyone.'

'Ah, well, it were a bit of a long shot anyhow. Still, it was a stroke of luck, seeing you in court. So you're housekeeper and artist's model both, are you? Very nice too.' He glanced up at the eighteenth-century façade. 'Bit of a step up from that other place you were living, eh?'

'I don't live here,' she told him.

'Don't you? Still, you're looking well on it, wherever you live – you're right bonny.'

Embarrassed, she said: 'I never knew you were a reporter. You didn't tell me that.'

'Before I went in the Army, I'd been an office-boy at the *Sheffield Telegraph*. When I were demobbed, they took me back and gave me a chance to try my hand at the bread-and-butter stuff – garden-parties, funerals, magistrates courts. I managed to make a go of it somehow, and I moved down south about three months back.'

'But you hated London. You said you'd never come back.'

'Well, I was offered a job on the *News*, you see – that were too good to turn down.'

'I'm very glad for you.'

'Are you? My girl-friend wasn't all that chuffed.'

'Oh, I didn't know—'

''Course you didn't know – how could you? Ah, well, her and me, we were going steady till this job came along. Still, as long as I can manage to wangle a long weekend at home every now and then, she'll not complain.'

'I see. Well . . .' Shifting from one foot to the other she said: 'Mr Wade will be wondering what's become of me.'

'Before you go, I just wanted to tell you I'm sorry about the last time – if I said anything out of place.'

'No, I'm sorry too. It was a dreadful mistake.'

'Well, we'll say no more about it. Best forgotten, eh? Any road, it's been nice talking to you, Jo. And good luck.'

She watched him walk away down the street, then went back to the studio.

Russell glanced up. 'You managed to get rid of him at last, did you?'

'Yes, I got rid of him.' She rubbed her hands together. 'It's still cold, isn't it?'

'Let's go upstairs. We'll be more comfortable there.' Russell put his arm around her. 'We'll have some tea, to warm ourselves up.'

But something made her draw back, saying: 'Not now . . . I must go. I'll come in tomorrow morning. The usual time?'

'All right.' As she went towards the door, he called after her: 'Are you sure you won't change your mind?'

'Yes. I'll see you tomorrow. Goodnight.'

At the Rope Walk, she found a letter waiting for her on the hall table, addressed in a neat, feminine hand. She did not recognise it, but when she saw the Chelsea postmark, she guessed who it was from. She hadn't seen Vee's handwriting since they were both children.

Up in her room, she tore open the envelope.

Dear Jo,
When you left that morning, you said you would ring me. When the days went by and you didn't phone, I got very worried. Then I saw a piece in one of the papers about the actress who was married to Russell Wade, and I realised things must have become difficult for you. But that was weeks ago now, and I still haven't heard from you.

I would have rung you, but I was afraid Mr Wade might answer the phone, so in the end I decided to write to you instead. Please telephone if you can. After meeting you that day, I couldn't bear to lose you again.

I know there's going to be an inquest, but I couldn't make out from the newspaper exactly what happened. Did Mrs Wade kill herself?

I am thinking of you all the time.

With all my love, V.

The address and telephone number were printed at the top of the letter. Jo rummaged for a handful of coppers, then went out again to the nearest phonebox.

An unfamiliar voice answered, announcing the number and asking: 'Who do you wish to speak to?'

'Miss—' In the nick of time, she stopped and began again: 'Miss Coburn, please, Miss Vanessa Coburn.'

'May I tell Miss Coburn who is calling?'

'Jo Wells – Josephine Wells.'

'Miss Josephine Wells. Hold the line, please.'

After a long wait, Jo heard Vee saying in the far distance: 'It's all right, I'll take it in here.' Then Vee's voice in her ear, saying: 'Jo, is that you?'

'Is this a bad time?'

'We were just sitting down to dinner, but you can ring me any time you like. What's happening? Are you all right?'

'I'm fine. I'm sorry I didn't phone before, but it's been such a nightmare – well, you know about that.'

'Not really, only that bit in the papers. When's the inquest?'

'It was today. It's all over now, thank goodness.'

'What did they say about that woman killing herself? Was it because of, you know . . .'

Jo said sharply: 'She didn't kill herself. It was an accident. She'd had too much to drink, and she took too many sleeping-pills by mistake.'

'Oh . . .' Vee did not sound totally convinced. 'So what's going to happen now?'

'Nothing's going to happen. I told you – it's over.'

Vee lowered her voice. 'I meant about you and him. Is that still going on?'

Jo was beginning to feel angry. 'Nothing's going on. I'm going back to work there, because he needs a full-time housekeeper now. That's all.'

Vee still sounded doubtful. 'Do you think that's a good idea? I mean, living with him, just the two of you. You know how people talk.'

'I'm not going to live there – I've still got my room at the Rope Walk. I shall just go in during the day, to cook and clean.'

'Well, I hope it works out for you. When am I going to see you? Could we have lunch together one day?'

'No, I'm sorry, Vee. I'm going to be very busy.'

'But you don't work every day, surely? He must give you some time off – weekends, or something?'

'We haven't planned it properly yet. There's so much to be done.'

'But I must see you.'

'Yes, all right, but I must get things sorted out first. I'll give you a ring.'

'Yes, but *when*?'

'I don't *know* when! I'll see you soon, but not yet.'

At Cheyne Walk, Vee put the phone down slowly. It was a relief to know Jo was all right, but all the same . . . Trying to put on a cheerful face, she returned to the dining-room.

Elspeth Coburn and Alec were at the table. They looked up as she entered the room, and Aunt Elspeth asked: 'Who was it, dear?'

'Oh, nobody you know. Someone I met in the park the other day.'

Alec said with mock solemnity: 'What's all this? A boy-friend? He's got a cheek, I must say, picking my sister up in the park!'

'It's not a boy-friend. Her name's Josephine Wells; she's very nice.'

'Of course she is, dear,' said Aunt Elspeth. 'Stop teasing, Alec. Now come and sit down, before your soup gets cold.'

Later that evening, Jo lay on her bed, trying to read a library-book, but she found it hard to concentrate. Her attention was distracted by sounds from other parts of the house: somewhere a wireless was playing much too loudly, a breeze rattled her window-panes, and there was a clatter of footsteps on the stairs. When they reached the landing, Jo heard a muffled conversation outside her door, followed by a discreet knock.

'Who is it?' she asked, putting aside her book.

Peggy Hooper poked her head in, saying brightly: 'All on your own-i-o? That's good – you've got a visitor. I found him wandering about in the street, looking for company, so I asked him if he'd like to come back, but he's not all that interested in me. Seemingly he's an old friend of yours.'

Jo sat up. 'Who is it?'

Then she saw Russell standing in the doorway, under the landing light.

'Hello, Jo,' he said. 'I'd like to talk to you.'

'That's right, dear, in you go,' said Peggy. 'I'll pop off and leave you in peace.' And she disappeared, shutting the door behind her.

'So,' said Russell. 'Here we are.' He pursed his lips, swaying slightly, but trying to appear completely nonchalant.

'I think you ought to go home,' said Jo.

'Can't do that – I haven't got a home,' he told her. 'It's just a house full of empty rooms. I couldn't stand it any longer, so I went out for a walk. Dropped into the pub for a while, but that didn't do any good. Why wouldn't you stay with me tonight, Jo? I wanted you to.'

'You know why,' she told him. 'It wouldn't have been right.'

'It would have been the best thing in the world. That's why I went out for a couple of drinks. I wanted you so badly. I love you, Jo.'

'I know, I love you too – very much – but—'

'Don't say "but", don't say anything. Just let me stay here.' He moved closer. 'I don't want to be on my own tonight, Jo, help me.'

She opened her arms to him and they lay on the bed, holding one another, comforting one another.

Tonight his love-making was slow and clumsy, and their roles were reversed; he needed her to lead the way – he was the helpless child, she was the tender, caring mother. When he had found the relief he needed, he fell asleep in her arms, spent and satisfied.

She lay awake for a long time, cradling him. For her, tonight had been nothing but a fleeting moment of satisfaction, and as soon as that was over, all her anxieties had come flooding back.

She could not understand what was happening; at the heart of their passion tonight, at the moment of climax, she had not been thinking of Russell at all.

During the weeks that followed, she found herself thinking of Pete Hobden again and again. She bought the *Evening News* every day, searching for the piece he had written about Russell and the inquest, but she never found it.

Chapter Ten

THE OLD YEAR CRAWLED AWAY to die – frozen and grey, and mourned by nobody – but the new year was no more appealing. January seemed to last for ever; time itself was embedded in ice.

Jo's life too was at a standstill. When she was working in Russell's flat, hoovering or washing-up, he would sometimes put his arms round her; occasionally they kissed, but without passion. He never suggested spending another night at the Rope Walk – they had not found her narrow bed very comfortable, and he had given up asking her to stay at Galleon House. Perhaps he was losing interest in her.

His mind appeared to be on other things. She thought he might be making plans for a new project, and she wished he would; he was always restless and discontented when he wasn't working.

Late one afternoon, when she was leaving Galleon House, Reggie Bentley hailed her enthusiastically: 'Jo! I haven't seen you for ages.'

'No, I've been busy,' she told him. 'I expect we both have.'

'Oh, yes, always got to keep the pot boiling, you know. Matter of fact, I've been hoping I'd see you. Come in, sit down – if you can find somewhere to sit.'

His studio was as untidy as ever, but he cleared a heap of papers and photographs from a battered armchair.

'That's one of the reasons I wanted to talk to you. How about modelling for my next *Woman's Own* serial?'

'Oh, Reggie, I'd love to, but I can't.'

She explained that Russell was employing her as a full-time housekeeper now; she worked all day and every day except Sundays.

'What a waste! Do you mean to say you're not even modelling for him?'

'Well, he says he'll use me when he starts his next piece of work – only I don't know when that will be.'

'Well, I call it a wicked waste of talent.' Reggie paused, then asked awkwardly: 'So how are things now – between you and him?'

'Russell's been a very good friend to me,' she said, carefully. 'That's how we are now – good friends.'

Reggie sighed. 'It must have been a terrible shock for him – well, for both of you – poor old Laura popping off like that, but let's face it, she could be very tiresome sometimes.' He lowered his voice. 'I've often wondered – did she leave a note?'

'A note?'

'A farewell letter, a curtain speech . . . Most of them can't resist having the last word.'

'What do you mean, "them"?'

'Suicides.'

'She didn't. It was an accident – didn't you see the papers?'

'Oh, yes, but they hushed it up, didn't they? I suppose Russell got rid of the farewell note. I don't blame him, mind you, saves a lot of trouble all round.'

Appalled, Jo protested: 'Reggie, there never was a suicide note. I was the one who found her, that morning, when I went to take in her breakfast. I was the first person to see her, lying there.'

As she spoke, she saw once more the lifeless face, the gaping mouth, cold hands clutching an empty glass that shone in the morning sunlight, and she repeated: 'There wasn't any note – I'm certain of that.'

'Unless Russell had been into her room, before you got there? He could have taken it.'

'I'm sure he didn't. You're only guessing.'

'Yes, I'm guessing, but I do know she threatened to kill herself that night – I heard her.'

'What? When?'

'I was here, working late, because I'd got a commission promised for the following morning. I'd just packed up, ready to leave, when I opened that door, and heard them yelling at each other.'

'You heard them – from the top flat? That's impossible!'

144

'They weren't upstairs, at least, Russell wasn't. He was halfway down the staircase and she was standing on the top landing, screaming at him: "Come back! If you go I'll kill myself, I swear I will!" And he shouted back: "That's the best news I've heard for a long time" – and went on running downstairs. She yelled: "You bastard!" then the front door banged, and a moment later the upstairs door slammed as well. So I got out as quickly as I could and went home.'

Slowly, Jo said: 'Are you sure about that?'

'Absolutely positive. When I heard next day that she'd taken an overdose, I wasn't exactly surprised. The only surprise was when they called it "accidental death".'

When she left Reggie, Jo went straight back to the top-floor flat. She found Russell in the living-room, pouring himself a large whisky.

As briefly as possible, she told him what Reggie had said, finishing: 'He never said anything about it – I think he felt sorry for you. But I have to know, is it true?'

Russell took a gulp of whisky, then said hoarsely: 'Give or take a word or two, he gave you a pretty fair account of my last conversation with Laura.' Then, glancing at Jo: 'Why are you looking like that?'

'How do you expect me to look? You lied in court. You were on oath, and you lied.'

'I told you, I wanted to hush things up for your sake.'

'But it wasn't only for my sake, was it? You lied to me as well. You said she would never have committed suicide, it wasn't in her nature.'

'I said that because it was true! Oh, she threatened to kill herself sometimes – it was just blackmail, when she couldn't get her own way. The first few times, I believed her, but I soon realised she had no intention of going through with it. It was just another chance to play a big tragic scene, with the spotlights on her.'

'Only this time, she did it.'

'No! The verdict was right – it was a sheer bloody accident! She never intended it to happen, but she was so drunk, she didn't know how many pills she'd taken. She was like the boy who cried "Wolf" – but this time the big bad wolf caught up with her.'

She saw that he was shaking – whether from grief or anger she could not tell. She did not even know if he was lying to her now. She didn't know anything.

'I'm sorry,' she said, wearily. 'I'd better go.'

He put out his hand, barring the way. 'That's not fair. You can't come in here, stirring things up all over again, bringing it all back, and then walk out on me. You can't leave me like this, Jo, not tonight. I won't let you!'

'No, I'm very tired. We're both tired.'

She tried to pull away, but he was too strong for her. 'Let's go to bed. We won't talk about Laura, we won't talk at all – we'll make love and forget everything else.'

She managed to struggle free, and backed away from him. 'I told you, I've got to go.'

'Why? What's the matter?'

'I – I'm late for something. I can't explain now.'

'Don't you love me any more?' He went on, with rising anger: 'Is that what this is all about? Answer me, God damn it!'

He began to move towards her, his green eyes black with fury, and for the first time she felt afraid of him. She turned and ran – out of the flat, and down the staircase – and she did not stop running until she was in her own little room, safe and sound.

Only nothing was safe any more . . . Because she was late.

Next morning, when she went back to work at Galleon House, Russell was very sullen. She took the breakfast tray to his bedroom as usual, and said: 'Good morning.'

Opening a bleary eye, he grunted: 'What's the weather like?'

'Grey, but at least it's not actually raining.'

'Oh, God.' He burrowed further down under the blankets. 'I think I'll stay in bed today, I'm not feeling too good. Leave the tray there – I'll have it later.'

So he was still in a bad mood. Closing the door quietly behind her, she went out, trying to think of something to give him for his lunch, something that might cheer him up. With rationing stricter than ever, it wasn't going to be easy.

Scouting through the shops in Battersea High Street, she suddenly remembered fish – a nice piece of plaice might appeal to him. Heading for the fish shop across the road, she stepped off the pavement—

With a scream of brakes, a sports car pulled up, inches away from her, and the driver shouted: 'Can't you look where you're going?'

He was a young man in his late twenties, bare-headed, with blond curls and a dashing red scarf round his neck. He would have been quite handsome if he had not been scowling.

'Why can't you look where you're going?' he barked.

He was interrupted by the young lady beside him, who exclaimed with delight: 'Jo, it's you! Alec, shut up and pull over to the kerb.'

Bewildered, Alec Coburn obeyed, and Vee jumped out of the car, hugging Jo and saying: 'I've been so worried about you – how are you?'

'Oh, not so bad. What are you doing, this side of the river?'

Vee explained: 'We're on our way to visit some friends of Alec's, at Wimbledon. Oh, I haven't introduced you. Alec, this is Jo Wells; she's the friend I met in Battersea Park. What a bit of luck, running into you like this. Where are you off to? Can we give you a lift?'

'Not really. I've got some shopping to do, thanks all the same, Vee—' Jo began, and was instantly corrected.

'Van, everyone calls me Van, don't they, Alec? Listen, I must talk to you. When can I see you? Come to tea on Sunday – you know where we live. Say four o'clock?'

Jo was beginning to feel more cheerful. 'Thank you, Van, I'll look forward to it.'

Watching them drive off in a cloud of exhaust-fumes, she felt a stab of envy. How lucky Vee was, to have found herself a new family. Then she pulled herself together. She had been lucky too – she had found Vee again. Vee or Van, it didn't matter – she wasn't alone any more.

But then, as she carried on with her shopping, she felt the hairs at the back of her neck prickling slightly. Because she was not alone – somebody was following her.

By Saturday, Russell was feeling a little better. At lunchtime, he told Jo that he was expecting visitors during the afternoon, and wouldn't be needing her.

She was both disappointed and relieved: she had something to tell him, and she wasn't sure how he would take it. This half-holiday was a welcome reprieve, though she knew she was only postponing the problem. Sooner or later, she would have to face it.

Now she had a whole afternoon to herself, with nothing to do. The sky was overcast, but a pale, watery sun was doing its best to break through. It might be nice to take a stroll in the park.

Walking along Battersea Church Road, she felt the same uncanny sensation: once more, she knew that she was being followed. She looked back. About ten yards behind her, a young man was walking in the same direction, wearing the olive-drab uniform of the United States Army. There were a great many Americans in Britain nowadays, though they mostly congregated around the Servicemen's club off Piccadilly Circus, known as 'Rainbow Corner'. They rarely ventured as far as Battersea.

Jo had noticed an American soldier in the High Street the other morning – could this be the same man?

At that moment, a number 34 tram rattled to a halt at the corner of Battersea Bridge Road. On the spur of the moment she boarded it and bought a ticket. The conductor punched her ticket and rang the bell, giving the driver the signal to start up again.

As the tram moved off, clanking and clanging along the rails, Jo heard another passenger jump aboard; looking back, she saw that the American soldier was lounging in one of the side seats, his legs stretched out across the gangway.

She tried to think what she should do. Of course it might be just a coincidence – he didn't look like a dangerous man – but on the other hand it might not. As the tram slowed down for the next stop, she recognised a grim red-brick building looming up ahead: Battersea Police Station.

That settled it. She stood up and walked back along the gangway, stepping over the American's legs. As the tram juddered to a stop she got off and began to walk briskly along the pavement, towards the police station.

Almost immediately, she heard footsteps behind her; one swift glance over her shoulder confirmed her fears – he was catching up fast.

Determined not to let him see that she was scared, she turned and faced him. 'Are you following me?' she asked.

His face broke into a broad grin, as he exclaimed: 'That I am, baby, that I am.'

Taken aback, she stammered: 'Well, you – you'd better stop it, that's all. Because I'm going to report you to the police!'

'What for?' The young man's eyes crinkled up with laughter. 'I never heard of any law against admiring a beautiful girl.'

'This isn't the first time. I've seen you before, haven't I? You've been following me for days!'

'Boy, you've got sharp eyes. I guess I just couldn't help myself – just one look, and you stole my heart away, honey. How's about letting me buy you a friendly drink?'

He was so eager to please, she almost smiled, but she retorted: 'Certainly not. Anyway, the pubs are shut.'

'Shucks, I keep forgetting these crazy regulations over here. OK, I'll buy you a cup of coffee, or would you sooner have tea?'

'Neither, thank you very much. I just want you to stop bothering me and go away!'

'Sure, I'll go, as long as you come with me. Whaddaya say we both take a walk? Seeing you've got nothing special to do.'

'What makes you think that?'

'I know you weren't going any place in particular, else you wouldn't have got on that streetcar, then jumped right off again.'

'I was trying to get away from you!' She tried to sound indignant, but when he laughed, she found herself laughing too. 'You're a terrible man!'

'You see? You're getting to know me already. All we gotta do now is introduce ourselves.' He held out his hand, cheerfully confident. 'The name's Scott, Don Scott, glad to know you, Miss – Miss . . .?'

She gave in and shook hands. 'Jo Wells. How do you do?'

'I'm doing great, Jo. Hey, listen, where were you heading, before I made you change your plans?'

'If you must know, I was on my way to the park.'

'Terrific. I like parks. Why don't you lead the way?'

She knew she shouldn't – everyone said that the American troops were not to be trusted – but his impish humour was warming on a bleak afternoon.

'All right, then,' she said. 'Just for half an hour.'

The sun was shining brightly now, and they found a drift of snowdrops under the trees.

'Whaddaya know? Springtime's on its way, even in England,' said Don.

He kept asking her questions, and as the conversation unfolded she told him something about her life: the loss of the family in the war, and her various exploits since she left Agar Road. When she went on to tell him about her work at Galleon House – first as a model, now as a housekeeper – he was very interested.

'Russell Wade? I never heard of him, but I guess he's famous over here, huh? D'you reckon you could introduce me some time?'

'I don't know. He's not what you'd call the sociable type. And this isn't a very good moment, either.'

She explained that Russell's wife had died recently, though she didn't go into any details, and Don said: 'That's too bad. But I'd sure like to get his autograph, so's I can tell Mom I met a real live celebrity. Maybe later, you could fix it?'

'We'll see. How long are you going to be over here?'

'About a year, I reckon. I'm stationed at a big US Army Base near Buck-ing-ham' – giving equal weight to every syllable – 'but I mostly get a weekend pass, three weeks in four.'

He told her that he came from a big family in Texas; his daddy managed a cattle-ranch, while Mom stayed home and raised the youngsters. Don was the eldest, with two younger brothers and a kid sister.

'You're lucky,' said Jo. 'Having a big family like that.'

He understood at once. 'Ouch, that wasn't very smart of me, was it? Still, if it's a family you're looking for, you could marry me, and have a share in my folks back home!'

She smiled. 'I'm afraid I can't get away this week, I've got to start the spring-cleaning.' Then she saw that he was looking at her in an oddly speculative way, and added: 'You were joking, I hope?'

'Maybe I was – and maybe I wasn't.' The smile returned. 'You never can tell.'

His sense of humour was sometimes disconcerting, but she certainly enjoyed his company. When at last she said she had to go, he asked her what she had planned for the evening – did she care for dancing?

'It's very kind of you, but I can't.' Everything was happening much too fast. She improvised rapidly: 'I've promised to visit some friends this evening. I'm sorry, I really must go now.'

He insisted on escorting her, and by the time they reached the Rope Walk, it was almost dark, but he behaved with strict propriety, and shook hands again when they parted.

'Thanks for taking pity on a lonesome GI,' he said. 'Will I see you again? How's about tomorrow?'

She was able to tell him, truthfully, that she already had a date tomorrow, and he shrugged. 'Well, OK – but now I know where you live, I'll be calling round again some time. Maybe next weekend, if that's OK?'

Her thoughts were pulling her in different directions, but to her surprise, she realised that she wanted to meet him again.

'Thank you,' she said. 'I'd like that.'

On Sunday at four o'clock she rang the doorbell at the house in Cheyne Walk. She looked forward to seeing her sister, but she was apprehensive at the prospect of meeting Vee's other family.

A maid in a cap and apron opened the door, and when Jo gave her name, the girl smiled and said: 'Miss Coburn is expecting you. May I take your hat and coat?'

She helped Jo off with her old winter coat and woolly hat, then led the way upstairs to the first-floor drawing-room. To her relief, Jo found Vee on her own, with tea-things laid out on a low table.

As soon as the maid left the room, Vee kissed her. 'It's so good to see you. I've been thinking about you so much.'

Seeing there were only two cups and saucers there, Jo said: 'I was afraid the whole family would be here.'

'No, it's just us. Alec's playing golf at Sunningdale, and Aunt Elspeth's gone to visit a friend in hospital. Anyway, you don't have to be shy, they're both lovely people. You liked Alec, didn't you?'

Jo protested: 'I only talked to him for a moment – I couldn't really tell.'

Vee's face fell. 'It's funny, that's more or less what he said about you . . . Do help yourself to a sandwich. They're a sort of cheese spread.'

Jo bit into the sandwich, then said: 'Mmmm – delicious. You do have interesting things to eat. I don't know how you manage it, with ration-books and all that. It takes me ages to shop for Russell, and then I have to fall back on dried egg and tins of Spam, as often as not.'

'I think it's just a question of knowing where to go,' Vee said vaguely. 'And knowing the right people – that helps.'

A silence fell. After a while, Vee exclaimed: 'I can't understand why you and Alec didn't take to one another! You're my two favourite people in the whole world – I felt sure you'd like each other!'

Jo laughed. 'It might have helped if I hadn't thrown myself in front of his car!'

'Yes, that wasn't a very good start,' Vee admitted. 'I expect that's why he was a bit standoffish. He's not like that as a rule – everybody likes him.'

Then Jo understood everything, and she exclaimed: 'Oh, Vee, I'm sorry, I should have realised.'

'Realised what?'

'You're in love with him, aren't you?'

Vee looked stricken. 'Is it that obvious?'

'Only to me. I'm sure nobody else would ever guess.'

Vee bit her lip. 'I have to be so careful when I'm with him. I just pray he never finds out. I love him so much, and it's driving me mad.'

'Don't be unhappy.' Jo put her arms round her. 'I'm sure it will all work out in the end.'

'How can it? I'm his sister.'

'Just tell them the truth, then you won't have to make a secret of the way you feel.'

'That's impossible! They'd be simply furious. They'd just tell me to pack my bags and get out . . . Except I haven't got anything to pack – everything belongs to them. I've been sponging on them, living under false pretences.'

'If Alec's half as nice as you say, he'll understand. And if not, then he doesn't deserve you, and you'll be well shot of him. You've got to come clean – what's the good of running away from the truth?'

For a few seconds, Vee considered the possibility – but then she shook her head.

'It's no good, I can't. I couldn't face them. I'm not brave enough.' She blew her nose. 'I'm sorry, I shouldn't have poured it all out like that, only it was so marvellous, being able to tell someone.'

'I know what you mean.' Jo hesitated for a moment, then went on. 'You see, I've got something to tell you as well . . . Something I haven't got the guts to tell anybody else.'

'Something to do with Russell?'

Jo smiled ruefully. 'Yes, it's to do with him. He's not going to like it, but—' She took a deep breath. 'I think I'm going to have a baby.'

Chapter Eleven

'A BABY?' Vee stared at her, unable at first to take in all the implications. 'Oh, how awful. Whatever are you going to do?'

'I don't know. I've tried to think about it sensibly, but it's such a muddle. Besides, I'm not sure yet. I've only missed once.'

'Oh, well, that might not mean anything. You could just be anaemic or something. People do miss, sometimes.'

'I don't – at least, I never have.'

Vee hesitated, then asked delicately: 'Do you know who – ?'

'Of course! It was Russell!' Absurdly, Jo felt a sudden flash of anger. 'There's never been anyone else.'

'I'm sorry – only you said that stopped, after his wife died.'

'Well, yes. Only he came to the Rope Walk one night. He was very unhappy, and I let him stay. It must have been then.'

'Have you told him?'

'No. I didn't want to say anything until I knew for sure.'

Vee considered this, then put another question: 'Do you think he'll marry you?'

Uncomfortable under this interrogation, Jo stood up and moved restlessly around the room, looking at various ornaments – a tropical sea-shell, unknown faces in elaborate silver frames – picking things up and then putting them down again.

'He might, I suppose,' she said at last. 'But probably not.'

'But, he loves you, doesn't he? And you love him?'

'I used to think so, but – I'm not sure now. And if he married me out of duty, what sort of life would that be, for either of us?' Her voice cracked. 'Oh, why did this have to happen now?'

Seeing that she was near breaking-point, Vee changed her tone. 'It'll be all right. Come and sit down. Try not to worry.'

'That's a daft thing to say! How can I help worrying?'

Steering her back to the chair by the fire, Vee repeated firmly: 'Come on, you mustn't get upset. After all, it doesn't have to happen. There's still time.'

'You think it might be just a false alarm?'

'There's that, too. But even if you are pregnant, you don't have to go through with it, do you?'

Jo was startled. 'You mean – get rid of it?'

'If it comes to that. Well, it's a possibility, isn't it? People do, you know. When I was at school in Scotland, there was a girl who had to leave in the middle of term – we all knew why. They called it "a necessary operation for medical reasons", but it wasn't really. I expect Mr Wade would pay for it, wouldn't he?'

'I haven't the faintest idea.'

'Well, I think you ought to talk to him about it. You're going to have to, sooner or later, so—'

She broke off as the door opened and an elderly lady entered the room. Finding the girls together, she apologised. 'Van dear, forgive me for interrupting your little tea-party. I just wanted to tell you I'm back. Poor dear Marjorie is making a good recovery, but she's still very weak, so I didn't stay long.' Advancing upon Jo with out-stretched hand, the newcomer added with a smile: 'I don't believe we've met, have we? Won't you introduce us, Van?'

'Of course – this is my friend Jo Wells. Jo, this is my Aunt Elspeth.'

'How do you do, my dear? I'm so pleased to meet you.'

Elspeth Coburn must have been in her late sixties, but she was still erect and slender, and her handshake was firm; her clothes were tweedy and serviceable, timeless rather than fashionable, and beneath her silver hair her complexion was fresh and smooth, like that of a much younger woman. Only the wrinkles around her steel-grey eyes betrayed her age.

'Do sit down, both of you, and finish your tea. Is there any left in the pot?' Without waiting for a reply, she pressed a bell-push beside the fireplace: 'I was offered tea at the hospital – very kind of them, but it's never the same, is it? I imagine they make it in one of those urns.' Her voice had a marked Scottish lilt, every word precisely accented, with perfect clarity and total assurance. When the maid appeared, she said pleasantly: 'Another cup and saucer, please, Alice, and some extra scones.'

Settling herself in her favourite armchair, she addressed Jo again: 'Now let me see, you must be the friend Van met in Battersea Park? Is that right?'

'Yes, we were both walking there one afternoon, and we happened to get into conversation,' explained Jo, feeling very self-conscious.

'Ah, yes, it's so nice to meet someone new, when you find you both strike on the same box, so to speak. Do you live near the park too?'

'Not as near as this.' Through the window, Jo could see the tops of the trees over the river. 'But not far – just off Battersea Church Road.'

'Oh, yes, St Mary's, a very handsome building. I've driven past, but never visited it. I'm Church of Scotland myself. I used to go to St Columba's in Pont Street until it was blown to pieces in one of the raids. But I hear it's to be rebuilt at last, God willing. So you attend St Mary's, do you?'

'Well – no, not really.'

'I see.' Aunt Elspeth smiled kindly. 'No doubt you're kept very busy. Vanessa tells me you are the housekeeper to a distinguished sculptor? That must be very interesting. I confess I don't know a great deal about art, but I used to paint in water-colours when I was a wee girl.'

She enquired after Jo's family, and expressed her sympathy on hearing of the death of her parents. 'How very shocking. And have you no brothers or sisters?'

Without looking at Vee, Jo replied: 'I had one brother – and one sister – but the night of the raid, they both – went . . .'

The conversation turned to more general topics: the long winter, the drabness of rationing and 'utility' clothes and furniture, and on a brighter note, the recent christening of the King and Queen's first grandchild, the little Prince Charles.

'I just pray that it will be a happy omen for all of us – another Bonny Prince Charlie!' said Aunt Elspeth. 'I do believe a new baby brings its own blessings with it, don't you?'

'I – I've never really thought about it.' Jo gathered herself up. 'If you'll excuse me, I really should be going now. It's been a lovely afternoon. Thank you very much – Van – and you too, Miss Coburn.'

'It's been a great pleasure, my dear. You must come again very soon.'

Vee too got up. 'I'll come down and see you off. Ring me when you can spare a minute, then we'll make a date for you to come again. We always seem to have so much to talk about.'

Later, Vee returned to the drawing-room, where her aunt was finishing off a scone, and said: 'Thank you for being so nice to her – she was feeling rather shy.'

'I thought she was charming – a very good type of girl, for a Londoner.' Elspeth Coburn wiped her fingers on a lace napkin, adding: 'Though to be perfectly honest, I'd recommend you to leave a little time before you invite her again.'

'What do you mean?'

'It's very good of you to take the girl up and show her a little kindness, but you mustn't let yourself become too involved. It always makes for difficulties in the long run, and it won't do the girl any favours if you go putting ideas into her head.'

'I don't understand. I thought you liked her.'

'So I do, but you mustn't encourage her to think she can become a close friend, dear. You have nothing in common – different backgrounds, different outlooks on life – she's not our kind of person, is she?'

'I've never heard anything so ridiculous. I thought the war had stopped that sort of nonsense. Jo Wells is a very nice person, and – and a very good friend!'

Aunt Elspeth sighed. 'Your generous heart does you credit, dear, but I'm just warning you: you're laying up trouble for yourself, and I don't want to see you get hurt – either of you.'

All the way back to the Rope Walk, one phrase ran through Jo's head – 'a new baby brings its own blessings.'

The old lady had been very pleasant, but she would have liked a little more time with Vee. Their discussion had been left unresolved; she still didn't know what to do.

That evening, she made up her mind to ask advice elsewhere.

When the other tenants had gone out and the house was quiet, she went downstairs and tapped on the half-open kitchen door.

'Come in, Jo,' said Sarah. 'I was hoping you might pop in for a chat. With everyone else being out, I could do with a bit of company.'

Tibbles, who had been curled up on Sarah's lap, lifted his head and glared at his mistress balefully, then rolled off, walked across the rug with his tail stiffly aloft, and jumped up on to Jo's lap instead. Circling round two or three times and kneading her with pincushion paws, he settled down and started to purr.

'I've hurt his feelings,' said Sarah. 'Oh, well, I expect he'll get over it next time I put down a saucer of milk . . . So, how's the world treating you, my dear?'

'Oh, I'm all right . . . More or less.'

'More than all right?' Sarah pursued. 'Or less than all right?'

'A bit less, at the moment.'

'Oh? And how's Russell?'

Jo shrugged. 'He has good days and bad days.'

'Yes, he's a moody creature. Always was and always will be. And he gets worse as he grows older. When he's in one of his moods, he takes it out on you, eh?'

'It's not that so much . . .' Jo plunged in. 'Can I ask you something?'

'Of course. I mightn't give you an answer, but you can ask.'

'Well, I was thinking, about the other girls in this house. Do any of them ever – get into trouble?'

'Most of 'em are sharp enough not to take any chances.' Sarah brought those huge, luminous eyes to bear upon Jo. 'Got yourself in the family way, have you? With Russell, I suppose?'

'I'm afraid so. I missed, last month.'

'Well, there could be different reasons for that. You don't want to go jumping to conclusions.'

'I know, but what if it's the same next time? What do you think I ought to do about it?'

'I'm not much of a one for giving advice. What do you want to do? Marry Russell and live happy ever after?'

'He might not want to.'

'You haven't told him yet?'

'No – not till I know, one way or the other. But even then, I'm not sure what I really want.' She went on stroking the cat, and Tibbles expressed his approval. 'That's why I asked about the other girls.

Have any of them ever . . . ?'

'Had an abortion? It has been known.'

'I thought so. So – if I need to – you might be able to tell me what to do, where to go?'

'I could tell you where to go. I couldn't tell you what to do. Nobody can tell you a thing like that.'

Hearing something in Sarah's voice – a different edge, a long-remembered unhappiness – Jo dared to ask: 'Have you – ever . . . ?'

'Yes, when I was about your age.'

'What was it like?'

'It wasn't any picnic, as I remember. But things are different nowadays. They make it a lot easier than it was in my time – leastways, they do if you can afford it.'

'I don't mean "Did it hurt?" I meant, what was it like afterwards – did you wish you hadn't done it?'

'No, not then. I just wanted to get on with my life as if it had never happened. I was so impatient – couldn't wait – never could wait for anything. But later on, much later, when I got a bit older and I saw the way my life was turning out, then I began to think different. No, I never regretted it then, but now there isn't a day goes by when I don't wonder what it might have been like, if I hadn't done it. I suppose I'll go on wondering that for the rest of my life.'

There was a long silence, broken only by the cat's purring. At last Sarah continued: 'That's not to say I wouldn't help you, if that's what you decide. Only you must think it over very carefully – and then let me know. And before you finally make your mind up, you must tell Russell. That's only fair.'

On Monday morning, when she went to work at Galleon House, Jo made two or three attempts to broach the subject, but it was extremely difficult – Russell was in one of his distant moods. For the time being, she gave up the attempt, deciding to try again later; perhaps he'd be in a more receptive frame of mind after lunch.

When he had scanned *The Times* and finished his morning coffee, he went down to the studio, saying he wanted to mull over some new ideas, so Jo set to work in the living-room. She had just begun to polish the coffee-table when to her surprise he came back.

'Hello!' said Jo. 'That was quick – did you forget something?'

He took the duster from her hand, and put the lid back on the tin of polish, then said: 'No, I've got something for you. I think you'd better sit down.'

He led her to an armchair, then produced an envelope, stamped and postmarked, explaining: 'I found this downstairs, on the mat. It must have come by the second post. It's addressed to you.' She held out her hand. He did not give it to her immediately, but added: 'It might be bad news.'

'Bad news?'

Then he showed her the envelope – it had a black border.

At a loss, Jo took it and read her own name, and the address of Galleon House, written in a round, slapdash hand she did not know. She tore open the envelope and took out a printed card, with the necessary details filled in along dotted lines in the same, unformed handwriting:

> It is with great sorrow that we have to announce the funeral of
> MR NORMAN JOHN BONE
> which is to take place at
> ALL SAINTS' CHURCH, PRINCE OF WALES DRIVE, BATTERSEA
> on
> MONDAY, 24 JANUARY 1949, AT 11.30 A.M.
> Your presence would be much appreciated,
> and your prayers are requested.
> R.I.P.

Russell asked gently: 'Was it someone close to you?'

'It's my Uncle Norman. I hardly knew him, really – he was in the Navy, so he was away a lot of the time. Seems funny, doesn't it? He got all through the war without so much as a scratch, and now it's all over, he . . .'

She ran out of words. Russell sat beside her on the sofa, but he did not try to touch her.

'I'm sorry,' he said. 'I know you don't have much family left – that must make it harder for you.'

'Yes, there's just his wife, my Aunt Topsy – his widow, I mean – and their daughter . . .' Then, remembering suddenly: 'Oh, you met them once – they came here, when my photo was in the paper.'

He said wryly: 'As I recollect, she didn't exactly approve of me.'

'She's never been very easy to get on with. I haven't seen her for ages, but all the same, when something like this happens . . .'

'At least she let you know about the funeral. Will you go?'

'I suppose so. It's a week today, Monday morning, but what about your lunch?'

'To hell with my lunch.' He held her hand. 'Of course you must go.'

'Thank you.' He was being so kind, unexpectedly kind, she went on quickly: 'Russell, I've got something to tell you.'

'Something about your family?'

'Something about us.'

In the end, telling him turned out to be quite easy. When she had finished, she waited for him to say something, but he was very silent.

Standing up, he walked across the room to the white piano, where the photographs of Laura had once been on display. Now they were put away in a box, on the top shelf of a cupboard in Russell's bedroom.

Without turning to look at her, he asked: 'What do you want to do?'

'I don't know yet. I don't know what would be best. I think I can find a doctor who'd help, if I decide – if we decide – not to go on . . . Not to have the baby.'

He turned round, his face dark with anger. 'Don't say that! It's my child too. Of course you will have the baby – why shouldn't you?'

'It's not very easy, for a girl on her own . . .' she began.

'Don't be a fool – you won't be on your own,' he told her harshly. 'I'll do my duty. You won't be short of money, if that's what worries you.'

'It's not only that. There's more to it than money.'

'I suppose you want a husband as well – is that it? Keep it nice and respectable, so the neighbours won't gossip. All right, if that's what you want, I'll marry you.'

Looking into his eyes, she saw they were no longer green, but black. Once before when he was in a rage she had noticed the same transformation; then she had put it down to a trick of the light, but today she saw it was not an illusion. His pupils seemed to be enormous, with only a narrow rim of green iris – and once again she felt afraid of him.

'Well?' he snapped. 'Will I do for a husband? Will you have me?'

'I don't know.' She could not give him an answer, but tried to smile, showing him she was not afraid. 'I need time to think. We don't have to decide right away. Perhaps it will turn out to be a mistake, then we shan't have to worry. Let's leave it a little longer.'

He frowned. 'I don't understand you. At one time you were always talking about the family you lost. Isn't this a heaven-sent opportunity to start again? To raise a family of our own? I'd have thought that would be your dream come true.'

She heard the irony in his tone, and said quietly: 'I know. I don't understand myself, sometimes.'

How could she tell him she was frightened, when she didn't even know what she was frightened of?

'So tell me, what's happened?' Vee wanted to know.

Jo had made hot-buttered toast at the gas-fire in her room; now she divided it between them and began: 'Nothing much.' She took a bite of toast, and said with her mouth full: 'Nothing's happened. I still don't know about the baby.'

'When you rang up, you sounded as if it were important, that's why I came round.'

'I'm sorry. I would have come to Cheyne Walk, only you said it wasn't convenient.'

'Well, no, it wasn't.' Vee looked uncomfortable. 'Aunt Elspeth can be a bit difficult sometimes, when I invite friends.'

Jo caught on quickly. 'Didn't she approve of me? Oh, dear, and I thought I'd made such a good impression, too.'

'Oh, it's not just you,' Vee explained – not entirely truthfully. 'She's the same about everybody. She scolds Alec sometimes, when his golfing chums make too much noise.'

'I didn't make too much noise, did I?'

'Of course not! But she does have her funny little ways. The other day she told Alec he treated the house like a hotel, dropping in and out at all hours. I felt so sorry for him. After all, he is nearly twenty-seven. Anyway, I thought I'd better not tread on her pet corns at the moment!'

'I see.' Jo wiped some melted butter from her chin. 'Actually, when I told you nothing had happened, that's not quite true. Two things have happened, and one of them is about the baby. I finally managed to tell Russell.'

'What did he say?'

'He wants me to have it. He's asked me to marry him.'

'And you said yes?'

'I told him it would be better to wait. I said I'd think it over.'

Vee studied her. 'You don't seem very pleased about it. I'd have thought you'd be delighted.'

'The trouble is, I'm not sure I want to marry him. It doesn't seem right to do it just because of the baby.'

'Well, I suppose you could have it adopted,' Vee suggested.

Indignantly, Jo exclaimed: 'Give my baby away? I couldn't do that. If I have the baby, I'll keep it – that's one thing I do know!'

After a moment, Vee began again: 'You said two things had happened. What's the other thing?'

'Oh, yes . . .' Jo stretched up and took the black-edged card from the mantelpiece. 'This arrived at Galleon House.'

Vee read it quickly, then said: 'Poor Uncle Norman – he can't have been that old. How did it happen, do you know?'

'I don't know anything except what it says there. I haven't heard from Auntie Topsy for ages.'

'Still, she sent you the card – that's something. Will you go? To the funeral, I mean?'

'I think I ought to.' Tentatively, Jo added: 'I don't suppose you'd come with me?'

Vee stared at her. 'Oh, no. How could I?'

'We could sit at the back of the church. If anyone asks, I'll just say you're a friend of mine.'

'Suppose Auntie Topsy recognises me?'

Jo tried to argue, but there was a tap at the door and Peggy Hooper called out: 'Jo, are you decent? You've got a visitor.'

The two girls looked at one another, and Jo called back: 'Who is it?'

Peggy opened the door saying cheerfully: 'What's it matter? He's tall, dark and handsome, and he's a Yank. Some people have all the luck!' Then, nodding casually at Vee: 'Hello, dear – we met before, didn't we? Sorry to barge in, Jo, but there's a GI on the doorstep, asking if you're at home. What shall I tell him?'

'It must be Don. He said he might call in – I forgot.'

'Look, if you don't want to be bothered, you can always push him in my direction, darling,' Peggy teased her. 'I'll take good care of him, believe you me! No, all right, I'm only kidding.'

Giggling, she ran downstairs.

Vee stared at Jo. 'An American soldier? As if you hadn't got enough problems already!'

'It's nothing like that. We went for a walk in the park, that's all.'

They heard footsteps on the stairs. Don burst in, carrying a large paper sack.

'Hi! I thought I'd drop by—' He broke off. 'You've got company.'

'That's all right. Vee, this is Don Scott. Don, this is – a friend of mine.'

'Vanessa Coburn.' Vee shook hands with him. 'How do you do, Mr Scott?'

'Glad to know you. Look, if you're busy, just say the word and I'll vamoose. I'd been planning on taking you out some place, but I could call back later.' Looking from one girl to the other, he added: 'Do you smoke?'

Vee answered: 'I like the odd cigarette now and then.'

Jo said: 'I don't as a rule, but if you want to—'

'It's not that. I picked up a few items from the P/X – maybe you could share 'em between you?' And to Vee: 'I hope you like American cigarettes, Vanessa?'

He unpacked the paper sack, tipping out cartons of Lucky Strikes and Camels, chocolate Hershey bars and gumdrops and – most precious of all – half a dozen pairs of nylons.

'It's like Christmas!' said Jo. 'Don, you shouldn't—'

'Don't give it another thought,' he told her. 'My pleasure.'

'And I can't even offer you a drink, unless you'd like a cup of tea?'

'Don't go to any trouble on my account. Listen, why don't I take you both out?'

On Saturday nights, the saloon bar at the Woodman in Battersea High Street was always packed; an elderly man was banging out popular songs at a tinny upright piano, and the customers were joining in the choruses.

'Wow! This is really something!' said Don, as they walked in. 'A real cockney singalong. I guess you two are both cockneys?'

'I am,' said Jo, smiling mischievously at Vee. 'But she isn't.'

'I don't get it.' Don was at a loss. 'What's the difference? You're both Londoners.'

'Yes, but she lives on the other side of the river,' Jo told him. 'The posh side.'

Don grinned. 'What we call the right side of the tracks, huh? Anyway, lemme get the drinks. What'll it be?'

When he went to the bar, Vee asked Jo: 'Why did he invite me along? Doesn't he want you all to himself?'

'He's not like that,' replied Jo. 'He's a very sociable person – and very generous.'

'He's that, certainly.' Vee glanced under the table, where her share of the American bounty was packed into the paper sack. 'The family are never going to believe this. But I must say he's rather charming, in his way.'

By the time Don returned, the pianist was working his way through the old music-hall numbers; the crowd were bellowing 'The Old Bull and Bush' and 'Oh, You Beautiful Doll', and the girls listened, remembering the old favourites.

Vee said dreamily: 'When I was little, I had a great big beautiful doll . . . I wonder what happened to her.'

Without stopping to think, Jo exclaimed: 'Of course – *Bella!* – I'd forgotten her.'

Vee turned to her eagerly. 'Do you remember Bella?'

Puzzled, Don asked: 'You two knew each other when you were kids?'

They fell silent, then Vee murmured uneasily: 'No, not exactly . . .'

Jo suggested: 'You must have mentioned your doll before, and I suddenly remembered the name.'

She felt ashamed. How could she have forgotten Bella, packed away in her room at the Rope Walk? She couldn't explain now, in front of Don. The next time she saw Vee, she would have a surprise for her.

At last Vee said she had to go – her family would be worried if she stayed out late. Don insisted on calling a cab, explaining that he had promised to meet some buddies in Piccadilly. He could drop both girls off along the way.

The taxi reached the Rope Walk very quickly, and when Jo got out, Don told her he might be on guard-duty next weekend, but he'd surely be back in two weeks' time. Then the cab drove on over the bridge and along Cheyne Walk, pulling up outside Vee's front door.

She picked up her sack of presents and thanked Don again, half-expecting he might make a grab for her, but he simply said: 'We must do this again some time. We could take in a show, maybe?'

'Well, that sounds very nice, but – are you sure you want me there as well?'

'It wouldn't be the same without you!' he told her. 'You know the old saying: two's company, but three's a party!'

Then he helped her out of the taxi, watching with a smile as she let herself into the house. When the door closed, he gazed up at the imposing façade, studying it carefully. He was still smiling when he climbed back into the cab.

On the morning of the funeral, Jo made an early start. She stopped to buy some white tulips; they might help to cheer Aunt Topsy a little.

Carrying them in the crook of her arm, she took the short cut through the park. Near the children's playground, she saw a couple coming towards her; the man was wheeling a pushchair with a toddler in it, and as Jo stepped aside to let them pass he suddenly exclaimed: 'Jo! It is you, isn't it?' He peered at her through steel-rimmed spectacles and grasped her hand. 'Don't say you've forgotten me? Malcolm Jones, from Bryden Brothers – remember?'

'I'm sorry, I was miles away. How are you, Malcolm?'

It was almost four years since she saw him last, but he seemed much older; his hair had begun to recede at the temples.

'I'm very well, thanks.'

He remembered the young woman at his side. 'Oh, 'scuse me. My wife, Pat. Pat, this is an old friend of mine – Jo Wells.'

Mrs Jones had bright eyes like a robin; smiling, she said: 'Pleased to meet you. And this is our little girl, Sandra – say hello, Sandra.'

The child stared up at Jo, dumbstruck.

'There now, and she's a regular little chatterbox at home,' Malcolm explained. 'I expect we've taken her by surprise.'

'You've taken me by surprise as well,' Jo told him. 'I didn't know you were a family man. Last time I saw you, you'd just been called up.'

'That's going back a bit! Yes, I did my National Service. That's

166

where I met Pat – she was in the ATS. When we got married, we were both in uniform. Sandra's going to be three next July.' Modestly, he added: 'And by that time we're hoping she'll have a little brother or sister!'

Jo, who had been trying not to stare too obviously at Pat's waistline, said: 'Oh, that's nice – congratulations!'

Politely, Malcolm enquired: 'How about you, Jo? Are you married, or anything?'

'No, I'm not married, or anything.' She changed the subject. 'What are you doing these days? I suppose you didn't go back to Brydens when you were demobbed?'

He frowned slightly. 'Yes, I did as a matter of fact. Why not?'

'Well, meeting you here, on a Monday morning . . .'

'I was due some time off on account of working late over Christmas, so Pat and me decided to come out and stretch our legs. Oh, yes, Brydens have been very good to me – they've made me a floorwalker now.'

'He's the youngest floorwalker they ever had,' Pat chimed in proudly.

For want of anything better to say, Jo asked: 'How's Nora? Is she still at Brydens too?'

Pat glanced from one to the other. 'Nora who?'

'Nora Topping – you don't know her,' replied Malcolm. 'No, she took up with some rich chap and went abroad. The girls at work were full of it . . . I'm surprised you didn't hear. Perhaps you don't patronise Brydens these days?'

'No, I haven't been back since . . .' Jo glanced at her watch. 'Oh, dear, I'll have to be getting along. I'm on my way to Agar Road and I mustn't be late.' She began to move away. 'It's been so nice to meet you.'

'Agar Road? That's not far from us, is it, Malc?' said Pat. 'We're in Blenheim Terrace. Is that where you live – Agar Road?'

'No, my aunt lives there. I'm going to—' Jo broke off. She couldn't stop and explain about the funeral now.

'But you still live in Battersea, do you?' Pat went on. 'You must come round for tea one afternoon, then we can have a nice long chat. Give me your address. Malc, have you got a pencil?'

'Don't worry, it's easy to remember,' said Jo. 'Number One, the

Rope Walk . . . Now I really must run. See you soon!'

It felt very odd, seeing Malcolm after all this time. They didn't have a great deal in common, but he'd been very pleasant, and Pat seemed anxious to keep in touch.

Leaving the park, she quickened her pace – under the railway bridge and up the slope past the Dogs' Home; the Power Station chimneys looked like gigantic pillars, holding up a heavy canopy of cloud.

When she reached Agar Road, she saw that the blinds had been drawn as a mark of respect. She rattled the knocker gently, and the front door was opened by Mr Mulligan, wearing a shabby black frock-coat and a pair of baggy black trousers.

His face creased into a smile and he gave Jo a smacking kiss, exclaiming: 'Is it yourself? Come along in – your auntie will be glad to see you.' Standing aside, he added in an undertone: 'She's not been her old self lately, I'm sorry to say.'

From force of habit, Jo was making for the back kitchen, but he redirected her. 'Not in there – she's in the parlour.'

Topsy Bone was seated in the best armchair, with Mr Penberthy hovering over her solicitously. They were both in funeral attire: Mr Penberthy had put on the pinstripe suit he wore to the office, and Aunt Topsy's high-collared black dress made her complexion yellow and waxen.

'What are you doing here?' she asked Jo accusingly.

'I came to see you, Auntie, to tell you how sorry I was to hear about Uncle Norman . . . And to give you these.'

Jo offered her the tulips. Topsy did not take them, but said flatly: 'You ought to have sent them to the undertakers, with the other floral tributes. Wreaths and crosses always go to the funeral parlour – didn't you know that?'

'These aren't floral tributes,' said Jo. 'They're for you.'

Behind her, Mr Mulligan said softly: 'A very nice thought – don't you agree, Mrs Bone?'

'Flowers, for me? I never heard of such a thing.' Topsy tossed her head, but she accepted the bouquet. 'I suppose you can afford to throw your money away on such things.' Then, raising her voice to a quivering shriek, she called: 'Chrissie, fetch me a vase out of the cupboard under the sink – a big one!'

Jo looked round. 'Where is Chrissie?'

168

'Upstairs, getting ready to go to church. Give her a shout, Mr Mulligan, we don't want to be late.'

'No need to trouble her, Mrs Bone, dear. I'll see to it.'

Mr Mulligan toddled off with the tulips, and Topsy turned to her niece.

'It's a long time since you set foot in this house, and no mistake. But there, that's gratitude for you.' She glanced up at Mr Penberthy for support. 'And after all I did for her when she was a kiddie, too.'

Mr Penberthy wagged his head. 'Sharper than a serpent's tooth is a thankless child, but the ungrateful never prosper.'

Jo tried hard to be patient. 'Last time we met, you made it pretty clear that I wasn't welcome here.'

'I never said that!' snapped Topsy. 'I was hoping you'd see the error of your ways, but I suppose that was too much to ask. You're still carrying on with that artist chap, no doubt?'

'I'm still his housekeeper, if that's what you mean.'

'Housekeeper indeed! That's not what I'd call it. I saw in the papers as how his wife had passed on, so I suppose you've moved in with him now, eh?'

'No, I haven't.' Jo was determined not to lose her temper. 'I go to work at Galleon House every morning, and at the end of the afternoon I go home again.'

'I'm glad to hear it, I'm sure.' Topsy sniffed, and changed the subject. 'So how did you find out about your poor uncle? Who told you?'

'You sent me a card, Auntie,' Jo reminded her. 'Don't you remember?'

'I never did.' Topsy knitted her brows. 'I didn't think you'd want to know. I said as much to you, didn't I, Mr Penberthy?'

'You did indeed, you said it would be a pity to waste the stamp.'

From the doorway, a small voice said: 'Did you call me, Ma?'

Chrissie, at eleven, was not a pretty child; dressed in a white blouse and black gym-slip, her arms and legs looked long and gawky. Like her mother, she was very pale, and in contrast to her carroty hair, her freckles had taken on a strange greenish tone.

Seeing Jo, she exclaimed happily: 'Oh, you did come!'

Topsy rounded on her angrily. 'So it was you, was it? You sent her that funeral card without telling me!'

'Somebody had to. Well, she is family . . .'

'Thank you, Chris,' said Jo. 'But how did you know where to send it?'

'I remembered that time we came to see you, me and Ma.'

'She never stopped talking about that blessed day for months.' Catching her breath, Topsy was overcome by a coughing fit. 'Now look what you've done. Fetch me a glass of water.'

As Chrissie obeyed, Topsy added grudgingly: 'I suppose you had a right to know about your uncle.'

'Yes, but how did it happen? Was he away at sea?'

'No, he was home on leave, right here in the kitchen.' It was obviously a story she had told over and over again. 'I'd just come back from the shops, and he was sitting at the kitchen table, reading the *Daily Mirror*. I told him to shift himself so I could unpack my groceries, and he said: "Righty-ho". He was just standing up when he gave me this funny look, and then he fell down. Being as it was a Saturday, Chrissie was home, so I sent her round to the doctor, but it wasn't no good. He'd gone before the doctor got here . . . Heart, it was; it just gave out all of a sudden. I'll never forget the way he looked at me: "Righty-ho," he said – those were his last words, "Righty-ho" . . .'

After a moment Jo said: 'You must miss him very much.'

'Well, yes. People think I must've got used to living on my own, with him being away at sea so much, but it's not the same. I always knew he was there, if anything happened. If I needed him, he'd come back. But this time he's gone for good . . .'

Mr Penberthy began to intone: 'How true the old saying is – in the midst of life, we are in death'.

Jo felt like saying: 'Oh, do shut up, for goodness' sake!' Instead, she asked her aunt: 'Would you like me to make you a cup of tea?'

'There isn't time. The hired car will be here any minute.' With some difficulty, Topsy levered herself up from her chair. 'You'll come to church with us, will you? It's going to be a squeeze in the back of the car, mind.'

'If there's isn't enough room, I can walk.'

'You'll do no such thing. Whatever would people say? We must all go together – Chrissie can sit on your lap.'

Then Chrissie appeared with a tumbler of water, followed by

Mr Mulligan carrying the vase of tulips and saying: 'Isn't this fine, now? All together again, to give him a good send-off.'

It was very strange to be sitting in the front pew with Aunt Topsy and Mr Penberthy. Jo felt as if she were fifteen years old again.

Mr Mulligan had seen them off from the front gate. He couldn't attend the ceremony himself as he 'didn't belong to the same club', but he had promised to light a candle for Uncle Norman.

Jo hadn't been inside a church for years. Aunt Topsy was never a regular churchgoer, and after Mum died Jo had stopped thinking about God. Now, as she sat and stared at the altar, old memories began to revive, one by one: church on Sunday mornings, with Mum and Vee and little Charlie; hymns in morning assembly at school; 'All Things Bright and Beautiful' . . . And the figure on the cross – the one she had stopped believing in.

And yet . . . Another, more recent memory came to the surface; the memory of a murky afternoon in Battersea Park, when ghosts from the past seemed to be following her, and she had been so frightened. In that moment, she had found herself praying to the God she did not believe in – and He had come to her rescue. Not only that – she had found Vee again, after so many lonely years.

With the rest of the congregation, Jo stood up as the clergyman in his white surplice and black stole began to recite: 'I am the resurrection and the life, saith the Lord; he that believeth in me, though he were dead, yet shall he live . . .'

That's what it was all about. Gradually, Jo began to realise that this was what God meant: life.

'. . . And whosoever liveth and believeth in me shall never die.'

Above the altar the stained glass in the windows glowed brightly; the sun had managed to break through. It might not last, it might be only a moment, but it was a moment Jo would never forget.

Chapter Twelve

ANOTHER LETTER ARRIVED, addressed in an unfamiliar handwriting – spiky characters sloping in different directions. The postmark was a United States military camp near Wendover, Bucks. Jo tore open the envelope and read:

> *Howya doing? Like I thought, I got landed with guard duty through this weekend, and now I'm stir-crazy, if you know what that means, and I'm looking forward to my next trip to London Town. I'm gonna get me some tickets for a show, so you and Vanessa had better be ready for a great Saturday night! I'll meet you both at the Woodman pub around six p.m. Saturday – OK?*
>
> *Be seeing ya – Don.*

When Jo rang her, Vee said: 'I wonder which theatre he's picked. I hope it's not something I've seen already.'

Jo smiled. 'I haven't been to a theatre since Mum took us to that pantomime at the Chelsea Palace – do you remember?'

'I can't stop and talk now, we're expecting some friends. Shall I meet you on Saturday at the Woodman?'

'I'd sooner come and collect you at Cheyne Walk, then we can talk before we meet Don.'

Vee sounded troubled. 'I'm not sure. Perhaps I should come to the Rope Walk.'

'No, it had better be Cheyne Walk, because I've got something to give you. Otherwise you'll have to cart it round with you all the evening.'

'What sort of something?'

'It's a surprise – you'll see. You can tell Aunt Elspeth that I'll wipe my shoes on the mat. I won't stay long, and I promise to talk proper!'

Vee laughed. 'All right then, come here at five o'clock on Saturday.' Then she lowered her voice. 'By the way, have you got any more news about – you know – any further developments?'

'No, no developments so far. But I've decided, whatever happens, it's going to be all right.'

'I don't understand.'

'I don't understand it either,' Jo couldn't explain. 'Somehow I just know it will.'

When she went to work next morning, she found Russell in a very good mood. He too asked if she had any news, and when she said no, he was obviously delighted.

'Couldn't be better,' he assured her. 'I've had a brilliant idea! Let's go down to the studio right away.'

'But what about your breakfast?'

'I made myself some breakfast. I was up at the crack of dawn, ready to start work.'

As they went downstairs, Jo asked: 'Is this going to be another dryad or naiad or whatever they're called?'

'Not likely, I'm sick and tired of classical myths. I still haven't managed to find a buyer for the water-nymph. Battersea Borough Council thanked me kindly for my suggestion, but regretted that the river-frontage is strictly controlled by some damn regulation or other. What they really mean is that they're too damn stingy to pay for a work of art.'

'So what are you going to do?'

'I've sent the poor girl into storage with some of my other pieces. But never mind, my new idea is going to be a regular knock-out.'

When they entered the studio, he told her to undress; he wanted to make some preliminary sketches. While she was behind the screen he continued: 'This won't be just one piece, it's going to be a whole series: four, six, a dozen, perhaps. I don't know yet. I've decided to make a record of you, all through the pregnancy; a young

173

mother-to-be, right up to the moment of birth . . . What do you think?'

'It sounds very good, but we still don't know for sure that I am pregnant.'

He brushed this aside. 'I can tell from the look of you. I can see the signs of new life already. There's a glow to your skin, a look in your eye, the way you move. No doubt about it – you're going to have our baby.'

Setting up his easel, he pinned a sheet of paper to the drawing-board, then broke off to add: 'I shan't be working in clay this time; it's not the right medium.'

Jo emerged, pulling the dressing-gown around her. 'Not in clay?'

He indicated some blocks of wood on the work-bench; roughly trimmed, but otherwise untouched.

'I used to do a lot of carving at one time. There's something special about wood. It's more difficult, because you can't make a single mistake, but it's the finest material of the lot. It's a living thing – natural, smooth, vibrant . . . Even the smell of raw wood is an inspiration.'

He helped her off with the old silk robe, and encouraged her to try several poses, then settled upon the simplest of all: she sat on a cushion with her legs curled under her, her hands slightly parted over her stomach and her head bowed, looking down upon the miracle that had just begun.

Working swiftly and surely, he produced a series of drawings. One in particular pleased him, turning the line of her head, neck and spine into a single curve, like the arched back of a contented cat.

'That's enough for one morning,' he said at last. 'Put some clothes on, and I'll stand you lunch at the pub. We've got to go out and celebrate! This is a champagne occasion!'

'That's very kind of you,' she said. 'But I'll be just as happy with fizzy lemon, really. I don't see why people make so much fuss about champagne.'

'That's because you've never had enough of it,' Russell told her firmly. 'I helped you to make a baby, and now you're helping me to make a masterpiece. If that doesn't call for a celebration, I don't know what does!'

*

By Saturday morning, Russell was making good progress. He had outlined the final shape on the top and four sides of a piece of limewood, roughly digging out the spaces with a spoon-shaped gouge. The work was slow and difficult, and Jo had to be very patient, but she enjoyed the steady rhythm of the mallet on the blade, and the smell of fresh wood-shavings that curled away and dropped like petals.

'We're two of a kind, you and I,' said Russell, running his hand lovingly over the grain of the wood. 'Both doing the same job.'

'How do you mean?' she asked.

'Within you, there's someone waiting to be born – and it's the same with carving. I can feel the figure under my hands, hidden inside the wood. I have to uncover it gradually and bring it out into the light.'

Jo understood, and enjoyed the sensation of kinship between them. At this moment, they seemed to be closer than ever before – closer even than when they were making love.

At last he glanced at his watch and laid aside the long, delicate chisel he had been using to mark out the next stage of the work.

'Nearly midday,' he said, then added hopefully: 'Do you feel like carrying on this afternoon?'

'It's Saturday,' she reminded him.

'Yes, I know, but I hate to stop when it's going well. Could you spare some extra time? You're not doing anything special, are you?'

She had to explain that she couldn't give up the afternoon; she had to get ready to meet some friends, because they were going to a theatre.

He grunted his displeasure. 'Pity . . . what about tomorrow? We could put in the whole day, if you're not busy? As it's a Sunday, I'd pay you double, of course.'

Jo was reluctant to give up her one free day, and she didn't care about the money, but he was so keen to get on, she didn't like to disappoint him.

'All right, I'll work tomorrow,' she told him.

'Bless you, you're a good girl.'

As she left the dais, slipping into the dressing-gown, he kissed her. It was a warm, affectionate kiss, and she felt a surge of hope.

Perhaps he was right – perhaps this was the beginning of a new understanding between them. That really would be a cause for celebration.

As it turned out, there was nothing to celebrate.

She was in her bedroom at the Rope Walk, getting ready to go out again, when she because aware of the change within her, and very soon her suspicions were confirmed. It had only been a false alarm after all; there would be no baby.

For a long while she lay on her bed, thinking over her situation. First and foremost, she had a sense of relief – yet there was an undercurrent of sadness in it as well. She realised just how much she wanted to have a child, though she had never admitted it, even to herself, and now it was not going to happen.

But it would be better this way, she told herself; better for her, better for the child too, really. What sort of life could she have given a son or a daughter? If she had married Russell, what kind of family would they have been? No, it was better like this.

She did not know how Russell would react to the news, but one thing was certain: his vision of a series of statues – the progressive sequence – had become impossible. She felt sure he would be angry and disappointed about that, and she dreaded having to tell him.

But she would think about that tomorrow – this evening she was going to meet Vee. Pulling herself together, she began to get dressed.

As she walked down the last flight of stairs, the front door swung open and she met Sarah coming in from the shops, carrying a string-bag full of groceries.

Looking up the stairwell to make sure she wasn't overheard, she said: 'I'm just going out, but I must tell you something first.'

Sarah put her head a little on one side, and said: 'So, there's no baby? Is that it?'

'How did you know?' Jo tried to make light of it. 'You must be a witch!'

The old woman considered this seriously. 'No, I don't think so, I just guessed, somehow. Well, how do you feel about that?'

'I don't know yet. I'm glad, really – at least, I think I am.'

'Of course you are.' Sarah patted her shoulder. 'You're a lucky girl.' And she set off down the passage.

Jo lingered for a moment, calling after her softly: 'Suppose it had turned out the other way? What would you have said to me then?'

'The same,' replied Sarah, over her shoulder, and disappeared into her kitchen.

★

The maid who answered the door at Cheyne Walk said: 'Miss Vanessa is expecting you, miss. She's just changing, but she asked me to show you up to her room.'

'Oh, don't bother, I know the way—' began Jo; then, seeing the girl's look of astonishment, she corrected herself: 'At least, I expect I do. It's on the second floor, isn't it?'

Upstairs, Vee was still wriggling into a 'New Look' dress – plum-coloured, with a very full skirt, a tight bodice and a strapless top.

'Oh, good, you're early,' said Vee, fumbling behind her back. 'You can help zip me up. I thought I'd better dress up a little, for the theatre.'

Sitting at her dressing-table, she began to put on her make-up. Jo watched her applying her lipstick, and for a moment she had a weird feeling, as if something very important were about to happen – as if she were going to hear some dramatic news – but the moment slipped away like quicksilver. Whatever it might have been, it had gone already.

Anyway, there was news to be told, and she must do the telling.

Catching Vee's eye in the mirror, she said quietly: 'By the way, I thought you'd like to know – I'm not pregnant.'

Vee was very glad to hear it. 'Thank goodness! I thought all along it was probably anaemia or something. You ought to get your doctor to put you on a course of iron pills.'

'I don't need any pills. Besides, I haven't got a doctor.'

'I thought everybody had a doctor nowadays, since this National Health thing started.' Vee frowned. 'All the same, you really should get your name on somebody's list, just in case anything happened.'

'I'm fine, nothing's going to happen.' Jo produced the carrier-bag she had brought with her from the Rope Walk. 'I told you I was bringing you a surprise. Don't you want to know what it is?'

'Yes, lovely.' Vee put the finishing touches to her face. 'You're very naughty, wasting your money on presents. It isn't my birthday yet.'

'I didn't buy this; it belongs to you already. I mean, it used to . . . A long while ago.'

Intrigued, Vee peeped inside the bag, and drew out the doll she had not seen since that night in May, nearly eight years ago.

Jo waited for her to say something. She did not know what she expected, but Vee did not react at all. For some time, she did not speak or smile; she just turned the doll over and over, studying it.

At last Jo prompted her: 'You know who it is, don't you? You recognise her?'

'Of course I do – it's Bella.'

'Your beloved Bella. The other day you said you wondered what had happened to her, and I felt awful because I'd had her all the time. I've been looking after her ever since – since the bombing . . . I kept her, because I was sure I'd find you again one day.'

'Thank you very much.' Still expressionless, Vee put the doll down and turned back to the mirror. Picking up a string of pearls, she went on: 'Do you think I should wear these, or would that be a bit ostentatious? I don't want your American friend to think I'm showing off.'

Jo felt deflated. 'I don't know . . . They look very nice.'

'Yes, they are rather gorgeous, aren't they? Alec gave them to me on my last birthday. I think I'll wear them. It's either the pearls or Aunt Elspeth's gold chain with the locket – I've got to have something round my neck, or I'll look half-naked. Oh, bother this catch, it's so fiddly. Be an angel and do it up for me.'

Standing behind her, Jo obeyed, then asked: 'Weren't you pleased to see Bella again? I thought it would be a nice surprise.'

'Yes, wonderful. I said thank you, didn't I?'

'I know, but – you used to love her so much.'

'I was a child then; I'm a different person now.'

'Yes . . . Perhaps it was silly of me to keep her all this time. I've got Charlie's teddy at home, too.'

'You hung on to Chockie as well?' Vee stared at her. 'You are extraordinary.'

'It would have seemed awful to chuck them away just because they were only toys. But I suppose you're right. Charlie must have outgrown teddy-bears by now. I mean, if he's—'

Then the door opened and Aunt Elspeth walked in without knocking.

'Van, dear, and Jo, too – how nice. I'm so glad I caught you. Van tells me you're taking her to a theatre this evening?'

'Well, it's a friend of ours actually,' Jo explained. 'He's taking us both out.'

'Oh, I must have misunderstood.' Aunt Elspeth threw a swift

glance at Vee, then continued smoothly: 'A friend? Anyone I know, dear?'

'I don't think so,' began Vee, and Jo chimed in: 'He's more a friend of mine, really. His name's Don Scott – he's an American stationed over here.'

'How very kind of Mr Scott. But then people always say the Americans are so generous, don't they? Which theatre are you going to?'

'I don't know yet, it'll be a surprise,' answered Jo. Her eye fell on Bella, lying on Vee's eiderdown with both arms outstretched to heaven and her moving eyelids closed.

Following Jo's gaze, Aunt Elspeth exclaimed: 'What a pretty doll. Where did that come from, Van?'

'It was a present – Jo brought it.' Vee stood up. 'I'm afraid we can't stop. We're meeting Mr Scott, and we mustn't be late.'

'Oh, no, that would never do. Don't let me keep you. But before you go . . .' Aunt Elspeth produced a little pair of opera-glasses, made of brass and ivory. 'I thought, if you're going to one of the larger theatres, these might come in handy. I'm sorry I only have one pair; you'll have to take turns.'

'Thank you,' said Vee, putting them into her handbag. 'I don't know what time I'll be back – you won't wait up, will you?'

'No, dear, of course not, though I'll probably be sitting up reading, anyway. If you see a light in my room, do put your head round the door. I shall want to hear all about it.'

'All right, if it's not too late.' Vee drew Jo towards the door. 'We must dash.'

When they left the house, she muttered: 'I know she thinks it's her duty to keep an eye on me, but she's getting worse. She always wants to know where I'm going, and who I'm with.'

'You are only sixteen,' Jo pointed out.

'I'm very nearly seventeen!' retorted Vee. 'Come on, let's try and pick up a cab. We mustn't keep our generous American waiting!'

The Woodman was already crowded with Saturday-night revellers when they arrived, but Don had managed to bag the same table as last time.

When he brought their drinks, he raised his glass in a toast, saying in a clipped, throaty accent unlike his own: 'Here's looking at you, kids.' Seeing their blank stares, he reverted to his own voice: 'You don't go for Bogart impersonations?'

Jo said: 'Humphrey Bogart? The film star?'

'You mean to say you never saw *Casablanca*? One of the all-time greats. I saw it during the war . . . '43 or '44, something like that.'

The girls shook their heads, and Vee explained: 'I was in the wilds of Scotland. The nearest cinema was fifteen miles away.'

'I was in Battersea, but Auntie Topsy didn't approve of throwing money away on the pictures,' said Jo.

'Too bad, you missed a darn good movie. Keep a look-out for it if it ever shows up again.' Don grinned. 'Anyways, here's looking at you – both of you – 'cos you're worth looking at, believe me.'

Jo noticed that he raised his glass in Vee's direction as he spoke.

Vee smiled, demurely. 'We do our best. It's not every day we get taken to the theatre, is it, Jo?'

'No, I wish I'd changed into something more dressy—'

Don interrupted. 'Don't give it another thought. Where we're going, I reckon they're not too particular.'

'Why, where are you taking us?'

'You'll find out!' He chuckled, and emptied his glass in a single gulp. 'Same again all round?'

'Oh, no, really . . .' Vee nursed her drink. 'If we're going all the way to the West End, shouldn't we be making a move? What time does the play begin?'

'There's no hurry, we're not going uptown.' Don pulled out three tickets. 'Front-row dress circle for the Grand Theatre, Clapham Junction. And it's not exactly a play, it's what you folks call a pantomime.'

'*Cinderella*! I saw the posters,' exclaimed Jo. 'We haven't been to a pantomime for years, have we Vee? Van, I mean . . .'

Vee tried to look equally delighted. 'I don't believe I have. What an original idea, Don. What made you think of it?'

'We don't have pantomime back home, but since it's an old British custom, you'll have to explain it to me.'

It took a good deal of explanation, and when they had finished, he was still confused.

'So the boy is played by a girl, right? And the dame is really a guy?'

He shook his head. '"Hellzapoppin" never dreamed up anything like this!'

When they reached the theatre on St John's Hill, the auditorium was only half full, but Jo explained: 'It's been on since Christmas – audiences have fallen off by now.'

Even so, Don was impressed. 'I'd say there must be near on a thousand people here. It's a lot bigger than I thought.'

'I expect it will be turned into a cinema eventually,' Vee remarked. 'That's happening everywhere. I suppose it's inevitable really.'

'Well, it's a theatre now, and I'm going to enjoy it!' said Jo. 'I haven't been to a pantomime for donkey's years, and then we had to come out before the end because my little sister was afraid of the Demon King, and Mum had to take us home.'

She nudged Vee, who looked straight ahead, tight-lipped, while Don said: 'They have demons in pantomime? You never told me that!'

'Oh, sorry. Yes, there's always a Fairy Queen and a Demon King – it's all part of the tradition.'

'Sssh!' said Vee. 'It's going to begin.'

The pit orchestra took their places. The footlights threw a golden glow along the red velvet curtains, the house-lights dimmed, and the curtain rose on the opening scene, the village green, where a happy band of peasantry – mostly girls – were singing and dancing around a wobbly maypole. Nobody in the audience could hear the words of the song, but that didn't seem to matter.

When the villagers dispersed, left and right, behind a flat oak tree and an equally flat cottage painted with hollyhocks, Prince Charming appeared, followed by Dandini.

Don whispered to Jo: '*Two* girls dressed up as guys? You never mentioned that, either.'

'Sorry, the one with the gold braid and glitter is the Prince, and the other one is his manservant, Dandini.'

'Yes, but why are they—'

'Ssh! You must listen, or you won't understand what's happening. This is where they put on each other's coats because they've decided to change places.'

By the interval, Don was completely lost. Vee and Jo were having a very good time – laughing at the Ugly Sisters, joining in the chorus song with Buttons, and gasping with admiration when the pumpkin blew up in a dazzling cloud of flash-powder and turned into a golden coach, drawn by four grubby Shetland ponies.

'Oh, I am enjoying this,' said Jo, as the house lights went up for the interval.

'You look a bit dazed,' Vee told Don. 'And I'm not surprised.'

'Do we have time to go to the bar?' he asked. 'Maybe I'll see things clearer with a drink inside me.' An awful thought struck him: 'Hey, do they sell liquor during a kids' show? It's not all soda-pop and Cokes?'

They reassured him and made their way to the circle bar, where Don took a long gulp of gin and tonic and began to fire questions at them: 'Why did they stop the whole darn show just so the guy in the buttons could teach us to sing that number about having an egg for our tea? And why did they go in the kitchen with the Brokers Men and start baking a cake and throwing all that flour at each other?'

Jo began to say: 'That's traditional too—' then broke off, staring across the table. Vee was holding a glass of orangeade; her lipstick had left a faint red smudge on the rim of the glass.

'What is it?' asked Vee. 'Have I got a smut on my nose?'

'No, it – it's just . . .' But she couldn't explain. 'It's nothing.'

In an instant, the vague anxiety that had haunted her for so long had become crystal clear; now she understood why she had felt an uneasy premonition as she watched Vee putting on her lipstick.

Lipstick on the glass . . . Why hadn't she thought of it before?

She was back in Laura Stanway's bedroom, on that dreadful morning, last autumn – pulling open the curtains, letting in the sunshine, turning towards the bed and seeing Laura lying there, stiff and still, her hands clasping the glass . . . And now she knew what was wrong.

Sunlight had glittered on the empty glass, bright and sparkling, without a mark on it; Laura's mouth was still painted in glossy red, but there was no trace of lipstick on the glass.

Which meant someone else had been in the bedroom that night. Someone had taken the glass from her, washed it out, then put it back in her hands—

'Jo!' Vee's voice cut in sharply. 'What's wrong?'

'Nothing's wrong, I'm fine. It's just a bit stuffy in here . . . Don't worry, I'll be all right in a minute.'

When the warning bell rang to mark the end of the interval, she hardly heard it; there were too many warning bells ringing in her head.

For Jo, the second half of the show passed almost unnoticed; the raucous comics, the speciality acts and the amazing xylophonist were like shadows – even the happy ending when the entire company walked down the palace steps seemed miles away, as she wrestled with the nightmare problem.

When they left the theatre, shivering in the cold night air, Don said: 'That's one night I'm never gonna forget! If I hadn't seen it with my own eyes, I'd never believe it.'

'But it was rather fun, wasn't it?' Vee asked him. 'I mean, you enjoyed it, didn't you?'

'Sure, like Cinderella, I had a ball! In fact, it was a kind of an extra celebration for me.'

'Why? What are you celebrating?'

'I'm counting the days till I'm a free man again,' he told her. 'In a month or two, I'll say goodbye to the darn uniform for ever!'

'Oh, I am sorry – no, I don't mean that – of course I'm glad for you, but I suppose you'll be going home to America?'

'Maybe not. I've got some leave due to me, and I'm figuring on spending it over here. In fact, if things work out, I could even settle right here in London – for keeps.'

'Why would you want to do that?'

'That's a good question. Could be I've fallen in love,' he said.

Vee gasped. 'In love?'

'Sure!' He grinned. 'I'm in love with England – didn't you know?'

He hailed a passing cab, and instructed the driver: 'Rope Walk, Battersea, then on to Cheyne Walk, OK?'

Sitting on one of the folding seats, he apologised. 'I wish I could ask you both out to supper and make a night of it, but there's this guy I've gotta meet. It's kind of a business deal – somebody back home asked me to do him a favour. But if this deal comes off, we're really gonna hit the high spots next time I see you, and that's a promise!'

When they reached the Rope Walk, Jo said goodnight. She was glad to be alone – she had a lot to think about.

The taxi drove on over the bridge, pulling up at the tall house in

Cheyne Walk. As Vee reached for the door-handle, Don pulled her towards him.

'Don't go, not for a moment,' he said. 'Wish me luck, baby – I'm gonna need it tonight.'

When he kissed her, his sudden outburst of passion took her by surprise. She felt the tension within him, hard and taut. Sometimes, at parties or charity balls, young men had kissed her and tried ineptly to explore her body, but this was very different; more thrilling – and more dangerous.

When he let her go, he touched her face gently, and whispered: 'Jeez, you're gorgeous. I can't get you out of my mind.'

With that, he jumped out of the cab and paid off the driver, then held the door for her while she stepped down on to the pavement. Guiltily, she glanced up at the house. There were lights burning at the first-floor windows.

As the taxi purred away into the night, she said breathlessly: 'Thank you again for a wonderful evening.'

He tried to take her in his arms, but she held back. 'Please, they haven't gone to bed – they might see us.'

'OK, why don't I come in and see them instead? Just to show I'm not some sort of weirdo! I'd like your folks to know I'm a pretty good guy – someone they can trust.'

'Oh, I'm not sure . . .'

'Listen, they're gonna have to get used to the idea some time, so why not now? The sooner they get to know me, the better.' He smiled. 'That is, if you want to go on seeing me?'

Her heart was beating very fast. 'You know I do, only – they live in a different world.'

'Oh, come on, the Old World gets along just fine with the New World these days; that's one good thing to come out of the war. Why don't I come in and say hello?'

So Vee let herself be persuaded, warning him that he mustn't stay long.

When she led him into the drawing-room, Alec and Aunt Elspeth were playing bezique at the green baize card-table. They looked up in astonishment at the sight of Don – and at Vee, with her lipstick smudged, and her hair slightly ruffled.

She performed the introductions, and Alec rose to the occasion.

'Good evening, Mr Scott. Good of you to look in.'

'How do you do?' Aunt Elspeth smiled politely. 'Won't you sit down? Alec, dear, I'm sure Mr Scott would like a drink.'

'That would be a great privilege, ma'am, believe me, but don't let me break up the game.'

'Oh, don't worry about that. It's high time we stopped; I'd no idea it was so late.'

They exchanged small-talk for ten minutes. Aunt Elspeth enquired how long Don had been in England, and wondered what he thought of it, and Alec asked how much longer he would be stationed over here?

'Not too long. I was telling Vanessa, my discharge papers should be through real soon.'

Vee chimed in: 'Don's thinking of staying on for a while. He might even decide to settle down in England.'

'That's right, I really like the English way of life. Maybe I'll stop in London for a while, and see if I can get me a regular job.'

'What kind of work do you do, Mr Scott?' asked Miss Coburn. 'When you're not in the Army, I mean?'

'I guess you'd call me a rolling stone, ma'am. I can turn my hand to most anything in buying and selling – I'm just a natural-born tradesman.'

Seeing the smile freeze on her aunt's lips, Vee hastened to explain: 'He means a businessman – in fact, he's working on some deals already, aren't you, Don?'

Putting down his glass, Don exclaimed: 'You know what? I just had me a great idea. When I get out of uniform, I'll be looking for some place to live. Now maybe I'm stepping way out of line, but would there be any chance of renting a room from you folks?' He looked round the room appreciatively, and directed a dazzling smile at Aunt Elspeth. 'You've got a really lovely place here, ma'am. The minute I walked in, I felt right at home. I wouldn't stop too long, you understand, just a short while, till I find an apartment of my own. Whaddaya say?'

There was a deathly silence, then Aunt Elspeth stood up and said kindly: 'What a charming idea, but I'm afraid it's long past my bedtime. Van dear, I'm sure you're tired as well. Let's say goodnight and leave the gentlemen to talk things over.'

Shaking hands with Don once more, she added: 'So nice of you to drop in, Mr Scott. Come along, Van.'

When the door closed, Alec picked up the decanter, saying pleasantly: 'Can I top you up, old man?'

'I'm sorry? Oh, yeah – maybe you could freshen my drink a little.'

They drank in silence, and then Alec began, carefully: 'As the aunt said, perhaps we should talk about this idea of yours.'

'Sure, how does it grab you?'

'May I speak frankly? I'm afraid it's really out of the question.'

'Hey, now wait a minute, I'm not expecting you to let me live here for free, I can afford to pay room-rent.'

'It's not a question of money. We don't let rooms – we never have, and I can't imagine that we ever will.'

'But the old lady said we should talk it over.'

'I think I know what Miss Coburn wished me to say to you. She didn't want to embarrass you in front of my sister.'

'Why not? Maybe Vanessa might have a few things to say.'

'Possibly, but she can be easily swayed. That's one of the reasons why we wouldn't be keen for you to stay here as a guest. She's not much more than a schoolgirl, you know.'

'Don't give me that – she's a young woman.'

'Yes, very young for her age in some ways. You probably know she had a traumatic childhood. Her aunt has tried to shelter her ever since. You may think she's been too sheltered, but that's why I must ask you to look for lodgings elsewhere.'

Don stood up. 'You're telling me to get the hell out – is that it?'

Alec rose too, a head taller and a good deal broader than Don.

'Since you mention it, yes, I think that might be the best solution. Don't encourage Van to build a casual friendship into something else. I wouldn't want her to get hurt.'

Don slammed his glass down on to the green baize table, and a dozen playing-cards fluttered to the carpet. Without another word, he turned and walked out of the room, down the stairs, and out of the house.

Jo went into Russell's studio on Sunday morning, intending to tell him at once that she was no longer pregnant, but her thoughts were so confused and unhappy, she did not know how to begin.

To make it more difficult, he greeted her enthusiastically: 'Thanks for coming round on your day off – I'm very grateful. Let's not waste any time. Get your clothes off, and we'll make a start.'

Following his orders automatically, she went behind the screen. She would have to tell him presently; soon, very soon – when she could think more clearly – but not yet.

While she took up her pose, Russell went on: 'Did you have a good night out? Where did you go?'

The previous evening seemed a million miles away. She found it hard to remember what had happened: 'Oh, yes, it was very nice. We went to the pantomime at the Grand.'

Russell laughed: 'Dear God, whose bright idea was that?'

'Don – Don Scott.'

His smiled hardened. 'And who is Don Scott?'

'He's an American GI stationed over here. He'd never seen a pantomime before.'

'I had the impression you were going with several friends?'

'Just three of us: Don and me, and Vanessa. She's a girl I know,' Jo finished lamely.

'And what did you do after the theatre? Stayed up half the night, I suppose? I thought you looked rather tired.'

'We didn't go anywhere afterwards. We just went home.'

'You and the American?'

'Of course not!' Jo felt herself beginning to blush. 'It was nothing like that. I went back to the Rope Walk quite early, but I couldn't get to sleep for a long time.'

'Perhaps you were over-excited.' Russell frowned with concentration, as he went on tapping the mallet on the chisel, punctuating his comments by pecking away small scrolls of limewood. 'I'd have thought . . . in your condition . . . you ought to take things easy . . . for the sake of the baby—' He broke off sharply. 'Don't lift your head! Now you've lost the pose.'

'I've got something to tell you.' She blurted it out: 'There isn't any baby. I only found out yesterday afternoon. I wanted to tell you, but I didn't know how. I'm sorry.'

Slowly, he laid aside the chisel, and the intense concentration drained from his face. He stood for some time, staring at her, then muttered: 'I'm sorry too. It's bad news.'

'I knew you'd be upset, because of the statue, your idea.'

'Never mind the idea.' He mopped his face with a piece of rag from the work-bench, and she saw that he had begun to sweat. 'You're quite well, in yourself, I mean? There's nothing wrong?'

'Oh, no, I'm perfectly all right.'

'That's good.' He wiped his hands. 'It's only a setback, after all. There's plenty of time for you to have another baby.'

Deep within her, Jo felt an icy stab of fear.

'What do you mean?' she asked.

'We can still get married – we can still begin a family. Next time you must take good care of yourself, then I can start on this again . . .' He stroked the newly cut wood with a loving touch. 'We can pick up where we left off.'

She looked at him helplessly, and he asked: 'What's the matter? Don't you understand? I'm asking you to marry me.'

She saw his green eyes darkening – and she saw the empty glass in Laura's hands. There had been no one else in the flat that night; no one else could have gone into Laura's room; no one else could have washed out the glass and put it back. No one but Russell.

The cold fear grew within her, freezing and paralysing her. With a great effort she managed to force out a few words: 'No, I can't – I can't marry you. I'm sorry.'

'You can't marry me?' There was a lengthy pause, then: 'You mean you won't?'

Now his eyes were black; she saw he was in the grip of anger. His hands shook as he picked up the chisel again.

'You don't love me, is that what you're trying to say? Oh, yes, I'm beginning to understand. When you found out you weren't going to have a child, you couldn't wait, could you? You'd sooner run off to some Yankee soldier, someone young and good-looking—'

'No, Russell, it's nothing to do with—'

But he would not listen. In the throes of his passion, he could not even hear what she said, but moved slowly towards her, gripping the long chisel. Jo wanted to run away, but there was no escape – she was naked and defenceless. As it was Sunday, there was nobody else in the house. If she screamed, there would be no one to hear.

When the razor-sharp blade came up to her throat, she tried to pray, but her brain seemed to be frozen, and she could not remember the words.

Chapter Thirteen

JO HAD STOPPED THINKING. There was nothing in her head except the certainty that she was about to die. This was the end; time had run out, and in a moment it would all be over.

But if time had stopped, Russell had stopped too. He stood with the chisel poised, and his face suddenly contorted. He let go of the chisel, which clattered on to the bare boards, and swore violently, then rubbed his right hand in his left, massaging it.

'I can't – I can't—' He turned away, instinctively burying his hand in his armpit.

'Have you cut yourself?' she asked – stupidly, because she knew his hand had been nowhere near the end of the chisel.

'No, of course not . . .'

He threw himself into the chair on the dais and sat there, rocking to and fro, obviously in great pain.

Swiftly, she picked up the chisel and put it on the work-bench, then pulled on the old dressing-gown, knotting it around her. Now she felt less vulnerable. In a moment their positions had been reversed: she was in charge of the situation, and he was helpless.

'What's the matter?' she asked. 'Is it cramp?'

'A kind of cramp, only ten times worse,' he muttered, rocking and grimacing. 'I've had these attacks before, but never as bad as this.'

'Should I call a doctor?'

'No, don't bother. I've seen Hawthorne already. He says it's bloody arthritis, and there's nothing he can do about it. When these spasms come, I just have to put up with them.'

'I didn't know.' She sat on the edge of the dais, close to him. 'You never said anything.'

'What's the point? Most of the time I can cope with it. But this was the worst yet.'

'Can I get you something? Aspirin, a hot drink?'

'It's easing off now.' He puffed out his cheeks. 'Oof! It comes from years of handling wet clay. I suppose the joints and muscles are staging some sort of protest. I've got to accept the fact that it will gradually get worse, until I can't use my hands at all.'

'But there must be something the doctors can do?'

'Hawthorne says there's no cure, as yet. If I'd stuck to wood-carving all my life, I might have got away with that.'

'I'm sorry,' she said, uselessly. 'So very sorry.'

He put out his good hand, touching her hair. 'I'm sorry I lost my temper. I shouldn't have gone for you like that. Did I scare you?'

'I thought for a minute . . .' She shook her head. 'It doesn't matter.'

'You thought what?' He looked at her; his face was still shadowed with pain. 'You thought I was going to attack you?'

She lowered her head, afraid that he might read her mind. 'I – I didn't know.'

'You can't really believe I'd do a thing like that?'

'You were angry, and I was frightened – I couldn't think straight.'

'My dearest girl.' His hand rested on her shoulder. 'I've not been well lately – you know I get these bad moods – but I'd never do anything to hurt you. It was only because I thought you wanted to leave me.' Putting his hand beneath her chin, he lifted her face to him and asked softly: 'Are you going to leave me?'

His eyes were grey-green now, tired and hurt, but there was no black anger in them.

'No, I won't leave you,' she said. 'I won't marry you, but I'll look after you.'

His lips puckered into that dubious expression she knew so well, and he added suspiciously: 'You're not saying that because you feel sorry for me? I don't want your damned pity.'

'It's not pity,' she said. 'I want to help you – that's what I'm here for.'

'I don't understand.'

'Helping is the only thing I'm any good at. If I can't help somebody, what's the use of me?'

★

The days went by, and the pattern of Jo's life continued. Sometimes, while she was cooking Russell's lunch, or ironing his shirts, she remembered how terrified she had been, when she thought she was on the edge of eternity. Now it seemed absurd. Yet from time to time she could not help thinking of Laura's death, and the empty glass . . .

It was the last week of February, and she remembered that on Friday it would be Vee's birthday. On Thursday, when she went shopping in the High Street, she chose a birthday card, then called in at the greengrocer's and bought a pot-plant – a coral-pink azalea, just coming into flower. The card had a view of distant figures under leafy trees, strolling among flower-beds, which she hoped might remind Vee of Battersea Park.

On her way back to Galleon House, she was astonished to find Don Scott walking in the same direction.

'Hello!' she exclaimed. 'What are you doing here?'

He grinned his usual grin. 'Coming to see you – what else?'

'But today's Thursday—'

'There was a wagon driving down to pick up supplies, so I hitched a ride. I've only got a few hours – the wagon's leaving at half after six – but when I hit town I said to myself: "OK, what do I do now?" and the answer came back: "Go see Jo!" . . . So here I am.'

'That's very nice, but I have to work; I must take the shopping in and get lunch ready for Mr Wade. I'll be busy all day.'

'I shoulda figured that. Ah, what the hell? Lemme help carry the groceries.'

He took the shopping-bag. Glancing at the pot-plant, he commented: 'That's real pretty – is it going to decorate the great man's table?'

'No, this is for Vee, as a matter of fact. It's her birthday tomorrow. I didn't know what to give her, so I just bought a card – and this azalea.'

'Her birthday? No kidding! How old will that make her?'

'Seventeen.' When they reached Galleon House, Jo opened the garden gate and said: 'I'm sorry to be unsociable, but I must go in now.'

'What time do you finish work?'

'Not till five, and then I'm going over to Cheyne Walk, to leave the card and the flowers for tomorrow.'

'Hey, listen, why don't I go pick up some little gift myself? When you're free we can go around there together, how about that?'

'But you've got to leave London at half-past six. You don't want to hang round all the afternoon, just for the sake of—'

'Who says I don't? I've got nothing better to do, and it's always good spending time with you, babe. I'll be here at five, OK?'

'Well, if you're sure . . .' She walked up the little garden path, and he followed her. 'I'll see you then.'

As she unlocked the door, he said thoughtfully: 'Remember what I said, the day I met you? I told you I'd like to say hello to Mr Wade, 'cos I'd never met a real live artist. D'you think he'd let me drop by, for a coupla minutes? I'd sure like to get his autograph.'

'Oh, I don't know, he might be busy . . .'

'You can ask, can't you? He can only tell me to go to hell!'

'I suppose so,' she said reluctantly, and Don walked into the hall, looking around him.

'Wow . . .' His jaw sagged. 'How old is this place?'

'I don't know exactly. Eighteenth century, something like that.'

He shook his head in amazement. 'You know what? It's the oldest goddam house I ever was in. Wait till I tell the folks!'

'Well, you'd better stay here for a minute. I'll go and have a word with Mr Wade.'

But when Jo was halfway up the stairs, she met Russell on his way down. He greeted her cheerfully. 'I thought I'd go and tidy up some odds and ends in the studio. I might even take another look at the work I started on the—' Then he stopped, frowning past her at Don, below them in the hall. 'Who's this?'

'He's a friend of mine – he helped me carry the shopping,' she explained awkwardly, 'and he'd very much like to meet you.'

'How very civil of him.' Russell brushed past her on his way down the stairs. 'I see you're in the American armed forces, Mr – er—?'

'Scott.' Don stepped forward with his hand out. 'The name's Don Scott.'

'Yes, I thought it might be. Miss Wells has mentioned you once or twice. But I can't imagine why you should wish to meet me, Mr Scott?'

'I just wanted to say hello. I never met a famous artist before.'

'And now you have.' Russell did not appear to see Don's outstretched hand. 'I'm afraid our meeting must be very brief; I have some work to do. You'll excuse me, I'm sure.'

Dismissing the unwelcome interruption, he began to move on, but Don detained him, saying: 'I won't keep you more than a minute, sir, but I'd be honoured if you'd give me your autograph. It'll be something to show the folks back home.'

Russell looked at him with such disdain, Don's usual self-possession deserted him, and he retreated slightly, adding: 'That's if you've no objection—?'

'Forgive me, Mr Scott. I am not a film star, or a popular celebrity. I do not sign autographs.'

With that, he walked into the studio and slammed the door.

Jo hurried downstairs, saying: 'I did warn you. He can be difficult with people he doesn't know, especially when he's working.'

'Yeah. He didn't exactly take a shine to me, did he? Oh, well, some other time, maybe.'

'I'm sorry.' Jo picked up the shopping basket and the plant. 'Now I really must go.'

'You won't forget I'm coming back at five?' Don asked. 'Don't worry, I won't come in! I'll be waiting on the sidewalk. See ya, babe.' And he walked out, whistling.

Jo smiled. He was like one of those kelly dolls: you could push him down, but he bobbed up again right away.

When Russell returned to the flat at midday, Jo asked if he had managed to get any work done, and he replied: 'Yes, I had some thoughts about that carving. It's not half bad . . . I think I could still make something out of it. Perhaps we could have another modelling session, one of these days?'

'Of course, if that's what you want.'

As he sat down to lunch, he continued casually: 'I hope I wasn't too short with your American friend. But I'm always wary of these celebrity-hounds. Why on earth should he want my autograph? I don't suppose he's ever seen any of my work, has he?'

'Probably not,' admitted Jo.

'Well, there you are, the whole thing's nonsense! Still, I didn't mean to hurt his feelings, particularly as he's a friend of yours.'

'Oh, I expect he'll get over it,' said Jo. 'I explained that you were busy; I'm sure he understood.'

When Jo had finished her day's work, she found Don outside, waiting for her, and they set out for Cheyne Walk together.

This time, he carried the azalea, and Jo asked: 'Did you manage to find a present for Vee – Vanessa, I mean?'

'Sure did. I went into the Beauty Department at Selfridges and picked up some perfume.' He said 'per-*fume*' instead of '*per*-fume', which made it sound very glamorous. 'I just hope she likes it.'

'I'm sure she will. What kind did you get?'

'Darned if I can remember, and if I did, I couldn't pronounce it. Some French name, imported from Paris.'

'It must have been terribly expensive.'

'Hell, birthdays only come once a year!' Then he added in a different tone: 'Sometimes you call her Vee, and sometimes Vanessa – how come?'

'Oh, that. I've always called her Vee; it's sort of a nickname. But I try to call her Vanessa when she's with her family.'

As they reached the Coburns' house, a sports-car drew up with a squeal of brakes and Alec jumped out.

'Hello there!' Greeting Jo, he glanced coolly at Don.

'Oh, Don, this is Vanessa's brother Alec,' she explained. 'Don's a friend of mine – from America.'

'We've already met. Mr Scott was kind enough to bring Van home after your theatre party,' said Alec. Eyeing the potted plant, he continued: 'But I'm afraid you've had a wasted journey. She's gone to some tea-party with Aunt Elspeth – I don't know what time they'll be back.'

'That's all right. I only came round to leave this – for tomorrow.'

Alec looked puzzled. 'Tomorrow?'

'I've got something for her myself,' said Don, pulling out a package wrapped in shiny gold paper and tied with a ribbon. 'The girl in the shop said they don't gift-wrap purchases over here, but I talked her into gussying it up some. Not bad, huh?'

'It looks very grand,' said Jo. 'Oh, I brought her a card as well – I nearly forgot.' She produced it from her bag. 'I've written "Not To Be Opened Till Tomorrow" on the envelope.'

Alec asked: 'Am I being very stupid? Is tomorrow a special occasion?'

They both stared at him, and Don asked: 'Wouldn't you call a birthday a special occasion?'

Then Jo realised what a fool she had been. It hadn't occurred to her that Vee's birthday would hardly be the same day as Vanessa's.

Alec shook his head. 'I think we're talking at cross-purposes. Van's birthday is the seventh of May.'

'Oh – yes, of course . . .' Jo stammered. 'I must have mixed her up with someone else. How silly.'

'No problem!' Don slipped the gift-wrapped package into his pocket again: 'We'll have to hang on to the presents till then, I guess.'

'I'll keep the card,' said Jo. 'But she might as well have the azalea now; it may not be flowering by May! Would you explain that I got mixed up about the date? Tell her it was all my fault.'

'Very well, I'll tell her.' Nursing the potted plant, Alec watched them walk away, and frowned.

As they turned the corner, Jo apologised to Don. 'Sorry – how could I be such an idiot? Thanks to me, you've had a wasted afternoon.'

'I wouldn't say that.' Don shrugged it off. 'Now we know when her birthday is, we've got plenty of time to plan something real good. Tell her to keep that weekend free – we're gonna give her a real night out!'

'And a pair of lamb chops.' The butcher slapped two skinny chops on to the scales, weighed them, and wrapped them. 'Will there be anything else, miss?'

'I wish there were,' said Jo. 'But I've only got two ration books.'

It was Saturday morning, and the weekend shopping was always a problem. By now the meat ration had been reduced to eight pennyworth of meat, per person, per week; it did not stretch far.

The butcher glanced conspiratorially around; there was no one about except for his wife behind the cash desk, and a young woman outside, gazing at the meagre display in the window.

Lowering his voice, he said: 'Seeing you're a reg'lar customer, I've got some nice sausages under the counter, miss. Come from a farm down Essex way – friends of the wife's brother. Best quality pork, and no questions asked.'

The offer was too good to resist. Jo left the shop a few moments later with a guilty conscience and a light heart, and the young woman outside stopped her, saying: 'I saw that! It would serve you right if I called a policeman.'

'Vee!' Jo laughed. 'You scared me. What are you doing here?'

'I knew you went shopping in the High Street. I had to talk to you.'

As they fell into step, Jo asked: 'Is something wrong?'

'Not exactly, though it could have been! Thanks for the azalea, by the way. I suppose I should have written to thank you, but when Alec told me what happened, I could have strangled you! How could you be so thoughtless?'

'As soon as I said it, I realised what I'd done – but I managed to talk my way out of it. I said I'd mixed you up with someone else.'

'Luckily he believed you – he's a trusting soul. And it was a very nice present, so I've almost forgiven you. But do stop and think, another time.'

'I'll try.' Jo glanced at her sister. 'Is that it? Did you come all this way, just to tick me off?'

'Well, no . . . I suppose I could have phoned, but I don't like ringing Galleon House, in case Russell Wade answers. You don't have a phone at your digs, do you?'

'There is one, but Sarah doesn't let people use it, unless it's an emergency. What's wrong?'

'I don't know – that's the trouble. Apparently there was a nasty scene when Don took me home after the pantomime. Did he tell you about it?'

'No. When we went round, Alec mentioned something about meeting Don that night, but I never really understood what happened.'

Vee launched into the story of the night's events; leaving out what happened in the taxi, she told Jo how Don suggested moving in to Cheyne Walk.

'Aunt Elspeth whisked me out of the room very quickly, and next morning Alec told us that they'd both agreed it wouldn't really be a good idea . . . Though Don seemed terribly keen on it at the time.'

'Hadn't he talked it over with you first?'

'Not a word. He'd been quite – friendly – on the way home, but he never said anything about moving in.'

'Men can take you by surprise sometimes,' said Jo, with feeling. 'So, how do you feel about him now?'

'I don't know what I feel. I haven't heard from him since. In fact I'm beginning to wonder if I'll ever hear from him again. So if you happen to run into him, perhaps you could ask him to ring me? Would you mind?'

When Jo got back to the Rope Walk, she found a postcard waiting for her – a sepia photo of the rose-garden in Battersea Park. On the back was a message in a neat, feminine hand:

12 Blenheim Terrace, S.W.8

Dear Jo, it was very nice to meet you. We would be very pleased if you could come to tea this weekend. We're always free on Sundays because of Malcolm's day off. Would tomorrow afternoon at three be too short notice? If you can't manage it, how about next weekend?
    Yours, Pat Jones. P.S. Malcolm sends his regards.

The invitation was so friendly, Jo decided to accept it. Malcolm was more relaxed than he used to be, Pat was a nice, sociable girl, and they both seemed so cheerful. Jo felt she was surrounded by people with problems; an afternoon in the company of two contented, uncomplicated people would make a nice change.

On Sunday morning she called in at the tobacconist's in the High Street and bought a small box of chocolates, and at three o'clock she presented herself at number 12 Blenheim Terrace.

It was in the middle of a short terrace of two-storey houses, identical to thousands of others built at the turn of the century: red-brick, with a shallow bay window on the ground floor and a little porch above the front door. Jo could tell at a glance that it would have a parlour at the front and a kitchen behind that; upstairs there would be two bedrooms, front and back, and a tiny boxroom. As Jo rang the bell she guessed that the wallpapers would be beige or dark brown, with patterned lino on the hall floor and a turkey-red stair-carpet.

Pat opened the door almost immediately, saying: 'Oh, good, you found us all right. Come in, Jo, make yourself at home.'

The layout of the house was just what Jo had expected, but the walls had been painted leaf-green, with a frieze of daisies along the top. The lino was covered by a navy-blue slip rug, and the jute matting on the stairs was a bold, bright orange.

'Mind the pram!' Pat warned her. 'I'm always laddering my stockings, trying to squeeze past. The pushchair lives in the kitchen, but we had to hang on to the pram, of course.'

'When's the new baby due?' Jo asked.

'About the end of May, give or take a week. I'll be glad when it's over: Sandra's getting to be such a big girl now, she's no lightweight if I have to carry her around as well!'

She picked up some scattered toys, including a teddy-bear, battered and obviously much-loved; with a pang, Jo remembered Chockie. Seeing her expression, Pat apologised: 'I know, don't say it, the place looks a mess – that's what happens when you start a family.'

'I was just thinking how smart it is,' said Jo. 'So lovely and bright.'

Pat called out: 'Hear that, Malc? Your friend approves of my efforts – so there!' She led the way along the narrow hall, adding: 'He's in the kitchen, helping Sandra finish her dinner.'

They found Malcolm with his daughter on his lap, trying to coax her to accept a spoonful of greens.

'Hello, Jo, nice to see you,' he said. 'Sorry about this – her ladyship's eaten her corned beef hash, but she's not so keen on cabbage.'

'Don't want it!' Sandra pushed the plate away. Malcolm caught it in the nick of time.

'I think that means she's had enough. Where's the face-flannel?' said Pat. 'I'll just give her a quick once-over, then we'll be ready.'

Sandra protested vigorously as her mother wiped traces of gravy off her chubby cheeks, and Malcolm asked: 'How about the washing-up?'

'Oh, just put everything into the sink or we'll miss the best of the day.' Pat explained to Jo: 'We thought we should make the most of the weather. Do you feel like a stroll in the park, before tea?'

'Love to.' Jo handed over the chocolates. 'By the way, this is just a little something—'

'Oh, you shouldn't go wasting your ration on us.'

'I'm trying to cut down on sweets. If I spoil myself, I put on weight.'

'What rubbish, you're slim as a rake – but it's very kind of you—' began Pat.

Sandra stretched out eager, starfish hands, saying: 'Chockie for Sandra!'

'Chockie, yes . . .' Jo managed a smile. 'You've got to share them with Mum and Dad, mind.'

Ignoring their daughter's protests, Pat and Malcolm squeezed her into a one-piece romper-suit with a hood, then they strapped her into her pushchair and set out. As he wheeled her down the tiny front path, Malcolm sniffed the air, saying: 'There's a breeze getting up.'

'If the wind keeps the clouds off, it'll give the sun a chance,' Pat told him.

'I was just thinking, this might be a good day to bring the kite,' he said. 'Hang on a tick, would you? I'll just pop in and fetch it.'

Pat lowered her voice as he disappeared inside the house: 'We bought Sandra a kite at Christmas, but the only time we took it to the park, there wasn't enough wind to get it off the ground. Perhaps we'll have better luck this time.'

Malcolm returned with a red, yellow and blue kite, saying to Pat: 'You carry this, I'll take the chair. We don't want you straining yourself in your condition, do we?'

As they set off along Nine Elms Road, Jo felt a pang of envy: this was how life should be. Last time she met the Jones family she had been almost sure that she was pregnant; now she knew she was not, she had a sense of loss.

They entered the park by the Queenstown Road gates, then skirted the lake, where Sunday anglers sat on folding stools, gazing fixedly at the dark grey-green waters as if they were hypnotised. A few yards away, a small boy wielding a fishing-net sat at the lake's edge with a jam-jar beside him, watching and waiting.

The sky had cleared, and winter sunshine was gilding the surface of the water. Early yellow crocuses blazed in the grass, and Jo said: 'It looks as if spring is on the way at last. Have you noticed how much nicer people are when the sun shines? This winter seems to have gone on so long – everyone's been miserable.'

'You never struck me as the miserable type,' remarked Malcolm. 'Just the opposite, I'd have said.'

'Well, we all have our ups and downs, don't we? Last time I saw you, I was a bit down. My uncle had just died, and I was taking some flowers round to my auntie, in Agar Road. She's practically the only relative I've got left now.'

Seeing a park bench, Pat suggested: 'Shall we sit down, Jo? We can talk, while Malc and Sandra fly the kite.'

So Malcolm wheeled the pushchair on to the grass, and tried to launch the kite. It took a long while. He ran into the wind as fast as he could, with the kite trailing after him, but every time he stopped it bobbed unsteadily upwards for a moment, then made a crash-landing.

Pat smiled as she watched him. 'He'll never give up till he gets it airborne. He's like that. He'll keep on working at it.'

'You must be two of a kind – doing all that painting and decorating,' said Jo. 'I'd never have the patience.'

'Well, when he's out at work I like to have something to keep me busy. How about you? What do you do – for a living, I mean?'

So Jo told her story briefly, without going into details, and when she had finished Pat said shyly: 'Can I ask you something? That girl you were talking about last time – Nora Topping. Malc had never mentioned her – I suppose she was his girl-friend, in the old days?'

Cautiously, Jo replied: 'I wouldn't say that. They happened to be together the first time I met them – they helped me get the job at Brydens. We went to the pictures once or twice, the three of us, but I don't think it was anything serious.'

Pat sighed. 'I think there was more to it than that. From something he said once, I got the impression he was very smitten with some girl in those days. Of course it was long before he met me, so I've got no reason to be jealous, but when you mentioned her name, and he didn't seem to want to talk about her, I guessed she must have been the one. What was she like?'

'I can't remember her very well after all this time. To be honest, I never liked her much; I don't think Malcolm did either . . . Anyway, you're worth ten of Nora Topping, and I'm sure he thinks so too.'

Pat relaxed. 'That's nice to know. I'm only being silly – I couldn't wish for a better husband. I was just curious – that's all.'

Jo interrupted her: 'Look – he's done it. The kite's flying at last!'

Out on the grass, Malcolm was enjoying his moment of triumph as the kite soared above him. Over his shoulder, he called to his daughter: 'Look, Sandra! Look at the pretty kite! Sandra . . .?'

Unfortunately the little girl, who had lost interest long ago, was fast asleep.

Irritated, Malcolm ran back to wake her, which proved to be a mistake. Pat and Jo tried to warn him, but it was too late. The kite swooped, side-slipped, and became entangled in the upper branches of a tree.

'Damn and blast!' he groaned. 'I'll never get it down now.'

The girls hurried across to join him, and Pat reminded him mildly: 'Malc, try and watch your language in front of Sandra.'

'Never mind Sandra – she's asleep!' he grumbled. 'How am I going to get the blasted thing down? I'll need a ladder to get up there.'

''Scuse me,' said a high, confident voice. 'I think I can reach it.'

It was the small boy with the fishing-net and the jam-jar – which now contained a couple of tiddlers. Satisfied with the day's catch, he was on his way home.

'Think so?' said Malcolm doubtfully. 'It's pretty high up.'

'I'm good at climbing,' said the boy. 'If you give me a leg-up on to the bottom branch, I can manage the rest.'

He was as good as his word; once in the tree, he climbed like a monkey. Reaching the kite, he disentangled the string and lowered it carefully to Malcolm at the foot of the tree. Then he scrambled down and jumped to the ground, saying: 'There you are – I told you it would be OK.'

'Thanks very much, very good of you.' Malcolm fumbled in his pocket and produced a sixpence. 'Here, something for your trouble.'

'Ta, but it wasn't any trouble,' said the boy, picking up his jam-jar and fishing-net. 'Be seeing you!'

And he set off, whistling. He could not have been more than ten or eleven, but he was so self-possessed, he seemed older than his years.

When Malcolm returned to the others, Pat asked: 'Who was that?'

'I dunno – just a boy. But he was a big help, climbing up like that. I couldn't have done it. I wonder where he comes from.'

'Must be local,' said Pat. 'Good-looking boy, too – didn't you think so, Jo?'

'Was he?' Jo shook her head. 'I didn't get a proper look at him.'

Malcolm was examining the kite. 'Bit of luck it didn't get torn. I could fly it again, if you like, 'cos Sandra missed it the first time.'

'I think we'd better leave it for another day,' Pat suggested. 'I don't know about you, but I fancy a cup of tea.'

They left by the Queenstown Road gates again; at the same moment, the boy was going out at the other end of the park, opposite Battersea Hospital, then he made for Latchmere Road, carefully holding his jam-jar so as not to disturb the tiddlers.

By the time he reached Lavender Hill it was almost dark. There were no lights on the stairwell as he climbed the stone steps to the second floor and entered the flat.

'What time do you call this?' asked his father, looking over the top of the *News of the World*.

His mother bustled out of the kitchen. 'I told you to be back by four. We were getting quite worried.'

'Sorry, I had to stop and help somebody,' the boy explained. 'This bloke was flying a kite, see, and it got caught in a tree, so I nipped up and got it down for him – that's what made me late.' He produced his sixpence. 'Look what he gave me.'

His mother was horrified. 'How many more times do you have to be told? You're not to take money from strangers – money or sweets, understand?'

His father pounced on the coin. 'And you're not spending it. This goes straight in your money-box, saving up for that bicycle – all right?'

'All right . . .' The boy was more interested in the contents of the jam-jar. 'Look what I caught – two of 'em this time.'

'Nasty-looking things!' His mother clucked disapprovingly. 'And who's going to look after them when we go away? That's what I'd like to know.'

The boy brightened up. 'When are we going? Will it be this week?'

'Easy now, son, I haven't heard yet,' said Dad. 'But I'm expecting a letter tomorrow.'

'I've heard that one before,' said Mum darkly. 'Now get that jam-jar out of my way and help me lay the table. It's time for tea.'

Jo had enjoyed her visit to Blenheim Terrace. When she left, Pat said: 'You must come again, mustn't she, Malc?'

She promised that she would, but on the long walk home, she began to have second thoughts – the afternoon had unsettled her somehow.

By the time she reached the Rope Walk she was feeling tired; turning her key in the lock, she entered the house. Sarah came out of the kitchen, saying: 'Oh, there you are, dear. I wasn't sure how long you'd be. You've got a visitor.'

Jo thought of Russell, and her heart sank; had he gone on a

lunchtime pub-crawl, and finished up here? Warily, she asked: 'Who is it?'

A man appeared, framed in the kitchen doorway, silhouetted against the light, but she recognised him instantly.

'Hello, Jo,' said Pete Hobden.

'Hello,' she repeated blankly. 'What do you want?'

'I want to talk to you – d'you mind?'

She had forgotten the soft warmth of that north-country accent, and it lit a flame within her, but she replied evenly: 'Depends what you want to talk about.'

'Oh, this and that, odds and bobs. I've been here nigh on an hour; Mrs Venus was good enough to brew a pot of tea while I waited.'

'I was glad of your company,' said Sarah. 'It's not often I get visitors – well, not good-looking young men, and not after dark!'

Pete grinned at Jo. 'So can you spare me a few minutes? Private, like?'

'You'd better come upstairs.'

When they reached Jo's room, Pete asked: 'All right if I tek me coat off? Or I'll not feel the benefit when I go out, as my old Gran used to say. D'you mind if I sit on the end of the bed? That chair looks a bit spindly to me. So how're you keeping, how's life?'

She told him that her life wasn't too bad, and soon it was going to be better. 'Very soon now – tomorrow, perhaps.'

'Why, what's happening tomorrow?'

'I don't know, but something good's bound to happen soon. I've made that my motto: "Happy tomorrow" – that's what I'm going to be!'

He didn't even smile. She asked how he was getting on at the *Evening News*, but he didn't seemed inclined to talk about that. After a pause, she asked after his girl-friend in Sheffield, and Pete said gruffly that she was pretty fair, considering.

Then he asked Jo: 'How about your friend? How's he doing?'

'You mean Mr Wade? He's a lot better than he was. He started on another sculpture, a few weeks ago, wood-carving this time.'

'No, not him. I meant your other friend – the American. Feller by the name of Scott, I believe? Donald Scott?'

Jo stared at him. 'How do you know about Don?'

'I'm a Journalist, ent I? It's my business to know things. I know he nips down to London most weekends. Sometimes he teks you out on the razzle, you and your friend – am I right?'

Jo swallowed hard, then said: 'You've been following me.'

'Not you – him. He's the one I were after. It came as a big surprise when he turned out to be a pal of yours! Funny how you 'n' me keep running across one another, eh?'

'Why were you following Don?'

'I shouldn't rightly be telling you this, but mebbe it's best you should know. They've put me on to the Crime Desk since last I saw you, and we're trying to chase up this black-market racket. There's millions of pounds changing hands all the time, and some of these American chappies are into it. Only we're still trying to get some real proof – facts, that's what I need.'

'Are you saying Don's mixed up in it? That's ridiculous.'

But a chill of doubt made her shiver.

'What's ridiculous about it? They've got loads of stuff at those Army PX stores, or whatever they call 'em – cigarettes, nylons, petrol, sides of beef, pounds of butter – they're rolling in it! All they need are the right contacts in the black-market chain, and Bob's your flippin' uncle!'

Jo remembered the business deal Don had talked about, and turned on Pete furiously. 'How dare you accuse my friends of being criminals!' She grew more and more angry. 'You've been spying on us, haven't you? And you're so damn proud of yourself. You make me sick!'

'I'm only tipping you off, for your own good,' Pete tried to explain. 'I wouldn't want you getting into trouble along with him.'

'Thanks a lot, but you needn't bother about me, I can take care of myself! Now get out of here. Go back to your newspaper and don't ever come near me again!'

He left without another word. She listened to his footsteps descending the stairs. She heard him crossing the hall; she heard the front door open and close – and then she sank on to the bed, burying her face in the pillows so nobody should hear her crying.

Some weeks later, she was hoovering the living-room carpet at Galleon House when the telephone rang. She picked it up at once, because Russell was having an after-lunch nap in his bedroom. At the other end of the line, Vee said: 'Can you talk, or is he in the room?'

'No, he's having forty winks. I mustn't talk for long.'

'I'll try to be quick, but I had to tell you. Don's written to me; the letter arrived this morning. It's rather peculiar.'

'Why? What's it about?'

'Oh, my birthday, mostly – I mean, my other birthday, May the seventh. It's a Saturday, and he wants to take us both out.'

'Well, what's wrong with that? It's very nice of him.'

'Yes, but – his letter struck me as a bit peculiar. Parts of it are – rather personal.'

'Do you mean it's a love letter?'

'I don't know – it's difficult to tell, he exaggerates so much. I mean, about the night out, he says we'll have a "real whirl", whatever that means. He's going to take us to the best restaurant in town and buy us champagne.'

Remembering, Jo smiled. 'It's funny the way men go on about champagne, isn't it?'

'But do you suppose it's some sort of joke? He can't possibly afford that sort of thing, can he?'

'I don't know, unless—' Jo remembered another conversation. 'He was talking about some business deal. He said if it came off, he'd take us somewhere special.'

'Yes, I know, but I can never decide whether Don really means what he says. Alec's convinced he's up to no good – what do you think?'

Jo found herself growing indignant again: 'Alec's got no right to say that, when he's got no proof. Don's never done anything wrong, has he? Just because he isn't English, people say nasty things behind his back—'

At that moment, Jo saw a moving shadow in the mirror over the fireplace; Russell was standing in the doorway, listening.

Breaking off immediately she said: 'I'm sorry, I've got to go. I'll talk to you again soon.'

When she replaced the receiver, Russell said dryly: 'I do beg your pardon. I didn't mean to interrupt your conversation.'

'I'm sorry if the phone woke you; it was a friend of mine. Nothing important.'

'You made it sound fairly important. I gather it was that American you were defending so passionately?'

'Yes – I don't think it's right to criticise people when they've done nothing wrong.' She turned away. 'Excuse me, I must finish the hoovering.'

She switched on the vacuum-cleaner again; at once Russell stretched across her and switched it off at the wall-socket.

'You're in love with him, aren't you?' he asked.

'No, I'm not! He's a good friend, that's all, but I'm not in love with him – I'm not in love with anyone. May I get on with my work now?'

Before he could reply, the bell in the hall rang loudly; someone was downstairs at the front door.

'We seem to be plagued by interruptions,' said Russell. 'I'm not expecting any visitors – are you?'

'It's probably somebody selling something. I'll go and see.'

Jo ran downstairs. When she opened the front door, at first she didn't recognise the girl on the step: her freckled face was pale and drawn, and her red-rimmed eyes looked as if she had been crying, but her bright red hair was unmistakable.

Jo exclaimed: 'Chrissie, whatever's the matter?'

The girl took a deep breath, and began: 'I'm sorry, I shouldn't come bothering you, but I didn't know where else to go. Can I talk to you, Jo?'

'Of course you can – come in. What's happened?'

Scared but determined, Chrissie Bone walked into the hall, and said: 'It – it's about Ma.'

'Oh, I'm sorry, is she ill again?'

'She was ill – very ill. The doctor wanted to send her to hospital, but she wouldn't have it – well, you know what she's like—' Chrissie broke off and tears welled up in her eyes. 'What she *was* like . . . It happened last night, all of a sudden. She just sort of – died . . . And I don't know what to do . . .'

Chapter Fourteen

WHEN JO AND CHRISSIE reached Agar Road, a long black limousine was driving away from the house.

Chrissie was holding her hand, and Jo felt her grip tighten as she said: 'That'll be the undertakers' men. They said they'd come round – to take Ma away.'

Jo stared at her. 'You called in the undertakers?'

'I was going to, but Mr Penberthy said he'd do it. He said it had to be a grown-up.'

Mr Mulligan came to meet them in the passage, holding out his hands. 'Me darlin' girl, is it yourself? I knew you wouldn't let us down, Jo. This poor child's had too much to do already, the past weeks.'

Mr Penberthy emerged from the front parlour, saying: 'It's unfortunate you missed the undertakers. No doubt you wanted to pay your last respects—'

Jo cut in: 'Chris, why don't you pop upstairs and take your coat off? I'll be up in a minute, to help you make up a bed for me.'

Chrissie beamed. 'Oh, good – you're going to stay the night.'

She ran upstairs, and as soon as she was out of earshot, Jo continued: 'I'm sorry, Mr Penberthy, I interrupted you.'

'If you wish to see the deceased, perhaps you should call round to the funeral parlour. You might still be in time.'

'No, thank you,' said Jo.

She had never forgotten her own mother, lifeless beside her in the ambulance, or the sight of Laura Stanway sprawled across the bed . . .

She had no wish to see any more corpses.

'Thank you for dealing with the undertakers,' she went on.

'I felt it was my duty.' Mr Penberthy fetched a sealed envelope from the mantelpiece. 'This is the death certificate, signed by the doctor first thing this morning. It has to be taken to the Registrar's Office. They will issue a green form, which must be taken to the undertakers.'

'Do you want me to do that?'

'I think it would be appropriate. Mr Mulligan said he felt sure you would be here shortly, so I thought it better to leave you to deal with everything. You are a blood relative, after all.' He cleared his throat, and continued in the solemn tone he always adopted whenever money was discussed: 'According to the law, the person who calls in the undertaker becomes responsible for paying the costs. And while I was happy to do my duty by the late Mrs Bone, I shall pass the bill to you for settlement when it comes in. No doubt it can be defrayed from the good lady's estate?'

'Oh, yes – certainly.'

Mr Mulligan muttered: 'Time enough to think of such things later, old man. Why don't I go and put the kettle on? Let's all have a cup of tea.'

Mr Penberthy watched him leave the room, then whispered: 'It's all very well for Mulligan. He doesn't seem to realise that I had to telephone the office and take a day off work. He doesn't appreciate that this is costing me money!'

'Of course.' Jo picked up the carrier-bag she had brought with her. 'I'll just run up and give Chris a hand. Excuse me.'

She felt quite breathless – so much had happened in the last hour, since Chrissie's arrival at Galleon House. She had explained the situation to Russell; obviously the girl couldn't be expected to deal with this crisis on her own.

'There must be somebody there who can handle things, surely?' he argued.

'No, there are just two elderly men living in the house – Aunt Topsy's lodgers. She's family; Russell, I must go and help.'

She had thrown a nightie and a toothbrush into a bag, then set out with Chrissie, catching a tram along Battersea Park Road. On the way, she encouraged the girl to tell her exactly what had happened.

'Like I said, Ma hadn't been well for a long time. The doctor said it was pleurisy, and she had to stop in bed, so I stayed home from school to look after her. Mr Mulligan helped with the housework and the shopping, and I did the cooking – but I let him peel the potatoes.'

'You cooked all the meals?'

'I'd done it before. After you moved out, Ma let me help in the house. I used to do the breakfasts before I went to school, and sometimes I made the tea as well, when I got home. Fried Spam, scrambled egg – things like that.'

'And you're only – what? Eleven?'

'I'll be twelve very soon,' Chris said proudly. 'So when Ma was ill I just carried on. When the pleurisy turned into pneumonia, the doctor tried to send her to hospital, but she wouldn't go. She said she'd be better off in her own home, but then, last night, she just sort of – stopped. When I took her in a cup of tea this morning, I could see she – she wasn't there any more, somehow.'

'I know what you mean,' said Jo. 'I once saw somebody like that.'

'Anyhow, I told Mr Mulligan and he woke Mr Penberthy up, and Mr Penberthy got dressed and went out to the phone-box. The doctor came round right away, and then he signed the bit of paper and told me it was all over. He said her heart had just wore out, like. And she died in her sleep, so it didn't hurt or anything. That was good, wasn't it?'

'Very good.' Jo put her arm round the girl's shoulders. 'Did he say anything else?'

'He asked who my nearest relative was, so I told him I'd got a grown-up cousin. I was sure you'd know what to do.'

When Mr Mulligan brought the tea, they sat round the parlour table, and Jo made a list of things to be done.

'First of all, I must go to the Registrar's Office with the certificate. Then I'd better see the vicar at All Saints about fixing a date.'

'And the bank manager,' suggested Mr Penberthy. 'I suppose Mrs Bone had a bank account?'

'Yes, she did,' said Chrissie. 'She's got a chequebook in the top drawer of her dressing-table, and a lot of other stuff – Dad's papers from the Navy, and her pension book and so on.'

'You won't forget what I said?' asked Mr Penberthy. 'The little matter of the funeral expenses?'

'I won't forget.' Jo glanced at the mantelpiece clock. 'Half past four. I'd better be making a move if I'm going to get to the Registrar's Office before it shuts.'

'Would you like me to come with you?' Chrissie offered.

'No, don't bother. Oh, what about tea?' Jo found her purse and gave Chrissie a ten-shilling note. 'Run round to the shops and find something nice for all of us. Whatever you like – I'll leave it to you.'

Chris brightened up and went to fetch her coat.

Mr Penberthy sighed heavily. 'That's all very well, but we should think a little further ahead, surely? What's going to happen to this house, without an owner? What will happen to us?'

'Never mind us!' said Mr Mulligan. 'It's that child we should be thinking of. What's to happen to her?'

'I've been thinking about that,' said Jo. 'Later on this evening, when Chrissie's gone to bed, we can talk it over.'

At the Registrar's Office in Southlands, off the High Street, a motherly lady in spectacles questioned Jo kindly, doing her best to be helpful and sympathetic.

'Yes, I see,' she said, crossing out what she had written and beginning again. 'Let me get this right – you are Mrs Bone's next-of-kin?'

'No, I'm her niece. Her next-of-kin is her daughter, Christine.'

'But I thought you were Christine?'

'No, I'm Josephine Wells, Chrissie's cousin. Mrs Bone was my aunt.'

'Oh, yes, that's right, you told me that before, didn't you? But her daughter, Christine – isn't she with you?'

'No. She's only eleven; I thought it might be rather an ordeal for her.'

'Oh, yes, quite right. Isn't there anyone else? What about Mr Bone?'

'He died at the end of January – Mr Norman Bone – you must have got all the details here already.'

'Have we? We deal with so many people, you'd be surprised.' The lady looked sad and solemn. 'Oh, dear, so your little sister is all alone now?'

'Not my sister, my cousin. She's not alone: there are two lodgers in the house, and I'll be staying there myself tonight.'

'But you don't live there permanently?'

'No, I gave you my address – number one, the Rope Walk.'

'Oh, yes . . .' With a faraway look, the lady chewed the end of her pen. 'That poor child . . . You'll have to get on to Welfare.'

'I beg your pardon?'

'The Welfare Department at the Town Hall. My friend Miss Frinton is in charge of Child Welfare; she'll have to be informed.'

'Why is that?'

'Well, they'll look after the poor little mite – I expect she'll be taken into care.' The lady scribbled something on a piece of paper. 'There, give that to Miss Frinton and say I sent you. Now, where had we got to? Oh, yes, the green form. You must take it to the undertakers; that gives them the authority to proceed with the arrangements for your mother's funeral.'

'My aunt – Mrs Bone was my aunt.'

'Oh, was she? That's funny, I seem to have written down "Daughter" under "Next-of-kin" . . . I wonder why?'

When Jo left the Registrar's Office, she ran for a bus that would take her up to Clapham Junction, but just missed it. There was no knowing how long she would have to wait for the next one, so she decided to walk.

By the time she reached the Junction and climbed the slope of Lavender Hill, her legs were aching. Passing the windows of Bryden Brothers, she peered in, hoping to catch a glimpse of Malcolm in his floorwalker's attire, but there was no sign of him.

At the Town Hall, a uniformed porter was closing the double doors, and she tried to slip past him, but he put up his hand: 'No admittance to the general public now, it's closing-time.'

'I must see Miss Frinton in the Welfare Department – I've got a note from the Registrar.'

The porter said: 'Then you're out of luck – she's just left.'

'But this is important, isn't there anyone else I could see?'

'I told you, the offices are closed. Come back tomorrow.'

So that was that – she'd walked all this way for nothing. As she left the Town Hall, she almost collided with a small boy running past; he had a battered-looking satchel slung over one shoulder, and was obviously on his way home from school, but Jo didn't give him a second glance, and the boy was in too much of a hurry to notice her at all.

*

He put on a last burst of speed, then turned into a side street. Diving through an open doorway, he clattered up the echoing stone stairs and burst into the flat, out of breath.

His mum began to scold him: 'What time do you call this, then? Where have you been?'

'School,' he panted. 'I was kept in.'

'Whatever for?'

'Teacher made me stay behind after the bell and write a hundred lines – "I must learn to pay attention and stop talking in class" . . . It wasn't my fault: one of the big boys took my pencil-sharpener, and I was telling him to give it me back, that's all . . . I really hate that teacher, he always picks on me.'

'I'm sure he doesn't. Go and wash your hands before tea.'

'He does pick on me, honest.'

From his armchair in the corner, his dad growled: 'Do as you're told, and don't talk back to your mother.'

The small boy stood his ground. 'But he does! He gets ratty because I don't know about the rotten Spanish Armada. I can't help it if I wasn't there when they did Queen Elizabeth, can I? I hate this school. I wish I was still going to Manchester – we did woodwork in Manchester. Or Portsmouth – they took us swimming at Portsmouth. I wish we were in Portsmouth now.'

His father grunted: 'Never mind. We'll go back there, one of these fine days, I promise. Now run along and wash your hands.'

In the doorway, the boy turned back to enquire: 'I s'pose that means you haven't heard anything yet – about a job?'

'No, son. Not yet.'

The boy nodded, and went out without another word.

As the door closed, Mum said: 'He worries when you're out of work.'

Folding up the newspaper, her husband muttered: 'I've been looking through the small ads again, but there's nothing suitable.'

'You can go round to the Labour, can't you? It'd be better than hanging about doing nothing, wouldn't it?'

Dad shook his head. 'They won't have anything in my line. If the worst comes to the worst, I'll just have to sell the van, that's all.'

Mum was horrified: 'Oh, no, love. We've got to keep the van – how could we manage without it?'

'If we have to, Miguel will see us right. We'll manage somehow.'

Although Christine had had the bedroom to herself since Jo moved out, the second bedstead was still there, and as she settled down for the night, Chris said: 'You'll come to bed soon, won't you? It'll be nice to have you here.' As Jo left the room, she added: 'Are you just staying one night?'

'I don't know. I'm still working for Mr Wade. I took some time off today, but he'll expect me there tomorrow.'

'If you ask him, wouldn't he let you stay two nights?'

'We'll see,' said Jo.

Downstairs, Mr Penberthy was sipping barley-water. When Jo walked in, he asked: 'What happened this afternoon? Everthing in order, I hope?'

'Yes. The funeral will be on Friday – two-thirty at All Saints.'

He tut-tutted. 'That means taking another half-day off this week – most inconvenient.'

'And what about the youngster?' asked Mr Mulligan. 'What's to happen to her?'

'The lady at the Registrar's advised me to go to the Welfare Department. She said Chris might have to be taken into care. They'd find her a place with foster-parents, I suppose.'

'Is that what the Welfare said?'

'I didn't get there, it was too late. I'll call in some time tomorrow, to sort things out.'

Mr Penberthy said: 'If the child leaves, what will happen to this house? Where would we go?'

Mr Mulligan asked Jo: 'Could you not move back here? I'm sure we could manage pretty well between us – a regular happy family. What d'you say?'

Mr Penberthy demurred. 'I'm not sure that it would be entirely legal. Since Miss Wells is not yet twenty-one, she may not be considered eligible to take on the responsibility.'

'Ah, who's to know?' exclaimed Mr Mulligan. 'She's a grown girl. If she's not old enough to take charge of the house, I don't know who is! What d'you think, me darlin'?'

'I don't know . . .' Jo smothered a yawn; it had been an exhausting day. 'Let me think it over, will you? We'll talk about it tomorrow.'

When she went upstairs, Chrissie was already asleep. Jo undressed quickly and slipped into her own bed, but there were so many thoughts going through her head, and so many problems, she lay awake for a long time.

Russell sniffed. 'I've never heard anything so absurd in my life.'

'She's my cousin. She's got nobody else to look after her.'

'You said yourself, she'd be put into a foster-home.' He was sitting up in bed, propped against the pillows. Pulling out a handkerchief, he blew his nose. 'She'd be well cared for.'

'Do you want me to get you something from the chemist's?'

'No, no, don't fuss – it's only a cold. If I stay in bed for a day or two, I'll soon throw it off,' he told her irritably. 'And don't change the subject! I remember your cousin very clearly – a spoiled brat with ginger hair. You didn't even like her!'

'She's changed a lot since then, and she's had a very tough time: first her father dying, and now her mother . . . She hasn't been spoiled lately, I can promise you that.'

'That's neither here nor there. You can't wreck your own life for the sake of that child – she's not your responsibility.' He wiped his nose. 'Frankly, I should have thought you might feel some responsibility towards me. What would happen here if you went off and left me stranded?'

Jo tried to make allowances for the fact that he was feeling ill. He seemed to be shivering, and his face had an unhealthy pallor.

'I'm not going to leave you stranded,' she said firmly. 'I'll come round every morning, to do the shopping and cleaning and cook for you. After lunch I'll go back and take care of things at Agar Road. Don't worry, you're not going to be neglected.'

He grunted. 'Don't you think you're taking on too much? You'll wear yourself out.'

'No, I won't. Thousands of women go out to work and run a home as well. I'll manage.' She added. 'And I'm not doing it out of the kindness of my heart, by the way – I've still got to earn a living!'

'Yes, of course.' He leaned back, resting his aching head. 'What about modelling for me? Will you ever be able to fit that in?'

'I'll be glad to – if I can find the time.'

When Jo had finished washing up after lunch, she left the flat. Running downstairs, she was astonished to see Don waiting for her, sitting on an oak chest in the hall, dressed in a sports coat and a black turtleneck sweater.

'I didn't know you were here!' she exclaimed.

He jumped up. 'I guess I shoulda called, but I didn't want to rile your boss. Howya doing, babe?'

'Oh, I'm fine, but if you didn't ring the bell, how did you get in?'

'One of the artists here saw me hanging around and let me through – some guy called Bentley? I said I wanted to see you, and he said to go on up, but I told him I'd sooner wait. I figured you were busy. Are you all through now? D'you have time for a drink?'

'Don, I can't, I've got to get back to Agar Road. We can walk along together if you're going that way. Why aren't you in uniform – are you a civilian now?'

'I'm on three weeks' terminal leave. Sure I'll walk with you. What's with this Agar Road? What are you doing there? You can tell me to mind my own darn business if you want.'

As they walked through Battersea, she explained about her aunt's death, and her concern for Chris, and he shook his head: 'That poor kid. I shouldn't come pestering you like this; you've got enough to handle.'

'It's good to see you. What are you going to do with yourself? Have you made any plans?'

'Oh, I got a coupla ideas. Most of the time I just sit around, feeling sorry for myself.' He threw her a sidelong glance. 'I guess Vee told you what happened? How her brother upped and kicked me out?'

'She didn't put it quite like that.'

'No? Well, that's the way it was. I've tried to call her, but it seems like she's never at home. D'you suppose the maids have been told to choke me off, maybe? So I was wondering if you'd give her a message, huh?'

'I'll try,' she said awkwardly. 'But how will I get in touch with you? Should I write to you care of the army camp?'

'No, I found me a place to stay right here in town. I'll give you the number, you can call me there.'

'What do you want me to say to Vee?'

'Ask her if we've still got that date for May seventh – I said I'd take the both of you out on her birthday, remember? Tell her I still love her.'

Jo felt quite touched, and said: 'I'll tell her, but I'm not sure if it'll do any good.'

'That bad, huh? But I've got to see her again. You can understand that, can't you?'

'I can't promise anything – I'll do my best.'

She had already arranged to meet Vee in the park on Saturday afternoon, to tell her about Aunt Topsy – and Christine.

It was the end of April, but it felt like high summer. Jo and Vee sat on a bench overlooking the boating-lake. Muscular lads in shirtsleeves were showing off to admiring girls in sun-hats – some of them preferred to ship their oars and let the boats drift to rest under the bank, screened by overhanging willows, affectionately entwined.

Vee sighed. 'Do you ever get the feeling that everybody in the world has got somebody to love except you and me? I haven't heard from Don for weeks.'

Jo hesitated, then said: 'I have.'

Indignantly, Vee swung round to face her. 'You mean he rang you? I suppose now he's given me up, he's having a go at you instead—'

'Hang on – give me a chance, will you?' Half laughing, half annoyed, Jo felt as if they were children again, squabbling over a favourite toy. 'He didn't ring up, he dropped in at Galleon House. And he came round to ask me about you!'

Feeling rather foolish, Vee muttered: 'I'm sorry. What did he want?'

'He wants to talk to you – he still wants to take us out on your birthday.' Jo explained as well she could, finishing: 'I warned him, I wasn't sure whether you'd still want to.'

'Of course I do! Why couldn't he ring me himself?'

'Every time he rang, they said you were out – and I knew Alec told you he was up to no good, so I wondered if you'd decided to take his advice.'

'But you were the one who said it was all rubbish! You said it's not fair to accuse him without any proof. Don't tell me you've changed your mind?'

'Don can be very charming when he wants to . . . Anyhow, it's not up to me, is it? Look, I've written down his phone-number. Do you want to ring him, or shall I?'

Vee studied the scrap of paper. 'It's difficult to ring him from home – somebody might be listening. Would you do it? Say we'll see him next weekend. If we're both there, it will be all right.'

'You're not really sure about him either, are you?'

'I don't know. Alec's a very good judge of people, and if he thinks I shouldn't see Don . . .' Her eyes roamed over the loving couples, half hidden beneath the weeping willows. 'I do want to see him, but only if you're there as well. You will come with me, won't you?'

'If that's what you want, all right.'

'Thanks, Jo. I'll do the same for you some day.'

Jo sighed. 'Chance'd be a fine thing! The way my life's going, I don't suppose I'm likely to meet any young men for quite a while.'

'What makes you say that?'

So she explained about Christine, and the household at Agar Road. As soon as Vee understood what Jo was proposing to do, her reaction was very like Russell's.

'Oh, you can't. You'd be throwing your whole life away!'

'Don't exaggerate. Chris isn't a baby, she's growing up fast – before we know it, she'll be going steady with some young chap, and setting up a home of her own.'

'Oh, yes, and what will you be doing by then?'

Jo shrugged. 'How should I know? I'll just wait and see – let God surprise me.'

Vee looked doubtful. 'Do you still believe in all that?'

'Sometimes I do, sometimes I don't . . . I'm never quite sure.'

Vee nodded. 'I know, that's how I feel. But I'm sure about one thing: if you give up your freedom to look after Chrissie, you'll be making a terrible mistake. Do change your mind – before it's too late.'

'It's too late now, I've already told them. Chris needs me, so I've got to do what I can. She's family.'

On her way back to Agar Road, Jo stopped at a phone-box and rang Don's number.

When he lifted the receiver his voice was oddly cautious: 'Who is it?'

'Don! It's me – Jo.'

'Hi!' He seemed relieved. 'How's tricks?'

'Were you expecting somebody else?'

'Oh, no, I just thought it might be someone for – for the guy who lives here. Did you get to talk to Vee?'

'Yes, she says she'd like to meet you.'

He gave a war-whoop. 'Yahoo! You're fantastic!'

'Don't expect miracles. She'll talk to you, but she wants me to come along as well.'

'Sure – that's the whole idea! So it's a definite date for Saturday, right?'

'What time do you want us to meet you? Where and when?'

'I leave it to you. Any time, any place you say . . . How's about the Rope Walk?'

'That's no good – I'm leaving the Rope Walk tomorrow, and moving to Agar Road. Could we come to you? Where you are now?'

After a moment's thought he said: 'Sure, only don't make it too early, huh? Come around between six and seven, OK?'

'Fine, except I don't know where you live. Hang on, I've got the piece of paper with your number on. Let me write down the address.'

He dictated it. 'Three, Battersea Reach . . . D'you know Lombard Road?'

'It's one of the side roads off Vicarage Crescent, isn't it?'

'Right! Battersea Reach is a turning off Lombard Road, down by the river – you can't miss it. Drop by around six-thirty, Saturday, OK?'

Jo left the phone-box, and went on to Agar Road. She had slept there every night since Aunt Topsy died, sharing Chris's room; tomorrow she was going to move in permanently, and in due course she would clear out her aunt's room and make it her own. But not yet – it might be upsetting for Chris. For the time being, she would make do with a shared bedroom.

On Sunday morning she got up early and laid the kitchen table. The lodgers expected a cooked breakfast, and she wanted to do the job properly.

Mr Mulligan rubbed his hands and said: 'Sausage and bacon, eh? You're spoiling us, me darlin' – isn't that right, Mr Penberthy?'

Mr Penberthy mumbled something inaudible through a mouthful of toast, but it sounded appreciative.

Jo said: 'When I was cooking for Mr Wade, it was hard to make the rations stretch, but now I've got four ration-books to juggle with!'

'It's like an answer to a prayer, so it is,' said Mr Mulligan. 'I'll lay you ten to one Our Blessed Lady had a hand in it. Bringing you back where you belong, almost like you'd never been away.'

Almost like you'd never been away . . . As she sat looking at the two old gentlemen, the familiar pattern of the wallpaper and the chipped crockery she had washed and dried a thousand times, she began to feel as if she had never left Agar Road. Her time at Bryden Brothers, at the Greasy Spoon, at the Rope Walk and at Galleon House – these were only memories now. And her life with Russell – her first love affair, those moments of ecstasy and misery – were all fading like dreams. She told herself that she must not look back, she must look to the future . . . But what did the future hold for her?

She began to make plans for the coming week. She must notify the Town Hall of her change of address, and go to the solicitors with her aunt's papers. Topsy Bone had never made a will, so according to Mr Penberthy her estate would go in trust until Chris came of age. And she'd make a start on turning out the big bedroom: the clothes could go to the jumble sale.

And she had to go back to the Rope Walk once more.

After tea on Sunday evening, she went back there to pack up her clothes. Somehow she had accumulated a lot of other things during the last few years – bulky objects like the kettle and the teapot, and awkward shapes like the frying-pan and the toasting-fork. She had borrowed a hold-all from Agar Road, but when that was filled, she was left with a pathetic heap of items – Chockie the teddy-bear wouldn't fit in anywhere.

Knocking at the room next door, she found Peggy putting on her make-up.

'Hello, stranger!' Peggy exclaimed. 'Where have you been hiding yourself? I was beginning to think you'd dropped down dead.'

'Not quite.' Jo sat on the end of the bed as Peggy applied mascara to her lashes. 'I've come to say goodbye, 'cos I'm moving out.'

'Moving in with your gentleman-friend the artist, I suppose? I can't say I'm surprised. I thought you'd have done that long ago. Fancy staying in this dump, when you could have been living up there like Lady Muck!'

'I'm not going to Galleon House.' Jo explained once again about Topsy Bone's death, and the house at Agar Road. '. . . So I'll be looking after Chris and the lodgers, though I'll still housekeep for Russell – mornings only.'

Pegge gazed at her, open mouthed.

'You must be barmy!' she said. 'You're going to wear yourself out, my girl. You'll be on half-wages up the road, and not earning a penny from those old codgers and the kid – how are you going to manage? I don't know why you ever took up that housekeeping lark in the first place; you'd have been better off on the game, like the rest of us.'

Jo tried to laugh this off. 'You know I wasn't any good at that – scrubbing floors and peeling spuds is more my style. Anyway, I've told everybody. I can't back out now.'

'Well, there's no accounting for tastes. It's going to seem very funny, not being able to pop next door when I'm on the cadge.'

'I'm on the cadge myself this time – you couldn't let me have a couple of carrier bags, could you?'

''Course – there's plenty in that corner cupboard. Help yourself.'

When Jo opened the cupboard door, a small avalanche of paper bags fell out, together with odds and ends of string, empty bottles and jam-jars.

'That's what comes of growing up in the war,' Peggy explained. 'I don't throw anything away – well, you never know when you're going to run short.'

She added a dash of lipstick to her mouth, and flicked a last curl into place, saying: 'I'll have to love you and leave you now – duty calls!' She squeezed Jo in a casual embrace. 'Pop in and see us sometimes, won't you? Only not in the mornings, 'cos of me having a lie-in, and not in the evenings, 'cos I'll either be out or working, one or the other. But in between times I'll always be pleased to see you – okie-doke?'

'Okie-doke,' said Jo, and went back to finish her packing.

When it was done, the room looked very bare. She took a last look round, remembering Russell, who had once slept in that narrow bed – and Pete Hobden, who had not. Then she walked out, shutting the door behind her.

Leaving her baggage in the hall, she went along to the kitchen to pay the last instalment of her rent.

Tibbles rubbed himself against her legs, arching his back and glaring up at her with baleful yellow eyes.

'You've hurt his feelings because you're not sitting down and stroking him,' Sarah interpreted. 'I'll make us a cup of cocoa – you're not in a hurry, are you?'

'Thanks all the same, I'd better not.'

Sarah smiled: 'All right, dear, it's up to you. It's been nice having you here; I'm sorry you're leaving. There's not many I'd say that about.'

'It's not as if I were going for good. I can still drop in and say hello when I'm over this way, can't I?'

'You do that. Good luck, dear, and God bless.' She kissed Jo. Her wrinkled skin was as soft as a kid glove; the scent of patchouli lingered on Jo's cheek. 'I'll come and see you out.'

As Jo collected up her luggage, Sarah added: 'Would you like to give me your new address, in case any letters come? Or if anyone should ask after you?'

'I suppose that would be a good idea.' Jo sighed. 'But I'm not really expecting anything.'

Chapter Fifteen

'IT'S GOT TO BE HERE SOMEWHERE,' said Jo. 'This is Lombard Road, and Don said Battersea Reach was a turning off Lombard Road.'

'But it doesn't make sense. We've walked all the way to the end and back again,' Vee complained. 'There's no other road here, and no sign saying "Battersea Reach".'

For most of its length Lombard Road had grimy factories on one side, and a high, unbroken wall on the other. Above the wall, they could see towering cranes like giant birds, dipping their heads to the river. There were no side turnings; a single unmade track sloped down to the wharves along the shore.

'He did say it led to the river,' Jo remembered. 'It's got to be down there somewhere.'

'But there aren't any houses,' Vee pointed out. 'I expect you muddled up the name of the street.'

'I'm sure he said Battersea Reach. Come on, let's have a look.'

They picked their way along the stony track, which broadened into a kind of towpath at the river's edge. The tide was out, and shallow puddles lay on the mudflats, with engine-oil like rainbows gleaming on the surface.

'This is a waste of time,' grumbled Vee. 'There's nothing here but filthy old coal-barges. I'm going back.'

'Hang on a minute – they're not all barges,' said Jo.

At the end of the towpath, she had seen a little trio of boats that looked as if they might be permanently moored; there were gangplanks fixed to the shore, and one had wooden tubs of geraniums on deck. And there were numbers on the doors, a brass knocker, and a letter-box—

'They're houseboats!' she exclaimed triumphantly. 'One – two – three, Battersea Reach!'

'But Don would have told you if he was living on a boat.'

'Perhaps he wanted to surprise us.'

As they reached the gangplank of number 3 they had another surprise. The door opened, and a young man stepped out, but it wasn't Don.

'Reggie!' said Jo. 'Fancy seeing you here!'

He smiled uneasily. 'Have you come to see Don? You'll find him down below. He said he was expecting visitors this evening.'

'I didn't know you were a friend of Don's,' began Jo: 'Oh, sorry – Vee, this is Mr Bentley – he's got one of the studios at Galleon House. Reggie – this is my friend, Vanessa Coburn. It's funny we're all visiting Don at the same time.'

'Actually, I'm not a visitor.' Reggie was looking flustered. 'I – er – as a matter of fact, I live here. This is my boat.'

'I never knew that,' said Jo.

'Yes, I picked her up just after the war. She's a converted MTB.'

'MTB?'

'Motor-torpedo boat, war surplus. She pongs a bit at low tide, and when the tugs go past, you bounce up and down rather, but it's worth it for the view. We get stunning sunsets.' Still talking, he backed away along the towpath: 'Sorry I can't stop. Got to see a chap about a commission – the Life and Loves of Lady Hamilton. Shame you're not available for modelling nowadays, Jo. You'd have been my first choice!'

Then with a final wave, he disappeared into the distance.

'I suppose that's what they call the artistic temperament,' said Vee.

'He's really nice when you get to know him.' Jo looked thoughtful. 'Don did say something about meeting Reggie at the studios, but he never mentioned anything about living on his boat.'

Hearing voices, Don came up on deck to investigate, and greeted them with a big smile. 'Hi there! Come down to the saloon. Watch how you go, there's a lot of low beams.'

They followed him down a steep companionway into the central saloon, a long low room that occupied the full width of the boat. It had a padded seat all round the sides, and a clutter of furniture crammed in between; below decks, the whiff of Thames mud was blotted out by the smell of oil-paints. Half-finished canvases were stacked on the floor, and there were tubes of colour, dirty brushes and paint-rags everywhere, among a magpie's hoard of bric-à-brac: an engraved glass goblet, a vase of dying roses scattering their petals, a coffee-table with dirty plates and the left-over remains of a meal.

Jo was used to the state of Reggie's studio at Galleon House, but his living-quarters touched new heights – or depths – of disorder.

'Sit yourself down, Jo,' said Don. Then he threw his arms round Vee and launched into a fortissimo rendering of: 'Happy birthday, dear Vanessa, happy birthday to you!' sealing it with a kiss on the lips.

When he let her go, she was caught between embarrassment and happiness. 'Don, you're terrible. We don't make such a fuss about birthdays in England!'

'I believe in keeping up the good old American customs. Many happy returns to the Birthday Girl!' and he produced the gift-wrapped package which he had been saving since February.

When Vee opened it she was overwhelmed. 'Oh, you shouldn't – it's gorgeous. I simply don't know what to say!'

'You don't have to say a word, honey, the ceremony's over. Let's all settle back and have a drink. I made us a pitcher of martinis, good and dry.'

The martinis were more than dry. Jo realised they were practically neat gin, and managed to conceal her glass behind a volume of the *Encyclopaedia Britannica* as Don went on happily: 'I heard you talking with Reggie. I asked him to stay around this evening, but he had to go see someone. He's been real good to me.'

'I didn't even realise you knew each other,' said Jo.

'Didn't I tell you? Yeah, I ran into him one time when I dropped by the studios. We kinda got talking, and I told him I was looking for some place to stay when I was in town, so he brought me back here. It's sort of cramped for space, I guess, but Reggie has the captain's cabin, down thattaway – ' he pointed forward, towards the bows: 'and I got me a cute little cabin all to myself, back there.' He pointed towards the stern. 'It's squeezed in between the shower-room and what Reggie calls "the heads". It's fine and dandy, except when the plumbing backs up – but let's not talk about that!'

'I think it's a brilliant idea!' said Vee. 'So much nicer than living in a boring old house like everybody else.'

'Oh, sure, it's loads of fun, watching the world go by. Barges, steamers, kids in rowboats – sometimes there are swans, right up close – we feed 'em hunks of bread.' He checked his watch. 'Talking of feeding, maybe we should go find some place to eat?'

'I hope we're not going anywhere grand,' said Jo. 'I'm not really dressed for the Ritz!'

'You look terrific,' Don assured her. 'I thought maybe we'd walk over to Chelsea. There's a whole lot of eating-places along King's Road. Vee, what's your favourite?'

'I don't know – we don't often go to restaurants,' Vee explained, adding a warning note: 'I believe some of them are rather expensive.'

He laughed. 'When I'm with the two prettiest girls in town, money's no object!'

But when they went out on deck, he looked up at the sky and pulled a long face. 'Wouldn't you know it? See those big clouds coming up from the west? That's a sure sign of bad weather. And you haven't got raincoats. I'd never forgive myself if you got caught in a storm.'

'Couldn't we pick up a cab?' Vee suggested.

He shook his head. 'You don't find cabs in this neck of the woods. Aw, what the hell? Remember the old saying – "East, west, home's best" – why don't we stay home and eat right here?'

'You mean you're going to cook for us?' asked Jo.

'I'm not the world's greatest chef, but don't let that bother you. I'll run along and pick up some take-home eats. You two make yourselves at home. Pour some more drinks, and I'll be back before you know it.'

When they had settled themselves once more in the saloon, Vee said: 'You can't help liking him, can you?'

'In spite of everything Alec said?'

'Alec's not always right – we all make mistakes sometimes.'

Jo said cautiously: 'I don't think you should get too involved with him, that's all. I thought Alec was the only man in your life?'

'Yes, he is – at least, he was – but I know I was being silly. I'm trying to forget Alec, and think about Don instead.'

'We don't really know anything about him.'

'What do you mean? It's not very nice to criticise him when you're sitting here, drinking his drink, waiting for him to give us supper. Anyway, I don't remember you getting so high-and-mighty when you were having your little fling with Russell Wade. I just wish you'd married him when he asked you to, then you wouldn't be so jolly miserable all the time.'

'I'm not miserable, I'm trying to be sensible.'

'I don't call it very sensible, the way you're carrying on. If you were sensible, you wouldn't have moved back to Agar Road, to look after awful Chrissie and those horrible old men.'

'They're not that bad! And Chris is heaps nicer than she used to be. You ought to come round to tea one afternoon and meet her – I wish you would.'

'I told you before, I daren't risk it. Suppose she recognised me?'

'Chris was only three last time she saw you; she couldn't possibly remember. I'll just say you're a friend of mine. Well, that's true – we are friends . . . Even if we do get on each other's nerves sometimes!'

Vee relaxed slightly. 'All right, I'll come and visit that horrid house, if you really want me to.' Then she added: 'But I still think you'd have been better off marrying Russell Wade. Did you fall out of love with him or what?'

'It's hard to explain. I still love him, in a way, but I stopped being *in* love. Something happened that made me frightened of him.'

'Frightened? Why?'

'He gets into these awful black rages. One day we had a row, and he picked up a chisel. I thought he was going to cut my throat.'

'Oh, for heaven's sake! You must have known he wouldn't do that!'

'I'm not sure . . . I can never be quite sure about him.'

Jo went on to tell Vee everything she knew about the night Laura died: how Russell had been the only other person in the house, and how Laura's glass had been washed and dried carefully and put back into her hands, after her death.

'He must have done it – and there's only one reason for that. He was afraid the police would find his fingerprints on the glass. That means he put the sleeping-tablets into her drink.'

The saloon was silent; absorbed, neither of them noticed the shadow at the half-open porthole, or the sound of a footstep on the deck overhead.

At last Vee said: 'You never told him – about the glass?'

'Accuse him of murder? He'd only deny it – after all this time, it could never be proved.'

She broke off as Don came down the companionway with a bundle wrapped in newspaper, announcing: 'Fish and chips! Get it while it's hot!'

As he dished it on to the plates, Jo asked: 'Has it started to rain?'

'Not yet, but it's going to, any time now. This ain't exactly what I'd planned, but at least we're cosy and warm. And next time I take you out, it'll be the Ritz – I promise!' Changing his tone, he turned to Vee. 'If there's gonna be a next time? If you want to give me another chance?'

She smiled back. 'Of course – you know that.'

Much later, when Jo was getting into bed, she realised that it had never rained at all, and it crossed her mind that three portions of fish and chips must have saved Don a lot of money . . . But then she scolded herself for having a nasty, suspicious nature.

At Agar Road, Sunday dinner was the highlight of the week, and Jo usually made a stew, because with a generous mixture of vegetables it helped to stretch the meat ration and leftovers could be served up as soup. She always provided an old-fashioned pudding – jam roly-poly, or an apple pie.

When Aunt Topsy was alive, they had eaten in the kitchen, but Jo suggested they should have Sunday dinner in the parlour, to make it more of a special occasion – besides, the wireless set was in the parlour. There were some good programmes at midday on a Sunday, like *Two-Way Family Favourites* and *The Billy Cotton Band Show* – bright, cheerful music, with a few laughs.

One afternoon, when the meal was over and they were clearing away, a REME sergeant somewhere in Germany requested a special record, dedicated to his girl-friend: Glenn Miller's *American Patrol*.

Mr Mulligan tapped his feet to the lively quickstep, saying: 'I was a great dancer in my day! If I was a few years younger, I'd show the lot of yez. Come on, Jo, come along, Chrissie – let's see you trip the light fantastic!'

Taking the folded tablecloth from Chris, Jo danced round the table and tossed it into the sideboard drawer as she passed. Chris joined in and they quickstepped round the room, while Mr Mulligan clapped his hands, stamping out the rhythm – until the music stopped abruptly.

Mr Penberthy had switched off the wireless. 'Have you forgotten what day this is?' he demanded. 'Can't you treat the Sabbath with respect?'

'Ah, come on, they're only dancing!' protested Mr Mulligan.

Mr Penberthy's face was white with anger as he rounded on Jo. 'You should be ashamed – and you, Christine. How can you be so thoughtless, with your poor mother recently taken from us?'

Stricken, Chris gulped: 'I'm sorry,' then rushed out of the room and up the stairs.

Jo told Mr Penberthy: 'She's suffered enough lately, without you making her feeling worse.'

'I'll go and have a word with her.' Mr Mulligan heaved himself out of his chair. 'I'll tell her you didn't mean what you said. I'll say it's indigestion, on account of you bolting your food so quick!'

When he had gone, Jo asked: 'Wouldn't you rather see Chris looking happy, than have her weeping and wailing?'

Mr Penberthy replied stiffly: 'There are certain conventions which should be observed. I have lived in this house for a good many years, and I believe I know what Mrs Bone would have wished. I'm sorry to have to say this, but I fear I shall have to seek other accommodation.'

'There's no need for that. If I was rude, I apologise, but really—'

'No – hear me out,' he interrupted her. 'I have been contemplating this move for some time. I have a colleague at Ealing who has offered to provide me with board and lodging. The increase in fares will strain my resources, but you leave me no alternative. Please accept my notice; I shall move out by the end of the week.'

'Just because we've had a difference of opinion—'

'Not only that. In any case, this was hardly a suitable arrangement: you are a young lady, and I am a bachelor. There could have been gossip – people might have made personal remarks. I'm sure you understand.'

With that, the old gentleman stalked out of the room. For a moment Jo felt very angry, but then the sheer absurdity of the situation hit her, and she began to laugh.

Next morning, a postcard arrived at Agar Road; a picture of the Albert

Bridge, it had been addressed to Rope Walk and re-addressed by Sarah Venus in an almost illegible scrawl which must have given the postman a headache. The message said simply:

Dear Jo: Malcolm and I are very pleased to say that our family has now increased. Michael Bernard Jones was born on 24 April, weighing 6 lbs, 4 oz. If you have an hour to spare we would love you to meet the new addition. Drop in any time – I don't go out much! All the best – Pat.

After breakfast, Chris began to get ready for school. She was still subdued; Mr Penberthy's harsh reproof had upset her a good deal.

On the spur of the moment, Jo followed her along the hall and stopped her at the front door, saying: 'What time will you be coming home this afternoon? You haven't got games or anything?'

'No, the usual time – why?'

'I'm going round to see a friend of mine. If I meet you after school, would you like to come with me?'

'No, thanks. Your posh friends wouldn't want me butting in.'

'Her name's Pat Jones. She's got a new baby, only a couple of weeks old, and she's dying to show him off to everybody. Won't you keep me company?'

Chris, who had a weakness for very small children, said: 'All right, I'll see you at the school gates.'

She was in a more cheerful mood after school, and as they walked along to Blenheim Terrace, she wanted to know: 'Who's Pat Jones? You never talked about her before.'

'I haven't known her long, though I knew her husband years ago. Do you remember when I worked at Brydens? Malcolm Jones helped me get the job – he still works there.'

'Then he went and married someone else?' Chris's romantic imagination was fired immediately: 'That's rotten. Was he your boy-friend?'

'Certainly not! And before you start getting any ideas, I'm not at all jealous. Pat's very nice – you'll like her.'

When they arrived at number 12, the door was opened by Malcolm himself, and Jo stammered: 'Oh, hello – Pat's card said drop in any time . . . This is my cousin, Christine. I didn't expect you to be home so early – if it's not convenient, we can come back some other—'

'Don't be silly, come in!' beamed Malcolm. 'How d'you do, Christine?' He ushered them in to the front room, calling: 'We've got visitors!'

Pat was sitting on the sofa with a Moses basket beside her and a white bundle of baby on her lap. The last time Jo saw her, she had been plumply pretty – today she was radiant, her face shining with happiness.

Christine was introduced, and Sandra, who had been playing with building bricks on the floor, said clearly and distinctly: 'I'm Sandra and I'm nearly three. He's called Michael Bernard and he's my brother.'

'That's right,' Pat agreed. 'Michael after my dad and Bernard after Malcolm's, so that ought to keep everybody happy.' Then, seeing Chris's look of rapture, she added: 'Would you like to nurse him for a bit?'

'Can I really?' Awestruck, Chris took the baby on her lap with great care, and exclaimed: 'He's smiling at me!'

Determined not to be overlooked, Sandra broke in again: 'That isn't really Mike's cot – it's mine, isn't it, Mum? I had it first, but now I'm too big I've let him borrow it. I let him have my toys as well – some of them. Shall I go and find my fluffy rabbit, Mum? Would he like to play with it?'

'I don't think he's quite big enough for that, but you can show it to him if you like.'

'All right then, I'll go and fetch it.'

Sandra trotted off purposefully, and Jo asked: 'How does she feel about having a baby brother?'

'We're doing our best to explain that he belongs to all of us. We tell her he's her baby as well as ours,' said Pat. 'It's working pretty well, too. The only trouble is, she wants to take him to bed with her!'

'How lovely.' Jo quoted: ' "First a girl and then a boy" . . . You must be very pleased, Malcolm.'

He grinned sheepishly. 'Yes, I am. Mind you, I'd have been just as pleased if we'd had another girl.'

Pat interrupted: 'Don't believe a word of it. He's like a dog with two tails now there's another man in the family.' She looked at the clock on the mantelpiece. 'Have you got time to stop for a cuppa?'

'Well, we mustn't stay long, we've got to get back to Agar Road.' Jo turned to Chris: 'If we keep the old gents waiting for their tea, they'll never forgive us, will they?'

'Mr Mulligan won't mind,' said Chris, without taking her eyes off the baby. 'And Mr Penberthy's leaving, so it doesn't matter what he thinks.'

'That settles it then.' Jo smiled. 'We'll stay for tea, please.'

Pat stood up. 'Come and talk to me while I put the kettle on. We'll leave Malcolm and Chris to look after his lordship – all right, Malc?'

Before he could reply, Sandra returned, dragging a grubby toy rabbit by one ear, and announced firmly: 'I'll look after him – he's our family!'

Pat laughed, and took Jo into the back kitchen, which was festooned with damp nappies and baby-clothes. 'I'm not going to apologise for the mess, it's your own fault for coming round on washing-day – though with two kids in the house, practically every day's a washing-day here. I tried hanging it all outside to dry when the sun came out, but there were so many soots blowing in from the railway-sidings, I had to wash them all over again.'

As they waited for the kettle to boil, she went on: 'If you don't mind me asking, who are Mr Mulligan and Mr Whatsisname? And what are you doing at Agar Road? I thought you were living at the Rope Walk?'

Jo explained the reason for the move. When she had finished, Pat said: 'I must say, I take my hat off to you. How you manage to look after Christine and two lodgers and still work half-days, I just don't know. Oh, well, p'raps when my two get a bit older, I'll be able to take a job myself – though I don't know what Malcolm would have to say about it. He didn't mind when we were in the Army, but now we're in Civvy Street, he's got some rather old-fashioned ideas about a woman's place being in the home. Still, he's come up trumps lately, bless him – I couldn't have managed without him.'

'I wondered about that – how did he get off work this afternoon?'

'He'd got two weeks' holiday due to him, so he decided to take them now. Well, we weren't going away – it would cost too much money. P'raps later on we'll have a day-trip to Brighton. Are you and Chris planning to go away?'

'Oh, no,' said Jo. 'We're not going anywhere.'

When they took the tea-tray into the front room, Pat offered to put Michael back in his cot, saying to Chris: 'I expect you're getting tired of nursing him, aren't you?'

'Oh, no, I don't mind a bit,' said Chris, then glanced at Jo and said reluctantly: 'Unless – would you like to hold him, Jo? You haven't had a turn yet.'

'I'd love to.' Jo took the baby from her. He looked up at her with innocent blue eyes, searching her face, then found her little finger and curled his fist round it.

Feeling the warmth of his fragile body, she remembered that not so long ago, she had thought she might be pregnant herself, and was transfixed by a sudden yearning. Turning her head, she found Sandra at her elbow, watching her closely.

She seized the opportunity, saying: 'No, this isn't fair – it's Sandra's turn, not mine . . . You take him, love. Like you said, he's your family.'

Monday was washing-day at Lavender Hill, too.

Halfway up the stone staircase, the small boy remembered what day it was. Mum would be in a state – she always got hot and bothered on Mondays.

When he entered the flat, the soggy smell of steam and yellow soap came to meet him; shirts and vests and pants were drying over a clothes-horse on the hearthrug, and his mother emerged from the kitchen – her face red, her hair tied under a duster, her sleeves rolled up above the elbow.

'Oh, it's you,' she said. 'I thought it might be your dad.'

He followed her into the kitchen, where she was doing the ironing, and asked: 'Why – where's Dad gone?'

'He's out. And don't start pestering me with questions. If I scorch one of his shirts again, there'll be trouble!'

'Yes, but where is he? Out where?'

She set down the iron and wiped her face with the back of her hand: 'If you must know, he's gone up west.'

The boy's face lit up. 'About a job?'

'It might be. They rang up this morning, and asked him to go in to the office; there'd been an enquiry. Now don't go getting excited, that's all it was – just an enquiry.'

'I bet it's a job. They wouldn't have asked him to go in if it wasn't a job.' He rushed at her and hugged her. 'I bet it is!'

She ruffled his hair, then said quietly: 'I don't want to talk about it. It's bad luck if you expect things to happen – best not to count your chickens. Now leave me to finish my ironing. I was late starting the wash today, and I'm all behind like the old cow's tail. You can make yourself useful, laying the table.'

'What have we got for tea?'

'Spam and salad – and don't look at me like that, you know I don't have time to make a cooked meal of a Monday.'

The boy went back to the other room and opened the sideboard drawer, taking out a tablecloth and a handful of cutlery. He was just shaking out the cloth when he heard footsteps on the stairs; they approached the front door and stopped. The boy held his breath.

The door opened, and Dad walked in. He looked at the boy without speaking.

'Well?' said the boy.

Mum appeared in the kitchen doorway. 'Any news?'

A slow smile crept over Dad's face, and the boy shouted: 'It's a job – it is, isn't it? I said it was!'

Almost in a whisper, Mum asked: 'Is it – truly?'

Dad nodded. 'Starting next weekend. We've got to be in Coventry Friday night.'

Mum ran to him and threw her arms round him, then asked: 'But what about the van? We haven't got the van now.'

'It's all right, don't fuss.' He patted her shoulder. 'I've spoken to Miguel. I told you he'd see us right.'

On Friday afternoon, Jo was alone at Agar Road when there was a knock at the door. She had done her weekly shopping on her way back from Galleon House, and was now unloading two carrier-bags at the kitchen table. Rather puzzled, she went to the front door and opened it.

'Well, you did tell me to come to tea,' said Vee. 'And you're not on the phone here, are you?'

Jo ushered her in and Vee lowered her voice, asking: 'Is this a good moment? Tell me if it isn't and I'll disappear.'

'Couldn't be better. We've got the house to ourselves. Hang your hat and coat on the pegs – I've just got to put away the shopping.'

Entering the back-kitchen, Vee looked round her, then said: 'I simply don't believe it. It's just the same. After all these years, it's the same as ever.'

For a moment, Jo couldn't think what she meant, then realised: 'Of course, I was forgetting, you haven't been here since . . .'

'And nothing's changed – it's like stepping back in time.' Vee's legs were shaking, and she slumped into a chair.

'Some things have changed – Auntie Topsy had a new stove put in just after the war.'

'It all looks the same to me. I always hated this house, when Mum brought us round to tea . . .' Vee buried her face in her hands. 'It's frightening – the way it brings everything back.'

Jo put an arm round her: 'I can imagine . . . Sit quietly for a minute. You'll get used to it.'

Vee shook her head. 'I keep expecting Mum to come through that door.' Her eyes glistened with tears. 'I don't know how you can bear it.'

'It's different for me. I lived here for years, when I was growing up.'

'But you hated it – you said so. I don't understand how you could—' Vee broke off, listening, as a key turned in the front door. 'Who's that?'

Jo called out: 'Hello?'

The door slammed with a bang that rattled the house, and an Irish voice replied: 'It's meself, darlin' I've been stretchin' me legs for the good of me health.' Leaning heavily on a walking-stick, he entered the kitchen, and at once apologised. 'Glory be, you've a visitor. I didn't mean to intrude.'

'You're not intruding. Vee, this is Mr Mulligan—'

Vee cut in urgently: 'Vanessa – my name's Vanessa.'

'Oh, yes. Mr Mulligan, I'd like you to meet a friend of mine, Vanessa Coburn.'

Mr Mulligan doffed his old tweed cap before shaking hands. 'It's a pleasure and a privilege, Miss Coburn – or is it Mrs Coburn? Sure, you're only a slip of a girl, but these days there's no knowing!'

'I'm not married.' Vee smiled. 'Please call me Vanessa.'

'I will so, Vanessa – proud to make your acquaintance.' He glanced at Jo. 'But I've had a good walk, and I've a mind to put me feet up for an hour. You'll excuse me, I hope?'

With another flourish of his tweed cap, he retreated, and they heard him climbing the stairs, his walking-stick clattering against the banisters.

Vee groaned. 'I'd forgotten about the lodgers – why didn't you warn me? He was here when I was little – it's a miracle he didn't remember me!'

'Well, you have changed a bit since then!' said Jo. 'I wasn't expecting him. He stays out most afternoons – if it's wet, he goes to the reading-room at the library, and works his way through the papers.'

'There used to be two of them – another one—'

'Mr Penberthy's out at work; he never gets back till after six. Don't look so worried!'

'It's all very well saying that, but you're so careless – calling me "Vee" like that. Suppose you'd called me "Vee" in front of Chrissie? She'd guess right away – she knows you had a sister called Vee, doesn't she?'

'I'm not sure; we never talk much about the old days. Anyway, I'll call you Vanessa when she's here, I promise.'

'What time does she get home from school?'

'Any time now, but she couldn't possibly recognise you after all this time.' Jo filled the kettle, saying over her shoulder: 'You won't have to bother about Mr Penberthy after today – he's leaving this weekend.'

'Oh, why's that?'

'He said it wouldn't be proper for an eligible bachelor like him to live under the same roof as an unmarried lady like me. But the real reason is me having the wireless on too loud – he's a terrible old stick-in-the-mud.'

'So you'll be glad to get rid of him?'

'In a way, though it's going to make things difficult. There'll only be Mr Mulligan's rent coming in – two pounds a week – plus what I earn at Galleon House. I'll have to advertise for another lodger, but—'

'Do be careful, there are some awful people about. You'll have to make sure you get someone you can trust . . .' After a moment, Vee went on: 'I suppose – you haven't heard any more from Don, have you?'

'No . . . Funny – I was just thinking about him.'

'Must be telepathy.'

'Not really. It was what you said – about trusting people.'

'Oh, don't start that again! I do trust Don – only, since he can't ring me, I have to rely on you for messages. I wondered if he'd spoken to you since Saturday?'

'No, I haven't heard a word.'

'That's so like him, isn't it? Weeks go by, and then he turns up out of the blue, as if nothing had happened.'

When the kettle boiled Jo began to make the tea, saying: 'Let's take it into the front room, shall we?'

'In the parlour? We never had tea in there when we were little. Don't you remember, we weren't allowed to touch anything?'

'Well, I've tried to brighten the old place up a bit.'

Jo had taken down the lace curtains, and sunlight streamed through the windows; in the fireplace, a vase of lupins made a fine splash of colour.

Vee said: 'It's better than it was, though I still wouldn't want to live here. What's it like upstairs? Have you got Aunt Topsy's room?'

'Not yet – I'm getting Chris used to the idea gradually. I don't want to rush things.'

'So you're still sharing that little bedroom with her? You are good . . .' Vee hesitated, then went on: 'If you can't find anyone for the spare room, I could probably help out. I get a decent allowance for clothes and stuff – I could easily spare a few pounds every week.'

'That's very nice of you, but I'm sure I'll find someone.'

'But I'd like to help, really I would.' Vee lifted her head, listening to the sound of the front gate swinging open, and footsteps on the path. Anxiously, she mouthed: 'Chrissie?'

Jo nodded: 'She's got her own key, in case I'm out when she gets home.'

The front door opened and shut. Vee sat rigidly, waiting, and Chris walked into the room, saying: 'Oh, hello . . .'

Vee forced a smile, but said nothing.

Jo said easily: 'This is Vanessa Coburn, a friend of mine; she's just dropped in for tea. Why don't you get yourself a cup?'

'Right-ho.' With another thoughtful look at the visitor, Chris went off to the kitchen.

Vee whispered: 'I'm terrified.'

'Don't be.'

Chris returned with a cup, pulling up a chair, but never taking her

237

eyes off the stranger. Jo tried to think of something to say, but could come up with nothing better than: 'How was school today?'

'Same as usual – boring.' Suddenly Chris asked Vee directly: 'Have I seen you before?'

Vee opened her mouth, but was unable to speak, and Jo replied for her: 'Vanessa lives across the river. I met her in the park one day.'

'Oh . . .' Chris still seemed puzzled. 'I thought – you remind me of somebody, that's all.'

Vee heard herself saying in a strained, unreal voice: 'Somebody you used to know?'

'I can't remember.' Chris struggled to explain: 'It's like – trying to remember a dream after you wake up. It sort of disappears when you think about it.' She turned her attention to the plate of biscuits on the table: 'Can I have one? I'm starving – we had frogspawn for dinner again.'

Seeing Vee's horrified expression, Jo explained with a grin: 'Sago pudding. School dinners are rather unpopular.'

'Unpopular?' Chris echoed indignantly. 'They're disgusting!'

She launched into a long catalogue, listing the iniquities of school meals, and as the others joined in the discussion, the tension lifted and the danger was over.

Late that evening, Russell Wade was in his studio at Galleon House.

He felt disturbed and restless; it was a familiar sensation, and it haunted him more and more frequently. Each time it began, he tried to fight against it; perhaps, if he kept himself busy – if he could throw himself into his work – he might be able to resist temptation.

For some time he had been planning to collect up the photographs that had accumulated in his studio – pictures of his own sculpture, taken over the years. He had an idea that they would make a book – the sort of expensive volume some art publisher might care to bring out. Perhaps that would help to keep his reputation alive.

As he shuffled the pictures into some kind of sequence, he heard the front door open and shut, then the sound of someone crossing the hall. He listened as the next studio door was unlocked, and called out: 'Reggie? Is that you?'

There was no reply.

Going to investigate, he found the door of Studio Three wide open.

One green-shaded table-lamp had been switched on. By its light, Russell recognised the intruder – that American friend of Jo's.

'What the devil are you doing here?' he barked.

Don greeted him calmly. 'I was modelling for Mr Bentley this afternoon, and I left something behind. He lent me his keys, so I could come by and pick it up.'

'And have you found it, whatever it was?'

'No, it's not here.'

'In that case, I'd be extremely grateful if you'd clear out. I don't allow strangers to walk in and out without my permission. I shall have a few words to say to Mr Bentley tomorrow.'

Don switched off the light but stayed where he was. 'I wouldn't do that, if I were you,' he said.

Russell could no longer see his face, just a silhouette against the grey blur of the curtained window, but he could hear that the young man was smiling.

'What do you mean by that?' he asked.

'The fact is, Reggie went out to see some friends tonight, so I couldn't ask him for the keys – I just kinda borrowed them.' In the same casual drawl, he continued: 'Is anyone else around? Or is it just you and me?'

Russell answered without stopping to think: 'No, there's nobody here, but—'

'Great, then I can tell you the whole thing. I had to make sure you were on your own. That's what I came for, so's we could have a little chat – just the two of us.'

A tremor of fear ran through Russell, and he tried to deal with it by losing his temper. 'Leave this house immediately, or I'll call the police!'

'I wouldn't do that, not if I was you.' Don strolled out of the studio, his smile as brilliant as ever. 'What I've got to say, you wouldn't want the cops to hear.'

'What are you talking about?'

'About your wife. You see, I know what happened, the night she died.'

That was all he said. He just stood and smiled, while the world stopped turning and time stood still. At last Russell managed to say: 'I think perhaps we'd better go upstairs.'

They walked up to the top floor. Russell led the way into the living-room, then turned to face him: 'Look here, I don't know what Reggie's been telling you, but—'

'Reggie never said a thing.' Without waiting to be asked, Don sat in one of the big armchairs, making himself comfortable. 'I know all about you, Mr Wade. Hey, now, don't go upsetting yourself! Just sit right down and listen to me, 'cos I'm gonna be the best goddam friend you ever had.'

Next morning, Jo arrived at her usual time, and began to make Russell's breakfast, but something was bothering her.

From the moment she walked into the flat, she knew there was something different about it. She smelled stale tobacco smoke and fumes of alcohol; Russell must have had some people here last night. Picking up his breakfast tray, she hoped he would not wake up with a hangover and a bad temper.

As she left the kitchen she heard a door open at the other end of the passage – the door to the room that had once been Laura's . . .

The tray rattled in her hands as a figure emerged from the doorway, tousle-haired and yawning, dressed in a khaki undervest and shorts.

'Oh, hi there. I guess I'd better go put some clothes on,' Don mumbled, and disappeared again, shutting the door.

Jo leaned against the wall, startled, bewildered, and very angry. Breathing a little faster, she walked down the corridor and knocked at Russell's door.

'Come in.' He looked terrible – pale and haggard. 'Oh, it's you.'

'Yes – who did you expect it to be?'

He rolled over, burying his face in the pillows as she put the tray down. Gripping his shoulder, she shook him. 'Russell, sit up! I've got to talk to you.'

'It's too early,' he protested thickly. 'What's the matter?'

'I want to know why Don's here. I want to know what's going on.'

'Oh, you've seen him, have you?' Unhappily, he dragged himself into a sitting position, and tried to explain: 'Your friend turned up last night. He told me he needed somewhere to stay, so – I said he could stay here . . . For the time being.'

'Yes – but *why*? It doesn't make sense!'

'There's something you don't know.' He rubbed his bloodshot

eyes. 'I didn't find out myself till last night. The fact is, his name isn't Donald Scott, it's Donald Stanway. His father was Harold Stanway – Laura's first husband, in California.' He faced her at last. 'That's why he was so anxious to meet me – he's Laura's son.'

Unable to meet her eyes, he turned his head away, and she felt sure he wasn't telling her the truth, but she didn't know why.

Chapter Sixteen

'I'LL NEVER GET BACK to sleep now – I might as well go and run a bath.' Russell threw back the bedclothes and swung his feet to the floor: 'I thought you'd enjoy having your friend to stay for a while.'

'Perhaps I will, when I get used to the idea,' Jo said crisply. 'Am I supposed to make lunch for him as well?'

'Yes, why not? Have you any objections?'

'Why should I?' She regarded him steadily. 'It's your house – you can invite anyone you like.'

Later, when she went in to clean the living-room, she found Don with his feet up on one of the chintz sofas, leafing through a copy of *Picture Post*.

'Hi there!' He glanced up and smiled. 'Where's the great man?'

'Downstairs in the studio. I wouldn't go down if I were you. He doesn't like being disturbed when he's busy.'

'I won't disturb him.'

'I'm glad. But he won't be very pleased if he catches you with your feet on the sofa, leaving dirty marks on the cushions.'

Don did not move. 'It didn't seem to bother him any, last night.'

Jo turned away and started dusting – then saw that Laura's photographs were on top of the piano once more.

'I see the photos have come out of the cupboard,' she said, with an edge to her voice. 'Whose idea was it? Yours – or his?'

'His, of course. How would I know he had those pictures stashed away?'

She ran a finger over one of the silver frames. 'They're getting rather tarnished. I shall have to find some metal-polish.'

As she moved to the door, he asked: 'Are you mad at me or something?'

She shrugged her shoulders. 'What do you expect? If you're really Laura Stanway's son, you could have—'

'What makes you say "if"?' He dropped the magazine and stood up. 'Do you think I'm not?'

'It doesn't make any difference what I think, does it? The question is, does Russell believe it?'

He laughed suddenly. 'You think I'm conning the old man – is that it? D'you suppose this is some sort of game I'm playing?'

'I don't know. I'm no good at guessing-games.' When she looked into his eyes, he stared right back at her, giving nothing away. Holding her ground, she went on: 'Do you have any letters from her – any papers?'

'Any proof I'm his stepson?' He laughed again. 'Right this minute – no, I don't. But can you prove I'm not? Russell asked a whole slew of questions last night, and I got top grades. Dates, places – I knew 'em all.'

'Anyone could have found that out; there must be reference books. What about your family in Texas? Your father on the cattle-ranch, your mother, your brothers and sister—'

'Mom ran off with some talent-scout when I was two years old. Daddy died a few years later – broken-hearted, I guess. So I kinda made up a family for myself. You should know how it feels, when you got nobody.'

Jo was fighting a losing battle. 'If you're her son, why didn't you tell anyone until now? Why didn't you say anything, the first time we met?'

'I wasn't too sure what kind of welcome I'd get. She'd just died, remember? There was an inquest – I read about it in the newspapers. That's why I started coming down to London every chance I got, asking questions, and I found out you worked here.'

'And that's why you started following me. What a fool I was.'

'I took a real shine to you, Jo. The more I knew you, the more I liked you. You gotta believe me.'

'Have I? What about Vee? Did you take a shine to her too?' She made for the door. 'Excuse me, I've got to start getting your lunch ready.'

He called after her: 'Next time you speak to her, tell her I want to see her – tell her I love her. Will you do that thing?'

'I hope you don't mind me coming round like this,' Jo began.

She was in the saloon on the houseboat, and Reggie threw her a puzzled smile. 'Always a pleasure to see you, Jo, any time. I'm sorry the place is such a pig-sty; I generally clear up if I'm expecting visitors.'

'I suppose I should have come down when you were in the studio, but I was afraid Russell might hear us. This is – rather private.'

'Something about Russell?'

'Mostly about Don.'

'Don?' Reggie frowned. 'He's not living here any more. I don't even know where he's gone.'

'I do – he's moved into Galleon House. He's staying in Russell's flat.'

Reggie shook his head. 'Oh, no, Don would have said if he'd been planning—'

'I think it all happened very quickly.'

Jo went on to tell him what Russell had said. When she had finished, he repeated helplessly: 'Laura Stanway's son? I hadn't the remotest idea.'

'None of us knew about it. Didn't he ever say anything to you, about Laura? Anything at all?'

'No, he never talked about his family. When you come right down to it, I didn't really know much about him.'

'But surely, if he is her son, he'd have said something?'

'Are you saying it isn't true? Just some sort of trick he's playing?'

'I don't know what to think. I'm afraid I don't trust him any more.'

Reggie's shoulders slumped. 'You're quite right, of course – he's a bit of a rogue. Some days he'd be practically broke, asking me to lend him some money – other times he seemed to be rolling in it. Not just English money: dollars, guilders, French francs—'

'Did he ever pay back what he'd borrowed from you?'

'No. But he was very generous in other ways. He'd bring home bottles of scotch, or cigarettes, or great tins of meat. Black market, I suppose.'

Jo remembered Pete Hobden; he had tried to warn her, but she wouldn't listen.

'I say, are you all right? You've gone rather pale.' Reggie stood up. 'I expect it's the motion of the boat. When one of those tugs goes past, the old tub heaves up and down a bit. How about a nip of brandy?' He uncorked a half-full bottle which had been buried under a Spanish shawl. 'This was part of Don's loot, funnily enough. Let me find a clean glass.'

'No, please don't bother. I'm all right.'

She did feel rather sick, but it had nothing to do with the motion of the boat.

In Battersea Park, roses were bursting into bloom, and the summer blossomed into a heatwave.

Jo moved into Aunt Topsy's room at last, so she could go to bed with nothing on except a sheet, but even then she lay awake for hours, worrying about Russell – and Don.

After a particularly bad night, she decided she must talk to Vee. When Russell was in the studio and Don was having a bath, she phoned the house at Cheyne Walk.

One of the maids answered, and when Jo asked to speak to Vanessa, the girl said: 'I'm sorry, Miss Vanessa's gone out. Can I take a message?'

'Not really. Do you know when she'll be coming back?'

'Not till about tea-time, miss. She's lunching with friends, and I believe she's going to the baths this afternoon.'

'The baths?'

'The swimming baths, miss. I know she took her costume and a towel in her bag. She's been going almost every day since the heatwave started.'

'Do you know which baths she goes to?'

'The Chelsea Baths, miss, just up the road, in Chelsea Manor Street.'

'Oh, yes, it's near Chelsea Town Hall, isn't it?'

'That's right. You might catch her there – between three and half-past, I should think.'

'Three to half-past. Thank you. If she happens to ring before that, could you say I'll meet her there?'

'Very good, miss. If she does, I'll certainly tell her.'

Jo was planning a cold supper for Mr Mulligan and Chris in any case – it was too hot for a cooked meal. She had been going to turn out the parlour. Well, it would just have to make do with a lick and a promise for once.

Meanwhile there was plenty to do here. When Don finished his bath she must ask if he would be in to lunch – sometimes he lounged around the flat most of the day, sometimes he went out on business. She felt more comfortable when he went out.

Dusting the piano, she was unaware that Don had finished his bath. There were damp footprints along the corridor, and a wet patch outside the door showed where he had been standing, but by the time she left the drawing-room they had dried out.

She was peeling potatoes when he appeared in the kitchen doorway, and she asked: 'Will you be in to lunch?'

He said cheerfully: 'Don't bother about me, babe, I'm gonna be pretty busy. See you tomorrow morning.'

At three o'clock she was outside the Chelsea Baths, waiting for Vee. Swimmers were going in and out, and the man in the ticket-office eyed her curiously.

After a while it occurred to her that Vee might have turned up earlier and gone in already, so she went to the ticket-office and said: 'I've been waiting for a friend, but she might be inside. Can I go through and look for her?'

The man wore a blue uniform with metal buttons, and he took his duties very seriously.

'We don't admit spectators except on gala nights and contests. It's swimmers only. Costumes can be hired for a small deposit, also towels.'

She made up her mind. 'All right, I'll have both, please.'

Looking her up and down, he said: 'Small to medium,' and produced a rolled-up towel and a shapeless garment made of black wool.

The costume had been rinsed since it was last hired out, but it was still damp. The thought of climbing into it was unappealing, but she couldn't back out now. She found a cubicle and changed quickly; the wet wool clung to her skin, and she decided to jump into the water right away.

She could not find Vee at first. The pool was very crowded and the cold water was a shock, but it was a relief after the heat outside, and she swam a length of the bath, trying not to collide with anyone.

As she turned at the deep end, a breathless voice exclaimed: 'Fancy seeing you – what a coincidence!'

Vee's hair was tucked inside a bright red bathing-cap that matched her smart red swimsuit.

Treading water, Jo retorted: 'It's not a coincidence. When I phoned, the maid said I might find you here. We've got to talk.'

They climbed out of the bath, sitting on the tiled surround with their feet dangling in the water. As simply as possible, Jo explained what had happened. Vee stared at her incredulously.

'Russell's stepson? Why didn't he tell us?'

'He says he couldn't tell anyone till he knew what sort of welcome he'd get, but I don't believe he's Laura Stanway's son at all.'

'Why would he say so, if it isn't true?'

'Perhaps he was hoping he might do himself a bit of good.'

Vee looked very shocked. 'Don's not like that.'

'I'm sorry, Vee, I'm only just beginning to realise it myself. Don uses people for what he can get out of them.'

'What do you mean?'

'He used me as a way of getting to Russell. When he met you, he tried to use you as well – he tried to move into your house – he even used Reggie in the same way, but he moved out again when something better came along. And now he's got his hooks into Russell.'

Vee shook her head. 'You've got it all wrong, Jo. I think I know Don better than you do, and I'm sure—'

A shadow fell across them. They looked up, shading their eyes against the sunshine that poured down from the glass roof.

'That's right, angel,' said Don. 'I guess you know me better'n anyone.'

The white trunks he wore emphasised his tan. He flexed his muscles, as Jo asked him pointblank: 'How long have you been listening?'

'Just this second arrived.' He grinned. 'Don't worry – I didn't hear a thing.'

'But how did you know we were here?' Vee scrambled to her feet. 'I suppose the maid told you?'

'Nobody told me, babe, I just felt like taking a dip. C'mon, race you both to the shallow end, OK?'

Jo stood up too. 'I'm sorry, I have to go now. I'll talk to you another time, Vee. Goodbye, Don.'

And she walked off to the changing cubicles.

Don watched her go, then asked Vee: 'What's biting her all of a sudden? Was it something I said?'

'I don't think so.' Vee gave him a searching look. 'Tell me honestly, Don – are you sure you didn't know I was here?'

'How in hell could I have known?' He put his arm around her shoulders, and her skin tingled at his touch. 'I guess it's fate, bringing us together.'

Although Vee had offered to help, Jo was determined to pay her own way at Agar Road.

A local solicitor was sorting out the complexities of the estate, and of Chris's situation. She had a Navy pension due to her as the daughter of CPO Bone, and a trust was being set up by the family doctor and the vicar of All Saints, ensuring that the money would be paid into a bank on her behalf.

But for Jo, money would still be tight, so when Mr Penberthy moved out, she put a card in the window of the nearest Sub-Post Office, advertising for a new lodger: 'Comfortable room, breakfast and evening meal provided. Suit older man, ex-serviceman preferred.'

The last phrase was Mr Mulligan's idea; he had never really hit it off with Mr Penberthy.

At first the card produced no result, until one afternoon during the school holidays, when Chris had gone to the Park with Mr Mulligan, there was a thunderous knock at the door.

As soon as Jo opened it, a large, greasy man lurched past her, beaming mistily and saying: 'Gorra room to let, have yer?'

The smell of beer and sweat hung around him like a cloud, and Jo began to say: 'Well, I'm not sure if—'

'Wotcher mean, not sure? You gorra room or aincher?' he demanded.

'Yes, there is a room, but I—'

'Thass or'right then – I'll take it! Corp'ral Fred Fookes, ex Catering Corps, demobilised – me pals call me Fatso.'

'The trouble is . . .' Jo tried to invent an excuse: 'The room's more or less promised to someone else, so I'm afraid I—'

'Don't be afraid!' Fatso reeled into the front parlour and flopped into an armchair: 'You get shot of 'im, whoever he is. I'm the one yer looking for, 'cos I got something the others ain't got . . . I got sustifficates!'

'Oh, have you?'

'Best damn caterin' sustifficates you ever saw. Diplomas long as yer arm – you'd be surprised. An' I'll tell yer what I'm gonna do. I'm gonna do yer cookin' – all yer cookin' – fer free. No charge, out of the goodness of me heart – breakfast, supper, bangers and mash, spotted dick, brown windsor – the lot. An' in return you can knock a bit off of me rent, OK?'

'I'm afraid not. I was trying to tell you, the room's not vacant now. I'm very sorry.'

At that moment she heard a key turn in the lock, and the front door opened.

'That'll be the others coming in, wanting their tea.' She tried to haul him up on to his feet. 'You'll have to go now.'

He fended her off. 'I'm all ri', don't you bother 'bout me.'

Chris came in, closely followed by Mr Mulligan. Taking in the situation at a glance, he said: 'What in heaven's name is going on? Who are you?'

'Corp'ral Fred Fookes, call me Fatso.'

'And I'm Sergeant-Major Mulligan, so you'll stand to attention when you speak to me, Fookes! Get on your feet!'

Swaying, Fatso pulled himself up and stood to attention. 'Corp'ral Fookes reportin' for duty – *sah*!'

Jo explained: 'He came about the vacancy, but I told him that the room's already been taken, so—'

'Oh, has it?' Chris joined the conversation. 'You never told me.'

'It happened while you were out,' said Jo quickly. 'So I'm afraid Mr Fookes has had a wasted journey. I was just going to see him out.'

'You can leave that to me,' said Mr Mulligan, grimly. 'By the right – quick – march! One, two, one, two . . .'

Obediently, the big man stumbled out of the room and along the hall. On the doorstep, he called out to Jo: ''Ow about if I do the cookin' wivout yer knocking anyfing off of the rent? And thass me final offer!'

'I'm sorry. Goodbye, Mr Fookes!'

'Call me Fatso . . .' He threw her a last oily leer, and tumbled out of the house just before Mr Mulligan slammed the door.

'He was in the Catering Corps,' Jo explained. 'But I don't really think he'd have fitted in, do you?'

'Who's this other man you've let the room to?' Chris wanted to know.

'There isn't another man. Well, I had to say something, didn't I?' She turned to Mr Mulligan. 'I never knew you were a Sergeant-Major!'

Mr Mulligan winked. 'Ah, no – well, I had to say something, didn't I?'

He plumped up the cushions of the chair Mr Fookes had been sitting in, and took his place with an air of quiet satisfaction.

'Good for you!' said Jo. 'I'll put the kettle on.'

She was halfway to the kitchen when there was another knock at the door.

'Oh, not again!' she exclaimed. 'Don't bother, Mr Mulligan, I'll get rid of him this time.' Calling out: 'Won't you ever take no for an answer?' she opened the front door.

But it wasn't Mr Fookes. Vee was on the step with Don beside her, carrying a shopping-bag.

'I never take no for an answer,' he said. 'Hadn't you noticed?'

'We've invited ourselves to tea,' Vee chimed in. 'Is that all right?'

When they entered the parlour, Mr Mulligan struggled to his feet, saying: 'Miss Coburn – it's grand to see you. And you too, sir.'

Jo introduced them. Don shook hands with Mr Mulligan, then with Chris, telling her: 'My, but you're beautiful. I've heard a lot about you, Chrissie, but nobody told me you look like Rita Hayworth!'

Chris, who had been called 'Carrots' or 'Ginger' from the day she went to school, blushed with happiness.

'I know we shouldn't barge in uninvited,' Vee went on, 'but we've brought some goodies for everybody.'

She unpacked the shopping-bag, producing a Dundee cake stuffed with fruit and covered in almonds, saying: 'Aunt Elspeth has them sent down from Scotland. If you put it in a tin, it will keep for ages. And Don's got something for you too.'

Don lifted out the biggest tin Jo had ever seen. 'Smoked Virginia ham, cooked with persimmons and glazed with molasses – you're gonna love it.'

Jo said stiffly: 'That's very kind, but I couldn't possibly—'

'Don't be silly!' said Vee. 'Of course you must have it, and the cake as well.'

Chris looked reproachfully at Jo: 'It's for all of us – Miss Coburn said so.'

Unable to voice her suspicions about the Virginia ham, Jo muttered: 'No, it's too much, you're too generous.'

'Nonsense!' said Vee. 'Didn't you tell me it's Chrissie's birthday soon? We'll call this a birthday party in advance.'

Jo accepted defeat. 'Say thank you, Chris. You'd better put on your best dress, if it's going to be a party.'

'If you'll excuse me, I'll slip away upstairs meself,' said Mr Mulligan. 'Time for a wash-and-brush-up, eh?'

When Chris and Mr Mulligan had left the room, Vee said: 'This isn't just a social call, Jo. The presents are more of an olive branch.'

Don smiled: 'I wanna put things straight between us – if you'll give me the chance. I wanna be friends again.' With his arm round Vee, he concluded: 'We're very happy right now, and we want for you to be happy as well.'

'Thank you,' said Jo. There was nothing else to say.

Then they both kissed her, and Don said: 'Vee's had this terrific idea. Seeing it's gonna be Chrissie's birthday soon, she says we oughta take you both out.'

'Some time next week, isn't it?' asked Vee. 'There's a circus on Clapham Common, and we thought—'

'I guess the birthday girl might enjoy it, and I sure as heck would!' said Don eagerly. 'So whaddaya say?'

'Say yes, Jo!' Vee urged her. 'Let's go to the circus!'

Standing in the doorway, Chris added fervently: 'Say yes, Jo – please!'

A striped canvas tent had sprung up like a gigantic mushroom in the middle of Clapham Common, and only a few minutes before the performance, the crowds were still pouring in.

Don had booked in advance, and the birthday group were in cushioned seats, close to the sawdust ring. Sitting in the centre with Vee on one side of her and Jo on the other, Chris bounced up and down, willing the show to begin.

Don leaned across Vee, advising her: 'Take it easy now, don't go wishing the evening away! The sooner it starts, the sooner it'll be over.'

Vee laughed: 'Have a heart, darling! When you're twelve years old, you want everything to happen at once – isn't that right, Jo?'

Jo tried to smile. 'I can't remember what being twelve felt like. It was a long time ago.'

She had never liked circuses very much. Performing animals made her feel uncomfortable, and even as a child she had been repelled by the clowns' antics. This evening she had another reason for uneasiness; it was the first time she had heard Vee call Don 'darling', which implied a new intimacy between them.

As if he were reading her thoughts, Don teased her: 'You're not looking too cheerful, babe. What's wrong?'

'I expect it's the weather,' she said. 'It's getting me down, rather.'

The heatwave was still dragging on; today the setting sun was smothered by a ceiling of cloud, which seemed to press down upon her.

'Yes, I hope it doesn't rain tonight,' remarked Vee absently. 'We haven't brought raincoats or umbrellas.' Then, folding back the programme, she passed it over to Jo, saying in a meaning tone: 'Did you see this?'

Halfway down the list of artistes, Jo read: 'The Amazing Dando Family! World-famous aerialists and wire-walkers! The incredible Dickie Dando and the lovely Dorothy, defying the laws of gravity. Also introducing the new comedy sensation – Chockie! Chills – thrills – a barrel of fun!'

Jo looked at Vee. 'Chockie?'

As their eyes met, Vee nodded. 'That's what gave me the idea of coming here. I saw it in the newspaper.'

'Chockie?' Don leaned closer, trying to hear what they were saying. 'Who's Chockie?'

'I know!' exclaimed Chris. 'Chockie's the name of the teddy-bear in Jo's bedroom.'

'It said in the paper, he's only twelve years old,' Vee went on quietly. 'Quite a coincidence, don't you think?'

Don chuckled. 'OK, so there's a circus act with the same name as a teddy-bear? Big deal!'

'I just thought it was interesting,' said Vee lightly. 'I mean, it's not the sort of name you come across every day, is it?'

High above the entrance to the ring, a band of musicians in crimson uniforms lifted their instruments; the conductor picked up his baton in white-gloved hands. The first chords rang out, and a shiver of expectation ran down Jo's spine.

First, there was the grand march past, as all the artistes appeared, making a triumphal progress round the ring, bowing and smiling and waving at the children in the audience; lovely ladies in feathers and spangles, a Spanish acrobatic troupe, clowns in baggy trousers and comic hats, sleek horses prancing and nodding in time to the music, and the ringmaster in a top hat and tailcoat of shining gold.

Jo scanned the performers. She could see no one who might be the Amazing Dickie and Dorothy Dando – and no twelve-year-old boy.

But she went on hoping. The rest of the performance passed before her in a blur; she was on tenterhooks all the time, waiting for the Dando family to appear.

At last the ringmaster made the announcement she had been waiting for. A tightwire had been stretched between the two main tent-poles, and a man and a woman in sky-blue leotards shinned up the ladders at either side of the ring. Their act was expert and meticulous. Dicky Dando not only walked the tightwire, he danced, he fooled, he pretended to trip and fall, while a thousand people said 'Ooh!' with one voice, for there was no safety-net. Dorothy, a glamorous blonde, allowed him to carry her across in his arms, and was later propelled along the wire in a wheelbarrow; then she astounded everyone by performing a ballet dance with arabesques and effortless jetées in mid-air, returning to the tightwire on the points of her toes every time.

But the act was not over. Dickie Dando blew a whistle, and the spotlight picked out a tiny figure far below; a pint-sized clown in a patchwork suit much too big for him and a purple fright-wig on his head. Dickie pointed to the ladder, and the small boy began to climb.

He seemed to be the clumsiest boy in the world, for ever tripping over his own outsize shoes, missing his footing on the ladder, catching himself by his toes and hanging upside-down from one of the rungs. The audience held their breath, then burst into laughter and applause.

On the high wire, Dickie handed him a bouquet of roses and sent him across to deliver them to the lovely Dorothy. Chockie dropped the bouquet and caught it in mid-air; he fell off the wire and swung head-over-heels; he discovered an itch in the small of his back, and was so intent on scratching it, he lost his footing once more and only saved himself from falling by hauling a parasol from his baggy trousers, just in time to regain his balance.

Somehow he managed to lose the bouquet, and kept turning round in circles to look for it, unaware that the flowers were sticking out of his back pocket. By the time he reached the pedestal at the far end of the wire, the audience were limp with hilarity and terror. He handed the flowers to Dorothy, made a gallant bow, and promptly fell headfirst from the pedestal, only to be caught halfway to the ground by an invisible wire fastened round his waist. He was left dangling helplessly, until Dickie swung down on a trapeze to rescue him. When the trapeze swung up again, Dorothy joined her husband and her small son; reunited, the amazing Dando family acknowledged the storm of applause.

Jo still couldn't tell whether she recognised Charlie or not; disguised by the shapeless costume and the absurd wig, he was also plastered in a clown make-up, with chocolate-brown patches round both eyes.

Under the applause, Vee asked: 'What do you think? Could it be?'

'I can't tell. He was only three, last time we saw him.'

'Saw who? What's going on?' Don wanted to know.

Vee shook her head. 'I'll explain later.'

The show went on, and when the cast assembled for the grand finale, and all the artistes came on to take a bow, Mr and Mrs Dando brought their son with them – no longer a clown, but dressed in a sky-blue leotard like his parents, his face scrubbed and his hair neatly combed.

Jo gazed at the boy, then admitted reluctantly: 'It's hard to say . . . There's something about the way he smiles, but I really don't know.'

'For pete's sake, what are you talking about?' Don asked. 'Why are you so interested in the kid?'

Before Jo could answer, Chris chimed in: 'I bet I know! You're wondering if it could be Charlie, aren't you? I remember, you said that teddy-bear belonged to Charlie when he was little.'

Vee turned to Don. 'That's right. Jo told me she had a brother who disappeared in one of the air-raids. If he were still alive, he'd be the same age as that little boy.'

'But that's crazy, he's their son—'

'He could have been adopted.'

By now the artists had vanished, and the band was playing the audience out. As they followed the crowds through the exits, Jo said: 'You're probably right, Don. But I think I'll try and have a word with Mr and Mrs Dando, all the same.'

'Are you nuts? You can tell by looking at them, he's gotta be their son. They're all acrobats, it runs in the family.'

'All the same, let's go and find out,' Vee said.

Jo made enquiries and was directed to the caravans behind the Big Top.

This was the other side of show-business. They smelled the musky smell of caged animals, trodden grass and sawdust and perspiring bodies; they heard a babel of voices in different accents and unfamiliar languages, and at last they found the caravan they were looking for. It was a long modern trailer, with cut-glass patterns at the windows, and polished chrome fittings.

The door was opened by a swarthy man in vest and trousers, burly and barrel-chested; Jo recognised him as the anchor-man of the acrobatic troupe.

'I'm sorry, I think I've come to the wrong caravan,' she said. 'It was Mr Dando I wanted.'

'No, is all right, Mister Dando is here,' grunted the Spaniard. 'Hi, Dick! Is for you. Come, please.'

The others hung back when Jo entered; the van was already crowded, and there would not have been room for them all. Inside, sitting at a big mirror, Mrs Dando wiped off her make-up with cold cream. As the colour came away, Jo saw that she was middle-aged, much older than the glamorous blonde whom the audience had applauded.

Dickie Dando too looked tired and worn; the black dye from his hair was trickling down in rivulets on his brow – and as for Chockie . . .

He was wearing a white vest and pants; at twelve, he was embarrassed by the arrival of an unknown young lady, and pulled on an old dressing-gown, stained with greasepaint.

Jo felt suddenly awkward. Don was right – this was absurd. All the same, there was something about the boy, something in his face – or was it the way he held his head?

'I'm sorry to bother you.' Clearing her throat, she tried to explain. 'You're going to think this is a strange thing to ask, but – it's about your son . . .'

'You want a signed photo, do you?' Mr Dando spoke in a tired South London voice; a lifetime spent in show-business had softened the rough edges of cockney, leaving it oddly classless, not unlike Jo's own accent. 'Dottie, have you got one of the postcards?'

'No, it wasn't that,' Jo tried to explain: 'though I did enjoy the show. You were all very good – it was wonderful.'

'Yes, it went pretty well tonight, didn't it? I daresay you'd like his autograph anyway. Write your name for the young lady, Chockie.'

The boy signed the card with a flourish, then handed it to Jo.

'Thank you,' she said, searching his face for some clue, some response, but there was no hint of recognition.

'Chockie's an unusual name,' she said cautiously. 'I suppose – it's just a stage name?'

'Oh, no, he's always been called Chockie,' said Mr Dando. 'Ever since he was a baby – haven't you, son?'

Chockie nodded; he had heard all this so many times before.

Jo's courage failed her; with the Dando family staring at her, she dared not ask what she wanted to know. Instead, she blurted out: 'I just wondered – where Chockie was born.'

'Right here, in London.' Mr Dando was obviously puzzled. 'We come from this part of the world, just off Lavender Hill. This van isn't our home; Miguel lets us have the use of it as a dressing-room, because we live near by. Why – what makes you ask?'

'I suppose it's silly of me; it's just that – I used to know somebody, years ago, a boy called Charlie.' She realised how ridiculous it sounded. 'And – Chockie was the name of his teddy-bear . . .'

She looked again at the boy; he didn't show the slightest interest

Mr Dando's smile faded, and he rose to his feet. 'Let me get this straight. You thought we might have named our son after some kid's teddy-bear? Is that what you're saying?'

His wife stood up. 'We've had a long day, and we're all rather tired, so we'd be grateful if you'd push off and stop bothering us – do you mind?'

Mr Dando snatched the signed postcard from Jo's hand. 'We might as well keep this for someone who'll appreciate it – you didn't want it, did you? All you wanted was to come round here, stirring up trouble! Now clear out and leave us alone!'

Jo stumbled out of the caravan, thankful to lose herself in the darkness; the others were waiting for her.

'What happened?' Vee asked. 'Did you find out anything?'

'There was nothing to find out,' she answered. 'It was all a mistake.'

Vee put her arm round her and said: 'Come on, we'll take you home.'

'Sure thing,' said Don. 'Let's see if I can rustle up a cab, huh?'

He found one cruising along Clapham Common North Side, and they soon dropped Jo and Chris off at Agar Road. Chris thanked Don for the outing, saying it was the best birthday she'd ever had.

He grinned. 'Let's do it again next year, huh? That's a date!'

With her key in the front door, Jo called to Chris: 'Come on, it's time you were in bed, young lady!'

Remembering Rita Hayworth, Chris blew Don a kiss and ran up the path.

As the cab moved away, Don pulled Vee closer and murmured: 'High time you were in bed too, young lady . . . Time we both were.'

'Don't be naughty,' she whispered, but a thrill of anticipation ran through her as he began to fondle her. His long, deft fingers slid across her skin – stroking, arousing, deliciously tormenting . . .

'Oh, Don . . .' She breathed his name ecstatically. 'We shouldn't – we mustn't . . .'

'You know you don't mean that,' he told her. His voice vibrated softly in her ear; her body was aching for him, and he knew it.

'When we get back to your place, how's about I come in for a while?' he suggested. 'If the house is dark, we'll know they've gone to bed.'

'Suppose they heard us coming in?'

'We'll be quiet as mice,' he assured her. 'No one will ever know.'

His other hand was creeping up her thigh, making her weak with longing. She knew it was wrong, but it felt so right.

When the cab pulled up at Cheyne Walk, they saw that the first-floor windows were ablaze with light.

'It's no good,' sighed Vee, with a touch of relief. She knew what would have happened if she had let him into the house, and she wasn't sure that she was brave enough. 'Alec must be sitting up. I must go.'

'Not yet; stay here for a while.'

He was still trying to undress her, and she protested: 'You mustn't. Suppose the driver sees us?'

'He won't give a damn,' Don whispered.

As he pulled at her clothes, she struggled to escape. 'No, don't—'

Then they froze, as someone appeared under the portico, silhouetted against the lights of the entrance hall.

'It's Aunt Elspeth!' Vee gasped. 'She's come out to look for me.'

'Jeez, anyone'd think it's you that's twelve years old!' he grumbled, while Vee tried to make herself presentable.

When she climbed out of the taxi, her aunt came to meet her, and the cab roared away. Aunt Elspeth seized her hands, saying: 'Thank heavens you're back. I've been so worried.'

'It's not that late. I'm perfectly all right, honestly!'

Her aunt interrupted. 'I don't mean that – it's Alec, I'm afraid he's ill. He's shut himself up in his room, and he won't tell me what's wrong.'

Vee did not wait to hear any more. A hideous weight of guilt descended upon her; she still loved Alec more than anyone in the world. This was her punishment for those moments of shameful pleasure . . . She ran into the house and upstairs to Alec's room on the second floor, but the door was locked.

She knocked urgently. 'Alec, it's me. Can I come in?'

There was silence for several moments, and she was afraid he might be unconscious. She knocked again. 'Can you hear me?'

He answered in a muffled voice: 'Go away, I'm trying to sleep.'

'Aunt says you're ill. What's the matter?'

'I need to sleep. Why can't everybody leave me in peace?'

'I just want to help you.'

'You can't help me – nobody can bloody help me. Go away!'

He had never sworn at her before. Shattered, she went downstairs and met her aunt on the landing.

'Can't we ring the doctor at home?' she asked.

Aunt Elspeth shook her head. 'Alec says he doesn't want the doctor.'

'Never mind what he says,' Vee told her. 'He must see a doctor, whether he likes it or not. If you won't ring up, I will.'

On Sunday morning London was still sweltering. Matins at All Saints seemed to drag on unbearably, and when they came out Chris said to Jo: 'All that stuff about African missions – I thought the sermon was going on for ever.'

'Yes, I must admit I was thinking about – other things,' Jo confessed.

'About Chockie?'

'How did you know?'

'You've got that look in your eye. You're still wondering, aren't you?'

'I don't know. If they say he's their son, I suppose he must be. And yet – there's something else that keeps bothering me.'

'What's that?'

As they walked past the Dogs' Home, on their way back to Agar Road, Jo explained: 'Two things really. The first thing is – why did Mr Dando get so upset before he threw me out? He suddenly turned quite nasty and said something about me "coming round, stirring up trouble". All I did was ask a few silly questions – why should he call that stirring up trouble? Unless he's got something to hide?'

'I see.' Chris still sounded unconvinced. 'What's the other thing?'

'This is really daft – you'll say it's my imagination . . . But when I met that boy, I kept thinking he reminded me of someone, and last night I dreamed about Mum.'

'You mean your mum? Auntie Gracie?' Chris looked a little awestruck. 'Yes, that is peculiar . . .'

'No, I often dream about her. But last night, the way she turned her head and looked straight into my eyes – when I woke up, I realised that Chockie had a look of Mum about him. There, I told you it was daft.'

'I don't think it's daft,' said Chris. 'I think you ought to go and see them again, tell them the whole story and see what they say.'

'They'll probably have me locked up if I go on pestering them.'

'I'll come with you,' Chris offered. 'They can't lock us both up! And Charlie was my cousin . . . I mean, he *is* my cousin – if it really is him.'

Jo smiled. 'Thanks, love. But I don't know where they live.'

'Somewhere off Lavender Hill, you said.'

'That's all I've got to go on. I can't knock at every single house around Lavender Hill, can I?'

'Wait a bit, I've got an idea!'

They were passing a telephonebox, and Chris darted inside; Jo watched her pick up the A–K volume of the directory, riffling through the pages. A moment later she emerged, wreathed in smiles. 'Number seven, Devonshire Buildings, Theatre Street!' she announced proudly. 'That's off Lavender Hill, isn't it?'

'Chris, you're a genius!' Jo hugged her. 'What made you think of looking in the phonebook?'

'I thought, if they're theatre people, they're bound to be on the phone, and there can't be many people called Dando! Shall I write down the number? You can ring up and ask—'

'No,' said Jo. 'If they've got something to hide, it would be better to see them. I'll go round after dinner, as soon as we've done the washing-up.'

'I'll come with you,' said Chris. 'Just in case!'

Theatre Street was a steep, narrow road, squeezed in between the Town Hall and the old Shakespeare Theatre.

The Shakespeare had been built around the turn of the century as a cultural oasis, bringing 'art' to the masses; while Marie Lloyd and Little Tich played the Grand, the Shakespeare proudly presented stars of the legitimate theatre like Sarah Bernhardt and Mrs Patrick Campbell.

Within a few years the Shakespeare fell on hard times; in 1912 it became a cinema, and remained one until it was bombed – first in 1940, then again in 1944. After that, it closed down and was left to moulder away.

From the outside, it appeared to be more or less intact, but as Jo and Chris walked down Theatre Street, they saw that the windows were boarded up, and a few tattered posters clung to the walls. Swinging her carrier-bag, Jo glanced at the old stage door, half off its hinges, a scrawny pigeon perched on top of it. Disturbed by their footsteps, the bird spread its wings and flapped away, disappearing into the building.

'How will it get out?' Chris asked. 'It'll be dark in there.'

'I believe the roof has fallen in. Perhaps it can fly straight up to the sky.' Jo glanced up as she spoke; overhead, the sky was a bank of copper-coloured cloud, shot with purple. 'It's going to rain soon – I can feel it.'

Halfway down the street they found Devonshire Buildings, a block of Victorian tenements with a front door opening on to the street. Inside was an echoing stairwell, with stone steps climbing to three upper floors, and four flats on each floor.

Number 7 was on the second floor; there was no bell or knocker, so she rapped on the door panels. It was Chockie who opened the door. His eyes widened at the sight of Jo.

'Oh – it's you,' he said. His voice was uncertain; a childish treble on the edge of breaking into a deeper register. 'What do you want?'

'I'd like to see Mr and Mrs Dando, please,' said Jo.

He looked at Chris, and asked: 'Who's she?'

'This is my cousin, Christine,' Jo told him.

They were about the same age, and within an inch or so the same height; they eyed one another with open curiosity.

'Come in,' said the boy.

It seemed that the Dando family enjoyed a lie-in on a Sunday; at three in the afternoon, Mr Dando was still in his pyjamas, and Mrs Dando was dishing up a fried egg on toast.

They looked at Jo, and at one another, then Mrs Dando asked: 'How did you find out where we live?'

'Chris looked in the phonebook,' said Jo. 'I'm sorry to interrupt your meal, but—'

'If it's about the boy, we've got nothing to say to you,' began Mr Dando, in a threatening tone. 'You've no business walking in here like—'

Wearily, Mrs Dando said: 'It's no good, Dad. I told you, it was bound to happen some day. Have your breakfast while it's hot. Chockie – you've had yours; you can go out for a while. Not too far, mind.'

Chockie glanced at Chris. 'Can she come too?'

Mrs Dando turned to Jo. 'Is that all right?'

'Why not?' said Jo. 'If you'd like to, Chris?'

'OK,' said Chris.

They went out together, and Mrs Dando said: 'Finish your breakfast, Dad. You know you won't eat it if it gets cold.'

'I'm not hungry.' He pushed his plate away, then turned to Jo. 'Look here, why d'you keep bothering us? What's it all about?'

There was no turning back now.

Sitting uncomfortably on the edge of a hard kitchen chair, Jo told them what had happened that night in May, 1941: the bombs on Mill Street, and on the Emergency Aid Post – and her last sight of Charlie, laughing in the doorway as the bomb whistled down.

'Everybody said he must have been killed, but I never believed it. I wondered if he was still alive . . . And I'm still wondering.'

When she had finished speaking, the silence seemed to go on for ever. She heard a train rattling along the line to Clapham Junction – or was it a rumble of thunder?

At last Mrs Dando said: 'He doesn't know, you see.'

'No – and there's no reason for him to know, is there? Not ever!' said her husband fiercely.

'I think there is, Dad,' said his wife. 'Let's go and find him. I know where he'll be.'

'What – again?' Mr Dando stood up, and started to bluster: 'After all we've said to him? It's not safe, I've told him a hundred times.'

'That's where you'll find him, I bet you,' said Dorothy Dando. She held the door open for Jo. 'You'd better come too.'

They went down two flights of stone steps without another word, then began to climb the steep ascent of Theatre Street. When they reached the broken stage door, Dickie Dando put his shoulder to it, heaving it a little further open.

'This place is a death-trap,' he muttered. 'You get all sorts coming in – drunks and layabouts. I don't know why the boy keeps coming back here.

When she followed them inside, Jo understood at once.

Ruined and derelict, the old Shakespeare was still a theatre. As they stepped out on to the bare boards that used to be a stage, now worn and crumbling in places, she gazed about her. There was a huge gaping hole where the roof should have been; a few battens and lines still hung from the flies, but as she looked up she saw the lowering purple sky, and felt the first drops of rain upon her face.

But it was the auditorium that took her breath away. It was all there – the stalls, the circle, the gallery, the boxes held up by female caryatids in imitation marble; the rows of seats that had once been covered in crimson plush were ragged and mouldy now, and there were weeds pushing through the carpet in the aisles.

The actors had long since departed, yet this empty space remained a theatre; and in the centre of the stage Chockie was showing Chris how to do a back-somersault.

Dickie Dando called out: 'How many times do I have to tell you?'

Chockie turned to face his parents. 'She wanted to see the theatre.'

'Never mind that,' said Dorothy Dando. 'This lady's got something to tell you, son.'

Jo picked her way across the crumbling boards, and opened the carrier-bag she had brought with her.

'I've got something to give you,' she said. 'I think it might have belonged to you once.'

Then she pulled out the old teddy-bear and gave it to him.

He held it for a moment, staring into the boot-button eyes; slowly, as if moved by some power outside himself, he rubbed his cheek against the worn brown fur.

'Chockie . . .' he said huskily.

The first crack of thunder startled them, and the rain began to fall heavily, but nobody moved. When the lightning flashed, they saw tears as well as raindrops on the boy's face.

Dickie Dando turned on Jo. 'Now look what you've done. What did you want to go upsetting him for?'

Dorothy Dando put her hand on her husband's shoulder. 'No, Dad,' she said. 'He's got a right to know.'

Charlie raised his head; as the tears streamed down his cheeks he turned to Jo.

'Tell me,' he said.

Second Interlude

'Are you asleep, Dickie?' whispered Dorothy.

'With those ack-ack guns booming away every few minutes?' muttered her husband. 'Chance'd be a fine thing . . .'

'Some people are asleep. I can hear them snoring,' she said.

'Dead drunk, more like,' he told her. 'Saturday night – they were all in the boozer till turning-out time. I'm beginning to wish we'd followed their example.'

'You? When have you ever got squiffy? You told me the first time I met you, if you have more than one pint, it throws out your sense of balance.'

'True enough. I've seen many a good wire-walker come to grief 'cos he'd had one too many. Still, it's not as if we'd been working tonight.'

'Pity we weren't. We could have done a darn sight better than the Flying Fanshawes,' said Dorothy. 'That's for sure.'

'Oh, come on, they're not that bad. They got a good round when they took their bow.'

'Call that a good round? People were walking out. I could hardly hear the orchestra for the clatter of the tip-up seats. If you want my opinion, it wasn't worth coming all the way from Lavender Hill.'

'Well, they had a lot to put up with – the ruddy siren going off the minute they came on, and the manager asking if anybody wanted to leave the theatre. I suppose now we'll be stuck here till tomorrow morning.' Dickie peered at his watch; it was hard to read by the dim blue light in the public air-raid shelter, but he managed it at last. 'It's

264

tomorrow morning already . . . Just gone midnight.'

On Saturday, 10 May, 1941, the Dandos had come across the river to catch the variety show at the Chelsea Palace. Some friends of Dickie's were on the bill, and the second house on Saturday should have been the highspot of the week, but the theatre had been barely half-full.

'If we'd caught the number 34 over Battersea Bridge, we'd have been home in bed by now,' Dorothy grumbled.

'Pearl and Stan would never have forgiven us if we hadn't gone round afterwards.'

'Oh, yes? The minute they'd got their hats and coats on, they were out of that dressing-room like greased lightning.'

'Stands to reason, living at Golders Green – they had a taxi waiting.'

'All right for some,' sniffed Dorothy. 'You'd have thought they might have offered us a lift part of the way.'

'Have some sense – they were going in the opposite direction! Besides, they've got their little girl to think of.'

Dorothy pursed her lips: although the Fanshawes were in a hurry, they had found time to show off the latest photos of their baby daughter.

Dickie put his arm round his wife's shoulders, saying softly: 'Can't blame them for being proud parents, can you?'

When the Dandos were married in 1936, they wanted to start a family, but it never happened. They had both been examined by doctors and told that there was nothing physically wrong, but now Dickie was forty-one and Dorothy only three years younger, and time was running out for them.

Comforted by his embrace, she sighed: 'I wish we could go home.'

'Why don't we chance it?' he suggested. 'It's not that far. We'll walk it in half an hour.'

'With the raid still going on? If the wardens catch us, they'll make us go back in the shelter.'

'I haven't heard anything except ack-ack for the last half-hour.'

'You can still get killed if a lump of shrapnel hits you.'

'We'll keep close to the buildings. Anything's better than sitting around like this all night – let's give it a go, eh?'

So they left the shelter and began to walk along the King's Road, hand in hand, towards Oakley Street and the Albert Bridge. Dorothy glanced up at the night sky, criss-crossed with searchlights, and exclaimed: 'Dickie, look! It's starting to snow!'

'In May? Don't be daft!' Then he saw the big white flakes coming down: 'Blimey, it can't be . . .'

Putting out his hand, he let a flake settle on his palm; it wasn't ice-cold but faintly warm, and as he touched it, it collapsed into feathery white ash.

'It's paper,' he told her. 'Burnt paper.'

Afterwards, they heard that a paper-mill in Wandsworth had been hit by incendiaries; all along the river, flakes of white ash floated down in a fantastic snowfall.

Then they heard the long, piercing shriek of a bomb coming down. Dickie pulled Dorothy into the doorway of the Town Hall and threw his arms round her.

She felt the ground shake beneath her feet, and a great rush of air hit them like a sledgehammer. She shut her eyes, clutching her husband and wishing they were still in the shelter. Dickie could not speak – struck by the force of the blast, he was momentarily winded. A split second later, the sound of the explosion caught up with them.

Dorothy clapped her hands over her ears and gasped: 'Oh, my God – it sounded so near. Can you see anything?'

A thick fog of choking brickdust filled their eyes and lungs, blinding and choking them. Clinging together, they heard the aftermath of the explosion – minor crashes, bangs and tinkles, as loosened slates tumbled from rooftops and glass shattered on paving-stones.

For several minutes they remained where they were, while heavy rescue vehicles and ambulances raced towards the latest disaster.

'It was close, all right,' said Dickie at last. 'Let's take a look.'

He steered Dorothy across the road to the corner of Sydney Street, and as they peered through the dust cloud they saw shrouded lights: ARP workers were already going into action.

'Looks to me like St Luke's Hospital got clobbered,' said Dickie. 'Murdering bastards – dropping bombs on sick people, on babies . . .'

'Let's go back, Dickie, I don't like it—' Dorothy began, but he interrupted her.

'Hang on, there's something coming this way . . .'

She saw it too; a small, pale shape emerging from the murky haze.

266

'Blimey,' said Dicky Dando. 'It's a kid.'

The child was running down the street, straight towards them – a small boy, no more than three years old, completely naked. Unaware of the rubble and broken glass beneath his bare feet, he stretched out his arms – needing help, needing comfort.

His clothes had been torn from him by the blast, but there wasn't a scratch on him; alone in the world, he was trying to find something or someone he loved.

Dickie picked him up, sheltering him inside his coat. 'What's your name, son?' he asked.

The boy looked at him with wide, searching eyes. 'Chockie,' he said.

For the next six months, it was the only word he ever said.

By one a.m. they were in their flat at Devonshire Buildings, and Chockie was tucked up in the big double bed, fast asleep. They sat in the kitchen, talking quietly for fear of waking him.

'What are we going to do?' Dorothy answered her own question. 'I suppose we ought to take him to the police station first thing – they'll know what to do. His parents must be frantic.'

'If they're still alive,' said Dickie. 'If they were with him when the bomb came down, they're probably in kingdom come by now. If you ask me, it's a miracle Chockie got out in one piece.'

'But if he's got no mum or dad, what's to become of him?'

'He'll be put in an orphanage, I suppose.'

Dorothy said slowly: 'It doesn't seem right. Almost like sending him to prison, just because he hasn't got a mum and dad . . .'

'Maybe he has got a mum and dad,' said Dickie. 'Maybe it's us.'

She looked at him – but he could see that she understood. 'We couldn't – could we?'

'Maybe that's why he found us,' Dickie suggested. 'Maybe it was meant.'

'What will people say? The neighbours will start asking questions if we suddenly turn up with a three-year-old boy.'

'They're not going to find out. Don't you know what day it is?'

'Saturday, of course . . . No, I mean Sunday.'

'That right. We've got a train-call at two o'clock this afternoon.'

Ever since Easter, they had been 'resting', but now they were about to set out on a four-month tour; they had signed up with a big circus that operated mainly in the North of England and Scotland. It was the first time the Dandos had joined this particular company and there would be no one there who knew them.

'Who's going to think twice about it if we take the boy with us?' Dickie asked. 'And when we come back, if anybody wants to know where he came from, we'll say he's a distant relative, left an orphan in the raids, and we had to take him in because he hadn't got anyone else. That's God's truth, near enough. Anyhow, these days people have got other things on their minds; we'll tell them he's our son . . . Say we've adopted him.'

'Our adopted son . . .' For the first time that night, Dorothy smiled. 'Chockie Dando . . . I like the sound of it.'

'So do I. And I'll tell you another thing. In years to come, it's going to look very good on the bills. "The Amazing Dandos – and Chockie"!'

Chapter Seventeen

'COME IN, CHARLIE, sit down,' said Jo. 'You know Chris already.'

'Of course he does – we're cousins!' exclaimed Chris. 'I hope you like jam-tarts, Charlie. I made them.'

'And here's someone you don't know,' added Jo. 'This is a friend of mine . . . Vanessa Coburn.'

It was the first time Charlie had visited Agar Road; the Dandos had allowed him to come on his own. It was also the first time Vee had met her brother in over eight years, and she wanted to put her arms round him, but they simply shook hands.

Some weeks had passed since the reunion with Charlie on the stage of the old Shakespeare Theatre; afterwards, they had gone back to the Dandos' flat, where they talked for hours. It was a difficult meeting, for they all saw the situation from different points of view.

Dickie Dando's attitude was straightforward; he admitted that they had taken the law into their own hands by adopting Charlie without permission – or Chockie, as he continued to call him – but he also maintained that they had given him a better start in life and more loving care than he could have known in an institution.

Dorothy supported him in this, but for years she had been suppressing pangs of guilt, wondering whether Chockie's real parents might still be alive, mourning the loss of their son. Now she knew the boy had no other parents, her conscience eased a little, but in her heart Dorothy could not help feeling that Chockie's blood relatives had first claim upon him.

Like Dorothy, Jo's emotions were in conflict; she had known a moment of joy when she found Charlie again and knew that the quest was over – yet she did not want to destroy the Dandos' happiness.

The person most concerned had the least to say for himself.

Chockie had no memories of early childhood; perhaps they had been erased on the night of the air-raid. When he took the teddy-bear in his hands, long-forgotten emotions had come to the surface, but nothing much beyond that. He tried to remember, but he could not; he seemed to have a faint recollection of a house he once lived in, though he wasn't certain about it. If he could have visited the house again, it might have helped, but Mill Street had vanished long ago.

When Jo told him she was his big sister, he took her word for it; if he'd had a sister, she might very well have been someone like Jo.

When she showed him an old photograph of their mother, he studied it for a long time, then said: 'She's got a nice face . . . I sort of remember her – I think I do – but I couldn't say for sure.'

Today, though they told him he had often been to Agar Road when he was little, he shook his head. 'I might have done. I don't know . . . I'm sorry.'

Jo had taken time and trouble over the tea-party; as well as Chris's jam-tarts, there were two kinds of cake – Charlie used to like marzipan when he was little, so Vee had contributed a splendid sponge sandwich from Fortnum's, decorated with marzipan fruits, and Jo had used up a month's sweet ration to make a chocolate cake, iced with chocolate, and layered with chocolate-cream.

He said it was the best tea-party he'd ever been to. Then he wiped his mouth with a paper serviette, and asked: 'What's it all about, then? The tea, the cakes – all this? Now you've found me again, what do you want to do about it?'

This was the question Jo had been dreading, and she replied carefully: 'I don't know yet. I'm just very glad you're safe and well. But as for the future, that's up to you.'

'D'you want me to leave Mum and Dad, and come here instead?'

'I didn't say that—'

Chris broke in: 'Yes, that's what we want. He could, couldn't he, Jo? We've still got the spare room empty – that can be Charlie's room!'

'Do you mind calling me Chockie?' he asked. 'I can't get used to being called Charlie – it seems like you're talking about somebody else.'

'Chockie, then.' Chris went on quickly: 'You can come and live here any time you want – isn't that right, Jo?'

'Let's not rush things,' Jo said. 'We've got to give him time to get used to the idea of a new family. We must let him decide for himself . . . All right, Chockie?'

He nodded. 'I suppose so . . . It's a bit peculiar, finding I've got a sister I never even knew about.'

'I know, it must be difficult—' Jo began.

Chris interrupted: 'It wasn't just one sister – two sisters, Chockie.'

He looked blank. 'I thought you said you were my cousin?'

'I don't mean me; you had another sister once. She was called Vee – Vee for Vera.'

Chockie said slowly: 'Vee . . . Yes, there was somebody called Vee . . . I'm sure there was.'

Looking round the table, he turned to the lady in the smart frock, sitting next to Jo and saying nothing – and Vee held her breath.

'Vee for Vanessa, too,' he said at last. 'That's you, isn't it?'

Joyfully, Chris clapped her hands. 'I wondered about that, the first day you came here, but I thought you couldn't be, because Jo would have said.'

Vee buried her face in her hands, and Jo had to explain; gently, she told them Vee's story – the story of Vanessa Coburn who disappeared in the bombing, and Aunt Elspeth, and the house in Cheyne Walk.

When she had finished, Vee managed to pull herself together, though her voice was still heavy with tears. 'You make me so ashamed. I've gone on living a lie ever since . . . You were the lucky one, Charlie – Chockie, I mean – you never had to pretend.'

Jo touched Vee's shoulder. 'You mustn't blame yourself. You did what you thought was best.'

Chockie surprised them all by laughing suddenly. 'It's funny – first of all I only had a mum and a dad, now I've got two sisters and a cousin as well – a whole new family!'

'And a new home – if you want it,' Chris reminded him.

'Don't rush him,' Jo warned her. 'Take your time, Chockie. But if you decide to make this your home, we'll be very glad to have you here.'

Caught up in the excitement, he said eagerly: 'P'raps I will . . . 'Course, I'll have to talk to Mum and Dad first, but—'

'Which school do you go to?' Chris wanted to know. 'Is it near here?'

'I go to different schools. That's one of the things about being on the road – you go to school wherever you land up. A week here, a week there.'

'How do you manage?' Chris was fascinated. 'You'll be taking your exams next summer, won't you? Like me?'

'Will I?' He didn't take exams very seriously. 'I dunno about that.'

'You'll have a lot of catching-up to do,' said Jo.

'If you decide to stay here, I might be able to help. I could pay for you to have special coaching,' Vee suggested. 'Or we could send you to a private school.'

'Let's not get carried away!' said Jo. 'You must go home and talk it over with Mr and Mrs Dando first. Whatever happens, we've found each other again – that's the main thing.'

'There's something else,' Vee broke in, awkwardly. 'I've no right to ask, but – do you mind not telling anyone – about me? I couldn't face my family, I mean, the Coburn family, if they found out.'

'I'll have to tell Mum and Dad,' said Chockie. 'But I won't tell anybody else, I promise.'

'Thank you.' She glanced at her wristwatch. 'It's getting late. Alec's coming back today, and I must be there when he gets home.'

'I didn't know he'd been away,' said Jo.

'Yes, the specialist sent him off to a marvellous sanatorium – but he's much better now, and he's coming back today.'

'Alec is Vee's brother – the pretend one,' Chris explained to Chockie.

'What was the matter with him?' Chockie asked.

'It's something to do with his nerves,' Vee told him. 'A sort of delayed reaction after all those years in a German prison camp.' Gathering up her handbag and her raincoat, she prepared to leave. 'Goodbye, Chockie – I'll see you soon. And if you need any help – money, or anything – Jo knows how to get in touch with me.' She added a final plea. 'But you won't tell anyone else about me, will you? That's got to be a family secret.'

When Vee got back to Cheyne Walk, she found her aunt waiting for her in the hall, saying: 'Alec's here already. He caught an earlier train.

He says he's perfectly well, and he won't have to be looked after any more.'

'That's good news. Where is he – in the drawing-room?'

'No, he went up to his room to unpack.' As Vee made a move towards the staircase, her aunt stopped her. 'Where are you going?'

'Upstairs, to say welcome home and all that—'

Aunt Elspeth put a hand on her arm: 'I wouldn't do that – not yet. I think he wants to be left alone for a little while.'

Vee looked more closely at her aunt. 'If the doctors say he's perfectly well, there's nothing to worry about, surely?'

'I suppose not. Only, he still seems to be under a lot of strain – he's not his old self.'

'They wouldn't have sent him home if he wasn't well, would they? Look, I'll just pop in and say hello – I won't be long!' and she ran up the stairs two at a time.

She found him lying on the bed with his hands under his head, staring at the ceiling.

'Hello!' she exclaimed. 'Sorry I wasn't here when you—'

Without looking at her, he said angrily: 'Do you always walk into a room without knocking?'

She caught her breath, as if he had slapped her across the face, but she tried to keep her voice light as she said: 'Well, thanks – it's nice to see you too!'

He glanced at her and mumbled: 'Sorry, I didn't mean to snap – I'm just a bit tired. I had to change trains. You know what it's like.'

'It's a pity you couldn't have driven up to town.'

'Yes, I wish I'd had the car with me. We weren't allowed little luxuries like our own transport; that would have been too much to hope for.'

'Why, was it awful? I thought it was supposed to be so marvellous.'

'Oh, yes, a really high-class, three-star prison camp . . . Only I don't need any more prison-camps.'

'I'm sorry. I hadn't realised . . .'

When she sat on the side of the bed, he edged away slightly and asked: 'Did the Aunt send you up here to help me unpack?'

'No, but I will, if you like.'

'I don't like! I can't stand being treated like an invalid. I'm perfectly well – there's nothing wrong with me.' He rolled over, turning away

273

from her. 'Now push off and let me have forty winks, will you?'

'All right.' She stood up. 'I'll see you when you come down to supper.'

With his back to her, he said: 'I don't think I'll bother. Tell them to send up something on a tray. I'm not particularly hungry.'

Her heart sank. This was exactly the way he had behaved before he went to the sanatorium; nothing had changed.

He went on: 'Just stop fussing over me, everything's all right. I'm absolutely fine!'

'Are you? Are you really?'

'Yes, I . . .' He swallowed hard, as if the words stuck in his throat, then said flatly: 'If you really want to know, I feel bloody awful.'

'I'm so sorry.' She sat down again, overwhelmed with pity. 'But why did the doctors send you home if you're not really—'

'They didn't send me home. I sent myself home. And I'm not going back, no matter what anyone says. I couldn't stay there another minute, shut up like a prisoner.'

'Of course you couldn't.' She longed to comfort him, to throw her arms round him, but she must never do that. Greatly daring, she began to stroke his hair. 'They should have realised, you're not a prisoner any more.'

He uttered an extraordinary sound that was something between a laugh and a groan, and retorted: 'Oh, yes, I am. But it's got nothing to do with locks and keys. I'll always be a prisoner, as long as I live.'

'Don't say that!' Her hand moved on to his forehead, as if she could smooth out the lines of tension; his skin felt wonderfully smooth and soft under her fingertips. 'You need to rest, that's all, then you'll be your old self again.'

He jerked his head away from her. 'You don't understand, do you? This is the thing I'm trying to run away from, the prison I'll never get out of . . . *Myself* – my own damned self!'

'No, I don't understand. I wish I did . . . I wish I could help you.'

When he went on, his voice was hard and bitter: 'You can leave me in peace. That's all I want, a little space – breathing-space – time to sort myself out. No one can do that except me . . . Just leave me alone.'

There was no more to be said. When she reached the door, she turned and looked back, but he did not move or speak.

✶

'What's the time?' Chockie asked.

'Twenty to four,' said Dorothy Dando, laying the tea-table. 'And it's only five minutes since the last time you asked me. If you want to make yourself useful, you can go and fetch me the plate of iced fancies that's on the kitchen dresser, and stop asking silly questions!'

'Do as you're told, son,' said Dickie Dando, from his armchair. As soon as the boy left the room, he added mildly: 'No need to get yourself all of a doodah, old girl. Anyone'd think we'd got the King and Queen coming to tea this afternoon.'

'As good as!' said Dorothy. 'I want everything to look nice for her when she comes. She laid on a very good spread when Chockie went round there.' Glancing towards the kitchen door, she lowered her voice. 'I thought we'd agreed to stop calling him "son"? You did it again just now.'

'I never did!'

'Yes, you did, I heard you.'

'Well, it must have slipped out. Old habits die hard.'

Chockie appeared in the doorway with the plate of fancy cakes. As he put them on the table, he asked: 'Why don't you want to call me "son" any more?'

'You know very well why not,' said Dorothy. 'Don't go on and on about it.'

'Seems daft to me. I'm still your son, whatever happens, aren't I?'

'Not legally, you're not. In the eyes of the law you're the son of Mr and Mrs Wells, deceased. Strictly speaking, we've been your foster-parents all these years,' said Dorothy.

'Yes, but I can call you Mum and Dad, can't I? I mean, I'll still see you all the time. I'll be able to come back whenever I like – Jo said so.'

'Of course you can. You'll have two homes from now on – two families.'

'Except when you're off on tour,' Chockie pointed out.

'We'll send you postcards from wherever we are,' Dorothy said.

'It won't be the same though . . . I wish I could live at Agar Road and still go on touring with you as well.'

'You want jam on it, you do,' grunted Dickie.

'Thank goodness you reminded me.' Dorothy rushed off to the kitchen. 'I forgot the strawberry jam.'

Chockie looked hard at his foster-father. 'You're sure you want me to go to Agar Road, Dad?'

''Course we do.' Dickie met his gaze. 'It's what you need – proper schooling.'

'I suppose so . . . And I can always come back to the circus later on, can't I? After I've done my exams and all that?'

'Depends, doesn't it?' said Dickie, evasively. 'We must wait and see.'

'You mean, you might get somebody else to take my place in the act?'

'No, we won't do that—' Dickie had been about to add 'son', but he remembered in time.

'How are you going to manage without me?'

'We'll manage very nicely, thanks. You're not the star of the show, my lad. The Amazing Dandos were doing all right before you came on the scene, and don't you forget it!'

Dorothy returned, saying: 'Sorry I took so long. The cut-glass jam-dish needed washing.'

'What's wrong with leaving it in the jam-jar?' Dickie asked.

'Not when we've got company.' She ran her eye over the table. 'I hope we've got enough cake. Chockie said they had two kinds of cake as well as jam-tarts. I knew I should have made some of my rock-buns.' She had a sudden brainwave. 'Chockie, take my purse and run up to Barnard's and get a packet of ginger biscuits. Come straight back, mind, and be careful crossing the main road!'

'And you can get me an evening paper while you're at it,' said Dickie. 'One with the racing results.'

As Chockie set off, Dorothy called after him: 'Does your sister like ginger biscuits?'

'How should I know?' he shouted back. 'Anyhow, if she doesn't, there'll be all the more for us.'

They heard his footsteps clattering down the stone stairwell. After a moment, Dickie said: 'You shouldn't go upsetting yourself like this.'

'I can't help it, can I? This is a very important moment, for all of us. It's only natural for me to feel upset.'

'I thought you said you wanted whatever's best for Chockie?'

'So I do! If it's what he wants, and what his sister wants, then that's what I want, too.'

'I'm not so sure it's what he wants. You heard what he said. He wished he could live with his sister, but still go on touring with us as well.'

'That's just plain silly!' Dorothy set her jaw. 'He'll get used to a different kind of life after a while. He's got to buckle down to his lessons, if he's going to make something of himself.'

'He's been brought up in the business, Dottie. I think that's what he really wants.'

'You mean it's what you want . . .' Her voice softened. 'You're going to miss him something rotten, I know that.'

'We'll both miss him. And there's another thing – the act won't be the same without him. I told him he needn't think he's the star of the show, but of course he is. Having the kid made us different from all the other acts.'

'We did all right before Chockie came. We can manage without him.'

'We're not getting any younger, either of us . . .' Dickie paused, then went on: 'I didn't tell you this, but when I rang up about the winter season at Manchester Belle-Vue, the manager said he couldn't fit us in after all.'

'What? You said it was a definite booking.'

'I thought it was. But it seems like he's already booked another tightwire act, so he won't be needing us this year.'

'Who's he got instead of us – did he say? There's nobody else in our class, not with our experience.'

'There are new people coming up all the time – young chaps, straight out of the Army. He said he was sorry to hear we won't have Chockie with us; that's why he turned us down. The boy was the real draw, you see.'

'That's not true. You're still a top-liner, Dickie. We'll soon pick up another booking over Christmas, you'll see.'

'Let's hope so. But you know what I mean – the act will be different without him.'

She took his hand and squeezed it. 'Everything's going to be different without him.'

Then they heard someone tapping at the door of the flat, and a voice called: 'Anyone home? Can I come in?'

'Blimey, she's here already.' Raising his voice, Dickie went to meet the visitor. 'Come in, Miss Wells, you're bright and early!'

Jo apologised. 'I know, I'm sorry. I got here quicker than I thought. And the front door was ajar, so—'

'Chockie's just gone up the road,' said Dorothy, all smiles. 'He'll be back in a minute. Sit yourself down – that's the most comfy chair. How've you been keeping, dear?'

'I'm very well – we all are. Vee – Vanessa – sends her regards.' As an afterthought Jo added: 'I suppose Chockie told you – about my sister?'

Dorothy nodded. 'Quite a surprise, that was. But she stayed with her other family, didn't she? Not like Chockie.'

'No, well, the Coburns don't know the whole story, and she doesn't want to tell them. The situation's different.'

There was an awkward pause, then Dickie said bravely: 'I daresay this way's the best, really. Better to have everything out in the open, don't you think so?'

'Oh, yes, much better.' Jo had been nerving herself up to pose a difficult question, and now she plunged in: 'As a matter of fact, I'm glad Chockie's out, because there's something I want to ask you.'

The Dandos looked at Jo warily, wondering what fresh surprises she might have in store for them.

'It's about my sister – about Vanessa. You know she's offered to pay for Chockie to have private coaching with a tutor, so he can catch up on his schoolwork?'

'We couldn't help that.' Dorothy was on the defensive. 'When you're on the road the kids have to pick up what lessons they can.'

'Oh, I'm not blaming you – I'm sure it's worked out very well; but before he can sit his exams, he'll have a lot of work to make up. And Vee's found a very good tutor, living in Pimlico. He's available right away, and if he can take Chockie for six hours every day, Monday to Friday, he says he can get him up to a pass-level for his entrance exam by Christmas, which means he could start the new school in January. The teacher lives near Victoria Station, so it would be quite handy for Chockie. He can get a bus all the way, across Vauxhall Bridge . . . And the sooner he can start, the better.'

Dickie asked: 'How soon would you want him to move, then?'

'Well, the tutor would like him to begin next Monday – if that's not too much of a rush?'

The silence was broken by the clatter of Chockie's feet racing upstairs.

He burst in, carrying a packet of biscuits and a newspaper. Jo noticed that it was the *Evening News*, and remembered Pete Hobden.

Chockie smiled and said: 'Hello, Jo, how's things? Biscuits, Mum. Here's your paper, Dad.'

'Vee sends her love,' Jo told him. 'And so does Chris. She's looking forward to seeing you soon.'

Chockie pulled a chair out from the table. 'Tell her I'll pop round one of these days . . . I thought p'raps we could go to the park, take one of those rowing-boats out. Do you think she'd like that?'

'I'm sure she would – only you might not have much time for boating,' Jo warned him. 'It looks as if you're going to be busy.'

'What d'you mean?'

There was a loud crackle, as Dickie shook out his newspaper; clearing his throat, he began to read the headlines aloud: ' "The Pound Falls . . . Stock Exchange Sensations" . . . There's a turn-up for the book!' he commented wryly.

'What does it mean?' asked Dorothy.

'Sir Stafford Cripps has devalued the pound – that's what it says here: "The pound, which had been standing at 4 dollars 30 has now slipped to 2 dollars 80." '

'Oh, give it a rest, Dad. I'm sure it won't make any difference to people like us,' Dorothy exclaimed.

'Oh, yes, it will!' Dickie skimmed down the page. 'According to this, it'll mean a rise in the cost of living. From now on a fourpenny-ha'penny loaf is going to cost sixpence! This is going to hit every-body.'

Dorothy shook her head. 'People will go on wanting entertain-ment, no matter what. Remember how it was in the war? They needed cheering up then, didn't they? Oh, there'll always be work for people like you and me.'

'You'll be OK. You've got that booking at Manchester, haven't you?' said Chockie.

Dickie took some time to fold up his newspaper carefully as he replied: 'We might have. It's not definite yet.'

Dorothy took charge of the situation, addressing the visitor: 'I daresay you're ready for a nice cup of tea, aren't you, Miss Wells?'

'Thank you, but I wish you'd call me Jo.'

'Jo then. I'll just go and put the kettle on.'

In the middle of the tea-party the subject of schools cropped up again, and Dorothy said to Chockie: 'Your sister was telling us before you came in, she's got a surprise for you.'

'That's right!' Dickie squared his shoulders; it was a gesture Chockie had seen a thousand times. Dad always flexed his muscles like that before he stepped out on the tightwire. 'It seems you're in luck, my lad. This new teacher your sister's going to pay for – he can take you on sooner than we expected.'

'He'd like you to start lessons next Monday,' Jo explained. 'So if it's convenient, you could move in to Agar Road straight away. I left Chris getting your room ready when I came out.'

Dorothy caught her breath. 'You want to take him back – right now?'

'It's not going to take long to pack, is it?' said Dickie, talking a little faster than usual. 'That's one lesson you learn on the road – you must always be ready to move on.'

Chockie's face was expressionless. Pushing back his chair, he muttered: ''Scuse me, back in a jiffy.'

When he left the room, Dorothy said: 'He'll be getting his suitcase down. It won't take a minute.'

But in less than a minute Chockie returned, holding the brown teddy-bear.

He handed it to Jo, saying: 'I'd like you to take this, if you don't mind. Chris can have it, if she likes. I'm a bit old for teddy-bears.'

Jo understood at once, but Dickie scolded the boy: 'Don't be ungrateful. Jo's been keeping it for you all these years – you can make room for it in your bag, can't you?'

'I won't be needing a bag,' said Chockie. 'I'm not going.'

'Oh, no, that's not right. You can't turn down a chance like this—' began Dorothy, but Chockie put his arm round her.

'It's all right, Mum, I've been thinking it over. I don't want any special schooling. I don't want to go away. Far as I can see, it doesn't matter where I was born – this is my home. It's been my home as long as I can remember.'

Dickie broke in: 'Don't be daft, son, Jo's gone to a lot of trouble, finding you. You can't let her down.'

'I'm sorry, Jo. I know you're disappointed. But we'll still see each other, won't we? Now you know where I am, we'll keep in touch. But this is my mum and dad – they're my family . . . You understand, don't you?'

They all waited for Jo to say something. Somehow, she managed to smile.

'I understand,' she said. 'You're quite right . . . Of course you are.'

Chapter Eighteen

IN THE WEEKS THAT FOLLOWED, Jo felt completely lost. Life seemed to have no shape; she had no idea where she was going, and no map or compass to show her the way. Sunday mornings at All Saints gave her no guidance – the service was a pleasant ritual, and nothing more.

For so many years she had been determined to find her brother and sister and reunite the famiy. Now she had achieved her goal, it had come to nothing. Vee was a friend, certainly, but as for Chockie . . .

His decision to stay with the Dando family had hit her very hard. It had come as a big disappointment, and though he had promised to keep in touch, she knew that as soon as the next circus booking came along, the Amazing Dandos would take to the road once more.

The news had been an even bigger blow to Chris; she had set her heart on having Chockie as a resident at Agar Road. When Jo broke the news, she burst into tears and shut herself up in her room for the rest of the evening.

The trees in the park lost their leaves, London settled in the grip of winter, and Jo had nothing to look forward to. She clung to the hope that she might be 'happy tomorrow' – but tomorrow seemed to be a long time coming.

At Galleon House, she went through her daily routine automatic-ally, taking care not to become closely involved with either Russell or Don. She had the feeling that they were excluding her from their discussions, but that didn't bother her; they were almost like strangers now.

One morning, as she scrubbed the scummy ring of soapsuds from the side of the bath – Don never troubled to leave it clean – she caught sight of her wintry expression in the mirror and realised with a shock that she did not care much about anyone, any more.

'Stop feeling sorry for yourself!' she scolded her reflection. 'You're nineteen years old, and turning into a crabby old maid already! Give us a smile, can't you?'

She forced her lips into an unconvincing grin. Soon it would be Christmas, the first Christmas since Aunt Topsy died – she must try to make it as happy as possible for Chris. On the way home, she would buy some coloured paper and tonight they could make a start on the decorations.

When the bathroom was bright and shining, she went to the kitchen and began to get the lunch ready. Don usually went out nowadays – he was in his room, getting ready for one of his mysterious 'business meetings' – and Russell spent most mornings in bed, reading the papers and dozing. The change in the weather had made his arthritis worse; recently he had been laid low by one bug after another: a cough, a cold or a feverish chill.

When Jo knocked at his door, she found him sitting up in bed with the papers scattered over the eiderdown; he looked old and tired, unshaven and grey faced.

'How are you feeling?' she asked. 'Do you want lunch in the sitting-room, or shall I bring you a tray?'

'What is it?' he asked.

'Fish. I've got you a lovely piece of finnan haddock.'

'I'm not hungry, have it yourself.'

'You must eat something. Dr Hawthorne will be cross if you go starving yourself.'

'For God's sake don't nag! Hawthorne's useless – he knows nothing about medicine. If he hadn't prescribed those sleeping tablets for Laura—' He broke off, as if he were afraid of saying too much, then mumbled: 'I don't trust doctors, I'm better off without them. Bring me some bread and cheese; I'll have it later. And tell Don I want a word with him.'

When Jo delivered the message, Don flashed her a brilliant smile, knotted one of Russell's silk scarves round his neck, and said: 'I'll be right along. Whaddaya bet he wants me to go running some errand or other?'

Returning to the kitchen, she put the haddock in the fridge; Russell might fancy it tomorrow. As she was putting on her hat and coat, she heard a murmur of angry voices from Russell's bedroom; they were becoming quite heated.

She heard Don exclaim: 'Take it easy, willya?'

Russell shouted: 'You promised me, you bastard – you gave me your word.'

Don yelled back at him: 'Gimme a break, for Chrissake. I told you, you're gonna have it real soon, any day now. Just get off my back, willya?'

Russell cut in savagely: 'Shut that door. Suppose Jo heard you?'

'Jo's off out, and so am I; I got me a date. Believe me, everything's gonna be just fine.'

As Don passed the kitchen once more, Jo stopped him and asked: 'What are you up to?'

He asked mockingly: 'Since when have you started listening at keyholes?'

'That wasn't necessary – you were both shouting your heads off. Have you been borrowing money?'

'Would I do a thing like that?' Hand on heart, he declared solemnly: 'I haven't borrowed a single goddam cent, so help me!'

'What's going on, then? Tell me!'

'Sorry, sweetheart, no can do.' He shook his head. 'Big, big secret. Christmas is coming, remember?'

'What are you talking about?'

'While the old man's laid up, I'm being Santa's little messenger. If I tell you any more, it'll spoil the surprise.' He grinned wickedly. 'But I'll let you in on this: you better hang up a real big stocking the night before Christmas!'

She would not let him go so easily. 'I don't believe you,' she said bluntly. 'It didn't sound very Christmassy to me.'

'Yeah, that's the way he is. When he can't get what he wants, he starts raising hell. I try to make allowances – he's not a well man.' Straightening his jacket collar, he continued: 'Matter of fact, there's something I've been meaning to ask you, babe.'

'Oh? And what's that?'

'Have you talked with Vanessa lately? Is she avoiding me again?'

'I've hardly spoken to her. She's very worried about her brother.'

She told Don about Alec's breakdown, and he nodded slowly. 'I guess that could be it. Well, next time you see her, tell her I still love her, OK?'

'This is how you cut out the first angel. Carefully, now. Mind how you go round the halo and the wings . . . That's right, now unfold it, like a string of paper dolls . . . There – you see?'

Chris pulled the folded paper out, concertina-fashion, and found that she had created a whole line of Christmas angels, wing-tip to wing-tip.

'It's lovely,' she exclaimed proudly. 'Can I do another one?'

'Of course you can. We're going to have them all round the parlour, and I'll get some holly to go on top of the picture-frames, and some mistletoe to hang on the lamp in the hall. It's going to look very festive.'

'You don't suppose Chockie will think angels are soppy?' Chris asked.

'I'm sure he won't – if he comes. You know the Dandos are still hoping to get some work, over the holidays. Their agent is trying to fix up a few weeks for them, starting on Boxing Day.'

'As long as Chockie can come for Christmas Day, that will be all right.'

'Yes . . .' said Jo cautiously. 'Except he might prefer to stay with his mum and dad then. I don't suppose he'd want to leave them to have Christmas dinner all on their own.'

Chris's face darkened. 'They're not his mum and dad! We're his real family – he ought to spend Christmas with us.'

'That's up to him. Anyway, we're going to make our house look nice, whether he turns up or not.'

'It wouldn't be the same without Chockie,' said Chris, hunched up over another piece of crêpe paper, folding it over and sketching the angel outline.

'If Chockie has to work over Christmas, we'll have a special party later on, for him and Vee. We'll have our family party on New Year's Eve, or whenever they can both get away.' Jo began unravelling lengths of gold and silver tinsel as she went on: 'Mr Mulligan said he might be bringing a few of his cronies back from the pub to see the New Year in. If we're going to keep open house for a crowd of

Irishmen, that should be a night to remember!'

'Where's Mr Mulligan this evening?' Chris asked. 'I thought he was going to help with the decorations?'

'He'll be along presently; someone at the Thessaly Arms offered him a cut-price Christmas tree. So if you see a fir tree walking up Agar Road all by itself, you'll know it's Mr Mulligan on his way back from the pub!'

Chris laughed, then added: 'Oh, by the way, there's a letter for you on the mantelpiece. It came by the second post.'

'Oh, thanks. I expect it's an early Christmas card.'

Jo found it propped up against the clock and scanned it for clues. 'I don't know the writing – it's a terrible scrawl. I'm surprised the postman managed to make out the address.'

'It might be your landlady, the one at the Rope Walk.'

'Oh, dear old Sarah – yes, I suppose so . . . Or it could be someone answering our advert for the spare room.'

Since Chockie had decided not to move in, Jo had started advertising the room to let once again, much to Chris's disgust.

'I still think you ought to keep that room for Chockie,' she grumbled. 'Suppose he changes his mind, later on?'

'We'll cross that bridge when we come to it.' Jo tore open the envelope, then exclaimed: 'Talk of the devil! This is from Chockie!'

'Is it about the room?' Chris lit up like a fire blazing into flame. 'Show me!' She snatched the letter from Jo's hands. 'Fancy you not knowing his writing!' she added reproachfully.

'When I knew him, he was too young to write. What's he got to say?'

Chris began to read it aloud: ' "Dear Jo – this is to wish you a" – a something – it looks like "boggy drumstick" . . . Yes, it is dreadful writing – I can't make it out.'

'Let me try.' Jo took it back from her. ' "This is to wish you a happy Christmas and send my love to you and to Vee." '

'Is that all?' Chris sounded agonised.

'No, he goes on to say: "Please tell Chris I'm sorry I shan't be able to come and see you at Christmas." '

'What?' Her voice was tragic. 'But he must come.'

Reading ahead swiftly, Jo explained: 'He says the Dandos have had a stroke of luck, they've got a booking with an international circus.

Some other artist had to drop out at the last minute, so the Amazing Dandos are taking his place. Isn't that marvellous? I'm so glad.'

'But how long are they going to be away? When are we going to have our family party?'

'Let me see . . . Um . . . "Starting 16 December, we play a month in Brussels, two weeks in Paris, one week in Copenhagen and one in Amsterdam. Should be back in London late Fib" – Fib? No, Feb – "late February, unless the tour gets extended to Geneva and Luxembourg . . ." He can't spell Luxembourg, either, but never mind. "Sorry we shan't see you before we leave, but we're busy packing and rehearsing. Love to all, merry Christmas and happy New Year – your loving brother, Chockie." Well! Isn't that wonderful?'

Chris rounded on her. 'What's wonderful about it?'

'It's a terrific opportunity for him, travelling all over Europe – he'll be able to tell us about it when he gets back.'

'Yes, *when* . . . He didn't even wish me a happy Christmas.'

'He said he's sorry he won't see us, and he did send you his love.'

'He said "*love to all*"!' Chris refused to be comforted. 'That doesn't mean anything.'

'Try to look at it from their point of view. It's what they'd been praying for – a nice long tour, to make them lots of money.'

'I don't care. I wanted Chockie to come and live here . . . That's what I'd been praying for.' She crumpled up the string of paper angels. 'Angels are like Santa Claus. You stop believing in all that when you grow up.'

'I wouldn't say that. Prayers can help.'

'Oh, yes? When has praying ever helped you?'

'It helped me find Vee and Chockie, I'm sure of that.'

'Well, it hasn't done you much good since then, has it? You haven't seen Vee lately, and now Chockie's going away.' Trying to cover her own disappointment, Chrissie turned on Jo: 'It's all your fault he didn't come here! You were going to arrange it, but then you let it all go wrong . . .'

'He made up his own mind. There was nothing I could do about it.'

'You could have persuaded him if you'd really tried. I wish Vee had gone to see him instead of you – she always gets what she wants. I bet she'd have fixed it somehow!'

'I'm sorry you feel like that about it. Look, why don't I make us both some cocoa, then we'll get on with these decorations and—'

'Damn and blast the rotten decorations!' Chris swept the coloured paper off the table on to the floor. 'I don't care about mouldy bloody Christmas. I don't care about anything. I'm going out!'

'What do you mean? Out where?'

'For a walk! And don't try to come with me. I want to be on my own!'

Chris grabbed her hat and coat and ran down the hall, out into the darkness.

Sadly, Jo picked up the crêpe paper and went on making Christmas angels, but her heart wasn't in it.

As she worked, she wondered when Mr Mulligan would be coming home with his cut-price Christmas tree. Perhaps he would meet Chris on his way back, and manage to cheer her up. She hoped he would return soon – his cheerful blarney would be very welcome tonight – but she had a strong suspicion that she wouldn't see him until turning-out time.

Half an hour later, there was a knock at the door, and her spirits rose; he was always going out without his key nowadays.

She went along the passage and opened the door; but the man on the step, silhouetted against a street-lamp, was not carrying a fir-tree.

'Couldn't you get a Christmas tree after all?' she began, then realised that the newcomer was not Mr Mulligan; he was taller and broader, with square shoulders and curly hair.

'Evening, Jo,' said Pete Hobden, stepping into the circle of lamplight. 'Sorry to disappoint you, but I don't have a tree on me just at the moment; only Christmas wishes, and the compliments of the season – will that do?'

She opened her mouth, but the words would not come.

'Ent you going to ask me in?' he went on. 'I've called round on a little matter of business.'

'Business?' she repeated, stupidly.

'Aye, I've come in answer to your advert. I understand you've a room to let – is that right?'

'Oh, yes . . .' She took a deep breath. 'You'd better come inside.'

She stood aside to let him in, and he squeezed past her into the narrow hallway, then turned to her. They stood face to face in the soft lamplight.

'By gum, you're lovelier than ever,' he said.

Soon it would be the shortest day of the year, and by the time Chris got to Cheyne Walk it was almost dark. Across the Albert Bridge, the embankment was lit by tall lamp-standards set at intervals upon the river-wall, but she hung back among the shadows.

It had seemed such a good idea at first. The more she thought about it, the more certain she was that Vee would solve all their problems. She had decided to go straight to Vee and tell her what had happened. She would ask her to speak to Chockie, and get everything sorted out.

Only now, as she faced the tall house, her courage was beginning to fail her. She glanced up at the lighted windows, and felt her boldness and determination oozing away. How could she walk up those imposing steps and ring the bell at the front door?

She tried to tell herself she was being silly. She only had to ask to speak to Miss Vanessa Coburn, after all – there was no law against doing that. If she could just see Vee and explain it all to her, her cousin would understand. It was the only way to get Chockie to stay in London and move into Agar Road . . . But she couldn't bring herself to make the first move.

There was nothing for it but to go home again. Sick at heart, she turned away – slap-bang into someone standing behind her in the darkness.

'Well, hello!' said an American voice. 'Look who's here – little Miss Rita Hayworth in person.'

'Don!' Startled, she lost her balance, and he caught her in his arms. 'I didn't see you there.'

'I didn't see you, till you nearly knocked me off my feet!' he teased her, then exclaimed: 'Hey, what's wrong, babe? You're shaking.'

As he held her close to him, she began to feel a little better; his thick tweed coat was warm and comforting.

'I'm all right, really I am.'

'Sure you are,' he soothed her. 'But what are you doing here? Is Jo with you?'

'No, I came on my own. I thought I might be able to talk to Vee . . . Vanessa, I mean.'

'Is that so? And did you see her?'

'No . . . I was going to, but then I sort of changed my mind.'

'I don't get it. Were you supposed to be taking tea with her, or what?'

'No, she doesn't know I'm here, so . . . It seemed a bit rude to go in without being invited.'

'I know what you mean.' She could hear that he was smiling. 'I guess I had the same kind of feeling myself. Fact is, I've been trying to get hold of the girl all week, only she's never home when I call her, so I figured if I hung around, I might catch her going in or out . . . Pretty dumb idea, I guess. Jo told me Vee's brother is sick – that's why she stays at home, to look after him. Maybe we'd do better to write her a letter instead?'

Chris was uncomfortably reminded of Chockie: 'I hate letters! Nobody ever writes letters to me.' She felt tears of self-pity welling up inside and tried to hold them back. 'Excuse me. I've got to go now.'

She struggled to break free, but he held her tightly. 'Hey, what's the big idea? Don't you go upsetting yourself.'

'I – I can't help it . . .' Now she was crying in earnest, unable to stop. 'Please let go of me,' she sobbed. 'I think I've lost my handkerchief. I don't want to cry all over your coat.'

'The hell with my coat, you go ahead and cry all you want.' He pulled out a shiny silk handkerchief. 'Here, dry your tears with this, then try telling me what's wrong, huh?'

Still with his arm around her, he steered her away from Cheyne Walk and over the bridge, back to Battersea.

Pete Hobden set down his cup and pronounced his verdict: 'You mek a fair pot of tea, I'll say that for you.'

'Thank you,' said Jo.

It felt unreal, sitting in the parlour at Agar Road with Pete at the other side of the table. She'd apologised for the state of the room, scooping up the half-finished bands of angels and stuffing them away behind the best armchair. In order to give herself time to think, she had offered him a cup of tea.

Now they sat and stared at one another, and he began again: 'About this room you're advertising – it's still vacant, is it?'

'Oh, yes,' she replied without stopping to think, then cursed herself for not having the sense to lie about it.

'Could I have a look at it, then?' he asked.

'I don't know – I mean – I don't think so,' she stammered. 'I don't really think it would suit you.'

'That's for me to say, ent it?' He stood up. 'Will you lead the way?'

She could find no reason to refuse. Uncomfortably, she took him upstairs and showed him the small front room – the single bed, the upright chair, the wardrobe and chest-of-drawers, the washstand with its jug and basin – and she felt ashamed of its spartan simplicity.

'I'm sorry there's no fitted basin,' she heard herself apologising. 'I bring up a jug of hot water first thing. The toilet's on the half-landing. There's only enough water in the hot tank for one bath every morning, so we have to have a rota for using the bathroom.'

'I hope you don't have a rota for using the lavvy?' he asked solemnly.

She was not amused. 'I daresay it's not up to your standards,' she retorted indignantly. 'If you don't like it, you're very welcome to go and find something better.'

'Easy now, don't tek me up like that. I never said I didn't like it. Why don't we go downstairs and talk it over? Mebbe you could squeeze a second cup out of that teapot, an' all?'

Back in the parlour, they discussed the financial details. She explained that the rent including a cooked breakfast and an evening meal.

'I might not always be here of an evening – I work funny hours, often as not,' he told her. 'But I'd say this would suit me down to the ground. How soon could I move in, like?'

She made one more effort to fight back. 'I'm not so sure it would suit *me*! Why on earth do you want to move in here? You could find a room as good as this, or better, anywhere in London. What made you pick on Agar Road, of all places?'

'I reckoned as you'd be a pretty good landlady, and I had an idea we'd hit it off,' he replied calmly. 'I like you, Jo Wells. I allus did, right from the first go – you know that.'

Before Jo could think what to say to him, she was distracted by the sound of a key in the lock, and the return of Mr Mulligan from the pub. She went into the hall and helped him carry the tree into the parlour. He had had a couple of drinks, certainly, but he was no more than merry, and he had acquired a very fine Christmas tree.

'It's a beauty – you've done us proud,' she told him. 'Chris said there's a box of decorations in the loft somewhere. I'll go up and look for them later, when—'

She broke off as Pete rose to his feet, saying: 'Mebbe I could climb up and find it for you?'

'No, thanks, I can manage,' she said shortly. Seeing Mr Mulligan's astonishment, she was forced to introduce the two men. 'This is Mr Mulligan, who has the room across the landing, and this is Pete Hobden, who—'

'I can guess!' The old Irishman shook Pete's hand warmly. 'Delighted to make your acquaintance. You'll be our new lodger, am I right?'

Pete turned to Jo. 'Well, Jo? What do you say?'

To her surprise, Jo found that she could not argue any longer.

'Yes,' she said. 'This is our new lodger.'

A clammy fog was creeping in off the river, and Battersea Bridge Road was almost deserted as Don and Chris walked back. An occasional car crawled by them, throwing out a pale glow-worm light before it was swallowed up again in the darkness.

Gradually Chris's sobs quietened to an occasional sniff. For a while they walked on in silence, but then Don began again: 'Wanna tell me about it?' he urged her. 'Whatever it is?'

'It's about Chockie,' she said in a small voice.

For a moment he was puzzled. 'Something to do with candy bars?'

'No, *Chockie* – you know, we saw him at the circus, on the tightrope.'

'Oh, sure, the kid in the clown outfit. Jo thought he might have been her brother. Yes, I remember. What about him?'

'He is her brother. Didn't Vee tell you?'

'No kidding? Like I said, I haven't seen Vee for quite a while.'

'Well, Jo invited Chockie round to tea – Vee was there as well – they both wanted him to come and live with Jo and me at Agar Road, and – and I wanted him to, as well. We thought he was going to, but then he changed his mind. And now he's going away with the circus for months and months – to Paris and Belgium and all sorts of places – and nobody knows how long they'll be away, except he's not going to have Christmas with us after all . . .'

Her voice sounded dangerously close to breaking again, and Don said: 'That's too bad. And you're feeling pretty low about it – right?'

'Well, yes. I got very angry with Jo this evening. I told her she'd messed everything up. That's why I wanted to talk to Vee about it. I'm sure she could persuade those Dando people to let Chockie come and live with us.'

'Think so?' Don pondered this for a few moments, then said: 'Sorry, I don't get it. What's it got to do with Vee, anyhow?'

'Don't you understand? Chockie's her brother too – we know that now. He disappeared just like Vee, that night in the war when they got bombed, and now they've all found each other again . . .'

Suddenly an uncomfortable thought occurred to Chris, and she added: 'You do know about that, don't you? About Vee being Jo's sister? I mean, you're her boy-friend, she must have told you?'

He only paused for a split second, before saying easily: 'Sure, she told me something about it . . . Hey, you're shivering. Lemme put my coat around you. I guess it's big enough for the both of us.'

Unbuttoning his tweed overcoat, he wrapped it round her, sheltering her within its reassuring warmth, and she began to relax.

'This is nice,' she said. 'I do like your overcoat.'

'It's not exactly mine, I borrowed it from Mr Wade . . . Well, he doesn't get around much, these days.'

As they wandered on, he continued: 'Yeah, Vee told me she was Jo's sister, but she never really filled me in on all the details, and I didn't like to pry. But I guess you must know the whole story, huh? Like, she's not really Vanessa Coburn at all, she's Vanessa Wells – right?'

'Her real name's Vera – Vera Wells – only we call her Vee. I sort of remember her from when I was little,' Chris explained, feeling pleasantly important. It was nice to be able to tell Don things he didn't know.

She told him everything she could remember, and when she had finished, he said thoughtfully: 'No wonder she wants to keep it a secret from the Coburns. I guess they'd go bananas if they ever found out.'

'That's right. That's why we must never tell anyone,' Chris agreed. She felt almost happy at last, within the comforting shelter of Don's coat. 'I wouldn't have told you, only I guessed you knew about it already.'

'That's right,' he told her softly. 'In fact, it might be best if you don't tell Jo and Vee we've been talking about it. It's such a big secret, they might not like to think we'd discussed it behind their backs.'

When they stopped outside the Battersea General Hospital, at the corner of Prince of Wales Drive, Chris said: 'This is where I turn off to go to Agar Road, unless you'd like to come and have tea with us? I'm sure Jo would be pleased to see you.'

'No, I won't do that; she's probably busy. If I were you, I wouldn't even mention you'd met me this evening. Let's just pretend we never had this conversation, OK?'

'OK,' said Chris. 'But I'm glad we talked – I feel a lot better now. Thanks for listening.'

'It was my pleasure,' said Don.

Chapter Nineteen

OVER THE NEXT FEW WEEKS, Don continued to take pleasure in the secret Chris had given away.

It was like a precious stone he had found in a dustbin, carried home and polished carefully. Sometimes he would lie awake at night and think about this valuable secret, turning it round and round in his mind, studying it from every angle, admiring its brilliance and wondering what it might be worth.

He was in no hurry to squander his treasure – he was content to save it up for a rainy day. In the meantime, he had the thrill of possession and power. That was a pleasure indeed.

Christmas came and went. Jo remembered Don's hint about needing a large Christmas stocking to hold her present from Russell, and was rather puzzled when it turned out to be a generous cheque. When she mentioned this to Don, he explained that Russell had intended to buy her a fur coat, but they had finally decided it was too difficult to get the right size, so Russell had given her money instead.

Jo wasn't sure she believed this – remembering the angry quarrel she had overheard, she could hardly imagine they had been discussing a fur coat – but she was very grateful, particularly as she had never had the slightest desire to own one. It would have stayed in her wardrobe, reeking of mothballs and waiting for a special occasion that never arrived. She preferred to put the money to more practical use.

Chockie sent glittering Christmas and New Year cards from Brussels, followed by picture postcards from all the other cities that the Grand International Circus visited. Another card arrived at the beginning of April, explaining that the tour had been extended, and they would now be visiting Oslo, Stockholm and Moscow as well.

'By the time he gets back, he'll be the best-travelled boy in Europe!' said Jo, as she got the breakfast ready.

'So what?' Chris tossed her red curls. 'He can go round the whole blooming world if he wants to, see if I care!'

Jo knew how Chris was feeling. She could still remember her own misery on the night of VE Day, when she thought she would never see Pete Hobden again . . . And now here they were, living under the same roof, with no romantic nonsense between them to spoil things – a nice, straightforward friendship and nothing more.

Well, almost nothing . . . As she made some toast under the grill, she tried to analyse her feelings. She had to admit that she did feel a kind of excitement when Pete came home from work. Sometimes, when Chris had gone to bed and she was sitting in the parlour, waiting for Mr Mulligan to come back from the pub, she would find herself looking at Pete, sitting at the other side of the fireplace. He would glance up and catch her eye, and it seemed that some unspoken message passed between them, though nothing was said.

Well, they'd been through all that long ago, and it was much better like this: two grown-up people, enjoying each other's company without any stupid, messy complications. Besides, he'd already got a regular girl-friend in Sheffield, hadn't he? So there was no possible reason for her to expect anything other than—

'Look out!' exclaimed Chris. 'The toast!'

Too late, Jo snatched at the grill pan. The slices of bread were black, and the kitchen reeked of burnt toast.

'Stupid – I was miles away,' she said, throwing them into the bin under the sink. 'I'll have to do some more, and try to be careful.'

When Pete and Mr Mulligan came down to the parlour for breakfast, the toast-rack was filled with golden-brown slices, and the kitchen door was firmly shut, so they were none the wiser.

The wireless was switched on in the background, and the two men were listening to the early news. Today, as Alvar Liddell read the latest bulletin, they heard a rustle of paper from the loudspeaker, then he continued: 'Here is an additional news item that has just come in. It has been announced that yesterday evening at the port of Liverpool, following upon information previously received, investigating officers from the Customs and Excise Department boarded the twenty-thousand-ton transatlantic liner, SS *Franconia*, when it arrived from New York.'

Pete looked up, a cup of tea halfway to his lips.

'Hidden within the inner hull of the ship, and behind wall-panels in some of the first-class cabins, they uncovered a large quantity of nylon stockings with an estimated value on the black market of over £80,000, together with other contraband merchandise. Several arrests have been made, and further police proceedings are now under way.'

Jo turned to Pete and said: 'Sounds like work for you, doesn't it?'

Chris was immediately interested, and asked hopefully: 'Do you sell nylons, as well as newspapers?'

'He doesn't sell newspapers, Chris. I told you, Pete writes for the *Evening News*.'

'Sorry to disappoint you.' Pete smiled. 'I don't flog nylons meself, I only write about them.' Then, in answer to Jo's question: 'Yes, I reckon I'll have to follow this up. The police must have had a good tip-off.' He pushed back his chair. 'If you'll excuse me, ladies and gents, I think I'd best be getting me skates on.'

'You haven't had your second cup of tea,' Jo reminded him.

'I think I'll give it a miss, just this once. Something tells me I'm going to have a busy day today.' He went into the hall to fetch his hat and coat, saying: 'So long, Mr M. – ta-ta, Chris – see you tonight, Jo. Usual time, I hope, but you never know.'

Less than a mile away, in the upstairs flat at Galleon House, Don too had heard the news – not from a wireless-set, but by way of an early-morning telephone call. When he put the receiver down, his face was hard and angry.

He would have to move fast, to try and recoup his losses. Glancing at the window, he noticed raindrops were spattering the panes – an April shower – and his lips twisted into a smile.

Maybe this was the rainy day he'd been waiting for.

Vee was alone in the drawing-room, having a mid-morning cup of coffee, when Alec walked in.

'Hello,' she said.

She expected him to turn round and go straight out again – that was what he usually did – but he came to the middle of the room and put

The Times down on the table.

'Hello,' he said – and he was smiling. 'How are you?'

'Very well, thank you,' she replied. 'How are you?'

He stopped smiling at once. 'For heaven's sake don't start that again! I'm fed up with people asking how I am – hovering round me, taking my temperature, firing questions at me—'

She interrupted him: 'You said "How are you?" so I said "How are you?" I know they're silly questions, but I thought we were being polite!'

He considered this, then managed another smile, and for a moment she saw the easy, good-natured Alec she loved.

'Sorry, I'm still a bit quick on the trigger,' he admitted. 'Is there any coffee left in that pot?'

'Yes, I think so. I'll ring for another cup.'

She pressed the bell-push beside the fireplace. It was a long time since Alec had been like this. For months now he had kept everyone at arm's length, spending the day in his own room.

He wandered across to the window. The early showers had given way to sunlight; that seemed to be a good omen.

'Nice day,' he said.

'Yes, isn't it?' she agreed, and dared to add: 'Everything looks better when the sun shines.'

'Matter of fact, I'm feeling pretty good myself. I've decided what I'm going to do.'

'Do?'

'Well, I'm not completely crackers, you know, whatever the experts say! I realise I can't go on like this for ever, but it wasn't till this morning, when I was reading something in *The Times*, that I suddenly realised what I've got to do.'

'What do you mean?'

He indicated the newspaper. 'It's all there – read it for yourself. A piece about emigration – people going off to start a new life in Australia. That's where I'm going.'

She didn't know what to say. 'Oh – but . . .'

'It's the perfect answer! A new beginning, in a new place, where nobody knows me – somewhere to start all over again.' Seeing the look on her face, he frowned. 'Now what's the matter?'

'Well, it's just – how long would you go for?' she asked.

He laughed at her inability to understand. 'It's not a holiday trip. Emigration means staying there permanently . . . Why are you looking so shocked?'

'But, if you go and live there, I'd never see you—' She corrected herself quickly: 'We'd never see you.'

'I'd have thought you'd be glad to get rid of me. I know I've been a pain in the neck lately.'

'We love you – Aunt Elspeth loves you – it would break her heart if she thought—'

'If Aunt wants to see me so desperately, she can always fly out for a visit – later on, when I've settled in.'

'Alec, she's nearly seventy! Can you imagine her going halfway round the world in an aeroplane?'

His face darkened, and she saw that he was working himself up into a rage. 'I might have known you'd do your best to stop me. Why the hell do you have to keep interfering?'

She clenched her fists so tightly, the nails bit into her palms. 'I'm not. It's just – we'd miss you so much if you went away, and you'd miss us too, wouldn't you?'

'Grow up, can't you?' His temper flared. 'You talk like a child.'

The door opened, and a startled parlourmaid asked timidly: 'You rang, miss?'

'Oh, yes.' Vee tried to pull herself together. 'Could you fetch another cup, please?'

'Don't bother, I don't want any damn coffee. I'm going up to my room,' said Alec, and walked out.

As he did so, the telephone rang, and the maid answered it, glad to have something to do. She listened for a moment, then threw Vee a sidelong glance as she replied carefully: 'I'm sorry sir, Miss Coburn is unable to come to the telephone. Would you care to leave a message?'

'Who is it?' Vee asked.

The girl covered the mouthpiece with her hand: 'It's that American gentleman, miss, that's why I told him you—'

Impulsively, Vee changed her mind. She went across to the telephone, saying: 'It's all right, I'll take it.' As soon as the door closed, she said: 'Hello, Don? It's me.'

'And they say the age of miracles has passed!' His voice sounded thin and metallic, but as lively as ever. 'If you knew how many goddam times I've tried to call you . . .'

'I'm sorry, I've been very busy.'

'Sure, your brother's sick – Jo told me. Sorry about that.'

'Yes, it's been a difficult time. Was there something special, or did you just ring up for a chat?'

'Hell, no! I want to see you, for gosh sake. It's been so long. I want to take you out some night . . . I've missed you like hell.'

'I know, I've missed you too, but—'

'Don't give me that! I won't take "no" for an answer, and I won't take any "buts" either! Just name the time and place and I'll be there. How's about it? Yes or no?'

At that moment, she wanted more than anything to try and forget Alec, to stop agonising over him, to go out and enjoy herself.

Breathlessly, she said: 'All right, Don – yes. I'd love to see you.'

He turned up that evening on the dot of seven-thirty, and waited in the hall while the parlourmaid went up to inform Miss Vanessa that her visitor had arrived.

A few minutes later Vee came downstairs, wearing a glamorous ballerina-length dress, with her coat over her shoulders. She wasn't sure how to greet him. She was about to shake hands, but he pulled her towards him and kissed her – a real kiss, on the mouth.

'You look a million dollars,' he said.

She smiled. 'So do you.'

He wore a crisply ruffled shirt, a long jacket in bottle-green with black velvet collar and cuffs, and his hair was brushed up into a quiff, held with brilliantine.

'Can I offer you a drink, or do you want to leave straight away?' she asked. 'Have you got a taxi waiting?'

'No, we can pick up a cab along King's Road. I guess a quick slug would hit the spot, get the evening off to a good start, huh?'

'Yes, of course. The only thing is, Aunt Elspeth and Alec are in the drawing-room, but we can have a drink in the dining-room, if you like. I think there's some sherry on the sideboard – would that be all right?'

The long dining-table was already laid with two places, one at either side. Vee poured two small sherries; they sat together at the end of the table, and Don clinked his glass against hers.

'Here's to you 'n' me, babe,' he said. 'And to the future.'

Emptying his glass in a couple of swigs, he made smalltalk – about the weather, the rumour that petrol-rationing was due to end very soon, and another rumour, even more exciting, that the bobby-soxers' idol, Frank Sinatra, might be coming over shortly to appear at the London Palladium.

'If he does, I'll get us a couple of ringside seats for the first night!' he promised.

The dining-room door opened, and Alec walked in.

Ignoring Vee, he addressed his remarks to Don. 'The maid told us an American visitor had arrived. I was afraid it might be you,' he said, tight-lipped. 'I hoped I'd made it perfectly clear that you are not welcome here. What do I have to do to convince you?'

Don stood up, trying to smile. 'Hey, now, wait a minute, willya?'

'No, sir, I will not wait. I must ask you to leave this house.' A nervous tic galvanised one side of Alec's face, as if he were winking, but his voice was crisp and hard. 'Will you get out, or do I have to throw you out?'

'Alec, don't, please.' Vee too rose to her feet, but both men were talking at once.

'I'm here to see Vanessa, not you, buddy.'

'Unless you leave this house immediately—'

'What right have you got to pull rank on me?'

'I have every right. She is my sister, and I feel responsible for—'

'Listen, buster, I know you've just come out of the booby-hatch, but this is none of your goddam business.'

Alec threw himself on Don, who fell back against the table. The cloth was dragged sideways, sending glass and silver crashing to the floor, and Vee grabbed Alec's shoulders, screaming: 'Stop it – stop it at once!'

Alec released his hold on Don, who scrambled away, taking Vee's hand and saying: 'He's nutty as a fruitcake. We're getting outa here.'

Alec called after Vee: 'Don't listen to him, don't go.'

Pale with anger, she turned on him. 'I'd never have believed you could behave like this. I'm ashamed of you.'

Taking Don's arm, she walked out of the house.

After supper, Mr Mulligan visited the pub as usual, and Chris went upstairs to do her homework. She would be sitting her exams in a few months, and she put in several hours of revision every night.

Pete wiped up while Jo washed, then helped her put the dishes away. As they worked, they talked easily about nothing in particular; they both enjoyed these relaxed evenings together. When the job was done, they returned to the parlour and sat in their usual places, facing each other across the hearthrug.

'Shall I turn the wireless on?' she suggested. 'There might be something worth listening to.'

'I'd sooner listen to you,' he said. 'What sort of day have you had?'

'Oh, the same as usual – shopping, cooking, cleaning,' she replied. 'Chris came home from school in a bad mood because Chockie hadn't sent her a postcard . . . Just an ordinary day, really.'

'So much for Agar Road.' Pete paused, then went on: 'How about Galleon House? Any excitement there?'

She glanced at him, then replied: 'No, sorry to disappoint you.'

'What d'you mean by that?'

'I wondered if you were hoping for some more information about Don Scott,' she said coolly. 'I thought this might be your tactful way of asking me what he's up to nowadays?'

'Don Scott never even entered my head,' said Pete, then grinned. 'But since you've raised the subject, do you happen to know what he's up to?'

'I haven't the faintest idea,' she answered. 'And if I had, I wouldn't tell you. I'm not going to spy on people, just to provide you with a good story for your newspaper.'

'Be fair. Have I ever so much as hinted?'

'No, but that's the reason you moved in here, isn't it? You thought it might be a good way of keeping an eye on Galleon House.'

'I told you why I moved in,' he said, evenly. 'And it had nothing whatsoever to do with Don Scott or Galleon House – or the *Evening News* either. When I come home, I try to forget about my job.'

'So that's why you never bring a copy of the paper with you. I wondered about that, too.'

He shrugged. 'Like I said, I leave all that behind. When I come home, all I'm interested in is you.'

She tried to turn this aside as a joke. 'You'll have to think up a better reason. I'm not that interesting.'

'Oh, yes, you are,' he said softly. 'The most interesting, the most fascinating, the most beautiful girl I ever met. Is that good enough?'

At that moment the little front parlour became a place of magic, filled with light and warmth and happiness, yet she struggled to talk sensibly. 'What about the other girl?' she asked. 'The one in Sheffield?'

'I knew you'd ask me that, sooner or later,' he said. 'I suppose I'd best come clean. There is no other girl, in Sheffield or anywhere else. I just made her up.'

'But why? Why did you pretend?'

'I was afraid you'd think there was summat wrong with me, if I said I'd no girl of my own. If I'd said I'd fallen for you the moment I saw you, you'd have thought I was a proper barm-pot.'

'Oh, Pete.' She caught her breath, overcome by a sudden surge of joy. 'I don't know what to say . . .'

He stood up, holding out his arms to her. 'Do we have to say anything?'

Before she could reply, they heard Chris running downstairs.

As soon as she entered the room, she stopped dead, looked from one to the other, then said: 'What's the matter?'

'Nothing's the matter,' said Jo. 'Why should anything be the matter? I was just going to put the kettle on and make us a hot drink.' She stood up. 'Do you want a cup of cocoa?'

'Yes, ta,' said Chris. 'If you're making one.'

For the sake of something to say, Pete asked her: 'Finished your homework, then?'

'Yes, I've done enough for one evening. I've gone over the Repeal of the Corn Laws, and *The Merchant of Venice* . . . Is it all right if I put the wireless on? It's *ITMA* tonight.'

So they sat and drank their cocoa and listened to Tommy Handley and Mrs Mopp. Later, after Chris had gone to bed, Mr Mulligan came in, and they sat and talked to him instead. Later still, when the old man had retired for the night, Pete took Jo in his arms and kissed her.

'About time too,' he said. 'I think I've aged ten years, these last few hours.'

Jo looked at him with shining eyes, then sighed. 'It's very late . . . I really should go up as well.'

'When the house is quiet, can I come to your room?' he asked.

Jo shook her head. 'No, Pete . . . Not tonight.'

'Why not?' He drew back, studying her face. 'You still don't trust me?'

'It isn't that. Everything's happened so fast. We need time to think – time to understand each other. This time we've got to do it properly.'

He was silent for a moment, and then, reluctantly, he nodded.

'Happen you're right. Let's do it properly. After all, this is going to last for the rest of our lives.'

Vee shut her eyes tightly, then opened them again, making a great effort to focus, but her head was swimming. A song was blaring out through a loudspeaker; the same tune seemed to have been playing all evening:

> "Put another nickel in – in the nickelodeon,
>   All I want is loving you, and music, music, music . . ."

'Enjoying it?' asked Don.

They were sitting in a side alcove, with plates of cold chicken and wilting salad in front of them.

Vee articulated each word carefully: 'Sometimes I think you can have too much music.'

'I meant the food,' he explained.

'Oh – it's very nice,' she said. 'Only I'm not very hungry.'

Don poured some more champagne into her glass. 'Have another drink. That'll wash it down.'

He had insisted on bringing her to what he called 'the most exclusive dive in town', and she tried to tell herself she was enjoying it, but it was too noisy, too crowded, and too dark.

On a small dance-floor in the middle of the room, a dozen closely packed couples were trying to dance; others sat in shady alcoves, drinking, eating, or – as far as she could see – embracing one another.

'It's the hottest nightspot in town, believe me,' Don told her. 'You gotta be really somebody to get in here.'

To her relief, the loudspeakers faded, and the dancers returned to their tables; then a cymbal-crash made her jump. A pair of curtains whisked aside to reveal a three piece jazz band on a tiny stage, and four chorus-girls ran on to the dance-floor, going into an energetic tap-routine.

'Cabaret time,' said Don, refilling Vee's glass. 'Get a load of this!'

At the climax of their number, three of the girls turned on the fourth and tore off her scanty costume, piece by piece, while the audience cheered and applauded – whereupon the girl, now wearing nothing but a diamanté g-string and a dazzling smile, raised her arms in triumph, and all the lights went out.

Vee, who had never seen a strip-tease before, was determined not to let Don know she was shocked, and when he asked: 'How's about that then?' she answered politely: 'It was very good – quite unusual.'

He laughed and put his arm round her. 'You're a great girl, you know that? I'm just crazy about you, babe.'

Now a mature lady in a low-cut black dress joined the band and began to croon a song about Mona Lisa. Under cover of the darkness, Don began to caress Vee, murmuring: 'I love you, and I gotta hunch you love me . . . That's why I want you to marry me, sweetheart.'

At first she thought he was joking, but when he repeated it she whispered uncomfortably: 'Oh, no, I'm sorry – you're very nice. But I couldn't – it's impossible.'

'What's impossible about it?' he asked. 'We love each other, don't we?'

'I don't know . . . But anyway, my family would never agree.'

She was feeling hot and dizzy, and when he tried to refill her glass, she said: 'No, honestly. I've had too much already . . . I must go home.'

'You're not going home,' he told her. 'You're staying with me tonight. I want you to stay with me for keeps, baby.'

'Don't be silly.'

'Forget about your folks. Lemme take you away with me . . . We'll run away together, back to the States. We'll find us a judge, get ourselves married, and live happy ever after.'

She tried to struggle free. 'Don, you're talking nonsense. I've got to go home.'

'You mean you won't marry me?'

'Of course I won't – I can't. I've had a lovely evening, but it's over now, so—'

As she struggled to her feet, he pulled her down again, and she began to feel frightened.

'I got news for you,' he said. 'If you don't marry me, I'm gonna tell the Coburns all about you, Miss Vera Wells . . . You thought I didn't know about that, didn't you? But dear little Chrissie told me everything. And if you don't play ball, I'm going to blow your fairy-tale right through the goddam roof! Whaddaya say to that, princess?'

In one horrifying moment, Vee sobered up. A trickle of sweat ran down her spine. Her body felt cold and clammy, and she saw Don Scott as he really was.

'Will you excuse me?' she said, with icy precision. 'I think I'm going to be sick.'

The following day, when Jo got back to Agar Road after lunch, Vee was waiting on the doorstep.

'Hello, stranger—' she began. Then she saw Vee's expression. 'What is it? Tell me!'

Vee shook her head. 'In a minute . . . Let's go inside.'

Jo led the way into the parlour, saying: 'Sit down, tell me what's wrong. You look dreadful.'

'I was awake most of the night, worrying myself to death.'

So then Vee told her the whole story – untidily and out of sequence, forgetting some of the details, then adding them in later.

Jo listened in silence until she mentioned Chris, then interrupted: 'Chris told him? Oh, no, she'd never do that.'

'She must have. Nobody else knows about it, except Chockie, and he doesn't even know Don.' Her face crumpled up as she added: 'I wish I didn't.'

Jo dropped to her knees, gripping Vee's hands and saying: 'I'm so very sorry. I don't know what to say.'

'Say whatever you like. You tried to warn me about him, and I wouldn't listen. I thought I knew him better than you did – but I didn't.'

'I never dreamed of anything like this. What are you going to do?'

'I don't know! That's why I came round to see you. Tell me what I ought to do.'

'I don't know either, except you can't possibly marry him. I won't let you.'

'But if I don't, he'll tell them. I've got until Friday to make up my mind.'

'Friday?'

'There's going to be a party at Galleon House on Friday night, and I'm invited.'

Jo frowned. 'It's the first I've heard of it.'

'Didn't Mr Wade tell you? Don says I've got to be there, so he can announce our engagement. And if I don't go – if I don't do what he says . . .' She clung to Jo. 'Do you think he means it?'

Racking her brains, Jo asked: 'Would you mind if I told Pete?'

'Pete who?' Vee stared at her. 'You mean your new lodger? Why on earth do you want to tell him?'

'He's not just a lodger, he's a reporter for the *Evening News*, on the Crime Desk. He warned me that Don was mixed up with some black-market racket. He might be able to advise us what to do.'

Vee protested: 'I can't see what good it will do, telling a reporter! I don't want to be plastered all over the newspapers.'

'Pete won't print anything if I ask him not to – we can trust him.' Jo looked at the clock. 'Chris will be back soon, we'll find out what—'

Vee pulled herself up. 'I'd better be going. The way I feel at this moment, she's the last person I want to see.'

'All the same, it might be as well to find out how much she told Don. Can I ring you later at Cheyne Walk?'

'Yes, but be careful what you say, in case anyone's listening.'

After Vee had gone, Jo returned to the parlour, trying to make sense of the situation.

When Chris came home, she was surprised to find Jo sitting there, doing nothing.

'Aren't we having tea today?' she asked. 'You haven't laid the table.'

'Sorry, I had things to think about.'

'That's OK. I'll put the kettle on.'

She was on her way to the kitchen when Jo called her back, asking: 'Have you spoken to Don lately?'

'No, not for ages. I haven't seen him since before Christmas. Why?'

'Vee called in earlier. Apparently Don has found out about her being Vera Wells. She seemed to think you might have told him . . . You didn't, did you?'

'Of course I didn't.' Then Chris frowned. 'Well, I didn't exactly *tell* him. I accidentally happened to mention something, but he said it was all right, because Vee had already told him anyway.' She looked puzzled. 'Do you mean – Vee forgot she'd told him?'

'Something like that.' Jo sighed. 'I think I see how it happened, now.'

'Well, she must have done – he's her boy-friend, isn't he?'

'She thought he was,' agreed Jo. 'But she's not so sure now.'

Chris went into the kitchen, where she filled the kettle and lit the gas. A moment later she returned, holding a white envelope.

'This was on the kitchen table. It's got your name on it.'

Jo tore the envelope open. Inside was a single sheet of paper:

Don't bother about supper for me tonight. My Editor's sent me up north to chase that smuggling story. Don't know when I'll be back; expect me when you see me . . .

Love – Pete.

Slowly, Jo folded the paper. Why did he have to disappear today of all days, just when she needed his help? And he'd left no address or phone-number where she could reach him.

Then a thought occurred to her: his newspaper must know where he was – she would ask them where she could reach him.

Telling Chris she would be back very soon, she walked to the nearest phonebox, in Nine Elms Lane, hoping it would have the London directories.

She was in luck. She looked up the number in the 'A–K' book, and put her pennies in the coinbox, then dialled and waited. A girl's voice said: '*Evening News*'.

Jo pressed button A, asking: 'May I speak to someone on the Crime Desk, please?'

It was all so simple . . . Or it should have been.

A few minutes later she left the phonebox, completely dazed. The *Evening News* had never heard of Mr Peter Hobden; Peter Hobden had never worked on the Crime Desk – he was not employed by the *Evening News* in any capacity whatsoever. As far as the *Evening News* was concerned, Peter Hobden did not exist.

Jo walked slowly along Nine Elms Lane, hearing herself saying:

'We can trust him . . .' She had trusted Peter Hobden, and he had turned out to be just another liar.

She stared at the Power Station chimneys, towering above her, as if she had never seen them before. She was lost in a strange land. She did not know if she would ever find her way home.

Chapter Twenty

Jo stood at the kitchen sink with her hands plunged in a washing-up bowl, staring through the window at the Agar Road backyard, and seeing nothing.

It was Friday evening – the evening of the party at Galleon House. Russell had kept Jo busy all the morning, making cocktail snacks and polishing glasses. She asked if he wanted her to come back tonight and take charge of the food and drink, but he had told her it wouldn't be necessary. So she had come home as usual, and made tea for Chris and Mr Mulligan, and now she was doing the washing-up – but all she could think about was Vee. Would she be brave enough to tell the Coburns the truth?

When Chris burst into the kitchen and found Jo gazing into space, she exclaimed: 'You look as if you'd been struck all of a heap!'

Jo pulled herself together. 'I'm just finishing the washing-up. Would you like to lend a hand?'

'All right, but I'll have to be quick. I've got to be there at six.'

Jo was still in a daze. 'Why – where are you going?'

'Don't you remember? It's the night of the party!'

Now Jo was totally confused. 'You're not going to Galleon House?'

Chris laughed, and picked up a tea-cloth. 'The party at Bryden Brothers. I promised Pat and Malcolm I'd sit with Sandra and Mike while they go out tonight – you can't have forgotten that!'

'No, it just slipped my mind for a moment, that's all.'

During the last six months, Chris had become a regular visitor at the Jones's house; the two children had both taken to her. Several times, when Pat went on afternoon shopping expeditions, Chris had kept an eye on them, but this would be the first time that she had been in charge for an evening. It was a special occasion: Mrs Spenlow, a pillar of the Bryden Brothers establishment, was finally retiring, and the management were holding a buffet supper at the Falcon Hotel.

'I mustn't be late, whatever happens.' Chris polished the last plate. 'There, that's the lot. I'll have to go.'

As she went to fetch her coat, Jo said: 'Hang on – I'll come with you.'

Chris stared. 'Whatever for? Pat's going to help me bath them and put them to bed before she goes. It doesn't need both of us.'

Jo, who didn't want to be left on her own to worry about Vee, said: 'Yes, I know, but I'd like the walk.'

When they arrived at Blenheim Terrace, Pat greeted them warmly. 'Hello – are you going to keep each other company?'

Chris said quickly: 'She just came for the walk. She's not stopping, are you, Jo?'

'Oh, well, come in anyway and say hello to Malcolm.' Passing the hall mirror, Pat glanced ruefully at her reflection. 'I wasn't sure if I could squeeze into this dance-dress. I haven't worn it for ages, and I'm bulging in all the wrong places.

'You look smashing, and you know it,' Malcolm told her, from the front room. 'Stop fishing for compliments!'

'I'll look like a drowned rat by the time we finish bathing the kids,' Pat groaned, tying on an apron. 'Come on, Chris, help me scrub the little monsters.'

They went upstairs, and Jo heard squeals of delight, followed by energetic splashing.

'Sit yourself down,' said Malcolm, straightening his tie. 'It's only a small do, but the management will be there, so we've got to put on our best bibs and tuckers.'

'You make a very handsome couple,' Jo assured him.

He mumbled: 'I don't know about that, but I must say, Pat's a good girl. I'm a lucky man.' Sitting on the edge of the sofa, careful not to crease his trousers, he added: 'It's funny the way things work out, isn't it?'

'How do you mean?'

'Well, I was just thinking back to VE Day, the first time I met you.

Less than five years ago, but it's like another lifetime . . . I didn't even know Pat then.'

'No, you were going around with Nora Topping. Didn't you say she's living abroad now?'

'That's right. She got hooked on one of these Yanks – some young chap in the US Army – and when the war was over she went across to marry him. She must have been one of the first GI brides. I hope it turned out all right – but you do hear some tales, don't you? Girls going over, and finding that all the stories about big houses and Cadillacs were a load of eyewash . . . '

Trying to steer the conversation in another direction, Jo said the first thing that came into her head. 'Did you know Pat was quite worried about you and Nora? She asked me one day – she thought Nora was your big romance!'

Malcolm chuckled: 'Oh, lor', that's my silly fault. One day I let slip I'd fallen for someone else before Pat, and she was dead keen to know who it was, but I never told her . . . Just as well, as things turned out!'

'Why, what do you mean?'

'Well . . . ' He lowered his voice. 'You must have guessed I was nuts about you in those days.'

She stared at him. 'But that was never anything serious.'

'Maybe it wasn't for you – it was serious for me, all right! When they sacked you, it was like the bottom had dropped out of my world. I knew you hadn't done anything wrong, and I wanted to find you, but I didn't know where you'd gone. Then a week later I was in the Army, miles away. I've never forgiven myself.'

'Forgiven yourself?'

'For not doing something to help you. I knew you'd been treated badly. I should never have let it happen. There – now I've told you.'

He frowned at the pattern in the carpet, unable to look at her.

Rising from her chair, she said softly: 'I'm very glad you told me, Malcolm – thank you.' She leaned forward and kissed him, then said: 'Will you give my apologies to Pat? Say I had to go.'

'Oh, but aren't you going to stay on with Chris?'

'She doesn't want me, and there's something I've got to do, before it's too late. Have a lovely time. Tell Chris I'll see her when she comes home.'

Then she left the house, with Malcolm's words still ringing in her ears: 'I should never have let it happen . . . '

Vee's fingers slipped as she tried to fasten the hook-and-eye at the back of her dress. She had put off changing until the last minute, hoping against hope that something might happen which would settle the whole thing.

She had hung on to the thought that Jo might phone at the eleventh hour with some brilliant scheme that would save the situation. But the eleventh hour had come and gone.

In a state of abject misery, she had begun to dress for the party, and because she was in a hurry, her fingers were all thumbs: she had laddered one of her stockings, she smudged her make-up and had to start all over again, and now she couldn't do up this beastly hook-and-eye.

While she was still struggling, there was a knock at her bedroom door.

'Can I come in?' said Alec.

'Yes, come in,' she said. 'Could you fasten this hook for me? It's so fiddly.'

Scowling with concentration, he obeyed, grumbling about the silly way women's clothes were made. Why couldn't they fasten sensibly at the front, like men's suits? At last he let her go. 'There you are – it's done.'

'Thanks, you're a pet,' she told him, then added: 'I'm sorry – was there something you wanted?'

'No, it's only – the Aunt told me you were going out tonight.' He tried to speak casually, but the tic at the corner of his mouth betrayed him. 'Where are you off to?'

'Oh, just a party, that's all.'

'Anyone I know?'

She avoided a direct answer. 'I expect there'll be dozens of people I don't even know myself.'

'How about your American friend? Will he be there?'

She could not lie to Alec, yet she could not tell him the truth either. Helplessly, she tore at the hook-and-eye, then pulled off her dress and stepped out of it in her slip, saying in a choked voice: 'I've changed my mind. I'm not going.'

Alec stared at her. 'What's the matter?'

313

Tears were beginning to run down her cheeks. She brushed them away impatiently. 'Nothing's the matter! I've changed my mind, and now I'm going to change my clothes as well, so will you kindly get out of my room?'

'No, I bloody won't!' Alec picked up her dressing-gown, then draped it round her shoulders, saying: 'Put this on and sit down. I may be going off my head, but I'm not deaf and blind. I can see something's wrong, and you're going to tell me what it is.'

She turned her back on him. 'I asked you to leave this room. I've got nothing to say to you.'

'Stop being so damn stubborn!' He gripped her shoulders, and more than anything in the world, she longed to turn and face him, to bury herself in his arms, but she knew that would be the end of everything . . .

And then she remembered – this *was* the end of everything. She had disobeyed Don. At any minute the telephone might ring, and the whole pathetic story would come out.

Moving away from Alec, she sank on to the edge of the bed and wiped her eyes, then said flatly: 'I was lying . . . I have got something to say to you. You won't like it, but I'm going to tell you the truth.'

Jo had been hoping Vee would be late, and that she might catch her before she went into Galleon House, but the street was deserted. She stood on the pavement for a minute or two, waiting – praying – but there was no sign of Vee.

It was a raw, cold evening. According to the calendar, this was spring, but Jo sensed a touch of frost in the air, and realised that she was shivering.

There was only one thing to be done. She must go in and look for Vee.

Taking the front-door key from her bag, she crossed the tiny garden and entered the house. Everything was very quiet. She had been expecting a babble of noise and laughter, but she could hear nothing except some strains of music, far away.

Puzzled, she climbed the stairs, and walked into Russell's flat.

After the freezing temperature outside, the warmth of the flat came as a shock, and she was surprised by the pungent smell of incense. Nervous but still determined, she walked into the living room. The music was coming from the radiogram – flutes and harps and little bells created an oddly dreamlike sound.

There were half a dozen people in the room; it was terribly hot in there – the men had taken off their jackets and unbuttoned their shirts. There was only one woman, stretched out on the carpet; she had undressed down to her brassière and knickers, and appeared to be asleep. No one was taking the slightest notice of her.

There were half-empty bottles and glasses everywhere. On a low coffee-table, a vase contained a handful of joss-sticks, their ends glowing red, their smoke spiralling upwards in a blue haze.

Some of the men turned their heads languidly and stared at her; they all appeared to be half-drunk. One of them, an elderly man with silver hair and a goatee beard, screwed a monocle into his eye in order to take a closer look.

'My dear, you must forgive me, I fear I cannot remember your name,' said Sir Hugh Fern-Pryce, slurring his words. 'But I'd been hoping I might find you here. Come and amuse me, you fascinating creature.'

He held out his arms, but Jo backed away, saying: 'I'm looking for a friend – excuse me.'

He called after her plaintively: 'Come back, lovely girl – let me be your friend.'

Closing the door behind her, she looked back along the corridor, wondering where she would find Vee.

Somewhere a girl was laughing – a high-pitched, mindless giggle – and Jo made her way towards the sound. The door of Don's room opened, and a man walked out, putting one hand on the wall to support himself. He was wearing nothing but a pair of lemon silk drawers, but he smiled at Jo graciously.

'Well, well!' he exclaimed. 'And what have we here?'

She tried to edge past, but he caught her arm. He had doused himself in perfume which did not entirely mask the smell of his sweating body, and he began to recite in a deep, mellifluous tone: 'Come, live with me and be my love, and we will all love's pleasures prove . . .'

In a waking nightmare she struggled with him, and the alarming thing was that she felt she knew him, yet she was certain she had never met him before.

'Please – let me go,' she said.

As she spoke a naked girl tumbled out of the bedroom, colliding with them and gurgling: 'Oops! Sorry – got to find the lulu!'

Distracted, the stranger loosened his hold on Jo and she slipped away, into Don's room.

Lit by one guttering candle, there was just enough light for her to see a crowd of men and women in various stages of undress – groping, thrusting, crawling slowly over one another, like a writhing heap of eels.

Nobody spoke. The only sounds were laboured breathing and groans that could have meant pain or ecstasy. Somewhere among them, the girl who had been giggling helplessly was now sobbing, either from misery or exhaustion.

To Jo's relief Vee was nowhere to be seen, though she recognised some of the girls – they had been fellow-lodgers at the Rope Walk.

And Don was there. Their eyes met. In a fit of anger, he pulled himself up from the mass of anonymous bodies and threw on a dressing-gown.

Bundling her out into the passage, he said accusingly: 'This isn't your scene – you don't belong here.'

'Vee doesn't belong here either, but she said you'd invited her,' said Jo. 'Where is she?'

'How in hell should I know? She never showed up.'

'Thank God for that—' she began.

A cry of panic startled her. At the far end of the corridor, a girl burst out of Russell's room, pulling a sheet around her and calling: 'Help me – help me, somebody. Get a doctor!'

It was Peggy Hooper. Abandoning Don, Jo ran the length of the passage.

Peggy stared at her as if she were a ghost, exclaiming: 'Jo! You're the last person I expected.' Then she gabbled: 'Thank God you're here. Come in, quick, I think he's dying!' and she dragged Jo into the bedroom.

Russell was lying aross the bed, with his head lolling over the side. It was a long time since Jo had seen him naked, and she was shocked to discover how emaciated he was; his body had become the body of an old man. His mouth was open. A trickle of vomit ran down his chin, and his face was a leaden purple, his complexion suffused with blood.

'I think he's stopped breathing,' whispered Peggy.

Jo put her ear to his chest, then felt for his pulse, but she could find nothing.

'I'll get help,' she said, and ran to the telphone in the living-room.

The guests were sprawled about, just as she had left them, staring at her with lacklustre eyes as she dialled 999. When the operator answered, Jo began: 'Please send an ambulance right away to the top flat, Galleon House, at the corner of the Rope Walk and Battersea Church Road. Mr Russell Wade is seriously ill—'

Don came up behind her and tried to take the phone out of her hand, saying: 'Are you nuts? Hang up, for Chrissake.'

Pushing him away, she clung to the telephone, repeating: 'He's very seriously ill, please send somebody at once!'

When she replaced the receiver, Don had vanished. She went back to Russell's room and found Peggy in tears, coming to meet her.

'It's no good – he's done for,' she sobbed. 'He's dead, I know he is.'

' . . . And tonight I realised I couldn't go on pretending for ever. I decided I'd got to tell you, and – and now I have.'

It had taken Vee a long time to tell her story. It was very important not to leave anything out, and she felt very tired, but now it was over. She had stopped lying, and she would never have to be afraid of the truth again.

The room was silent, except for the quiet ticking of the little clock on her bedside table.

Alec sat quite still, as he had been since the beginning of her confession. He had only made one movement, and that was early on, when he understood what she was trying to tell him; then he had shifted slightly and put a hand to his head, so she could not see his face.

She waited for his anger, his reproaches – his disgust, even. Instead, he began to laugh; quietly at first, and then he threw back his head, laughing wholeheartedly.

Vee had not known what to expect, but it certainly wasn't this. 'It's not funny!' she exclaimed. 'How can you laugh about it?'

'I'm sorry – you don't understand,' he said, before another paroxysm convulsed him.

Furiously, she turned on him: 'Stop laughing at me!'

317

He turned and looked at her, caught between amusement and concern. 'I'm not laughing at you,' he said. 'I'd never do that.'

'What's so funny, then?' she asked.

'If I'm laughing at anyone, I'm laughing at myself,' he told her.

'I don't understand.'

'No, neither did I. For years I couldn't understand it, but now I do. I understand myself, and that's the best thing in the world.'

Bewildered, she stared at him. 'I thought you'd be very angry.'

'Did you? No, I'm not angry, not in the least.' Slowly, the laughter left his face, and he frowned slightly. 'There's only one thing I don't understand,' he continued. 'You were going to a party, weren't you? What made you change your mind? Why did you decide to tell me all this – tonight?'

So then she had to explain about Don as well, and his attempt at blackmail. As she talked, his expression darkened and he shook his head.

'I thought that was what you wanted,' he said. 'I thought you were in love with him.'

'Not really. I tried to tell myself I loved him, but I knew I didn't. I couldn't love him, because . . . ' She paused, then went on quietly: 'Because I was in love with somebody else.'

He said, slowly and haltingly: 'Would that be – anyone I know?'

Still she could not look at him. He crossed the room and knelt at her feet, putting his hand to her cheek, turning her face towards him.

'Are you trying to say – what I hope you're saying?' he asked.

Then they looked at one another, and there was no need to say anything at all. At that moment their lives began all over again.

'It's horrible,' said Peggy. 'I can't stand any more of this, looking at him lying there . . . Let's cover him up, for goodness' sake.'

The two girls had been sitting by Russell's bed, waiting, but when Peggy tried to pull the sheet over his face, Jo stopped her. 'Don't do that – we can't tell . . . I'm just praying the ambulance gets here in time.'

'Praying?' Peggy sniffed. 'Fat lot of good that's going to do now.' Then she stopped. 'Hang on – did you say "ambulance" . . . ?'

'Yes, I dialled 999. They said they'd send an ambulance right away.'

'You silly cow!' Frantically, Peggy began to pull on her clothes. 'I thought you were calling his doctor. That's what you should've done.'

'I thought 999 would be quicker.'

'You don't want this reported, do you? It'll have to be official now – you'll be kept here all night, answering bloody questions!' She pulled on her shoes. 'I'll go and find the others, and get them out of here.'

'What others?'

'The rest of 'em from the Rope Walk. Don got us to come round and liven things up a bit . . . ' At the sound of running footsteps on the stairs, she broke off. 'That's never the ambulance already? How did they get in?'

'I went down and opened the front door, to save time,' Jo explained. 'Even a few seconds might make a difference.'

Peggy began to run along the passage, calling: 'Renee – Patsy – Rose – get your clothes on! We've got to scarper!'

But as she passed the door of the flat, two uniformed men came in, and one of them asked: 'Are you the lady that telephoned?'

'That was me,' said Jo, coming to join them. 'Mr Wade's in his bedroom. It's along here.'

Peggy tried to squeeze past them. 'Let me get by, will you?'

'Not just yet, miss.' Taking Peggy firmly by the arm, the ambulance-man followed Jo into Russell's room. 'You might be needed here.'

A few minutes later, he sat back on his heels, then turned to his colleague. 'OK, Jack, you know what to do. Get on to the police.'

In the drawing-room at Cheyne Walk, Elspeth Coburn sat on the sofa. Alec had his arm round her shoulders, while Vee sat at her feet, saying: 'I'm sorry. I know this must be a terrible shock for you.'

Aunt Elspeth said slowly: 'Not altogether . . . There was a time – a long while ago – when I wondered about it. Sometimes, things you said troubled me, and I asked myself if, somehow, I'd made a mistake . . . But you were just a child, and you'd been through such a shocking experience, I told myself I was imagining things.'

Vee hung her head. 'Once I'd started, I had to go on. I wasn't brave enough to own up . . . It was wicked of me, I know that now.'

'Oh, no, my dear, you were never wicked. Vanessa had been taken from us, and you were sent to take her place. I'll always thank God for that.'

'You mean, you don't hate me?'

'How could I hate you? You're one of the family – isn't she, Alec?'

'Well, she's going to be.' He chose his words carefully. 'You see, Aunt, there are going to be some changes made. We'll have to tell all our friends – they're going to find out soon in any case.'

'What do you mean?' The old lady turned to him fearfully. 'Is there something else I don't know?'

'Don't worry, old darling – it's all good news from now on. For a start, you don't have to bother about your beloved nephew's mental state. I thought for a while I was going potty, but I'm not.'

Elspeth Coburn was totally bewildered. 'The specialist said he was very concerned about you.'

'I was very concerned about myself! I thought there was something seriously wrong when I realised I was falling in love with Van . . . Dammit, chaps don't fall in love with their sisters, do they? That sort of thing is rather frowned upon in polite society.'

While Aunt Elspeth was trying to get her breath back, Vee chimed in: 'I'd fallen in love with him, too. I loved him from the moment I saw him, when he came home from Germany! I loved him so much, and I couldn't even tell anybody – except Jo, of course.'

Now it was Alec's turn to look astonished. 'You told Jo Wells?'

'Oh, dear,' Vee remembered. 'That's something else you don't know . . .'

Although Jo's hands were trembling she managed to make a pot of coffee and pour out four cups.

The police had arrrived within minutes, and as soon as they entered the flat, they took charge of everything. A doctor and a detective inspector moved into Russell's bedroom, carrying out some mysterious tasks behind a closed door. For the time being the ambulancemen could do nothing, so they sat in the kitchen with Jo and Peggy, and drank coffee.

Without any warning, everything had changed. The flat, which had seemed crowded already, was crammed with people now. Guests, fuddled and frightened, were putting their clothes on under the scrutiny of uniformed policemen and policewomen. A little while ago, it had been unnaturally quiet; now there was a frantic hubbub as people pleaded and cried. Jo could not think clearly.

'I told you it'd be like this,' Peggy told her. 'I said we'd be here all night, once the law moved in. It'll be nothing but bloody questions from arseholes to breakfast-time!'

One of the ambulance-men snorted, and tried to turn it into a cough.

'But what's it all about?' asked Jo. 'What are the police doing here?'

'It's all on account of you and your precious 999 call!' Peggy told her. 'I'm surprised the perishing fire brigade didn't turn up as well!'

Taking pity on Jo, the ambulance driver said: 'We had to report it, miss, soon as we saw what was going on.'

'You mean the party?' Jo felt sorry for the silly people who were now so humiliated. 'I know it was all a bit nasty – getting sozzled, carrying on like that – but it's not a crime, is it?'

'It wasn't booze and sex that did for Mr Wade,' said the driver. 'Of course, we shan't know for certain till the autopsy, but I've no doubt in my mind it was the overdose that finished him off . . . Cocaine, heroin – whatever he was on.'

Jo's coffee slopped on to the table. 'He was taking drugs?'

Peggy looked at her with a mixture of scorn and pity. 'My God – you really didn't know, did you?'

Jo put her cup carefully in the saucer and stood up. 'Excuse me,' she said. 'I've just got to go out for a minute.'

'They won't let you. I've tried that—' began Peggy.

Jo ignored her. She wanted to shut herself up in the bathroom – to get away from the noise and the confusion and the horror of it all. But that too was impossible; a uniformed police-sergeant was hammering on the bathroom door and calling out: 'Come along, sir, if you please. I know you're in there!'

Another policeman was guiding Sir Hugh Fern-Pryce along the corridor, with a firm hand on the old gentleman's shoulder. Twitching with fear, Sir Hugh bleated: 'I have to go back and find my monocle. I must have dropped it somewhere.'

'If we come across it, sir, we'll send it on to the station after you.'

Sir Hugh tried to clutch at Jo. 'Where's Russell? He started all this. It's nothing to do with me.'

'Russell isn't here,' Jo told him, and her voice sounded thin and unreal. 'He's dead.'

Sir Hugh's mouth sagged open. 'I don't believe you. He's hiding somewhere, isn't he? This is some trick, to put all the blame on me.'

'Come along, sir, you'll only make things worse for yourself, talking like that,' said the constable, steering him away. 'They're waiting for you downstairs.'

As Sir Hugh was led away, the bathroom door opened and a man came out. Jo had seen him before, but he was no longer wearing a pair of lemon drawers. Now he was stark naked. His face was glistening with sweat, and sweat poured down his chest, but he still smiled the same fixed smile as he addressed the police-sergeant: 'Sorry to keep you waiting, my dear chap. The annoying thing is, I seem to have mislaid my clothes – could you help me find them?'

The sergeant called to a passing policewoman: 'Fetch this gentleman a blanket, will you?'

The stranger raised an eyebrow. 'That's hardly what I had in mind.'

'Better than nothing, sir. You'll be glad of it when you go out – there's a nasty nip in the air.'

'A kind thought, but I'd sooner wear my own togs, if it's all the same to you. They can't have gone far.'

As he strolled away, apparently unconcerned, Jo asked the sergeant: 'Who is that man? I've seen him before somewhere – I know his voice, too.'

The sergeant looked at her quizzically. 'I shouldn't wonder. You've probably heard him making speeches on the wireless, or seen him on the newsreels. Cabinet Ministers get themselves into the news pretty often, though not under these circumstances as a rule. He'll be lucky if he can hush up this little lot.'

Jo felt as if the world were turning upside-down. Of course, he was a famous politician – but what was he doing here? When she saw Russell, she must ask him—

Then she remembered that she could never ask Russell anything again.

Going into the bathroom, she locked the door. Until this moment, she hadn't taken in the fact of Russell's death. Now she began to sob, burying her face in her arms to muffle her tears.

She had no idea how long she stayed there. At last she pulled herself up, then ran some water into the wash-basin and bathed her eyes, trying to summon enough strength to face whatever else the night had in store.

In the kitchen, another policewoman asked her a stream of questions, taking down her answers in a notebook, establishing Jo's name, age, address, her status in the household and the fact that she had been responsible for calling the ambulance.

At last she said: 'Thank you, Miss Wells, much obliged. It's OK for you to go now. We know where to find you.'

Jo stood up. 'Thank you. What will happen about Mr Wade? Is he – still here?'

'They took him away in the ambulance. That's all taken care of. Now they're questioning the last of the guests. Most of them will be up in front of the magistrates in the morning.'

Suddenly Jo thought of Don and realised she hadn't seen him for hours, not since she made that phonecall. She was about to ask what had happened to him, but then she changed her mind. She felt too tired to stir up any more trouble tonight. Instead, she said simply: 'I'll be off then.'

'By the way, I hear there's some newspaper reporters outside,' said the policewoman. 'If they try to pester you, there's no need to tell them anything. Just keep on walking.'

'Reporters?' Jo stared. 'How on earth did the newspapers find out?

The young woman shrugged. 'You'd be surprised how quick the word gets round. These press people have their spies everywhere!'

When Jo got to the foot of the stairs, she found the Cabinet Minister ahead of her, escorted by two policemen. He was fully clothed now, with a blanket draped round his shoulders.

As they opened the front door, the darkness splintered. A flash-bulb exploded immediately in front of him. Instantly, he pulled the blanket over his head, but it was too late – the damage was done.

While the police hurried him into the Black Maria, Jo noticed a little group of bystanders by the garden gate, and among them she saw one face she knew only too well.

Her grief and shame and anger all bubbled up and boiled over, and she rushed towards Pete, scolding him furiously: 'How can you? How could anyone be so cheap and horrible? Digging out people's secrets, ruining their lives—'

He interrupted her. 'Hey-up, what's all this? What am I supposed to have done now?'

'You're a two-faced liar, the lowest kind of news-hound – and you're not good enough to work for the *Evening News*!'

'That's enough, miss, leave this to me.' The man on duty held her back, telling Peter: 'Move along, sir, you've no business here.'

'That's where you're wrong,' said Pete and dug into an inside pocket, producing a card from his wallet and showing it to the constable. 'Sergeant Hobden, Special Branch – Drug Squad. . . Who's in charge here?'

Chapter Twenty-One

'Where's Mr Mulligan?' asked Chris.

She had just finished laying the breakfast table when Jo brought in two grilled kippers.

'Gone to the paper shop – it's Saturday,' Jo reminded her.

Every Saturday morning, Mr Mulligan went out to buy a newspaper. Once a week he treated himself to a flutter on the horses, and he liked to study the list of runners, though he never laid out more than a few shillings.

'I've left his on the stove to keep hot.' Seeing Chris's nose wrinkle, Jo said: 'I thought you liked kippers?'

'They're OK, only I hate picking out all those tiny bones. I'd sooner have haddock.'

'Well, I'm sorry, there wasn't any. I got the last three kippers in the shop,' Jo told her sharply. 'You should think yourself lucky!'

Chris looked up and said: 'Sometimes you sound just like Ma.'

Jo sighed. 'Sorry . . . I'm a bit tired this morning.'

'I thought so. I heard you come in – you must have been ever so late,' said Chris. 'Where did you go?'

'Galleon House. I told you – Mr Wade was throwing a party.'

'I thought you weren't invited? Still, you must have enjoyed it, staying so late.'

'I didn't enjoy it at all.' Jo wondered how to explain. 'Mr Wade was – taken ill. I had to call an ambulance.'

Chris stared at her, round eyed. 'How awful. Is he all right now?'

'No, he isn't. By the time they got there he was dead.'

Then the front door opened and shut, and Mr Mulligan walked in. Tossing the newspaper to Jo, he took off his hat and coat, saying: 'Will you look at this? I declare I don't know what the world's coming to. A man like that – highly thought of.'

The photograph of the Cabinet Minister was on the front page; his face white, his eyes staring into the camera, caught in the glare of publicity.

'You'd expect a man in his position to be above such things,' Mr Mulligan continued. 'And that artist feller who lived there, would he be the one you worked for?'

Jo tried to focus on the newsprint, but the words ran together. Chris snatched the paper from her, saying: 'Show me!'

'No, don't, I'd rather you didn't—' Jo began, but Chris was already reading avidly.

'So you were there when it happened?' she asked breathlessly. 'What do they mean by "compromising circumstances"?'

'Some people had too much to drink and started behaving in a silly way,' Jo replied lamely.

'It says there's to be an inquest.' Mr Mulligan grimaced. 'And what's going to happen to you, I'd like to know?'

'Me?' Jo drew back defensively. 'It's got nothing to do with me.'

'It has so!' he contradicted her. 'The man was your employer, wasn't he? Now he's dead and gone, you'll be looking for another situation, I shouldn't wonder?'

'I hadn't even thought about that. It's all happened so suddenly.' Jo stood up. 'Your kipper's on the stove, keeping hot. I'll go and fetch it.'

'Don't you stir yourself, I'll see to it,' he said.

A few minutes later, while he was tucking into his kipper, Chris looked up from the newspaper, awestruck. 'It says here the police are proceeding with their enquiries. You never said the police were there too!'

'Yes, they turned up later,' said Jo flatly. 'Along with our ex-lodger, Mr Hobden.'

Mr Mulligan nearly choked on a mouthful of kipper. 'What in God's name was he doing there at all?'

Jo tried to speak calmly. 'You know he told us he was a newspaper-man? Well, that was his little joke – he's really in the police force.'

'Peter? A policeman?' shrilled Chris.

'And not just an ordinary policeman, a plain-clothes police sergeant. Oh, yes, he's full of surprises.'

'Well, I never! Did you talk to him?'

'Not much. By the time he arrived, I was ready to leave. He said he'd see me later, and I said it was after midnight, and I wanted to go home . . . Quite honestly, I didn't feel much like talking by that time.'

'I wonder he didn't come back here afterwards?' mused Mr Mulligan. 'Perhaps he'll drop in presently.'

'I don't think so,' said Jo. 'Now he's found out everything he wanted to know, I don't expect we'll be seeing him again.'

Chris wasn't listening. Still glued to the newspaper report, she said: 'Number one, the Rope Walk – isn't that where you used to live?'

'Yes – what about it?'

'It says that's where some of the guests came from.' She read aloud: '"Miss Peggy Hooper (34) told our reporter that she had been invited to join the so-called party, but stressed that she scarcely knew the late Russell Wade, saying: 'If I had realised what kind of party it was, I should never have accepted his invitation' . . . It is understood that Miss Hooper and her friends will be appearing in court later today. For further details see the Obituary Column on page seven."'

A sudden fear gripped Jo. 'Is that what it says? "Peggy Hooper – thirty-four"?'

A loud knock at the front door startled them all. Jo held her breath, then relaxed as she saw the postman in his peaked cap going past the front window. 'It's all right, it's only the post.'

'I'll go,' said Chris.

As she left the room, Mr Mulligan looked at Jo with concern. 'My darlin' girl, you're white as a sheet. What's wrong with you?'

'Suppose they put my name in the paper too? They print your age as well, don't they?' Jo asked.

'What does that matter? It's nothing to be ashamed of.'

Jo lowered her voice. 'You don't understand. If the police find out I'm under twenty-one, they'll say I'm not old enough to be responsible for Chris. They'll take her into care!'

She broke off as Chris returned, holding a picture postcard and saying: 'It's all for me – from Chockie! He says they'll be coming home any day now – he's looking forward to seeing me!'

★

327

There was a different policeman on duty outside Galleon House this morning, and when Jo opened the garden gate, he tried to prevent her from going in.

'Where d'you think you're going?' he said. 'Who are you?'

She explained that she worked for Mr Wade. To prove it, she produced her key-ring.

'I've got to go up to the flat. There'll be a lot to do, tidying up after last night.'

He seemed very dubious. 'I don't know about that . . . Inspector Ross is in charge now. You'll find him upstairs.'

She climbed the stairs, wondering if Peter Hobden would be there – hoping he would not, yet curious to hear what he had to say for himself.

There were several plain-clothes men in the flat, but Peter was not among them. Inspector Ross, a dour man with a ragged moustache, questioned her closely. 'What time did you arrive last night? Did Mr Wade invite you?'

'I don't know exactly what the time was – and I wasn't invited. I only came here because—' Then she realised she could not tell him the truth about that; she must not involve Vee in a police enquiry. She began again: 'I was hoping to see someone – a friend of mine.'

'A friend?' The Inspector seized upon this. 'Ah, that would be the American gentleman, I expect – Mr Scott?'

Clutching at straws, she lied. 'Yes, Don Scott.'

'Was he here when you arrived?'

'Yes, but almost at once, someone said Mr Wade had been taken ill. That's why I phoned for the ambulance.'

'And where was Mr Scott during all this?'

'When I rang off, he'd vanished. I never saw him again after that.'

'So that's why he did a bunk. Have you any idea where he is now?'

'No idea at all.'

'Oh, come on, Miss Wells, you were a close friend of Mr Scott – you introduced him to Mr Wade in the first place. You must have some idea of his whereabouts?'

'I'm sorry, I can't help you.'

'We're anxious to find anything he might have left behind. Perhaps you'd tell us if you can identify anything here that belonged to him?'

He took Jo into Don's room. Empty bottles and glasses, full ash-trays, rumpled bedclothes and items of underwear lay scattered about – but although Jo searched carefully, she could find nothing. Don had vanished completely, leaving no trace.

Every room in the flat looked the same – chaotic, soiled and trampled over by strangers.

'Shall I start clearing up now?' she asked.

'Oh, no, my chaps will be sorting through this lot for quite a while yet. You may as well take yourself off – there's nothing you can do here.'

She turned away. It would have helped her if she could have begun to clean the place, to make it the way it was when she first knew it . . . When she first knew Russell.

Slowly, she walked downstairs. On impulse, she opened the door of Russell's studio and went in.

She hadn't been in the studio for a long while, and neither had he; she couldn't remember the last time he had felt the urge to do some work.

Gazing round at the familiar objects – the easel, the tools on the work-bench, the maquettes on the shelves, all neglected, all abandoned – she felt unbearably sad.

She knew Russell was gone, though she could not quite believe it yet. She felt his presence so strongly – when she heard a footstep behind her, she turned, half expecting to see him walking through the door . . .

But it was only Reggie. He took her in his arms without a word.

'You've heard, then,' she said, when she could speak.

'I saw it in the papers, first thing this morning. I came round to see if there was anything I could do. I guessed you'd be here.'

'I'm surprised they let you in,' she said.

'They couldn't stop me. I pay rent for my studio – I've got a right to come in. I've been trying to work – it helps to have something to do.'

They sat on the edge of the modelling dais as he went on: 'Though I must admit I kept thinking about poor old Russell. I still don't know exactly what happened.'

Jo told him as much as she knew, and he said: 'I thought it was probably something like that. It must have been a terrible shock for you.'

'The worst of it is, I feel responsible. If I hadn't introduced him to Don in the first place . . . '

'If it hadn't been Don, it would have been someone else. I think Russell had been trying to find a way out for years. When he was young, he had a big, blazing talent, but it had begun to dry up. There's nothing so tragic as an artist who outlives his talent.' He put his arm around her. 'You really loved him, didn't you?'

'In the beginning, yes, I did – at least, I thought I did. I'll always be grateful to him. He taught me so much – he opened my eyes to all kinds of things I'd never known before . . . Painting, sculpture, all kinds of new ideas – and love, too . . . I never really thanked him for that.'

After a moment, Reggie asked: 'What are you going to do now?'

'I suppose when the police move out, I'll be able to clear up, in the flat, and down here. That's something I can do for him, at least. After that I'll have to start looking for somewhere else.'

'I wish I could offer you a job – God knows I could do with somebody to look after things and keep me neat and tidy – only I don't suppose I could afford to pay you what you're worth . . . But you'll keep in touch, won't you?'

'Oh, yes, Reggie, we'll keep in touch.'

'I'm looking forward to it,' said Chockie.

His father snorted: 'I dunno what you've got to look forward to!'

'He means coming home,' said Mrs Dando. 'I'm looking forward to it as well. I'm sure we all are.'

As they drove along Wandsworth Road, Dickie Dando stared bleakly out of the taxi window.

'You speak for yourself,' he muttered. 'After all the places we've been – Brussels, Paris, Copenhagen, Moscow even – how do you expect me to feel about coming back to Clapham Junction?'

'It's all been very interesting, but I wouldn't want to live there,' said Dorothy. 'I mean to say, there's no place like home, is there?'

They had arrived off the boat-train an hour ago, after an endless series of journeys across Europe, each stage longer and wearier than the one before. Now they were on the last leg of the trip; any minute now they would be home again.

'Besides, we've got friends here,' Charlie added, self-consciously

His mother glanced at him. 'You wouldn't be thinking about that young cousin of yours by any chance?'

'Yes, her, too,' he admitted. 'I mean to say, it's nice to be back in London.'

'You can keep London, far as I'm concerned!' said Dickie. 'I tell you, I wouldn't care if I never saw that blessed flat in Theatre Street again.'

They all lurched sideways when the cab screeched round the corner, past the ruins of the old Shakespeare Theatre.

'Nearly there,' said Dorothy, collecting her handbag and umbrella. 'Goodness only knows what it's going to cost us, taking a taxi all the way from Victoria. Talk about throwing money away!'

'Have a bit of common, for gawd's sake,' growled Dickie. 'What was I supposed to do with all the luggage? Hop on a bus?'

When they drew up outside Devonshire Buildings, it took several minutes to unload all the suitcases. The driver had to give them a hand with the huge cabin trunk.

'Thanks, old man. Much obliged, I'm sure.' Dickie peeled off a couple of notes in a lordly way, adding: 'Keep the change!'

It took several journeys up and down the stone steps before all the bags and baggage were up on the second floor. They left the cabin trunk till last, and then, with some difficulty, Mr Dando and Chockie lugged it upstairs between them.

'There – that's that,' said Dickie at last, panting but triumphant, as he fumbled through his pockets. 'Now then, what did I do with the front-door key?'

'Oh, Dad, don't say you left it in Moscow!' exclaimed Dorothy.

'No, it's OK, it was in my waistcoat pocket all the time.' He produced it with a flourish, and inserted it in the lock. 'Here we go!'

'Thank goodness for that,' sighed his wife. 'I wonder if there's any tea in the caddy? You can say what you like about travelling abroad; you never get a proper cup of tea.'

'Buck up, Dad,' said Chockie. 'What are you waiting for?'

'It's this key . . . ' Dickie frowned, took the key out and tried again. 'I can't get it to turn, somehow.'

'You're probably trying the wrong key,' said Dorothy.

'I ought to know my own door-key after all these years – anyhow, I've only got the one. But it won't seem to go in properly.'

He was still struggling with it when the front door across the landing creaked open and a voice said: 'You're wasting your time, Mr Dando.'

They all turned. A wispy little woman in a crossover pinny was standing with her arms folded, watching them.

'Hello, Mrs Willinger, nice to see you!' said Dorothy. 'How've you been keeping?'

'Mustn't grumble,' she said. 'I see you're home again, then?'

'Yes, we are, only I can't get this blessed key to work—' began Dickie.

'No, like I said, you can't get in. I'd have tried to drop you a line to let you know, if you'd left an address.'

'What do you mean, we can't get in?'

'We couldn't leave an address, 'cos we were travelling all the time,' Dorothy explained. 'Put a drop of oil in the lock, Dad. 'It's probably got rusty, not being used for so long.'

'It's not that,' said Mrs Willinger. 'It's the landlord – come round and changed the lock, he did.'

'Changed our lock, without asking us?' blustered Dickie. 'I'll have a few words to say about that.'

'He wants a word with you, an' all,' said Mrs Willinger. 'According to him, you went off without paying your rent. He said you're nearly five months in arrears.'

Open mouthed, Dorothy turned to her husband. 'Oh, Dick, you didn't, did you? How ever much do we owe him?'

Slowly, Mr Dando sank on to the cabin-trunk beside her, saying in a dazed voice: 'I don't know – I'm not sure.'

'It's over three hundred pounds,' said Mrs Willinger helpfully. 'He said he gave you fair warning. He put two reminders through the letter-box before he sent the final demand in red.'

'What's the good of that?' demanded Mr Dando. 'We were halfway across Europe then. What did he think we'd got in our luggage – carrier pigeons?'

'Oh, and your phone's been cut off as well,' said Mrs Willinger. 'But if you'd like to pop in for five minutes, I could make you a nice cup of tea – how about that?'

When Jo had tidied up the studio, she left Galleon House. Perhaps tomorrow the police would have finished; then she could come back and clean the flat as well.

She nodded to the policeman on duty as she opened the garden gate, and she was about to set off up Battersea Church Road when she became aware of a buzz of chatter. Looking along the Rope Walk, she saw a group of people at the other end of the street, and asked: 'What's going on there?'

'Newspaper-men and photographers,' the policeman told her. 'They've been hanging round ever since last night, trying to get a few words with the girls who live there.'

'At number one?' Jo asked. 'Sarah Venus's house?'

She started to run along the Rope Walk. The little crowd turned and stared as she tried to push her way through. At the front door, another burly policeman was standing guard.

'You can't come in here, miss,' he said. 'Nobody allowed in without permission.'

'I've got to see Mrs Venus!' Jo told him. 'She's a friend of mine.'

Some of the reporters sniggered, and a voice began to sing: 'Tell us the old, old story . . . '

Someone called out: 'I saw you last night. You're Wade's house-keeeper, aren't you?'

Someone else asked eagerly: 'Are you the one who found the body?'

A girl reporter cut in: 'Can I have an exclusive interview, Miss Wells? Look this way – get a picture, Nobby.'

Jo backed away, terrified by the greedy eyes fixed upon her: 'No, I can't – I don't want any—'

Behind her, the door opened and someone grabbed her, saying: 'Come in, Jo, you'll be all right.'

It was Peggy Hooper. Fighting off the hands that reached for her, Jo retreated into the house. The policeman began: 'You can't go in there, not unless you're a resident—'

'I used to be,' said Jo, and shut the door in his face.

In the hall, Peggy puffed out her cheeks and said: 'Well, this is a nice carry-on. I wish I'd never talked to those rotten sods – promised me money and all sorts, if I'd give 'em a few words. I should've known better!'

She raised her voice above the sound of fists hammering the door panels. 'Let's go upstairs, I can't hear myself think!'

She was about to lead the way when Jo heard someone calling: 'Jo –
Jo Wells! Is that you?'

Sarah Venus was standing at the kitchen doorway in her shabby
dressing-gown, hanging on to the door-post and looking very frail.

'Better go and see the old girl,' Peggy whispered. 'Come and talk to
me later on, eh?'

Jo nodded, and went down the hall.

She was taken aback by the change in Sarah. Her peroxided hair was
more grey than blonde, and though she had tried to do her face, she
had used too much powder, and her lipstick was crooked.

'It is you, isn't it?' she repeated anxiously, as Jo approached. 'I felt
sure I knew that voice.'

Looking more closely, Jo saw that those great, lustrous eyes were
misted and milky white, and she realised that Sarah was half-blind.

'I'm glad you're here . . . Tibbles, look who's come to see us!'

As soon as Jo sat down, the old tabby cat jumped on to her lap. He
only just made it, digging in his claws to keep from falling; Tibbles too
had aged since her last visit.

'This is a nice old mess we're in.' Sarah plumped down in her
armchair. 'What are we going to do about it, eh?'

'I don't know,' said Jo. 'I wish I did.'

'Peggy tells me you were there last night, when Russell died.' Sarah
shook her head. 'I'd never pictured you getting mixed up in anything
like that, somehow.'

'I wasn't supposed to be there. I called an ambulance, but it was too
late, and then the police turned up, and the photographers—'

'And now we're in all the papers, and they won't leave us alone.'
Sarah's voice cracked. 'I don't understand it. Somebody said the *News
of the World* would pay me a thousand pounds for my life story . . .'
She shook her head again, unable to comprehend a world in which
such things were possible. 'I'd sooner be dead.'

Jo reached across and squeezed Sarah's hand. 'Try not to think
about it. It'll blow over – they'll leave you alone presently.'

'But what about you?' Sarah asked. 'I heard them shouting at you.
What's going to become of you, now Russell's gone?'

'I'll manage.' Jo tried to soothe her. 'I expect I'll get a job as a
housekeeper somewhere else.'

Sarah gripped her hands. 'You could come and help me,' she said. 'I

334

need someone here. I can't look after the house by myself, not like I used to. I don't suppose I could pay you as much as Russell did, but I'd give you all I've got. Only I can't bear it any more, not on my own . . . Come and look after me, would you? Please?'

'I expect you could do with another cup,' said Mrs Willinger. 'I'll just get some hot water, to freshen the pot.'

When she left the little sitting-room, a silence fell. It had been difficult to discuss the situation while she was there, and even now it was hard to know where to begin.

At last Dorothy Dando said wryly: 'Well, Dad, you did say you wouldn't care if you never saw that flat again. It looks like you're going to get your wish.'

'Don't talk so daft,' muttered Dickie. 'Of course we'll see it again. The landlord can't chuck us out, not without giving us fair warning!'

'He did give us fair warning,' said Chockie. 'Mrs Willinger said there's two reminders and a final demand inside.'

'We can't help it if we weren't here, can we?' snapped Dickie. 'There's no law against going abroad in the way of business.'

'There's probably a law against not paying the rent,' Dorothy pointed out. 'Far as I can see, the only way to settle it is to pay him the three hundred pounds.'

'More than three hundred, she said—' Chockie threw in.

His father turned on him: 'You keep out of this!'

'Don't take it out on him, it's not his fault.' Dorothy protested.

'Oh, no, I'm well aware it's all my fault. Don't rub it in. The trouble is, we haven't got three hundred pounds.'

Chockie was shocked. 'You must have! You said we were earning good money on tour.'

'So we were, but the bills soon run up, when you're touring – living in digs and eating out all the time. I tried to put some money by, but – well, it's nowhere near three hundred, and that's a fact.'

'So what's going to happen?' Dorothy asked. 'Where are we going to go?'

Mrs Willinger, coming in with the teapot, said: 'These walls are like paper, I couldn't help overhearing. I'd offer to put you up, only this flat's not as big as yours; there's only the one bedroom. You're welcome to sleep on that old sofa, but I can't fit three of you in.'

'We wouldn't dream of imposing,' Dickie told her. 'And if the landlord found out, he'd be after me like a shot. No, we'll have to look elsewhere.'

'But there's all our stuff locked up inside the flat – furniture and pots and pans – that all belongs to us, doesn't it?' exclaimed Dorothy. 'How are we going to get it back?'

They stared into space, trying to find some way out, and then Chockie said: 'Dad, have you got tuppence on you?'

Dickie stuck his hand in his trouser pocket: 'Yes, I think I can just about run to that. Why?'

'Well, there's a phonebox up the road, and I've got an idea.'

When Jo got back to Agar Road, Chris met her in the hall, saying: 'Wherever have you been? I was getting so worried.'

'I stopped off on the way home to see poor old Sarah Venus. Would you believe it – she's offered me a job!'

'At the Rope Walk?' Chris looked shocked. 'You can't work there – people are saying dreadful things.'

'You shouldn't take any notice of what people say. I'm very fond of Sarah, and if she needs somebody to—'

Chris interrupted impatiently. 'Never mind that now. You're ever so late, and he's been here ages, waiting for you.'

From the parlour, Pete Hobden called out: 'Afternoon, Jo! I was beginning to think we'd lost you.'

Jo tried to keep her temper. 'Chris, would you mind going up to your room for a few minutes? Read a book or something – I want to speak to Mr Hobden in private.'

Reluctantly, Chris trailed upstairs and Jo went into the parlour.

Pete began: 'Before you say anything, I must ask you a question—'

Jo cut in: 'Before you say anything, I've got a question for you. Why did you tell me you were a reporter, when you've been a policeman all the time? How could you tell such lies?'

'Only one lie,' he said softly. 'I apologise for that, but I couldn't risk telling you the truth, could I? I had an idea Russell Wade was on drugs, and I suspected Don Scott of being a dealer, but I'd no proof. You were friendly with both men—'

'And you couldn't trust me enough to be honest with me, is that it?'

'It's nowt to do with trust. If I'd told you the truth, you might have given the game away without meaning to – that was a risk I couldn't afford to take.' He took a step towards her. 'Don't you think you might overlook it – just this once?'

Turning away, she said: 'I just wish you'd been straight with me.'

'I'm being straight now. And I'm here to ask you a straight question. Don Scott's disappeared, and we've got to find him as soon as possible. That's why I want you to tell me honestly – have you got any idea where he—'

It was not the question she had expected. Furiously, she flew at him: 'I'm sick of people asking me about Don Scott. I've already told Inspector Ross I don't know where he is! Why can't you stop pestering me?'

Gripping her wrists, he pulled her round to face him. 'I wouldn't be asking if it weren't a matter of life and death. I want to catch him before he wrecks any more lives. You've got to tell me everything you know about the bugger – every single thing you can remember, all right?'

His intensity was almost overwhelming. With an effort, she tried to think. 'I don't know – I don't remember. He never talked about himself much . . . Except for that rubbish about his mother.'

'What about his mother?'

'Oh, it's nothing. When he moved into Galleon House he pretended he was Laura Stanway's son. He said his father was Laura's first husband, Harold Stanway. Of course I never believed that for a minute, but—'

Peter let go of her suddenly.

'Donald Stanway . . . ' he said. 'Well, I'll be damned. Why the hell didn't you tell me that before?'

Grabbing his coat, he raced down the hall. The front door slammed so hard, it made the whole house shake.

Chris came running downstairs. 'What was that?' she asked. 'What happened?'

'I don't know,' said Jo.

Chapter Twenty-Two

WHEN THE DANDOS ARRIVED at Cheyne Walk and the cab had driven away, they stood beside their stack of luggage and looked up at the tall, stately house.

'Are you sure this is where the Coburns live?' Dorothy asked.

'Of course I'm sure,' said Chockie. 'I made Vee say it twice, to be on the safe side. This is the house, all right. It's bigger than I thought.'

'It seems a bit much, going in like this with all our luggage,' said Dickie uneasily. 'You don't suppose, when she said "Come over right away" she didn't really mean it . . .?'

'Of course she meant it! She's my sister, isn't she?' Chockie tried to sound confident, then spoiled it by adding: 'But don't say anything about that, 'cos nobody else knows. She said it will be all right for us to stay till we find somewhere else – they've got plenty of room.'

'You can say that again!' Dickie squared his shoulders. 'Ah, well, give us a hand with this ruddy trunk, will you?'

As they were dragging it up the steps, the front door opened and Vee appeared, saying: 'Hello! I saw you from the window.' She turned to the startled parlourmaid behind her. 'Alice, would you help with the suitcases?'

In the hall, Chockie said: 'This is my mum and dad,' and to his parents: 'This is Vee.'

Vee shook hands, smiling. 'I feel as if I know you already. Of course, I saw you all in the circus, on Clapham Common.'

The parlourmaid looked even more startled, and nearly dropped the suitcase she was carrying.

Then Elspeth Coburn came down with Alec, and Vee told the girl: 'Take that case up to the guest-rooms, would you? We'll see to the rest later,' then she launched into more introductions: 'This is my Aunt Elspeth – and Alec . . . Mr and Mrs Dando – and this is my brother Chockie.'

There was a gasp and a thump as the suitcase hit the floor, and they all began to talk at once.

Aunt Elspeth began: 'Oh, dear, Vee, do try to *think*.'

'Sorry, it sort of slipped out, but we'd agreed everyone will have to be told anyway, so—'

Alec told the maid: 'Leave that for now, Alice, we'll sort things out presently.' As the girl scuttled away, he continued: 'This is a great pleasure. Hello, Chockie, how are you?'

Confused, Chockie stared at him. 'I thought it was supposed to be a secret.'

'It was,' said Vee. 'But I'd kept the secret long enough, and we're very glad you've come to stay – isn't that right, Aunt?'

Prompted, Aunt Elspeth said: 'Yes, indeed, delighted,' and they shook hands all round. 'Well, now, shall we go upstairs?'

If the Dandos were still a little overawed, they would not show it. True performers, they struck up instant friendships with everyone they met.

In the drawing-room, Dickie rattled off a summary of their European tour, and the Coburns were very impressed.

'You certainly covered a lot of ground,' said Alec. 'I spent a few years in Europe myself, though I didn't manage to travel so extensively.'

'It certainly was an eye-opener,' agreed Dickie. 'They've got circuses over there like you never even dreamed of here in England. In terms of audience capacity alone – I mean to say, compared with the last show we did over here . . . ' He turned to Aunt Elspeth. 'I don't know whether you managed to catch us at Clapham Common last winter?'

Dorothy nudged him. 'Dad, I don't expect they go to circuses that much, do you, Miss Coburn?'

'Well, no, I must admit, not very often.'

'We don't only do tent shows,' Dickie hastened to explain. 'We did a fortnight at the Palladium a little while back, on the same bill as

Johnnie Ray – maybe you saw us there?'

'I'm afraid I missed that as well,' Aunt Elspeth apologised.

Alec came to her rescue, saying: 'I gather you had a setback when you got home? Vee told us something about a spot of bother with the landlord?'

Dickie tried to laugh it off. 'Yes, that was a slap in the chops, and no mistake!'

Dorothy was quick to defend her husband. 'We left London in such a rush, Dickie never had time to make arrangements about the rent.'

'I still say he had no call to go changing the locks like that when our backs were turned,' Dickie began.

'The worst of it is, all our belongings are inside the flat – all our valuables,' Dorothy explained. 'And we can't go in and get them.'

'There must be some way you can get in, surely?' asked Alec.

'Not without taking the front door off its hinges,' said Dickie. 'I can't think of anything else.'

For some time Chockie hadn't said a word, but now he spoke up. 'I bet I could do it,' he said.

On Sunday evening, Jo was alone at Agar Road.

Mr Mulligan was down at the pub as usual, and Chris had gone to the Granada cinema with one of her school-friends, to see *Samson and Delilah*.

Realising that Jo was still feeling very low, she had suggested: 'Why don't you come as well? It's got Hedy Lamarr and Victor Mature – you'd enjoy it.'

'I don't think I'll bother, thanks all the same. Mind you come straight home when it's over.'

Jo had thought about going to Evensong at All Saints, but now she'd left it too late; she hated going in after the service had started.

Somehow she had not felt like going out of the house today, and she didn't know why. Idly, she switched on the wireless to listen to *Grand Hotel* with Albert Sandler and the Palm Court Orchestra, but her attention kept wandering, and after a while she turned if off again.

When she heard a key turn in the front door, she realised why she had stayed at home all day; without knowing it, she had been waiting for this to happen.

Pete Hobden came in and put his overnight case down on the table.

'Evening,' he said, taking off his hat and coat.

'So you're back then,' she said, and was immediately furious with herself for saying anything so obvious.

'That's right,' he said, sitting down in his armchair.

She indicated the suitcase. 'And this time you're staying?' she asked.

'Most likely.' He nodded briefly. 'Oh, we picked up your American friend this afternoon.'

'He's not my friend.'

'I reckon he's nobody's friend – he'll not be missed. But give credit where it's due. We wouldn't have found him if it hadn't been for you.'

She looked up sharply. 'What do you mean?'

'We'd been on the wrong track, looking for an American service-man called Don Scott, who'd vanished into thin air. Yesterday you put me right, and we started looking for Donald Stanway instead – a deserter, as it turned out. He'd had a narrow squeak back in the States, a few years since – stole a lot of money and went on the run. Next thing anyone knew, he'd signed on in the US Army as Don Scott, and flown over here. But he hung on to his papers – his passport and all that – just in case. Now the heat was on, he was all set to slip out of the country under his own name. Likely he'd have got away with it an' all, if you hadn't set us right.'

'You mean he really was Laura Stanway's son?'

'He was that. It's probably the only time he ever told you the truth, and you didn't believe him.'

She tried to think back. 'Russell told me Don was Laura's son, but somehow it didn't ring true. I felt sure he was hiding something.'

'Oh, aye, he was hiding summat all right. You see, Don read about his mum's death in the newspapers – the inquest and all that. Not being one to miss a trick, he sniffed out that there might have been something fishy about her death, so he came down to London and began asking a few questions. That's when he met you.'

'Yes. I was very stupid, wasn't I?'

'You weren't to know. Later on, he tackled Russell Wade. I've no doubt he tried to get him to cough up a share of Mum's estate, not realising by the time she died Laura Stanway had spent every cent she ever had – there was nothing left. But our Don had been pushing drugs for a while, and as soon as he met Russell, he spotted he was an addict. So he offered to supply him. He charged him a hefty price, of course, but Russell would have paid any money to get hold of the stuff.'

'Is that why he behaved so strangely? I knew he'd become very moody – happy one minute, and in a black rage the next – I just thought he was ill.'

'So he was – in the last stages of his addiction – and in the end it killed him.'

'Then Don was no better than a murderer.' Suddenly Jo asked: 'You don't suppose he could have killed Laura as well, do you? If he thought he was going to inherit some money?'

Peter shook his head. 'Nice try, but no goal. He didn't even know where Laura was till he read about the inquest.' He went on in a different tone: 'So you don't believe Laura's death was an accident? What gave you that idea?'

She told him about the glass tumbler in Laura's hand, with no trace of lipstick on it, and he nodded thoughtfully: 'Interesting. Pity there's no way of checking it now. If you're right, who d'you think might have done it?'

Jo said unhappily: 'It must have been Russell. There wasn't anyone else. He admitted he'd been out drinking that night. I suppose when he came home from the pub they quarrelled as usual, and he put the pills in her glass. Afterwards he wiped it to remove his fingerprints, but he forgot about the lipstick. I didn't want to believe he could have done such a thing, but I knew it had to be him, really.'

'No – it couldn't have been.' Pete's voice was very quiet, with an edge to it that she had never heard before. 'You see, what you didn't know was – he had an alibi.'

'An alibi? No, he didn't.'

'I'm sorry to contradict you. I checked our records carefully. Russell Wade didn't go to a pub that evening; he went to a party – a proper classy affair it was too, somewhere off Park Lane. The guests were very important people. I reckon most of 'em were druggies as well, although nobody realised that at the time. Any road, there were at least a dozen people to swear that Russell Wade had been there all night. He didn't leave the party till dawn, then he went home to bed – just before you arrived to start your day's work and found Laura's body. According to the medical evidence, she'd been dead for several hours by then, so he couldn't have killed her.'

'But that doesn't make sense. Somebody killed her, somebody washed out that glass – and it had to be Russell. He was the only person who had a key. Nobody else could have got in to the flat.'

There was a long silence before Pete said: 'Wrong again, there was another key . . . Your key.'

Then there was an even longer silence. At last Jo said: 'Are you saying I did it? You believe I killed Laura Stanway?'

'I don't know, do I? You were in love with her husband. You had the motive, and you had the opportunity. That's all I'm saying.'

'It's not true . . . ' She got the words out with difficulty. 'I couldn't have done it, not possibly. You see, I had an alibi that night, as well.'

'You were at the Rope Walk, only two minutes away.'

'No, I wasn't. The night Laura died I was out all night, staying with a friend.'

He leaned forward, his eyes ice-cold and ice-hard: 'What friend?'

She hesitated. 'I can't tell you that.'

'Why can't you?' His barely concealed anger lashed her like a whip. 'Didn't you even ask his name?'

She turned her head away. 'It's not what you're thinking. I'd gone to see a girl I knew. It got very late, so I stayed the night.'

'All right, then – what's her name?'

That was when she realised the trap she had dug for herself.

'I can't tell you that either,' she said. 'She's – someone who wouldn't want to get mixed up in this. You'll just have to take my word for it.'

Slowly, he stood up.

'Remember what you said to me yesterday?' he asked, and his voice was so low, it was almost a whisper. 'Seems like it's my turn to say it to you.'

'Say what?'

He collected his hat and coat and picked up his overnight case, before he reminded her: ' "I just wish you'd been straight with me . . . " '

She managed to say: 'I thought you were staying here tonight?'

His words came back along the narrow hallway: 'So did I.'

'I don't like it,' said Vee.

'He'll be all right,' Dorothy Dando assured her.

Mrs Willinger next door said: 'But suppose anyone sees him

343

climbing out of that window? Suppose they should report it to the police? I'm the one what'll get into trouble for helping you!'

'Nobody's going to see.' Dorothy tried to soothe her. 'There'll be no one about, this time of day.'

When Chockie first outlined his idea, it sounded absurdly simple.

All the principal rooms at the rear of Devonshire Buildings had shallow bay windows, in an attempt to try and let in as much light as possible; they were overshadowed by a huge furniture repository in Latchmere Road, and sunshine rarely filtered down into the narrow space between the buildings. There was no garden behind the flats; only a cramped, sooty yard where the dustbins were kept.

Remembering those rows of bay windows, Chockie had said: 'I can climb out of Mrs Willinger's kitchen on to her window-sill, and step across to the little sill outside her bathroom, then hang on to the drainpipes while I get over to the window-sill outside *our* bathroom. That old window-catch has been broken for ages – remember how it used to rattle? I can pull it open from outside and climb in, then all I've got to do is open our front door from the inside – it'll be dead easy!'

Vee felt a twinge of fear, and said: 'I don't like the sound of it – you'd be taking a terrible risk.'

'The boy will be in and out in two ticks – nobody will be any the wiser,' said Dickie proudly. 'I reckon we've got a right to break into our own flat. That's our stuff the landlord's got locked up in there, don't forget!'

'I didn't mean that exactly . . . I meant, is it safe? Balancing on window-sills, two storeys up – suppose he falls off?'

Chockie looked at his sister and said: 'I'm a pro, aren't I? I've been climbing and balancing since I was five years old. There's nothing to it, is there, Dad? Isn't that right, Mum?'

And his parents had agreed. The only snag would be if the landlord had gone in while they were away and mended the bathroom window-catch, but it wasn't very likely.

Even so, Vee had said: 'I'm not letting you do it on your own. We'll come too, won't we, Alec? You might need some help.'

So here they were, in Mrs Willinger's sitting-room, watching Chockie make his preparations.

Alec had brought a coil of rope, and although Chockie had objected – ('You'll be sending for a safety-net next!') – Dickie overruled him.

'It won't do any harm, and if it keeps them happy, son, what's wrong with that?'

He helped Alec fasten one end of the rope round Chockie's waist, then they tied the other end to one leg of Mrs Willinger's sideboard, which agitated her still more.

'Suppose he was to fall, and that sideboard turned over – what about my best china?' she wanted to know.

'It won't turn over. Like the rock of Gibraltar, your sideboard is,' Dickie told her. 'To make double sure, we'll tie a couple of loops round our waists as well, OK, Mr Coburn?'

'Fine by me,' said Alec, and the two men lashed themselves to the rope. 'Right, Chockie, are you ready?'

'I'm ready,' said Chockie, so Alec slid up the sash-window and Dickie helped the boy to climb out.

'Mind my aspidistra!' exclaimed Mrs Willinger, but no one paid any attention. Chockie took a firm foothold on the sill, then began to sidle round, outside the bay window.

'Don't look down!' called Vee.

'He knows what he's doing – stop fussing,' Alec told her.

The gap between the sitting-room and the bathroom was only about eighteen inches, but Chockie had to brace himself to take that step.

He soon discovered that this was more difficult than walking the tightwire. On the wire, you were free to move – with space on either side, you could balance yourself; on these narrow ledges, with a brick wall nudging him as if it were trying to push him off, he felt cramped.

Under the Big Top, he would have been twice as far from the ground, and felt completely confident; now, for the first time, he was afraid of falling.

From the window of the sitting-room, the others watched. Nobody spoke; Dickie and Dorothy realised that the boy was finding it difficult, and Alec and Vee could sense their anxiety. As he inched his way along the small sill outside Mrs Willinger's bathroom, Dorothy asked: 'Would you mind if I put the kettle on? I think I fancy a nice cup of tea.'

She went out without waiting for an answer. Scandalised, Mrs Willinger turned to Vee. 'How can she leave the boy at a time like this? Talk about hard-hearted!'

'I wouldn't say that,' retorted Vee. 'In fact, I think I'll see if she needs any help.'

The kitchen window did not have a bay, just a simple sash-window facing the blank wall of the warehouse opposite. Dorothy filled the kettle and began to lay out the teacups.

Vee heard them rattle in the saucers, and said: 'You're nervous too, aren't you? I'd have thought you'd be used to it.'

'In the show, we rehearse until we get it right,' said Dorothy. 'But he's on his own out there, with no rehearsal . . . I couldn't watch.'

'I know. I wish I'd never agreed to this. It's crazy – he's risking his life to get into that flat. It's not worth it!'

They they heard Mrs Willinger utter a piercing shriek.

'Oh, my God!' said Dorothy, as they ran back into the sitting-room.

'He's fallen, he fell off the window-sill!' gabbled Mrs Willinger. 'He's broken his neck, I know he has—'

'Nonsense,' said Alec briskly. 'Come on, Dick, heave-ho!'

The two men took the strain and hauled the rope in, hand over fist.

'He's no great weight,' said Dickie. 'One, two, three – *hup*!'

'What happened?' asked Dorothy.

'He'd just got to the tricky part – the long stretch between the two bathrooms, with no sill to stand on and nothing but drainpipes to hang on to,' Dickie explained breathlessly as they pulled on the rope.

'It wasn't his fault,' said Alec. 'Just as he stepped across the gap, a damn great pigeon fluttered down, on to the same window-sill. It swerved off at the last moment, but it was enough to throw him off-balance, and down he went.'

'Is he hurt?' Vee asked urgently.

'We'll soon know,' said Alec, between his teeth. 'Hooray and up he rises . . . '

With a last heave they pulled Chockie up and dragged him in. He had a graze down one side of his face and a reddish bruise on his forehead, but he said with a shaky laugh: 'No bones broken. The worst bit was dangling at the end of the rope – I smacked into the wall before I could stop myself! But it won't happen again – I'll make sure there aren't any pigeons about next time.'

'You're not going out there again!' gasped Vee. 'Alec, don't let him, it's too dangerous—'

'Rubbish!' said Chockie. 'There's nothing to it!'

'I won't let you—' began Vee, but Dorothy took her by the arm.

'Come into the kitchen, dear,' she said. 'I expect that kettle's boiling by now.'

In the kitchen, she shut the door and faced Vee, saying: 'I know how you feel, but we've got to let him go. He's got to try it straight away, otherwise he might lose his nerve. He might never go on the highwire again.'

'Would that matter so very much?' said Vee angrily. 'It's his life I'm talking about.'

'You're quite right, it *is* his life. It's what he does better than anything, and he loves it. You wouldn't stop him doing that, would you?'

Chockie was already outside Mrs Willinger's bathroom. When he reached the big gap, it seemed wider than ever. He glanced up at the rooftops; there were no pigeons to be seen.

Gauging the distance as well as he could, he stretched out until he was holding on to the drainpipes, bounced on the balls of his feet a couple of times, then propelled himself into space.

And then he was safe, outside his own bathroom window. He stood still for a moment, taking two or three deep breaths to steady himself. Then he felt for the edge of the window, and dug his finger-nails into the frame. The broken latch gave way, and he eased the window open. Throwing a last grin over his shoulder, he scrambled in and untied the rope from his waist, then gave his audience a 'thumbs-up' sign.

Dickie slapped Alec on the back, and called to the women in the kitchen: 'He's made it. Now then, where's that cup of tea?'

Five minutes later, Chockie walked out of the Dandos' flat, carrying a jewel-box from his mother's dressing-table, his father's cuff-links, their wedding photographs and a marriage certificate, assorted mail which he had found on the doormat, including a few Christmas cards which had arrived after they left London, a canteen of cutlery that had been a wedding present and, most precious of all, the album containing the family's press-cuttings.

'Is there anything else you want?' he asked. 'Now the door's open, I suppose there's nothing to stop us taking some of the furniture as well.'

'Yes, that's an idea—' said Dickie.

Vee interrupted him. 'That final demand you were talking about – is that with the rest of the mail?'

'This looks like it.' Dickie tore open the buff envelope and whistled. 'Blimey, three hundred and twenty-five pounds!'

'I'll look after that,' said Vee, taking it from him. 'My chequebook's in my bag. Tell me where the landlord is and I'll settle it right away.'

'Oh, no, you can't – we couldn't let you—' Dickie mumbled.

'Shut up!' said Vee. 'If it makes you feel embarrassed, we'll call it a loan. I only wish I'd thought of this before.'

Dorothy started to argue: 'It's very nice of you, but there's no reason for you to help us.'

'Oh, yes, there is,' said Vee. 'Chockie's my brother, and your son – that makes us all one family, doesn't it?'

'Of course it does!' agreed Alec. 'Dammit, one of these fine days, that young hero's going to be my brother-in-law!'

Tibbles sniffed the bowl under the kitchen sink, then walked away.

'What's the matter, puss?' asked Sarah Venus. 'Don't you like it?'

By way of reply, he turned his back, pointing his tail at the bowl in a marked manner.

Jo came in to put away the dustpan and brush, saying: 'I've done the stairs and the landings – is there anything else before I go?'

'No, dear, except Tibbles seems to have gone right off his food. I hope he's not sickening for something.'

Hearing his name, Tibbles rubbed himself against Jo's legs, miaowing indignantly.

'Aren't you happy?' Jo stroked his head. 'That's not like you.'

Sarah said: 'I put down some catfood for him, but he won't touch it. Do you think it's gone off?'

Jo inspected the bowl, then smiled. 'You must have opened the wrong tin – it's baked beans, not catfood.'

Sarah groaned: 'My trouble is, I'm blind as a bat, as well as dotty!'

Jo threw out the beans and found the tin of catfood. 'I told you, you should get some glasses!'

Sarah changed the subject. 'I was thinking I might toddle round to the High Street. Did you happen to notice if there's anyone still hanging about outside?'

'Three or four, last time I looked. I wouldn't go out if I were you. If

348

there's something you need from the shops, I can—'

'No, I was only going to the Post Office for my pension. I'll leave it till tomorrow. Perhaps the newspapers will have lost interest in us by then.'

'I don't think the people out there are reporters, just nosey-parkers.'

'Then if we take no notice, they'll go away. At least they're not doing us any harm.'

Jo said nothing. She was glad Sarah had not seen the filthy words daubed aross the walls and door this morning – it had taken her half an hour to clean them off.

Aware of her silence, Sarah went on: 'It's worse for you than anyone. You were so close to Russell. I know you're unhappy.'

'It's not only Russell, it's a lot of different things . . . ' Jo didn't want to tell Sarah about Pete Hobden, and she tried to keep her voice light. 'But I'm sure things will get better. Tibbles is happy now, that's a start!'

With his head in the food-bowl, Tibbles was making up for lost time. Putting on her coat and knotting her headscarf, Jo continued: 'If there's nothing else, I think I'll push off. See you tomorrow morning, the usual time.'

'Goodnight, dear, God bless.'

As Jo went along the passage a voice whispered: 'Have you got a minute?'

Peggy was hanging over the landing banisters. When she went up the stairs, Peggy thrust an envelope into her hand, saying: 'Do me a favour, give Sarah this tomorrow morning, would you?'

'All right, but why not give it to her yourself? She's in the kitchen.'

'I'd rather not. You can explain it to her better than I can.'

'Explain what? What is it?'

'It's my money, my rent up to the end of the week . . . I'm leaving.'

'That's a bit sudden, isn't it?'

'Well, you see, I met a pal of mine last night. She's got a flat in Shepherd Market and she asked me if I'd like to move in with her. She used to share with another girl, only she had a bit of trouble with the law so her room's vacant now, and my pal's been looking for somebody to take her place – and I said I would. I'm moving out this evening.'

'You're not even going to say goodbye?'

'I wouldn't know what to say. Sarah's always been good to me, and I don't like leaving her like this, but – all those people outside, staring at you and calling out . . . I can't stick it any longer.'

'I know what you mean.'

'I just want to get right away and start again. You will explain to her, won't you? Tell her I'm really sorry.'

Jo felt like saying: 'So you should be. If it wasn't for you and your pals, Sarah wouldn't be in this mess!' but what was the use?

'All right.' She slipped the envelope into her bag. 'I'll tell her.'

Peggy beamed. 'I'm glad I caught you. I wanted to say bye-bye and – you know, good luck and all that. I'm really pleased you've come back here. Sarah needs someone to look after her.' She leaned forward and kissed Jo, then said brightly: 'Ta-ta for now. Don't do anything I wouldn't do!'

And she ran upstairs, to the top floor.

As soon as Jo opened the front door, the people on the pavement pressed forward, staring at her. Someone said: 'I bet she's one of them, you can always tell . . .Little tart.'

'It's what they all are – dirty little tarts, the lot of 'em.'

Jo pushed past and walked on quickly to the end of the road. Behind her, a man laughed, and a moment later an empty milk-bottle smashed against the wall. Instinctively, she put up a hand to shield her face, as the fragments tinkled on to the pavement.

When she lowered her hand, she saw Pete Hobden standing on the corner outside Galleon House.

'Afternoon,' he said. 'Chris said I'd probably find you here.'

She slackened her pace. 'Chris?' A sudden anger blazed up in her. 'Have you been questioning her too?'

'I called at Agar Road on the chance of seeing you, and Chris said as you'd gone back to the Rope Walk – working for the old lady, she said.'

'Any objections?'

'Not the most comfortable place right now, I'd have thought, but that's up to you.' He fell into step beside her. 'So you're on your way back to Agar Road now? Mind if I go with you?'

'I can't very well stop you, can I?' She stared straight ahead as they strode along Battersea Church Road, beside the river, and screwed up her eyes against the dazzle from the water. 'Is this official business?'

she asked. 'Or are you off-duty?'

'Bit of both, you might say.'

'Oh, yes, I ought to know by now, you're never off-duty.'

They walked on in a silence broken only by the sound of their own footsteps and the shrieks of gulls, wheeling and swooping overhead.

Studying her profile, he said at last: 'Your eyes are red. Have you been crying?'

'No, the sunlight hurts my eyes.'

'I thought you might be feeling miserable.'

'What if I am?'

'I'm sorry. That's why I came to find you, to apologise about last night. I think I passed a few remarks that weren't called for.'

'Did you?' She lifted her chin. 'I really can't remember.'

'Perhaps I ought to explain. I told you I'd been to Agar Road this afternoon. I thought there was a party going on – I've never seen so many people in your front parlour.'

She swung round to face him. 'People? What people?'

'Chris, of course, and a young chap called Chockie Dando – funny name, that. His mum and dad were there, an' all, and another couple – Mr Alec Coburn and a young lady called Vanessa – only Chris calls her Vee.'

'I don't understand. What were they doing there? Something must have gone wrong.'

She began to run. By now they had reached the corner of Battersea Bridge Road, and if Pete hadn't grabbed her she would have dashed out among the traffic.

'Hey-up, what are you trying to do – kill yourself?' He hung on to her until the lights changed, and then they crossed over.

'There's no need to get upset,' he continued, as they walked along Park Gate Road. 'They were having a high old time. Seemingly the Dandos had just got back from abroad. Chris was right pleased to see them – she and the boy were getting on like a house afire . . . She tells me he's her cousin.'

Jo frowned. 'But what was Vee doing there? Vanessa Coburn, I mean – and Alec . . .? They didn't even know the Dandos.'

'Well, they do now! They told me the whole story. It seems like Miss Coburn is Chris's cousin too – she's not really a Coburn at all. In fact, her and this chap Alec are engaged to be married.'

Jo tried to take this in. 'You mean – Alec knows all about her? And *you* know?'

'Well, I got a bit confused to start with, but I think I've sorted it out now. Vee and young Chockie, they're the sister and brother you lost in the war, right? And now you've found 'em again?'

She nodded slowly. 'Yes. But I didn't think Vee would ever tell anyone. That's what I—'

When she broke off, he carried on: 'That's what you couldn't say last night? It was your sister you were staying with, the night Laura Stanway died?'

'Did Vee tell you that?'

'No, it didn't even cross my mind till later. Then it struck me sudden-like – it was her you were on about, wasn't it? Your alibi?'

'Yes, it was . . . I'm glad you know.'

When they reached Albert Bridge Road, the park gates were wide open.

'Shall we tek the short cut through the park?' Pete suggested.

'If you like.'

It had turned into a glorious evening; the trees and shrubs looked newly painted in their fresh green. Children played on the grass, and couples strolled along the paths. It was like the first day of summer.

'Pretty place, this,' remarked Pete. 'I've always had a soft spot for Battersea Park – let's hope they don't go and spoil it, next year.'

'Why, what's happening next year?' asked Jo.

'1951 – the Festival of Britain, they call it. Hadn't you heard?'

'There was a man talking about it on the wireless, but I thought he said it was going to be somewhere near Waterloo.'

'Aye, the Exhibition, but that's only the serious part. The fun and games are going to be here in Battersea. They're planning to turn the park into the Festival Pleasure Gardens. Fun-fairs and fountains and scenic railways – very nice, if you like that kind of thing. Meself, I prefer it like it is now.'

They walked together through the rose-garden. All around them, the first buds were pushing through the leaves.

'Seems like it's going to be a good year for roses,' Pete said, then, with a change of tone: 'So I thought you'd like to know your alibi was OK. You don't have to worry.'

They stopped by an ornamental pool, looking down at the goldfish sliding among the water-lilies.

'I wasn't worried,' said Jo. 'I knew I'd got an alibi. You were the one who was worried about it.'

'I wouldn't say worried exactly, but I had to make sure.'

'Did you really think I might have killed Laura?'

'No! 'Course I didn't . . . But it was that business about the keys to the flat, you see. If Mr Wade didn't get home till morning, that only left your key.'

'And now you know I stayed with Vee that night, it couldn't have been my key either . . . Unless you still think I'm lying?'

Pete looked at her, then said uncomfortably: 'I suppose there must have been a third key – one that nobody knew about . . . '

'You're still not quite certain, are you?' Jo would not let it rest there. 'You'd like to feel sure about me, but you'll never be happy till you get some real proof.'

'I'm a policeman, ent I? We're always looking for proof.'

'Yes, that's why you kept following me, looking for proof about Don . . . Only I thought it was because you loved me.'

'I did love you!' he insisted, then corrected himself: 'I *do* love you.'

'No, you were right the first time. You did love me – before all this happened. And I loved you too, until everything went wrong . . . Why couldn't you tell me you were a policeman?'

'Why couldn't you tell me about your sister?' he countered. 'Maybe we didn't trust each other enough. Maybe there were too many secrets.'

High overhead, birds were singing their hearts out in the trees – a chorus of joy, in praise of life and love and springtime – but to Jo it was nothing but a meaningless babble of noise.

Slowly, Pete stepped back. 'I'm really sorry,' he said. 'Mebbe you'd best go home without me, after all. And in case you want to advertise that spare room of yours, I shan't be needing it any more . . . Goodbye, Jo.'

Then he turned and walked away.

Chapter Twenty-Three

WEEK BY WEEK, the house in the Rope Walk grew emptier. Peggy Hooper had been the first to leave, and the others were following her example.

The exodus did not happen immediately; most of the girls had very little money and it was hard to scrape together enough for a month's rent in advance somewhere else. Those who had woken up to see their faces in the popular newspapers discovered that respectable landladies were not willing to take them in, but they eventually found places where no questions were asked, and slipped away into anonymity.

Jo found that as the number of lodgers dwindled, the task of keeping the house clean became more difficult. It had never been easy, for the old house had not been repaired for several years; damp seeped down through the roof, dry rot crept up from the basement, and however often she swept and polished, grime and dust seemed to reappear overnight.

When the house was full, the girls had looked after their own rooms; now every time someone moved out, it became Jo's responsibility to keep the empty room neat and tidy, ready for any prospective tenant.

Not that there were many of those.

Jo had the job of showing the empty rooms, and soon learned to recognise the enquiries that were not serious – inquisitive callers eager for a peep behind the scenes at the house of ill-repute.

To make matters worse, some months after Russell's death, there was a revival of interest when a Sunday paper published the details of his will. Jo was surprised and touched – and more than a little embarrassed – to learn that she had been left a thousand pounds. In the weeks that followed, callers pretending to look for accommodation would slip in remarks like: 'You're the one he left his money to, aren't you? Is is true he bumped off his wife because of you?'

When Christmas came, the house was almost empty.

Jo did not have to plan a traditional Christmas dinner at Agar Road, because she and Chris had been invited to spend the day with the Dandos. At first Jo was worried about leaving Mr Mulligan – until Chris told her the old gentleman had plans of his own; he had arranged a little reunion with some old messmates from his Army days.

'In that case, I'll spend the day with Sarah,' said Jo. 'I'll send my apologies to Chockie and the Dandos – you can take my presents round with you, can't you? Otherwise Sarah will be all on her own.'

They had a quiet day together. Sarah, who seemed to live more and more in the past, recalled some of the exciting Christmases she'd had when she was young. Nowadays she preferred not to think about the present – or the future.

On New Year's Eve, Jo brought the old lady a bottle of port and they toasted one another, holding up the ruby-red glasses to the light.

'Here's to the Festival of Britain,' said Jo. 'Let's hope 1951 turns out better than 1950. Mr Herbert Morrison said the country deserves to give itself a pat on the back, whatever that means.'

'What for? Winning the war?' asked Sarah derisively. She took a sip of port and smacked her lips, saying: 'That's a drop of good stuff. P'raps it will give me enough Dutch courage to tell you . . . Jo, dear, you're not going to like this, but I can't carry on here. I'm running short of cash, and the house is nearly empty. That's why I've decided to sell up and move out.'

'Sell the house?'

'What's left of it. It's leasehold, you see, and there's not many years left to run, but I daresay I'll get a couple of thousand for it. That'll see me out. I'm nearly seventy-one – I won't be around much longer, thank God.'

Jo sighed. 'Seventy-one . . . I didn't know that. And I'm going to be twenty-one at the beginning of May – there's just fifty years between us.'

Sarah raised her glass again: 'Here's hoping you make better use of those fifty years than I did.' Narrowing her eyes, she tried to look around the little kitchen. 'It's a mercy my eyes aren't up to much. If I could see what the old place looks like now, it'd probably break my heart. I shan't be sorry to leave the Rope Walk.'

'But where will you go?' Jo asked.

'Bognor Regis. I've got a friend down there – Gwennie – I've known her all my life. We met in a life-class at the Chelsea School of Art; I was modelling, and she was a student. She was all set on becoming a great painter; of course it never happened – she got married and raised a family and that was the end of that. Now her husband's dead, and her children have gone off to America and Australia and goodness knows where, so she lives on her own in this private hotel at Bognor Regis. Between you and me it's more of an old folks' home really. She rings me up every now and then. She wants me to pack up and go down to join her, and I think the time's come to do it. It's not cheap, but with the money I get from selling the house, I reckon I can just about afford it.'

'Won't you miss London?' said Jo.

'Bound to, at first, but I daresay I'll get used to Bognor Regis, in time – perhaps the sea air will do me good.' She hesitated, then added: 'I'm going to miss you, Jo, and that's a fact.'

'She pretends she's looking forward to it, but she's dreading it really,' said Jo.

Seated at her dressing-table, Vee made up her lips, saying between each carmine stroke: 'She wouldn't go – unless she wanted to – would she?'

'She can't afford to carry on here. There's hardly any rent coming in now. She's got nothing to live on except her pension. Selling the house is the only way she can raise any money.'

'Poor dear. Still, if it's the only way out . . . ' Vee put down the lipstick and turned to face Jo. 'How do I look?'

'Lovely, you always do. But listen, I've had this brilliant idea. If she's got to go into a home, why don't we take over the lease and turn the Rope Walk into an old people's home? Then Sarah can stay where she is!'

'You mean, you and me?'

'Why not? I don't know how much it's going to cost – she said a couple of thousand – I've already got a thousand pounds in the bank, and you must be rolling in money. We could afford it between us, couldn't we?'

Vee stood up, putting on her fur coat. 'I'd love to be able to say yes, but I'm not going to be here much longer – in London, I mean.'

'Where are you going?'

'After the wedding, Alec and I are moving up to Scotland to reopen the family house. It's been shut up since the end of the war, and Alec's always dreamed of living there. There's some extra land available, and we're scraping together every penny we can to buy it, so he can start farming.'

'Oh, I didn't know . . . When are you getting married?'

'The end of April. We'll send you a card as soon as they come back from the printers . . . Actually, that's why I asked you to come shopping with me – you can help me choose my trousseau. I hate buying clothes on my own, and Aunt Elspeth's a darling but she's absolutely useless about undies. She thinks nice girls wear woolly vests and sensible knickers.'

Jo's hopes crumbled. 'So you'll be going to Scotland for good? Living there all the time?'

'Alec says it's the only place to bring up a family.' Vee smiled. 'He's awfully keen to start a family, and so am I.'

'Yes.' Jo thought of the family Vee and Alec would have. 'I'm so glad.'

Vee came over to her. 'What's the matter?'

'Nothing. I just – I didn't know you were going away.'

'Don't worry, we'll be popping backwards and forwards all the time, to see the Aunt – and you and Chockie and everybody. And you'll be able to visit us – you must come up for holidays!'

'I don't have holidays,' said Jo.

'Don't be silly, everybody has a holiday sometimes.' Vee pulled Jo on to her feet. 'We can't sit here all day, I've ordered the cab for two-thirty. Cheer up! I know, we'll buy something for you to wear at the wedding!'

'When exactly is it going to be?' Jo asked.

'April the 24th – Easter Saturday. Afterwards we'll drive straight up to Scotland – spring is simply glorious up there.'

★

On Easter Saturday, the weather in London was cold and grey, with a biting wind off the river.

The wedding took place at the Chelsea Registrar's Office, and was a very private ceremony, attended only by Aunt Elspeth and the best man, an old friend from Alec's RAF days. The Coburns had kept the whole thing as quiet as possible, hoping that the bizarre family history would not be picked up by the press. By this time a discreet firm of solicitors had straightened out the question of Vee's parentage and her name appeared on the marriage certificate as 'Vera (Vanessa) Wells', together with her correct date and place of birth, so no awkward questions were asked.

The wedding reception was held in a more elegant setting.

Some old friends of Aunt Elspeth's – Jo never discovered their surnames, but he was called Bunny and she was called Baba – had a house overlooking the river at Hammersmith, and as Easter Saturday also happened to be Boat Race day, they suggested that it might be nice to combine the wedding reception with a Boat Race party.

Only the Coburns' closest friends were invited, and some of those had sent their regrets – even now, the conventionally-minded found the thought of Alec's marriage to Vee faintly distasteful. Jo didn't know anyone there, except Chris and the Dandos.

'What are you looking so glum about?' Chockie asked Jo, when Alec and Vee had cut the cake, and everyone had drunk a toast to the bride and groom.

'I'm not very good with strangers,' replied Jo. 'I never know what to say to people.'

'You don't have to say anything,' said Chockie. 'You look smashing in that new dress – all you've got to do is stand there and smile. The fellers will do all the talking!'

She tried to smile, she tried to join in the general mood of festivity, but all she could think was that after today Vee would live in Scotland. She didn't know when she would see her again.

'How can you be so selfish?' she scolded herself. 'Vee and Alec are shining with happiness. You know what your trouble is, don't you? You're just plain jealous, because they've got each other, and you've got nobody . . . Nobody except Sarah, and soon she'll be going away as well.'

The room had tall windows along one side, looking across a paved terrace to the Thames, and she told herself that this was a beautiful house, full of beautiful people, and she was having a very nice time.

She passed Chockie and Chris; he must have said something funny, because she was laughing. Chris had been happier ever since Chockie returned to London; happier, and more sure of herself – more of a young woman. Jo realised that at thirteen Christine was growing up fast.

At the other end of the room, Dickie and Dorothy entertained a group of guests with tales of their continental tour. From where she stood, Jo could only catch the occasional word, but she could admire the way they shared the story between them; years of mutual reliance and affection had made the Amazing Dandos an amazing partnership.

Then Jo understood why she was feeling out of place. Wherever she looked, she saw men and women in couples, and she realised that she had been on her own for a long time.

Alec and Vee broke away from Bunny and Baba and came over to her, and Vee explained. 'We're just going to slip away and change – we've got to dash off very soon. We're so glad you could come. Are you having a good time?'

'Wonderful, thank you.' Jo glanced out of the windows; the wind was whipping the surface of the river into catspaws. 'I just wish the weather had been kinder. I thought we'd be able to go out and watch the Boat Race – I wanted to cheer the winners!'

Alec laughed: 'Not today – didn't you hear? Apparently the Oxford boat sank, and they had to call the race off, so there aren't any winners today.'

'Yes, there are.' Jo put one arm around Alec, and one round Vee. 'This is your day – you're the winners, and I'm very happy for you.'

On 3 June, the King and Queen visited the new exhibition site on the South Bank, and the Festival of Britain was declared open.

On 5 June, Jo Wells had her twenty-first birthday.

Chris asked her how she wanted to celebrate the great day and Chockie told her his mum and dad would be happy to throw a party for her, at the flat in Devonshire Buildings: 'They'll ask some of the tenting folk round – we could get up a concert if you like?'

'It's very kind of them, but what I'd really like would be to go and see the Festival at Waterloo. Why don't we make it a family outing?'

Vee and Alec were still settling down to their new life in Scotland, so in the end the party consisted of Jo, Chris, Chockie, Mr and Mrs Dando, and Mr Mulligan.

They had to queue up to get in, but Chris and Dorothy had made sandwiches, so they ate their picnic lunch while they waited. Only Mr Mulligan was able to sit down; guessing that there might be a certain amount of standing about, Jo had brought a folding camp-stool for him.

The old man was very grateful. 'It's the leg-joints that play me up, y'see,' he explained. 'The trouble is, I need a few squirts of the oil-can for me poor old knees!'

He was becoming very lame now; he could only get out for his daily constitutional with the aid of two walking-sticks, and he rarely ventured further than the pub.

'Would you think there'd be a bar in this place at all?' he asked hopefully. 'Like I said, a little lubrication wouldn't come amiss.'

'I don't know about that,' said Jo. 'But I expect we can get tea or coffee, or lemonade.'

'Lemonade . . .' Mr Mulligan sighed heavily. 'Ah, well, I suppose that'd be better than nothing . . . Just!'

When they got inside the exhibition grounds at last, they were all bewildered; there was so much to see, and so many people there, pushing and jostling. Looming over everything, the Dome of Discovery shone in the sunlight, housing the latest scientific and technological marvels.

The Skylon soared upwards, a gigantic aluminium javelin hung between heaven and earth, mysteriously suspended above the ground without anything to support it, as far as they could see.

'What's it meant to be?' asked Dorothy.

'It's the emblem of the Festival,' Jo told her. 'I think its supposed to symbolise Britain today.'

'Very appropriate,' said Dickie. 'Seeing it's got no visible means of support.'

'Let's take a look in the Dome of Discovery,' said Chockie. 'Are you coming with us, Mr Mulligan?'

'I think I'll sit here and survey the wonders from a respectful distance, if it's all the same to you,' said the old man. 'Myself, I'm not that struck on science. It hadn't been invented in my young days, and we got on very well without it.'

'All right, then, here's the little stool,' said Jo. 'Would you like me to get you a cup of coffee?'

'I would not, thank you kindly,' snorted the old man. 'I see they're charging ninepence for coffee – daylight robbery, I call it!'

They left him glowering at the marvels of science, and entered the Dome.

It was all very fascinating, but after a while Jo and Chris followed Mr Mulligan's example; finding a vacant bench, they sat down to wait for the others, and Chris asked: 'Well, are you enjoying your birthday?'

'Oh, yes, I've had some wonderful presents.'

Chris, who had given her a silver bracelet, said: 'I wish I could have bought you something really grand, like diamonds. If you could have anything you wanted in the whole world, what would you wish for?'

Jo thought for a moment, then said: 'What I'd like more than anything would be to buy the house in the Rope Walk.'

She began to tell Chris about her dream of turning the house into an old people's home, so Sarah could go on living there, then added impulsively: 'How about you and me going into partnership? I never thought of it before, but I've got some money in the bank, and if you sold Agar Road, I'm sure we could manage it somehow. Mr Mulligan could move there as well – we'd all stay together.'

Chris shook her head. 'Not Mr Mulligan. Didn't he tell you? He'll be moving out soon.'

'Leaving Agar Road? But – where's he going?'

'You know those old Army friends of his? They're Chelsea Pensioners from the Royal Hospital, across the river. They said he ought to apply as well, and this morning he told me he's been accepted.'

'He never said anything to me.'

'Perhaps he thought it might spoil your birthday. He's really looking forward to it – talking over old times with his mates. I think he fancies himself in that red uniform! Besides, the Rope Walk wouldn't be very suitable for old people – all those stairs.'

'I never thought of that.' Jo felt rather foolish. 'You're quite right. How are we going to manage at Agar Road? I'll have to start advertising for some new lodgers.'

'I've been meaning to talk to you about that. Mrs Dando was saying the other day they've never been very happy since they moved back into Devonshire Buildings. Mrs Willinger told all the neighbours how they got behind with the rent – it isn't very nice for them, being gossiped about. So I thought, seeing we'll have two rooms going begging, p'raps they could have one, and Chockie could have the other . . . If that's all right with you?'

'Oh, yes – of course . . . Perfectly all right,' said Jo.

'I'm glad. Anyway, I wouldn't really fancy moving to the Rope Walk – Agar Road's always been my home.'

She broke off as the Dandos returned. Dickie and Dorothy were arguing again.

'I've never been so embarrassed!' Dorothy appealed to Jo. 'D'you know what he just did? He went up to one of the officials and said this scientific stuff was all very well, but you can have too much of a good thing.'

'I said they ought to employ a few professionals to provide a bit of light relief, that's all,' said Dickie, defensively.

'Good old Dad!' grinned Chockie. 'He only offered to put up a tightwire between the Skylon and the Dome of Discovery, and offered to do the act twice daily – that's all!'

'I didn't know where to put myself,' said Dorothy. 'The man said at the end of the month they're opening the Pleasure Gardens at Battersea for that kind of thing, and he told Dad he ought to apply there instead.'

'All right, there's no need to go on and on about it,' muttered Dickie. Turning to Jo, he asked: 'Well, how's the birthday girl? Having a good day?'

'Yes, it's all lovely.'

She couldn't tell him she wasn't enjoying it, but it didn't seem like her birthday any more. It was just another day, like all the rest.

The following morning she went to work at the Rope Walk, confessing that her plan to take over the lease had collapsed completely.

'That's a weight off my mind, dear,' said Sarah. 'I didn't like to say anything, but I can tell you now – the agent rang up a few days ago and told me he's had an offer for the house.'

'So you're selling it?'

'I won't get as much as I'd hoped, but then you never do, do you? As long as I'm careful, I'm sure I shall manage at Bognor Regis.'

'How soon will it happen?'

'I've said I'll pack up and go by the last day of June. That gives me a month to get myself ready. I'm afraid it's going to mean a lot of extra work for you.'

'That's all right, I don't mind,' said Jo, which was a lie – she minded very much, though not about the extra work.

Tibbles jumped on to her lap, gazing up soulfully into her face. When she stroked him, he purred sympathetically.

'What's going to happen about Tibbles?' she asked.

'Oh, he's coming with me. I wouldn't go if I couldn't take Tibbles! The hotel's very good like that. They know old people like to keep their pets with them. My friend Gwennie's got a cage full of canaries!'

'She'll have to keep her door shut, if Tibbles goes on the prowl.'

'Oh, his hunting days are over. He's like me now, ready to settle for a quiet life . . .I'm sure it'll all work out in the long run.'

Jo tried to look on the bright side. 'And I can come down and see you sometimes. I'll get a day-return ticket.'

'Yes, you do that.' Sarah thought for a moment, then went on: 'You asked me once if I'd miss London, and I said I would, but now I'm not so sure. I never go out these days. I might as well live in Timbuctoo for all I see of London. I think I'll be just as happy beside the seaside with Gwennie, talking over the happy times we used to have.' She groped for Jo's hand, and squeezed it. 'Still, good times or bad times – they all come to an end, sooner or later.'

When Jo left the Rope Walk that afternoon, she did not go straight home; she did not really have a home to go to. Yesterday, talking to Chris, she had discovered the big difference between them. Chris had her own home – a house she had always lived in – but Jo had nowhere on earth to call her own.

At the end of the street, she looked about her, and for want of anything better to do, she crossed the road and opened the gate into the churchyard of St Mary's.

Poised beside the Thames, Battersea Parish Church had all the dignity and calm certainty of the eighteenth century. With its spire like a signpost to heaven, it seemed indifferent to the passing of time – to the busy river traffic on one side, or the modern street on the other – and seemed to say: 'All this shall pass. I stand for something that outlasts time.'

Jo made her way among the graves and headstones, and found the west door was open.

She tried to remember how long it was since she had been to church or said her prayers; she went into one of the pews and knelt down, looking up at the clear, clean lines of the nave, the high altar and the stained-glass windows.

She tried to draw comfort from these witnesses to faith; she tried to open her mind and heart and pray for guidance – because she was afraid.

Time was running out so fast, and she could not hold on to it. It was racing away, beyond her grasp, and she was helpless.

Everyone seemed to be leaving her – some had left already. Even Chris was growing up so quickly. Soon she would not need Jo to look after her.

'And if nobody needs me any more, what's the use of me?' Closing her eyes and putting her hands together, she prayed: 'Our Father – help me . . . Please, God – help me . . .'

But she wasn't sure if anyone was listening.

Chapter Twenty-Four

'Is that the lot?' asked Sarah.

Jo looked round the kitchen. 'I think so – anyway, I hope so, because we've run out of boxes.'

She had spent all day packing up Sarah's possessions; the clothes, the make-up and jewellery, the personal belongings had all been put in suitcases, ready to go to Bognor Regis with her tomorrow.

There was far too much luggage for Sarah to take to Sussex by train, so she had decided to make a grand gesture and booked a hired car. When she left the Rope Walk for the last time on Saturday morning, she was going to go in style, comfortably settled in the back of a limousine, surrounded by bags and boxes, with Tibbles on her lap.

The contents of the kitchen had been something of a problem; it had taken hours to pack up all the saucepans, the pudding-basins, the remains of an expensive dinner-service, the teapot and the cracked cups, the cutlery, the kettle, the bread-board and the colander – all the things she would never need again, when she moved into a private hotel.

'Are you sure you've taken everything you want?' Sarah asked Jo. 'How about the coffee-percolator? It's quite a good one.'

'I'm already taking more stuff to Agar Road than I can carry in one go,' Jo told her. 'And we've got a coffee-pot anyway, we don't really need another one. I'll run it round with the other things to the church hall – they'll be glad of it for the jumble sale.'

'You did say the men were going to move the furniture out tomorrow?'

'Yes, the van's coming after you've gone. I'll be here to see to all that, you don't have to worry about it.'

The furniture had been the biggest problem of all. There were beds and wardrobes, tables and chairs from every room in the house. Sarah had urged Jo to take anything she wanted, but they couldn't really cram any more furniture into Agar Road. In the end Jo had found a local junk-dealer who had agreed to clear the house.

'I've wrapped all the ornaments up in newspaper and put them into the tea-chest,' she added. 'And the pictures and the mirrors are all stacked in the hall, ready to go . . . Except this one – I thought you might want to take it with you.'

She handed Sarah a small framed drawing; it was a charcoal sketch of a laughing girl with large, dark eyes, putting up her hair.

Holding it close to her eyes, Sarah sighed. 'Ah, yes . . . That's how I looked once upon a time. Do you know who drew this?'

'He hasn't signed it, but – was it Russell?'

'Russell Wade, the up-and-coming young artist . . .' Sarah nodded. 'Yes, I think I'd like to hang on to this one – thank you, dear. Put it in the basket with the bottle – it will be safe there.'

When she was turning out the kitchen, Jo had discovered a dusty bottle of champagne, and Sarah had decided to take it with her, to share with her old friend Gwennie when she arrived at Bognor Regis, and drink a toast to her new abode.

Sarah went on: 'You remembered to give my new address to the Post Office so they can forward any letters that come for me? Not that I'm expecting any letters – and if there are any, I shan't be able to read them! Oh, and you've arranged about turning off the electricity and the gas?'

'It's all taken care of. The Gas Board said they'll send a man round to read the meter either this evening or first thing tomorrow.'

'That's all right, then. You're a good girl, getting everything sorted out . . . By the way, where's Tibbles got to? I haven't seen him lately.'

Sarah was interrupted by the telephone-bell; the phone was on the little table beside her chair, and she picked up the receiver.

'Hello? Who's speaking? . . . Oh, yes, I see . . .' After a short pause, she went on: 'Yes, that will be quite convenient. I shall be here to let you in. I won't be going out this evening . . . Goodbye.'

When she rang off, she explained: 'The man asked if it would be all right for him to come round now, so I told him it would.' Then she broke off and asked suddenly: 'What was I saying just now? Oh, yes – Tibbles – it's not like him to go off on his own. Where do you suppose he's got to?'

'I don't think he likes all this upheaval. He's probably taken himself off to sulk in some quiet corner, out of the way. Do you want me to go and look for him?'

'I wish you would. I wonder if he's got wind of the move, and he's hiding somewhere. He's probably afraid he'll be packed up with the rest of the luggage.'

Jo set off to search the house, one floor at a time, looking into every room, but there was no sign of the old tabby cat. She called his name repeatedly, and listened for a 'miaow' in response, but she couldn't hear him.

As she climbed to the top of the house, her heart sank. The empty rooms looked so mournful and desolate, stripped of everything except the bare minimum of furniture, with nothing to show who had lived there – no sign of life at all.

'Tibbles? Tibbles, where are you?'

At last she reached the attic floor. She went first to the room that used to be Peggy's, but Tibbles was nowhere to be seen. Jo had left till last the room she'd occupied herself, feeling a kind of reluctance to enter it, but the door was ajar, and she made herself go in.

It was hard to believe she had ever lived here. She had sat on that bentwood chair, she had made toast by that gas-fire, and slept in that single bed, on that dingy mattress. Once, Russell had shared that bed with her – and in this room, she had refused to sleep with Pete Hobden.

As she remembered the past, the hair stirred at the back of her neck, and she felt a chilly draught upon her cheek. Turning to the window, she saw that the lower sash had been left slightly open.

She walked over to close it, and found Tibbles.

It was a dormer window, and the roof outside sloped down to a shallow parapet; stretched out upon the slates, Tibbles was enjoying the last rays of sunlight.

'You bad lad!' Jo said gently. 'Giving us such a fright – this is no time to start playing hide-and-seek. Come inside and don't be so silly, come on now!'

She pushed the window up a little more and reached out for him, but the cat twitched his tail a couple of times and slid a few inches further down the roof, just out of reach.

'Don't be so wicked! Come in, and I'll give you some supper!'

Tibbles took no notice. If he refused to budge, she realised she might have to climb out after him, and the thought terrified her. Suppose she slipped and fell? Suppose she tumbled over that low parapet, and crashed headfirst to the pavement below? She began to wish Chockie was with her; he wouldn't think twice about such a feat.

'Tibbles, do buck up, I can't hang about all night!'

Then she heard footsteps mounting the stairs – a brisk, firm tread. It couldn't possibly be Sarah – it must be the man from the Gas Board, but why was he coming up here when the meter was in the kitchen cupboard? Still, whatever he was after, he might have longer arms than she had. Perhaps he could reach out and grab Tibbles.

'I'm in here!' she called. 'Could you come and help me? The cat's out on the roof, and I can't get him to come in!'

Behind her, the door swung open—

'Hello there,' said Pete Hobden. 'Happen I'm a bit late, but – many happy returns of last month.'

She stared at him, unable to speak, and he added: 'Sorry if I startled you. You look like you'd seen a ghost.'

Jo took a deep breath and asked: 'What on earth are you doing here?'

'I rang up ten minutes since. The old lady said as it would be all right to come round, so here I am.'

'That was you on the phone? She never said.'

'I told her I wanted it to be a surprise, like . . . How are you, Jo?'

'I'm all right.' She couldn't think. Helplessly, she indicated the window. 'I was just trying to persuade the cat to come in.'

'Oh, aye? Out on the tiles, is he? Pete joined her and peered out. 'Here, puss, you're wanted!'

'It's no use calling him, I've already tried,' she began, and with that Tibbles rose, walked up the tiles in a nonchalant way and jumped across the window-sill into Jo's arms, purring. 'Well, honestly!' she exclaimed. 'Of all the cussed animals . . . Would you mind closing the window for me? I'd better take him downstairs before he goes missing again.'

Pete shut the window and fastened it, then said: 'Don't run away for a minute, I want to talk to you.'

'Oh, really? What is it this time – black-marketeers or drug-dealers? I don't suppose I'll be much help to you, I've been rather out of touch lately. Who are you chasing now?'

'You,' he said.

She stared at him. 'What for? I haven't done anything.'

'I know that. And I'm sorry I missed your birthday, but I was away on business on May 5th.'

'How do you know my birthday?' she demanded.

'It's on your records, along with everything else. Twenty-first, wasn't it? How did you celebrate it?'

'Excuse me, I'm going downstairs.' Carrying Tibbles, she led the way, saying over her shoulder: 'If you must know, I went to the Festival on the South Bank, with some friends.'

'Oh, aye? Doesn't sound much like fun to me. Have you tried the Pleasure Gardens yet?'

'No, I haven't, I've been rather busy.'

'Never mind, we'll soon put that right. I can tek you round there right now. We'll celebrate your birthday all over again, eh?'

As the sun went down, the sky turned from orange to greenish-blue and then to purple, and all the lights in Battersea Park came on – more and more of them: street-lights like yellow moons along the broad avenues, and tiny lights like stars twinkling among the trees, coloured lights submerged beneath the fountains, and in the funfair, a glitter of light all around them.

They took a ride on the scenic railway, and as the car crawled up the first ascent, Jo said: 'You still haven't told me why you came to the Rope Walk tonight – what's it all about?'

'Does it have to be about anything special? I wanted to talk to you, that's all.'

Then they reached the top, swung over it – hung in space for a split second – and dropped like a thunderbolt on the other side, while Jo squealed, and Pete held her so tightly, they could not talk at all.

And they didn't talk much when they went on the Rotor; standing obediently with a dozen strangers, their backs against the wall of the huge drum, they held hands as it began to revolve, spinning faster and faster until, unbelievably, the floor dropped away beneath their feet and they remained where they were, pinned to the wall by centrifugal force, unable to speak at all, unable to hear anything except the roar of the engine, and a hundred electric guitars hammering out the driving rhythms of 'How High the Moon'.

Even when they walked arm in arm through the floodlit gardens, they still found little to say; they stopped to admire the elaborate Guinness Clock, which opened up when it struck the hour, with quaint characters and animals popping out of various doors and windows, one after another, and a carillon playing a jaunty tune. There was so much going on, they didn't even notice what time it was, and they didn't care.

Then they heard another kind of music – a dreamy slow fox-trot coming from the dance-floor; through open archways they could see other couples swaying and circling.

'D'you want to go in and join them?' Pete asked.

Jo shook her head. 'I'd just as soon be out here.'

So they stayed where they were, and danced beneath the stars.

'Back to the beginning,' said Peter softly, as their bodies moved easily together. 'This is how it all started . . . VE Day, Trafalgar Square – remember?'

'We didn't talk much that time, either,' she said.

'Maybe we were right. Maybe we've talked too much since then.'

'Too much talk,' she agreed, looking into his eyes. 'And too many secrets.'

'Too many secrets,' he said. 'And not enough dancing.'

Afterwards, above the long promenade and the coloured fountains and the flagpoles, the firework display began.

When they got back to the Rope Walk it was very late, but Sarah was still awake, waiting for them. She had unwrapped three glasses, and she asked Pete to do the honours and open the champagne.

'What about your old friend Gwennie?' asked Jo. 'You were saving that for her.'

'To hell with my old friend Gwennie,' said Sarah. 'Tonight's the night for champagne.'

When Pete filled her glass, she raised it, saying: 'Here's to you, the pair of you. I don't know what happened this evening, and you don't have to tell me, but whatever it was, it must have been good.'

'We just went to the Pleasure Gardens, that's all,' said Jo. 'Nothing happened.'

'Yes, it did,' said Pete. 'We went back to the beginning.' Putting his arm round Jo, he added: 'It's taken us six years, but we got there in the end.'

'We spent too much time asking questions, not trusting one another,' said Jo. Sitting in that crowded, untidy kitchen, remembering the past, she said to Pete: 'I'll never forget the worst moment of all. You honestly thought I might have killed Laura Stanway, didn't you?'

'I never really believed that,' he said. 'I just couldn't understand who else could have done it.'

'Oh, well, if that's all you've got to worry about, I'll tell you,' said Sarah, peeping at them over the rim of her glass like a naughty child. 'I did it . . . Only you won't say anything to anybody, will you?'

No one spoke for a moment; only Tibbles, curled up on Sarah's lap, purred contentedly.

'You did it?' repeated Jo at last. 'But how? Why?'

'I had to do it, for Russell's sake.' Sarah raised her head, gazing up at the ceiling, but seeing the whole thing as clearly as if it were happening again, before her tired old eyes.

'The phone rang, and when I picked it up, it was Laura. She was very drunk, and very angry, and she wanted to speak to Russell. He'd gone out, and she thought he must be with you, Jo. I said he wasn't here, and you weren't here either. So she decided you'd both gone to some party, and she knew the kind of party Russell enjoyed. She was feeling very sorry for herself, rambling on and threatening to commit suicide, and then she hung up on me.

'Well, I went up to your room to make sure you weren't there. You'd left your door open, and your bag was lying on the table. So I decided to borrow your keys – the keys to Galleon House. I thought I'd better try and talk some sense into the silly woman.

'Of course I should have known better. When I let myself into the flat, Laura got hysterical. She hated me, she hated you – most of all she hated Russell. She was threatening to ring the newspapers and tell the world that her brilliant husband was a dirty lecher and a dope-addict. She kept on and on, planning her revenge on him, and getting through a bottle of scotch at the same time. She was too far gone to pour it into the glass, so she made me do it for her. That's when I saw the sleeping-pills beside her bed. I decided to help her do what she'd talked about so many times . . . I'd have done anything to help Russell.'

'You must have loved him very much,' said Jo, in a whisper.

'Oh, yes, I always loved him, from the very first day I started to model for him. I wasn't going to stand by and let Laura wreck his life. Every time I filled her glass, I put some more pills in and let them dissolve. She was so wrapped up in herself, she never noticed. When she finally dropped off to sleep, I washed the glass out and put it back in her hands, then I came home, popped the keys back in your bag, and went to bed . . . And that was that.'

It was after midnight when Jo and Pete left the house. As they walked towards the river, Jo asked: 'What are you going to do about it?'

'Nothing. Let's face it – we don't really know anything for sure. Whatever happened that night, it was a long time ago. Nothing could ever be proved now. And Sarah Venus is an old lady. Old ladies get muddled sometimes.'

Side by side, they leaned on the river wall, and watched a string of barges gliding by, their lights reflected in the calm water. The breeze blowing in from the estuary had a tang of salt.

'And tomorrow she's leaving London,' said Jo. 'Tomorrow, it will all be over.'

Pete swung round to face her. 'Tomorrow it'll be only just beginning,' he said, and slipped his hand into his pocket. 'I nearly forgot. I've brought you a little birthday present – better late than never, eh?'

It was a very small leather box; by the glow of the nearest street-lamp, she opened it. Inside was a engagement ring.

'Are you sure?' she asked. 'After all that's happened, are you really sure?'

'Never more sure of anything in my life,' he said. 'I need you, Jo. I've needed you for six years, and I want you to marry me.'

She looked up at him; it was too dark to see his face, but she knew that he was smiling. Above and beyond him, she could see the outline of the church spire, silhouetted against the stars, and she smiled back. Someone had been listening, after all.

'I'm sure too,' she said. 'How strange. All this time, I thought I wanted something quite different.'

'Did you? What was that?'

'Ever since I was a kid, I had this dream about finding my family and bringing them together again. I thought that was the most important thing in the world. And now I've found them, they've gone off in different directions, with different people.'

Upriver, a goods-train rattled across the railway-bridge, and in the distance the lonely hoot of a tug floated on the night air.

'That's right.' Pete put his hand on her shoulder. 'That's what families do when they grow up. Every family starts again, each new generation. Now it's our turn – we'll start our own family.'

'Oh, yes!' Of course that was the answer; they would begin again. 'We'll be happy tomorrow, won't we?'

'No . . . ' When he took her in his arms, it felt so right – it felt like coming home at last. 'We'll be happy today,' he said.